THE MAGIC LABYRINTH

THE MAGIC LABYRINTH

The Fourth Novel in the RIVERWORLD Series

Philip José Farmer

Published by
Berkley Publishing Corporation
Distributed by
G. P. Putnam's Sons, New York

Copyright © 1980 by Philip José Farmer

Library of Congress Cataloging in Publication Data

Farmer, Philip José.
  The magic labyrinth.

  (The Riverworld series; v. 4)
  I. Title.
PZ4.F234Mag   [PS3556.A72]   813'.54   80-144
ISBN 0-399-12381-4

Printed in the United States of America

For Harlan Ellison, Leslie Fiedler, and Norman Spinrad, alivest of the alive

Reason is Life's sole arbiter, the magic Labyrinth's single clue . . .

Where 'twill be man's to see the whole of what on Earth he sees in part . . .

—The Kasîdah of Hâjî Abdû Al-Yazdi

CONTENTS

Author's Foreword

Now ends the Riverworld series, all loose ends tied together into a sword-resisting Gordian knot, all the human mysteries revealed, the millions of miles of The River and the many years of quests and The Quest completed.

SECTION 1

The Mysterious Stranger

1

"EVERYBODY SHOULD FEAR ONLY ONE PERSON, AND THAT PERSON SHOULD be himself."

That was a favorite saying of the Operator.

The Operator had also spoken much of love, saying that the person most feared should also be much loved.

The man known to some as X or the Mysterious Stranger neither loved nor feared himself the most.

There were three people he had loved more than he loved anybody else.

His wife, now dead, he had loved but not as deeply as the other two.

His foster mother and the Operator he loved with equal intensity or at least he had once thought so.

His foster mother was lightyears away, and he did not have to deal with her as yet and might never. Now, if she knew what he was doing, she would be deeply ashamed and grieved. That he couldn't explain to her why he was doing this, and so justify himself, deeply grieved him.

The Operator he still loved but at the same time hated.

Now X waited, sometimes patiently, sometimes impatiently or angrily, for the fabled but real riverboat. He had missed the *Rex Grandissimus*. His only chance now was the *Mark Twain*.

If he didn't get aboard that boat . . . no, the thought was almost unendurable. He must.

Yet, when he did get on it, he might be in the greatest peril he'd ever been in, bar one. He knew that the Operator was down-River. The surface of his grail had shown him the Operator's location. But that had been the last information he would get from the map. The satellite had kept track of the Operator and the Ethicals, except for himself, and the agents in The Rivervalley, beaming its messages to the grail which was more than a grail. Then the map had faded from the gray surface, and X had known that something had malfunctioned in the satellite. From now on he could be surprised by the Operator, by the agents, and by the other Ethical.

Long ago, X had made arrangements to track all those from the tower and the underground chambers. He had secretly installed the mechanism in the satellite. The others would have put in a device to track him, of course. But his aura-distorter had fooled the mechanism. The distorter had also enabled him to lie to the council of twelve.

Now, he was as ignorant and helpless as the others.

However, if anybody on this world would be taken aboard by Clemens, even if the complement was full, it would be the Operator. One look at him, and Clemens would stop the boat and hail him aboard.

And when the *Mark Twain* came along, and he, X, managed to become a crew member, he would have to avoid the Operator until he could take him by surprise.

The disguise, good enough to fool even the other stranded Ethical, would not deceive that great intelligence. He would recognize X instantly, and then he, X, would have no chance. Strong and quick as he was, the Operator was stronger and quicker.

Moreover, the Operator would have a psychological advantage. X, face to face with the being he loved and hated, would be inhibited and might not be able to attack the Operator with the fury and vigor demanded.

Cowardly though it was, a detestable act, he would have to take the Operator from behind. But his detestable deeds had been many since he had set himself against the others, and he could do this. Though taught from early childhood to loathe violence, he had also been taught that violence was justified if his life was in peril. The resurrecting force which for all practical purposes made everyone on the Riverworld indestructible just did not enter into it. Resurrection no longer worked but even when it had he'd still forced himself to be violent. Despite what his mentors said, the end did justify the means. Besides, all those he'd killed would not be dead forever. At least, he'd thought so. But he'd not foreseen this situation.

The Ethical was living in a bamboo leaf-thatched hut on the bank of The River, the right bank if you faced upstream. He hadn't been there long. Now he sat on the thick short grass of the plain near the shore. There were approximately five hundred others around him, all waiting for lunchtime. At one time, there would have been seven hundred here, but, since the resurrections had ceased, the population had lessened. Accidents, mostly from encounters with the gigantic human-eating boat-smashing riverdragon fish, suicide, and murder, had accounted for most fatalities. Once, war had been the greatest death-maker, but there had been none in this area for many years. The would-be conquerors had been killed off, and now they would not be translated elsewhere along The River to make more trouble.

Also, the spread of the Church of the Second Chance, the Nichirenites, the Sufis, and other pacifistic religions and disciplines had had great effect in bringing peace.

Near the crowd was a mushroom-shaped structure of a red-flecked granite material. It was called a grailstone, though actually it was a highly electrically conductive metal. It had a broad base five feet high, and the top had a diameter of approximately fifty feet. On the surface of this were seven hundred depressions. In each one was a cylinder of gray metal, a device which converted energy discharged by the grailstone into food, liquor, and other items. The containers kept the vast population of the Riverworld, estimated to have been thirty-five to thirty-six billion at one time, from starving to death. Though the grail-provided food could be augmented by fish and acorn bread and the tips of young bamboo shoots, these were not enough to feed the dwellers of the narrow Valley, a valley which enclosed The River, ten million miles long.

The people by the stone chattered and laughed and kidded around. The Ethical did not speak to those near him; he was occupied with his thoughts. It had occurred to him that perhaps the malfunction of the satellite was not natural. Its tracking mechanism was designed to function for over a thousand years without breakdown. Had it failed because Piscator, the Japanese once named Ohara, had messed up something in the tower? Theoretically Piscator should have been destroyed by the various traps that he, X, had placed in the tower or been caught in a stasis field installed by the Operator. But Piscator was a Sufi, and he might have had the intelligence and perceptive powers to avoid these. That he could enter the tower showed that he was very ethically advanced. Not one in five million of the *candidates*, the resurrected Terrestrials, could have gone through the entrance on top. As for the one at the base, only that had been prepared by X, and only two knew about it until the expedition of ancient Egyptians had gotten to it. He'd been surprised and upset when he'd found their bodies in the secret room. Nor had he known then that one Egyptian had escaped and had been drowned and then translated back to The Valley until he'd heard the survivor's story, somewhat distorted and via who knew how many tellers? Apparently no agents had heard it until it was too late for them to transmit the news to the Ethicals in the tower.

What worried him now was that if Piscator had indeed been responsible for accidentally causing the tracker to malfunction, then he might somehow bring the Ethicals back to life. And if he did that . . . he, X, was done for.

He stared across the plain at the foothills covered with the long-bladed grass and trees of various kinds and the gloriously colored blooms of the vines on the ironwood trees and then past them to the unscalable mountains walling in The Valley. His fear and frustration made him angry again, but he quickly used the mental techniques to dissipate his anger. The energy, he knew, made his skin temperature rise for a hundredth of a degree Celsius for a few seconds. He felt somewhat relieved, though he knew that he'd be angry again. The trouble with the technique was that it didn't dissipate the source of his anger. He'd never be able to get rid of that, though he had appeared to do so to his mentors.

He shaded his eyes and glanced at the sun. Within a few minutes, the stone would vomit lightning and thunder along with the millions of others on both banks. He moved away from the stone and put the tips of his fingers in his ears. The noise would be deafening, and the sudden discharge still made one jump though you knew it was coming.

The sun reached its zenith.

There was an enormous roar and flashing upward of ravening blue white-shot electricity.

On the left bank, not the right.

Once before, the right-bank grailstones had failed to function.

Those on the right bank waited with apprehension and then increasing fear when the stones failed to spout their energy for dinnertime. And when they failed again at breakfast time, the consternation and anxiety became panic.

By the next day, the hungry people invaded the left bank en masse.

SECTION 2

Aboard the *Not For Hire*

2

THE FIRST TIME THAT SIR THOMAS MALORY DIED WAS ON EARTH IN A.D. 1471.

The English knight got through the terrible weeks after Resurrection Day without too many body wounds, though he suffered grievously from spiritual shock. He found the food in his "littel greal" fascinating. It reminded him of what he had written in *The Book of King Arthur* concerning Galahad and his fellow knights when they ate of the food provided by the Sangreal. ". . . ye shall be fed afore this table with sweetmeats that never knights tasted."

There *were* times when Malory thought he'd go mad. He'd always been tempted by madness, a state in which a person was both touched with holiness by God and invulnerable to the cares and woes of the world, not to mention his own. But a man who'd spent so many years in prison on Earth without going crazy had to be basically tough. One of the things that had kept his mind unclouded in prison had been his writing of the first English prose epic. Though he knew that his readers would be very few, and most of them would probably not like it, he did not care one whit. Unlike his first work, which had been based on the great French writers of the cycles about King Arthur of ancient Britain, this was about the rejections but final triumph of his sweet Jesu. Unlike so many once-devout Christians, Malory clung to his faith with fierce obliviousness to "facts"—in itself an indication that he had gone mad, if his critics were to be believed.

Twice slain by savage infidels, Malory ended up in an area inhabited on one side by Parthians and on the other by Englishmen.

The Parthians were ancient horsemen who got their name from their habit of shooting backwards from their steeds as they retreated. In other words, they always got in a parting shot. At least, that was the explanation for their name according to one informant. Malory suspected that the grinning fellow was pulling his leg, but it sounded good, so why not accept it.

The Englishmen were chiefly of the seventeenth century and spoke an English which Malory had trouble understanding. However, after all these years, they also spoke Esperanto, that tongue which the missionaries of the Church of the Second Chance used as a universal medium of communication. The land, now known as New Hope, was peaceful, though it had not always been so. Once it had been a number of small states which had had a savage battle with the medieval German and Spanish states up north. These had been led by a man called Kramer, nicknamed the Hammer. After he had been killed, a long peace had come to the land, and the states eventually became one. Malory settled down there and took as his hutmate Philippa Hobart, daughter of Sir Henry Hobart. Though there was no longer a giving in marriage, Malory insisted that they be married, and he got a friend who had been a Catholic priest to perform the old ceremony. Later, he reconverted both his wife and the priest to their native faith.

He was set back somewhat, though, when he heard that the true Jesu Christ had appeared in this area with a Hebrew woman who had known Moses in Egypt and during the exodus. Jesu had also been accompanied by a man named Thomas Mix, an American, the descendant of Europeans who had emigrated to the continent discovered only twenty-one years after Malory had died. Jesu and Mix had burned to death together in bonfires ignited by Kramer.

At first, Malory had denied that the man calling himself Yeshua could be the real Christ. He might be a Hebrew of Christ's time, but he was a fake.

Then Malory, after tracking down all the evidence he could of Yeshua's statements and the events of his martyrdom, decided that perhaps Christ had truly been present. So he incorporated the tale told by the locals into the epic he was now writing with ink and a pen formed from the bone of a fish on bamboo paper. Malory also decided to canonize the American, and so Mix became Saint Thomas the Steadfast of the White Hat.

After a while Malory and his disciples forgot that the sainthood was a fiction and came to believe that Saint Thomas was indeed roaming The Valley in quest of his master, sweet Jesu, in this world which was purgatory, though not exactly the middle state between earth and heaven portrayed by the priests of lost Earth.

The ex-priest who'd married Thomas and Philippa, as a bishop ordained on Earth and so in the direct line of priesthood from Saint Peter, was able to instruct others and to make priests of them. The little group of Roman Catholics, however, had a different attitude in one respect from that they'd had in their Terrestrial days. They were tolerant; they did not attempt to bring back the Inquisition nor did they burn suspected witches. If they had insisted on these old customs, they would have quickly been exiled or perhaps even killed.

Late one night, Thomas Malory was lying in bed and pondering on the next chapter of his epic. Suddenly, there was a great shouting outside and a noise as of many running. He sat up and called to Philippa, who awoke frightened and trembling. They went out then to ask what the commotion was about. The people questioned pointed upward into the cloudless sky made bright as a full moon by the packed stars and flaming cosmic-gas sheets.

High up were two strange objects silhouetted against the celestial blaze. One, much smaller, was composed of two parts, a larger sphere above the other. Though those on the ground could not see any linkage between the two, they got the impression that the two were connected because they moved at the same speed. Then a woman who knew of such things said that it looked like a balloon. Malory had never seen one, but he had heard descriptions of them from nineteenth- and twentieth-centurians, and this did indeed look like the description.

The other object, far greater, resembled a gigantic cigar.

The same woman said that this was an airship or dirigible or perhaps was a vessel of the unknowns who'd made this planet.

"Angels?" Malory muttered. "Why would they have to use an airship? They have wings."

He forgot about that and cried out with the others as the huge vessel of the air suddenly dived. And then he screamed with the others when the vessel exploded. Burning, it fell toward The River.

The balloon continued to travel northeastward, and after a while it was gone. Long before that, the flaming airship struck the water. Its skeletal framework sank almost at once, but some pieces of its skin burned for a few minutes before they, too, were extinguished.

3

NEITHER ANGELS NOR DEMONS HAD VOYAGED IN THAT VESSEL OF THE SKY. The man whom Malory and his wife pulled out of the water and rowed to shore in their boat was no more and no less human than they. He was a tall dark rapier-thin man with a big nose and a weak chin. His large black eyes stared at them in the torchlight, and he said nothing for a long while. After he had been carried into the community hall, dried off and covered with thick cloths, and had drunk some hot coffee, he said something in French and then spoke in Esperanto.

"How many survived?"

Malory said, "We don't know yet."

A few minutes later, the first of twenty-two corpses, some very charred, were brought to the bank. One of them was a woman's. Though the search continued through the night and part of the morning, these were all that were found. The Frenchman was the single survivor. Though he was weak and still in shock, he insisted on getting up and taking part in the search. When he saw the bodies by a grailstone, he burst into tears and sobbed for a long time. Malory took this as a good indication of the man's health. At least he wasn't in such deep trauma that he was unable to express his grief.

"Where have the others gone?" the stranger demanded.

Then his sorrow became rage, and he shook his fist at the skies and howled damnation at someone named Thorn. Later, he asked if anybody had seen or heard another aircraft, a helicopter. Many had.

"Which way did it go?" he said.

Some said that the machine making the strange chopping noise had gone down-River. Others said that it had gone up-River. Several days later, the report came that the machine had been seen sinking into The River two hundred miles upstream during a rainstorm. Only one person had witnessed that, and he claimed that a man had swum from the sinking craft. A message via drum was sent to the area asking if any strangers had suddenly appeared. The reply was that none had been located.

A number of grails were found floating on The River, and these were brought to the survivor. He identified one as his, and he ate a meal from it that afternoon. Several of the grails were "free" containers. That is, they could be opened by anybody, and these were confiscated by the state of New Hope.

The Frenchman then asked if any gigantic boats propelled by paddlewheels had passed this point. He was told that one had, the *Rex Grandissimus*, commanded by the infamous King John of England.

"Good," the man said. He thought for a while, then said, "I could just stay here and wait until the *Mark Twain* comes by. But I don't think I will. I'm going after Thorn."

By then, he felt recovered enough to talk about himself. And how he talked about himself!

"I am Savinien de Cyrano II de Bergerac," he said. "I prefer to be called Savinien, but for some reason most people prefer Cyrano. So I allow that small liberty. After all, later ages referred to me as Cyrano, and though it was a mistake, I am so famous that people cannot get used to my preference. They think they know better than I do.

"No doubt you've heard of me."

He regarded his hosts as if they should feel honored to have such a great man as their guest.

"It pains me to admit that I have not," Malory said.

"What? I was the greatest swordsman of my time, perhaps, no, undoubtedly, of all times. There is no reason for me to be modest. I do not hide my light under a bushel or, in fact, under anything. I was also the author of some remarkable literary works. I wrote books about trips to the sun and to the moon, very pointed and witty satire. My play, *The Pedant Out-Witted*, was, I understand, used with some modifications by a certain Monsieur Molière and presented as his own. Well, perhaps I exaggerate. Certainly he did use much of the comedy. I also understand that an Englishman named Jonathan Swift used some of my ideas in his *Gulliver's Travels*. I do not blame them, since I myself was not above using the ideas of others, though I improved upon them."

"That is all very well, sir," Malory said, forbearing to mention his own works. "But if it does not make you overwrought, you could tell us how you came here in that airship and what caused it to burst into flames."

De Bergerac was staying with the Malorys until an empty hut could be found or he could be loaned the tools to construct one for himself. At this time, though, he and his hosts and perhaps a hundred more were seated or standing by a big fire outside the hut.

It was a long tale, more fabulous even than the teller's own fictions or Malory's. Sir Thomas, however, had the feeling that the Frenchman was not telling all that had happened.

When the narrative was finished, Malory mused aloud, "Then it is true that there is a tower in the center of the north polar sea, the sea from whence flows The River and to which it returns? And it is true that whoever is responsible for this world lives in that tower? I wonder what happened to this Japanese, this Piscator? Did the residents of the tower, who surely must be angels, invite him to stay with them because, in a sense, he'd entered the gates of paradise? Or did they send him elsewhere, to some distant part of The River, perhaps?

"And this Thorn, what could account for his criminal behavior? Perhaps he was a demon in disguise."

De Bergerac laughed loudly and scornfully.

When he had stopped, he said, "There are no angels nor demons, my friend. I do not now maintain, as I did on Earth, that there is no God. But to admit to the existence of a Creator does not oblige one to believe in such myths as angels and demons."

Malory hotly insisted that there were indeed such. This led to an argument in the course of which the Frenchman walked away from his audience. He spent the night, from what Malory heard, in the hut of a woman who thought that if he was such a great swordsman he must also be a great lover. From her accounts, he was, though perhaps too much devoted to that fashion of making love which many thought reached its perfection, or nadir of degeneracy, in France. Malory was disgusted. But later that day de Bergerac appeared to apologize for his ingratitude to the man who'd saved his life.

"I should not have scoffed at you, my host, my savior. I tender you a thousand apologies, for which I hope to receive one forgiveness."

"You are forgiven," Malory said, sincerely. "Perhaps, though you forsook our Church on Earth and have blasphemed against God, you would care to attend the mass being said tonight for the souls of your departed comrades?"

"That is the least I can do," de Bergerac said.

During the mass, he wept copiously, so much so that after it Malory took advantage of his high emotions. He asked him if he was ready to return to God.

"I am not aware that I ever left Him, if He exists," the Frenchman said. "I was weeping with grief for those I loved on the *Parseval* and for those whom I did not love but respected. I was weeping with rage against Thorn or whatever his real name is. And I was also weeping because men and women are still ignorant and superstitious enough to believe in this flummery."

"You refer to the mass?" Malory said icily.

"Yes, forgive me again!" de Bergerac cried.

"Not until you truly repent," Malory said, "and if you address your repentance to that God whom you have offended so grievously."

"*Quelle merde!*" de Bergerac said. But a moment later he embraced Malory and kissed him on both cheeks. "How I wish that your belief was indeed fact! But if it were, then how could I forgive God!"

He bade adieu to Malory, saying that he would probably never see him again. Tomorrow morning, he was setting out up-River. Malory suspected that de Bergerac would have to steal a boat to do so, and he was right.

Malory often thought of the man who'd leaped from the burning dirigible, the man who had actually been to the tower which many spoke about but none had seen except for the Frenchman and his crewmates. Or if the story could be believed, a group of ancient Egyptians and a huge hairy subhuman.

Less than three years later, the second great paddlewheeled boat came by. This was even more huge than the *Rex* and it was more luxurious and faster and better armored and weaponed. But it was not called the *Mark Twain*. Its captain, Samuel Clemens, an American, had renamed it the *Not For Hire*. Apparently, he'd heard that King John was calling his own boat, the original *Not For Hire,* the *Rex Grandissimus*. So Clemens had taken back the name and ceremoniously had it painted on the hull.

The boat stopped off to recharge its batacitor and to charge its grails. Malory didn't get a chance to talk to the captain, but he did see him and his surprising bodyguard. Joe Miller was indeed an ogre, ten feet high and weighing eight hundred pounds. His body was not as hairy as Malory expected from the tales. He was no more hirsute than many men Malory had seen, though the hairs were longer. And he did have a face with massive prognathic jaws and a nose like a gigantic cucumber or a proboscis monkey's. Yet he had the look of intelligence.

4

ON DROVE THE PURSUER.

It was an hour to high noon. In another hour, the fabulous riverboat would be anchored, and a very thick aluminum cable would connect a copper cap placed over a grailstone to the batacitor in the vessel. When the stone delivered its tremendous voltage, the batacitor would be charged again and the grails on another copper plate in the boat would be filled with food, liquor, and other items.

Its hull was white except over the paddle boxes, or wheel guards, over the four paddlewheels. On these were painted in big black letters: *NOT FOR HIRE*. Under this in smaller letters: Samuel Clemens, Captain. And under this line, in still smaller letters: Owned & Operated By The Avengers, Inc.

Above the pilothouse was a jack staff flying a square light-blue flag on which was a scarlet phoenix.

From the stern or verge staff, leaning at a forty-five-degree angle from the stern of the lowest deck, was another flag with a light-blue field and bearing a scarlet phoenix.

Sam's boat was 550 feet and eight inches long. Its breadth over the paddleboxes, or paddlewheel guards, was 115 feet. Its draft was 18 feet when fully loaded.

There were five major decks. The lowest, the A or boiler deck, held various storage rooms, the enormous batacitor, which rose from a well into the next deck, the four electrical motors which drove the paddlewheels, and a huge boiler.

The batacitor was an enormous electrical device fifty feet wide and forty-three feet high. One of Sam's engineers had claimed it was a late twentieth-century invention. But, since the engineer had said he'd lived past 1983, Sam suspected that he was an agent. (He was long dead.)

The batacitor (from battery-capacitor) could take in the enormous voltage discharged from a grailstone within a second and deliver it all within a second or in a mere trickle, as required. It was the power source for the four massive paddlewheel motors and for the other electrical needs of the boat, including the air-conditioning.

The electrically heated boiler was sixty feet wide and thirty high and was used to heat water for the showers and to heat the cabins, to make alcohol, to power the steam machine guns and fighter-plane steam catapults, and to provide air for the compressed-air cannon and steam for the boat's whistles and the two smokestacks. The smokestacks were misnamed, since they only vented a steam which was colored to simulate smoke when Sam felt like putting on a show.

At water level in the rear of the boiler deck was a big door which could be raised to admit or let out the two launches and the torpedo-bomber.

The deck above, the B or main deck, was set back to provide an exterior passageway, called the promenade deck.

On the Mississippi riverboats which Sam had piloted when young, the lowest deck had been called the main deck and the one above that the boiler deck. But since the boiler in the *Not For Hire* had its base in the lowest deck, Sam had renamed that the boiler deck. And he called the one above it the main deck. It had been confusing at first for his pilots, who were accustomed to Terrestrial usage, but they had gotten used to it.

Sometimes, when the boat was anchored off the bank of a peaceable area, Sam gave the crew shore leave (except for the guards, of course). Then he would conduct a tour for the local high muckymucks. Dressed in a white fishskin-leather jacket, a long white kiltcloth, and white calf-length boots and wearing a white leather captain's hat, he would take his guests from top to bottom of the boat. Of course, he and some marines kept a sharp eye on them, since the contents of the *Not For Hire* must have proved very tempting to landlubbing stay-at-homes.

Puffing on a cigar between his sentences, Sam would explain everything, well, almost everything, to his curious party.

Having led them through the A or boiler deck, Sam would then take them up the steps to the B or main deck.

"Navy people would call this series of steps a ladder," he said. "But since most of my crew were landlubbers, and since we do have some real ladders aboard, I decided to call the stairways stairways. After all, you go up them on steps, not rungs. In the same spirit, I dictated, despite the outraged protests of naval veterans, that walls should not be called bulkheads but walls. However, I did allow a distinction between your ordinary door and hatches. Hatches are those thick airtight watertight doors which can be locked with a lever mechanism."

"And what kind of weapon is that?" a tourist would ask. He'd point at a long tubular duraluminum device looking like a cannon and mounted on a platform. Big plastic tubes ran into the breech.

"That's a steam machine gun, .80 caliber. It contains a complicated device which permits a stream of plastic bullets, fed through a pipe from below, to be fired at a rapid rate from the gun. Steam from the boiler provides the propulsive power."

Once, a person who'd been on the *Rex* said, "King John's boat has a .75-caliber steam machine gun, several of them."

"Yes. I designed those myself. But the son of a bitch stole the boat, and when I built this one, I made my guns bigger than his."

He showed them the rows of windows, "not ports but windows," along the exterior passageway. "Which some of my crew have the unmitigated ignorance or brazen gall to call corridors or even halls. Of course, they do that behind my back."

He took them into a cabin to impress upon them its commodiousness and luxuriousness.

"There are one hundred and twenty-eight cabins, each of which is fitted for two persons. Notice the snap-up bed, made from brass. Eye-ball the porcelain toilets, the shower stall with hot and cold running water, the wash basin with brass plumbing, the mirrors framed in brass, the oak bureaus. They're not very large, but then we don't carry many changes of clothes aboard. Notice also the weapons rack, which may hold pistols, rifles, spears, swords, and bows. The carpeting is made of human hairs. And pop your eyes out at the painting on the wall. It's an original by Motonobu, A.D. 1476 to 1559, the great Japanese painter who founded the style of painting called Kano. In the next cabin are some paintings by Zeuxis of Heraclea. There are ten in there. As a matter of fact it's Zeuxis' own cabin. He, as you may or may not know, was the great fifth-century B.C. painter born in Heraclea, a Greek colony in south Italy. It's said of him that he painted a bunch of grapes so realistically that birds tried to eat it. Zeuxis won't confirm or deny this tale. For myself, I prefer photographs, but I do have some paintings in my suite. One by a Pieter de Hooch, a Dutch painter of the seventeenth century. Near it is one by the Italian, Giovanni Fattori, A.D. 1825 to 1908. Poor fellow. It may be his final work, since he fell overboard during a party and was smashed to shreds by the paddlewheel. Even if he were resurrected, which isn't likely, he won't find pigments enough for a single painting anywhere but on this boat and the *Rex*."

Sam took them along the outside or promenade deck to the bow. Here was mounted an 88-millimeter cannon. So far, Sam said, it hadn't been used, and new gunpowder would soon have to be made to refill the charges.

"But when I catch up with the *Rex*, I'll blow Rotten John out of the water with this."

He also pointed out the rocket batteries on the promenade, heat-seeking missiles with a range of a mile and a half and carrying warheads of forty pounds of plastic explosive.

"If the cannons miss, these'll shred his ass."

One of the women tourists was well acquainted with Clemens' work and biographies about him. She spoke in a low voice to her companion. "I never realized that Mark Twain was so bloodthirsty."

"Madame," Sam said, having overheard her, "I am not bloodthirsty! I am the most pacifistic of men! I loathe violence, and the idea of war puts my bowels into an uproar. If you'd read my essays about war and those who love it, you'd know that. But I have been forced into this situation and many like it. To survive, you must lie better than the liars, deceive more than the deceivers, and kill the killers first! For me, it's sheer necessity, though justified! What would you do if King John had stolen your boat after you'd gone through years of search for iron and other metals to build your dream! And years of fighting others who wanted to take them away from you after you'd found them, and on every side treachery and murder, all directed against you! And what would you do if that John killed some of your good friends and your wife and then sped away laughing at you! Would you let him get away with it? I think not, not if you've got an ounce of courage."

"*Vengeance is mine, saith the Lord*," a man said.

"Yes. Maybe. But if there is a Lord, and He works His vengeance, how's He going to do it without using humans as His hands? Did you ever hear of any wicked person being struck down by lightning, except by accident? Lightning also strikes thousands of innocents every year, you know! No, He has to use human beings as His instruments, and who else is better qualified than me? Or more made by circumstances into His keen and purposefully designed tool?"

Sam was so upset that he had to send a marine up to the grand salon to get four ounces of bourbon to settle his nerves.

Before the drink was brought down to Sam, a tourist muttered, "Bullshit!"

"Throw that man off the boat!" Sam shouted. And it was done.

"You're a very angry man," the woman who knew his works said.

"Yes, ma'am, I am. And with good reason. I was angry on Earth, and I'm angry here."

The marine brought Sam's whiskey. He downed it quickly and then continued the tour with his good humor restored.

He led the group up the grand staircase to the grand salon. They paused in the entrance, and the tourists oohed and ahed. It was two hundred feet long and fifty wide and the ceiling was twenty feet above the floor. Along the center of the ceiling was a line of five huge cut-glass chandeliers. There were many windows making the huge room well lighted and many wall and ceiling lights and towering ornate brass floor lamps.

At the far end was a stage which Clemens said was used for live dramas and comedies and for orchestras. It also had a big screen which could be pulled down when movies were shown.

"We don't use chemically treated film to shoot these," he said. "We have electronic cameras. We make original films and also remake the classics of Earth. Tonight, for instance, we're showing *The Maltese Falcon*. We don't have any of the original cast except Mary Astor, whose real name is Lucille Langehanke, and she plays Sam Spade's secretary. Astor was, from what I've been told, miscast. But then I don't suppose most of you know what I'm talking about."

"I do," the woman who'd called him angry said. "Who played her part in your version?"

"An American actress, Alice Brady."

"And who played Sam Spade? I can't imagine anyone else but Humphrey Bogart in the role."

"Howard da Silva, another American actor. His real name was Howard Goldblatt, if I remember correctly. He's very grateful to get this role, since he claims he never had a chance to show his real acting ability on Earth. But he's sorry that his audience will be so small."

"Don't tell me the director is John Ford?"

"I never heard of him," Sam said. "Our director is Alexander Singer."

"I never heard of him."

"I suppose so. But I understand that he was well known in Hollywood circles."

Irked at what he considered an irrelevant interruption, he pointed out the sixty-foot-long polished oak bar on the port side and the neatly stacked row of liquor bottles and decanters. The group was quite impressed with these and the leadglass goblets. They were even more affected by the four grand pianos. Sam told them that he had aboard at least ten great pianists and five composers. For instance, Selim Palmgren (1878–1951), a Finnish composer and pianist who had been prominent in establishing the school of Finnish national music. There was also Giovanni Pierluigi da Palestrina (1526–1594), the great composer of madrigals and motets.

"Amadeus Mozart was once on this boat," Sam said. "He's a really great composer, some say the greatest. But he turned out to be such a failure as a human being, such a sneak and lecher and coward, that I kicked him off the boat."

"Mozart?" the woman said. "My God, Mozart! You beast, how could you treat such a wonderful composer, a genius, a god, like that?"

"Ma'am," Clemens said, "believe me, there was more than enough provocation. If you don't like my attitude, you may leave. A marine will escort you to shore."

"You're no fucking gentleman," the woman said.

"Oh, yes, I am."

5

THEY WENT DOWN A PASSAGEWAY TOWARD THE BOW, PASSING MORE cabins. The last one on the right-hand side was Clemens' suite, and he showed them that. Their exclamations of surprise and delight gratified Sam. Across from his cabin, he said, was that of his bodyguard, Joe Miller, and Joe's mate.

Beyond his quarters was a small room which contained an elevator. This led into the lowest of the three rooms of the pilothouse structure. This was the E deck or observation room, furnished with overstuffed chairs, lounges, and a small bar. There were also mounts in the windows for machine guns which shot plastic or wooden bullets.

The next room of the pilothouse structure was the F or cannon deck, called so because of the emplacement of four 20-millimeter steam cannons. These were fed ammunition by belts enclosed in a shaft which ran from the boiler deck.

The very highest deck, the pilothouse or control or G deck, was twice as large as the one beneath it.

"Big enough to hold a dance in," said Clemens, who didn't mind exaggeration at all, especially when he was the exaggerator.

He introduced them to the radio and radar operators, the chief executive officer, the communications officer, and the chief pilot. The latter was Henry Detweiller, a Frenchman who'd emigrated to the American Midwest in the early nineteenth century and become a river pilot, then a captain, and finally the owner of several steamboat companies. He'd died in Peoria, Illinois, in his palatial mansion.

The exec, John Byron, was an Englishman (1723–1786) who'd been a midshipman on Anson's famous naval expedition around the world but was shipwrecked off the coast of Chile. When he became an admiral, he earned the nickname of "Foulweather Jack" because every time his fleet put to sea it ran into very bad storms.

"He is also the grandfather of the famous or infamous poet, Lord Byron," Sam said. "Isn't that right, admiral?"

Byron, a small blond man with cold blue eyes, nodded.

"Admiral?" said the woman who'd been bugging Clemens. "But if you're the captain. . . ?"

Sam puffed on his cigar, then said, "Yes, I'm the only captain aboard. The next highest rank is full admiral and so on down. The chief of my air force, which consists of four pilots and six mechanics, is a general. So is the chief of my marines. The latter, by the way, was once a full general in the United States army during the Civil War. He's a full-blooded American Indian, a Seneca chief. Ely S. Parker or, to use his Iroquois name, Donehogawa, which means 'Keeper of the West Gate.' He is highly educated and was a construction engineer on Earth. He served on General Ulysses S. Grant's staff during the war."

Sam next explained the controls and instruments used by the pilot. He sat in a chair on each side of which were two long metal rods projecting from the floor. By moving the control sticks forward or backward, he could control the forward or backward rotations of the paddlewheels. Also, their rate of speed of turning. Before him was a panel with many dials and gauges and several oscilloscopes.

"One is a sonarscope," Sam said. "Reading that, the pilot can tell exactly how deep the bottom of The River is and how far from the bank the boat is and also if there are any dangerously large objects in the water. By switching that dial marked AUTO CRUISE to ON, he doesn't have to do a thing then except keep an eye on the sonarscope and another on the banks. If the automatic system should malfunction, he can switch to a backup system while the other is being repaired."

"Piloting must be easy," a man said.

"It is. But only an experienced pilot can handle emergencies, which is why most of them are Mississippi boat veterans."

He pointed out that the deck of the control room was ninety feet above the surface of The River. He also called to their attention that the pilothouse structure was, unlike that on the riverboats on Earth, located on the starboard side, not in the middle of the deck.

"Which makes the *Not For Hire* resemble an aircraft carrier even more."

They watched the marines drilling on the flight deck and the men and women busy practicing the martial arts, sword, spear, knife, and axe fighting, and archery.

"Every member of this crew, including myself, has to become proficient with all weapons. In addition, each person has to become fully qualified to handle any post. They go to school to learn electricity, electronics, plumbing, officering, and piloting. Half of them have taken lessons on the piano or with other musical instruments. This boat contains more individuals with more varied skills and professions than any other area on this planet."

"Does everybody take turns being the captain?" said the woman who'd angered him.

"No. That is the exception," Sam said, his thick eyebrows forming a frown. "I wouldn't want to put ideas into anybody's head."

He strode to the control panel and punched a button. Sirens began to wail, and the exec, John Byron, asked the communications officer to send the "Bridges, clearing" warning over the general intercom. Sam went to a starboard window and urged the others to gather by him. They gasped when they saw long thick metal beams slide out from the three lower decks.

"If we can't sink the *Rex*," Clemens said, "we'll board it over those bridges."

The woman said, "That's fine. But the crew of the *Rex* can also board your vessel on your own bridges."

Sam's blue-green eyes glared above his falcon nose.

However, the others of the group were so awed, so astounded, that Sam's hairy chest puffed from joy. He had always been fascinated by mechanical devices, and he liked others to share his enthusiasm. On Earth his interest in novel gadgets had been responsible for his going bankrupt. He'd put a fortune into the unworkable Paige typesetting machine.

The woman said, "But all this iron and aluminum and other metals? This planet is so mineral-poor. Where did you get these?"

"First," Sam said, pleased to recount his exploits, "a giant nickel-iron meteorite fell into The Valley. Do you remember when, many years ago, the grailstones on the right bank ceased operating? That was because the falling star severed the line.

"As you know, it was back in operation twenty-four hours later. So . . ."

"Who repaired it?" a man said. "I've heard all sorts of stories, but . . ."

"I was in the neighborhood, in a manner of speaking," Sam said. "In fact, the tidal wave of The River and the blast almost killed me and my companions."

He mentally winced then, not because of the near-fatality but because he remembered what he'd done later to one of his companions, the Norseman Erik Bloodaxe.

"So I can testify to the amazing but undeniable fact that not only had the line been repaired overnight, but the blasted land had also been restored. The grass and the trees and the stripped soil were all back."

"Who did it?"

"They had to be the beings who made this Rivervalley and resurrected us. I've heard that they are human beings like us, in fact, Earthmen who lived ages after we did. However . . ."

"No, not human beings," the man said. "Surely not. It was God who made all this for us."

"If you're so well acquainted with Him," Clemens said, "give me His address. I'd like to write Him."

He continued, "My group was the first to get to the site of the meteorite. The crater, which might have been as wide and deep as the famous one in Arizona, was buried by then. But we staked out a claim, and we began digging. Some time later, we heard that large deposits of bauxite and cryolite were under the land of a state down-River. Its citizens, however, had no means of digging it up or then using it. But my state, Parolando, could make aluminum from the ores after we'd fashioned iron tools. That state, Soul City, attacked us to get the iron. We beat them and confiscated the bauxite and cryolite. We also found that some other states relatively nearby had some copper and tin deposits. Also, some vanadium and tungsten. We traded our iron artifacts for these."

The woman, frowning, said, "Isn't it strange that there was so much metal in that area, and elsewhere there is almost none? It's quite a coincidence, isn't it, that you were looking for these metals and just happened to be in the neighborhood when the meteorite fell?"

"Maybe God directed me to that place," Sam said sneeringly.

No, he thought, it wasn't God. It was that Mysterious Stranger, the Ethical who called himself X, who had arranged, who knew how many thousands of years ago, that the deposits should be so concentrated in that area. And who then directed that meteorite to fall near them.

For what purpose? To build a riverboat and to provide weapons so that Sam could voyage up The River, perhaps for ten million miles, and get to the headwaters. And from there to the tower which reared high in the mists of the cold northpolar sea.

And then do what?

He didn't know. The Ethical was supposed to visit him again during a thunderstorm at night, as he always did. Apparently, he came at that time because the lightning interfered with the delicate instruments the Ethicals used to try to locate the renegade. He would give him more information. In the meantime, others visited by X, his chosen warriors, would find Sam and get on his boat and go with him up-River.

But things had gone awry.

He'd not seen or heard from the Mysterious Stranger again. He'd built his boat, and then his partner, King John Lackland, had hijacked it. Also, some years later, the "little resurrections," the "translations," had ceased, and permanent death had come to the dwellers in The Valley again.

Something had happened to the people in the tower, the Ethicals. Something must also have happened to the Mysterious Stranger.

But he, Clemens, was going to the headwaters anyway and then try to get into the tower. He knew how difficult the climbing of the mountains which circled the sea would be. Joe Miller, the titanthrop, had seen the tower from a path along the side of that towering range when he'd accompanied the Pharaoh Akhenaten. Joe had also seen a gigantic aircraft of some sort descend to the top of the tower. And then he'd tripped over a grail left by some unknown predecessor and had fallen to his death. After being resurrected to a place in The Valley, he'd met Sam and had told his strange tale to him.

The woman said, "What about this dirigible we've heard rumors of? Why didn't you go on that instead of the boat? You could have gotten to the headwaters in a few days instead of the thirty or forty years it'll take you on the boat."

That was a subject Sam didn't like to talk about. The truth was that no one had even thought of an airship until shortly before the *Not For Hire* was to set out. Then a German dirigible man named von Parseval had come along and asked why he hadn't built the ship.

Sam's chief engineer, Milton Firebrass, an ex-astronaut, had liked the suggestion. So he'd stayed behind when the *Not For Hire* left, and he'd constructed the floating vessel. He'd kept in radio contact with the boat, and when the ship did get to the tower, he'd reported that it was a little over a mile high and almost ten miles in diameter. The *Parseval* had landed on its top, but only one of its crew, a Japanese ex-blimp man and Sufi who called himself Piscator, had been able to enter. The others had been restrained by some invisible but tangible force. Before that, an officer named Barry Thorn had placed a bomb on the helicopter carrying Firebrass and some others on a scouting landing. He'd set the bomb off with a radio signal and then stolen a helicopter and flown off the dirigible. But he'd been wounded, and the copter had crashed at the base of the tower.

Thorn was brought back to the dirigible and questioned. He refused to give information, but he was visibly shocked when he heard that Piscator had gotten into the tower.

Clemens suspected that Thorn was either an Ethical or one of their subordinates, whom the X's recruits called agents.

He also had some suspicions that Firebrass had been one or the other. And perhaps the woman who'd died in the explosion of the helicopter, Anna Obrenova, had been an Ethical or agent.

Sam had concluded from his examination of all available evidence that something had long ago stranded a number of agents and perhaps some Ethicals in The Valley. X was probably one of them. Which meant that agents and Ethicals would have to use the same means as the Valley-dwellers to get to the tower. Which meant that there were probably some disguised agents or Ethicals or both on his boat. Which meant that there were probably also some on the *Rex*.

Just why the Ethicals and agents hadn't been able to use their aircraft to return to the tower, he didn't know.

By now he'd reasoned that anyone who claimed to have lived after A.D. 1983 was one of the beings responsible for the Riverworld. It was his idea that the post-1983 story was false and was a code which enabled them to recognize each other.

He also reasoned that some of them might have figured that X's recruits suspected this story-code. Therefore, they would be dropping that story.

Clemens said to the woman, "The airship was supposed to be a scout, to find out the lay of the land. Its captain was under orders, however, to get into the tower if it was possible. Then he was to return to the boat and pick up myself and some others. But no one but a Sufi philosopher named Piscator could get in, and he didn't come back out. On the way back, its captain, a woman named Jill Gulbirra, who took over when Firebrass was killed, sent a raiding expedition in a copter against the *Rex*. King John was captured, but he escaped by jumping from the copter. I don't know whether or not he survived. The aircraft flew back to the *Parseval* and continued on its course to the *Not For Hire*. Then Gulbirra reported sighting a very large balloon and was heading for it when Thorn got loose again. He flew off in a copter. Gulbirra, suspecting he'd planted a bomb, searched for it. None was found, but she couldn't take a chance that there wasn't one. She dived the dirigible toward the ground. She wanted to get her crew off just in case there was a bomb.

"Then she reported that there was an explosion. That was the last we heard from the *Parseval*."

The woman said, "We've heard rumors that it crashed many thousands of miles up-River. There was only one survivor."

"Only one! My God, who was he? Or she?"

"I don't know his name. But I heard that he was a Frenchman."

Sam groaned. There was just one Frenchman on the airship. Cyrano de Bergerac, with whom Sam's wife had fallen in love. Of all the crew, he was the only one whom Sam would not have sorrowed over.

6

IT WAS LATE AFTERNOON WHEN SAM SAW THE STRANGE BEING WHO WAS even more grotesque than Joe Miller. Joe was at least human, but this person had obviously not been born on Earth.

Sam knew at once that the being had to be one of the small group from a planet of Tau Ceti. His informant, the late Baron John de Greystock, had known one of them. According to his story, the Tau Cetans, in the early twenty-first century, had put into orbit a smaller vessel around Earth before descending in the great mothership to the surface. They'd been welcomed, but then one of them, Monat, had said on a TV talk show that the Cetans had the means for extending their lives to centuries. The Earthpeople had demanded that this knowledge be given them. When the Cetans had refused, saying that the Terrestrials would abuse the gift of longevity, mobs had lynched most of the Cetans and then stormed the spaceship. Reluctantly, Monat had activated a scanner on the satellite, and this had projected a beam which killed most of the human life on Earth. At least, Monat thought it would do so. He didn't see the results of his action. He, too, was torn apart by the mob.

He had set the death-beams into operation because he feared that Terrestrials would use the spaceship as a model to build more ships and then would go to his native planet and war against it, perhaps destroy all his people. He didn't know whether or not they would actually do that, but he couldn't take the chance.

The Cetan was standing up somewhat precariously in a narrow dugout and waving frantically at the *Not For Hire*. Obviously, he wanted aboard. So did a lot of people, Sam thought, but they don't get their wish. This, however, was, if not a horse of a different color, a biped neither bird or man. So Sam told the pilot to make a circle and then come alongside the dugout.

Presently, while the gaping crew lined the exterior passageways, the Cetan climbed a short ladder to the boiler deck. His companion, an ordinary-looking human male, followed him. The dugout drifted away to be grabbed by whoever got to it first.

Escorted by two marines and General Ely S. Parker himself, the two were soon in the control room. Sam, speaking Esperanto, shook their hands, introduced himself and the others, and then they introduced themselves.

"I am Monat Grrautut," the biped said in a deep rich voice.

"Jesus H. Christ!" Sam said. "The very one!"

Monat smiled, exposing human-looking teeth.

"Ah, then you've heard of me."

"You're the only Tau Cetan whose name I know," Sam said. "I've been scanning the banks for years for one of you, and I've never seen hair nor hide of any. And then to run smackdab into you yourself!"

"I'm not from a planet of Tau Ceti," Monat said. "That was the story we gave when we came to Earth. Actually, I'm from a planet of the star Arcturus. We misled the Terrestrials just in case they proved to be warlike and then . . ."

"Good thinking," Sam said. "Though you were a little tough on Earthpeople, as I understand. However, why did you stick to that story when you were resurrected here—without your permission?"

Monat shrugged. How humanlike, Sam thought.

"Habit, I suppose. Also, I wanted to make sure the Terrestrials still didn't represent a danger to my people."

"I can't blame you."

"When I knew positively that Earthpeople were no danger, I told the true story of my origin."

"Sure you did," Sam said and laughed. "Here. Have a cigar, you two."

Monat was six feet eight inches tall, thin, and pink-skinned. He wore only a kiltcloth, allowing most of his features to show, but concealing the most interesting to some. Greystock had said that the fellow's penis could pass for human and was circumcised, as were all men's on this world. His scrotum, however, was a knobby sac which contained a number of small testes.

His face was semihuman. Below a shaved skull and very high forehead were two thick black curly-haired eyebrows that ran down to his very prominent cheekbones and spread out to cover them. The eyes were a dark brown. Most of his nose was more handsome than Sam had seen on many people. But a thin membranous fringe a sixteenth of an inch long hung from the sides of his nostrils. The nose ended in a thick, deeply clefted pad of cartilage. His lips were doglike, thin, leathery, and black. His lobeless ears displayed quite unhuman convolutions.

Each hand bore three fingers and a long thumb on each, and he had four toes on each foot.

I don't suppose he'd scare anybody on skid row, Sam thought. Or in Congress.

His companion was an American born in 1918, deceased in 2008, when the Cetan or Arcturan beam swept Earth. His name was Peter Jairus Frigate, and he was about six feet tall, of muscular build, had black hair and green eyes and a not ugly face in front, but a rather craggy and short-jawed profile. Like Monat, he had a grail and a bundle of possessions and was armed with a stone knife, an axe, a bow, and a quiver of arrows.

Sam doubted very much that Monat was telling the truth about his place of birth or that Frigate was giving his right name. He doubted the story of anybody who said he'd lived past 1983. However, he wasn't going to say anything about that until he became well acquainted with these two.

After having a drink served to them, he personally led them to the officers' quarters near his suite.

"It just so happens that I'm short of three of my complement," he said. "There's a cabin available in the boiler deck. It's not a desirable location, so I'll roust out two junior officers from this cabin here. You can have theirs, and they can go below."

The man and the woman who had to surrender their cabin didn't look happy when they heard Sam's order, but they got out quickly.

That evening, they ate at the captain's table on china plates painted by an ancient Chinese artist and drank from cut-leadglass goblets. The dining utensils were a solid silver alloy.

Sam and the others, including the gigantic Joe Miller, listened intently to the stories of both newcomers about their adventures on the Riverworld. When Sam heard that they'd journeyed for a long while with Richard Francis Burton, the famous nineteenth-century explorer, linguist, translator, and author, he felt a shock run through him. The Ethical had told him that he'd also recruited Burton.

"Got any idea where he is?" he said calmly.

"No," Monat said. "We were separated during a battle and could not find him after it though we searched for him."

Sam urged Joe Miller to tell his story of the Egyptian expedition. Sam was getting impatient with his role of the polite questioner and host. He loved to dominate the conversation, but he wanted to see what effect Miller's tale had on the two.

When Joe finished, Monat said. "So! Then there *is* a tower in the polar sea!"

"Yeth, goddam it, that'th vhat I thaid," Joe said.

Sam intended to take at least a week hearing everything relevant they had to say about themselves. Then he would subject them to much more rigorous questioning.

Two days later, when the boat was anchored on the right bank at noon for recharging, the grailstones remained mute and flameless.

"Holy jumping Jesus!" Sam said. "Another meteorite?"

He didn't think that was the cause for the failure. The Ethical had told him that meteor-deflecting guards had been set up in space, and that the only reason the one had gotten through was because he'd managed to make the guards fail at just the right moment to permit the meteor to pass through them. The guards would still be out there, floating in space, ready to do their job.

But if the failure hadn't been caused by a meteorite, what had caused it?

Or was it another case of malfunction of the Ethicals' systems? People were no longer resurrected, which meant that something had gone wrong and unrepaired in the mechanism which converted the heat of the planet's core into electricity for the stones. Luckily, these were set in a parallel, not a series, arrangement. Otherwise, everybody would starve, not just those on the right bank.

Sam immediately ordered that the boat resume its course upstream. When it was near dusk the boat stopped at the left bank. Not unexpectedly, the locals did not agree to allow the use of a grailstone. There was a hell of a fight, a slaughter which sickened Sam. Frigate was one of those killed by a small rocket launched from the bank.

Then the starving desperates of the right bank invaded the left bank. They came in swarms that would not be stopped until so many had been killed that there was room enough on the stones for the grails of the survivors.

Not until the bodies no longer clogged the surface of The River did Clemens give the order to proceed upstream. A few days after that, he stopped long enough to replace those he'd lost in the bloodiness.

SECTION 3

Aboard the *Rex:* The Thread of Reason

7

IT WAS LOGHU AND ALICE WHO GOT BURTON AND THE OTHERS ONTO KING John's boat.

Their group had traveled up-River to the area at which the *Rex* had anchored for shore leave and repairs. They found the landing place temporarily overpopulated because of those curious to see the great vessel at close range, some of whom were also ambitious to get signed up as crew members. There were some vacancies aboard which rumor said had resulted when the captain had reprimanded too harshly six people whom he thought negligent in their duties. He didn't seem in any hurry to replace them.

When John came ashore, he was surrounded by twelve marines, who gave him plenty of elbow room. It was no secret, though, that King John had an eye for beautiful women. So Loghu, an exceedingly beautiful ancient Tokharian blonde, walked by him clad only in a short kiltcloth. John stopped his marines and began talking to her. He wasn't long in inviting her aboard for a tour of his boat. Though he didn't say so, he intimated that his grand suite might take the longest to inspect and that only he and Loghu should do the inspecting.

Loghu laughed and said that she might come aboard, but her friends would have to come with her. As for the tête-à-tête, she would consider it but would not make up her mind until she had seen everything on the vessel.

King John looked sour, but then he laughed and said that he would show her something that most people didn't get to see. Loghu was no fool and understood well what he meant. Nevertheless, she knew how desperately necessary it was to get aboard the *Rex*.

Thus Alice, Burton, Kazz, and Besst were also invited to the tour.

Burton was fuming since he did not wish to get John's ear by having Loghu behave like a slut. It was the only way, however. His previous declarations that he would find some way to get onto the boat, no matter what the obstacles, had been so much excess steam, impressive but useless. There was no other course to take that would get him more than a very temporary stay on the *Rex*.

Thus, Loghu had taken a very old and still effective method. Without actually saying so, she had suggested that she might be willing to share John's bed. Burton hadn't liked it. He felt like a whoremonger, and it also angered him that it was a woman who had done what he couldn't do. He wasn't as upset as he would have been on Earth or even here many years ago. This world had given him a good opportunity to see what women could do once the inhibitions and strictures of Terrestrial society had been removed. Moreover, it was he who had written: *Women the world over are what men have made them*. That might have been true in Victorian times, but it no longer applied.

While going back to the boat, Loghu introduced the others. All except Burton were using their native names. He had decided this time not to use his old half-Arab, half-Pathan guise, not to be Mirza Abdullah Bushiri or Abdul Hassan or any of the many similar guises he'd used on Earth and here. This time, for a reason he didn't explain to his companions, he was posing as Gwalchgwynn, a Dark-Age Welshman who'd lived when the Britons were making their final stand against the invading Angles, Saxons, and Jutes.

"It means 'White Hawk,' Your Majesty," he said.

"So?" John said. "You are very dark for a white hawk."

Kazz, the Neanderthal male, rumbled, "He is a great swordsman and marksman, Your Majesty. He would be a good fighter for you."

"Perhaps I'll give him a chance to demonstrate his skill sometime," John said.

John looked through lowered lids at Kazz. John was five feet four inches in stature, but he looked tall alongside the Neanderthal. Kazz was squat and big-boned, as all early Old Stone Agers were. His breadloaf-shaped head, the low slanting forehead, thick shelving brows, broad flat nose, and very protruding jaws didn't make him handsome. But he was not subhuman-appearing like the Neanderthals in illustrations or the early reconstructions in museums. He was hairy but no more than the most hirsute of Homo sapiens.

His mate, Besst, was several inches shorter than he and just as unprepossessing.

John was interested in the two of them, however. They were small, but their strength was enormous, and both male and female would be good warriors. The low brows did not necessarily front a low intelligence since the gamut of brilliance to stupidity was the same in Neanderthals as in that of modern humanity.

Half of John's complement was early Paleolithic.

John, nicknamed Lackland because for a long time he'd not been able to possess the states he claimed title to, was the younger brother of King Richard I the Lion-hearted, the monarch to whom the legendary Robin Hood remained loyal while John ruled England as regent. He had broad shoulders and an athletic sturdy frame, a heavy jaw, tawny hair, blue eyes, and a terrible temper, though that was nothing unusual for a medieval king. He'd had a very bad reputation during and after his death, though he was no worse than many kings before or since and better than his brother. Contemporary and later chroniclers united to present an unfair portrait of him. He was so loathed that it became a tradition that no one of the British royal family should be named John.

Richard had designated his nephew, Arthur of Brittany, as his heir. John had refused to accept this, and, while fighting Arthur, had captured him and then imprisoned him in the castle of Falaise and later in Rouen. There Richard's nephew disappeared under circumstances which made most people believe that John had slain him and then thrown the weighted body into the Seine. John had never denied or confirmed the accusations.

Another blot on his record, though no larger or blacker than that on the records of many monarchs, was the undeniable fact that he had caused to be starved to death the wife and son of an enemy, the Baron de Braose.

There were many more stories, some of which were true, about his evil deeds. But not until many centuries later did objective historians record that he had also done much good for England.

Burton didn't know much about John's life on the Riverworld except that he had stolen Samuel Clemens' boat. He also knew that it would not be discreet to mention this to John.

The monarch himself was their guide. He showed them almost everything from the lowest deck to the top, the boiler, main, hurricane, flight, and texas deck, an extension from the lower story of the two-story pilothouse. While they were in the pilothouse, Alice told the king that she was his descendant through his son, John of Gaunt.

"Indeed," he said. "Were you then a princess or a queen?"

"Not even of the nobility," she said. "Though I was of the gentry. My father was a relative of Baron Ravensworth. I was born in the Year of Our Lord 1852, when Victoria, another descendant of yours, was queen."

The king's tawny eyebrows rose.

"You are the first descendant of mine I've ever met. A very pretty one, too."

"Thank you, Sire."

Burton burned even more. Was John contemplating incest, however rarified the consanguinity might be?

John had apparently been considering taking all of them on as crewmembers, and Alice's distant kinship decided him. After they had gone to the grand salon for a drink, he told them that they could, if they wished, travel the river with him. He told them in detail, first, what the general duties of the crew were and what the discipline consisted of, and then demanded they swear an oath of fealty to him.

So far, John had not followed up on his intimations that Loghu go to bed with him, but he undoubtedly meant to. Burton asked if he could talk to the others privately for a minute. John graciously gave permission, and they went to a corner to talk.

"I don't mind," Loghu said. "I might even like it. I've never been mounted by a king. Anyway, I have no man now and I haven't since that bastard Frigate ran out on us. John isn't a bad looker at all, even if he is shorter than I am."

On Earth, Alice would have been horrified. But she'd seen too much and changed too much; most of her Victorian attitudes had long dissipated.

"As long as it's voluntary," she said, "then it's not wrong."

"I'd do it if it were wrong," Loghu said. "We have too much at stake for me to be squeamish."

"I don't like it," Burton said. He was relieved but didn't want to admit it. "But if we miss this boat, we may not get a chance to get on the other. I'd say that boarding the *Mark Twain* would be as difficult as it would be for a politician to get into Heaven."

"However, if he should mistreat you . . ."

"Oh, I can take care of myself," Loghu said. "If I can't throw that runt clear across the cabin, I've lost my touch. As a last resort I can crack his nuts."

Alice hadn't changed so much that she didn't blush.

"He might even make you his Number One mistress," Kazz said. "Haw! That'd make you queen then! Hail, Queen Loghu!"

"I'm more worried about his current mistress than I am about him," Loghu said. "John wouldn't stab me in the back, though he might try to take me in the rear, but his woman might put a knife in my spine."

"I still feel like a pimp," Burton said.

"Why should you? You don't own me."

They returned to John and told him that they wished to take the oath.

John ordered drinks for the occasion. After these, he had his executive officer, a huge late-twentieth-century Yank named Augustus Strubewell, make arrangements for the swearing-in that evening.

Two days later, the *Rex* up-anchored and set out up-River. Alice was attached as a nurse to the staff of one of the boat's physicians, a Doctor Doyle. Loghu was to be trained as a pilot, after which she would be officially a pilot second-class, extra. The duties would require only that she substitute if one of the second-class pilots was unavailable. She would have plenty of spare time unless John kept her busy in his suite, which he did for some time to come. The woman she dispossessed seemed to be angry about it, but was only pretending. She'd been getting as tired of John as he of her.

Kazz and Burton were ranked as privates in the marines. Kazz was an axeman; Burton, a pistoleer and rapiersman. Besst was put among the women archers.

One of the first things that Burton did was find out who on the boat claimed to have lived past A.D. 1983. There were four. One was Strubewell. He'd been with John when he hijacked the boat.

8

WHEN THE REVEREND MR. DODGSON, BETTER KNOWN AS LEWIS CAR-oll, wrote *Alice in Wonderland,* he prefaced it with a poem. It begins with "All in the golden afternoon" and compresses that famous journey by boat up the Isis during which Dodgson was teased by the real Alice into writing down the tale he'd composed to please the "cruel Three."

On that day of July 4, 1852, golden in memory only because it actually was cool and wet, Dodgson, who would be the Dodo in *Alice* and the White Knight in *Through the Looking-Glass,* was accompanied by Reverend Duckworth, who naturally became the Duck. Lorina, aged thirteen, was the Lory, and Alice, age ten, Dodgson's favorite, was of course Alice. Edith, the youngest sister, aged eight, would be the Eaglet.

The three little girls were the daughters of Bishop Liddell, whose surname rhymed with fiddle, as evidenced by a poem about the bishop sung by the rowdy Oxford students. Dodgson's verse refers to the girls in Latin ordinals according to the ages. Prima, Secunda, and Tertia.

It seemed to Alice now, as she stood in the middle of Richard's and her cabin, that she had in truth played the part of Secunda during her Earthly life. Certainly, on this world she was Secunda. Richard Burton regarded few men as his equal and no women, not even his wife and perhaps especially his wife, as equals.

She hadn't minded. She was dreamy, gentle, and introverted. As Dodgson had written of her:

> *Still she haunts me, phantomwise.*
> *Alice moving under skies*
> *Never seen by waking eyes.*

That would become true in more senses than Dodgson could have dreamed of. Now she was under a sky in which even at the blaze of noon she could see near the tops of the mountains the faint phantom glow of a few giant stars. And in the moonless night sky was the blaze of great gas sheets and enormous stars which shed the light of a full moon.

Under the light of day and night, she had been content, even eager, to have Richard make the decisions. These had often involved violence, and, contrary to her nature, she had fought like an Amazon. Though she did not have the physique of a Penthesilea, she did have the courage.

Life on the Riverworld had often been harsh, cruel, and bloody. After dying on Earth, she'd awakened naked and with all body hair shaven, in the body she'd had when she was twenty-five, though she'd died when eighty-two. Around her was not the room of the house in which she'd died, her sister Rhoda's in Westerham, Kent. Instead towering unbroken mountain ranges enclosed the plains and the foothills and the river in the middle of the valley. As far as she could see, people stood on the banks, all naked, hairless, young, and in shock, screaming, weeping, laughing hysterically, or in horror-struck silence.

She knew no one and had by impulse attached herself to Burton. However, one of the items in her grail was a chiclelike stick containing some sort of psychedelic substance. She'd chewed it, and then she and Burton had copulated furiously all night and also done things she then regarded as perverted and some things which she still did.

She'd loathed herself in the morning and felt like killing herself. Burton she'd hated as she'd never hated anyone. But she continued to stay with him since anyone she switched to might be worse. Also she had to admit that he too was under the gum's influence, and he did not press her to renew, as she then thought of it, their carnal acquaintance. Burton would have used an Anglo-Saxonism, as he called it, to describe their coupling.

In time she'd fallen in love with him—had, in fact, been in love that night—and they began living together. Living together was not exactly accurate since a good half of her time she spent by herself in their hut. Burton was the most restless man she'd ever known. After a week in one place he must be up and moving: From time to time they'd had quarrels, he doing most of the quarreling, though by now she could hold her own. Eventually he disappeared for years and returned with a story that turned out to be the essence of cock-and-bull.

She was very hurt when she finally found out that he'd kept his most important secret from her for years. He'd been visited one night by a robed and masked being who said that he was an *Ethical,* one of the Council which governed those responsible for the resurrections of thirty-five billion or so Terrestrials.

The story went that these Ethicals had raised humanity to life to perform certain experiments. They meant to let humankind die, never to be resurrected again. One of the Council, this Ethical, this "man," was secretly opposing this.

Burton was skeptical. But when the other Ethicals tried to seize him, Burton had run. He was forced to kill himself several times, utilizing the principle of resurrection, to get far away from his pursuers. After a while he decided that he might as well keep going. After 777 suicides, he awoke in the Council room of the twelve. These had told him what he knew already from X, that is, that there was a renegade among them. So far, they hadn't been able to detect who he or she was. But they would.

Now that they had caught him, they would keep him under permanent surveillance. The memory of his visits from the Ethicals, in fact, everything since he'd first known X, would be wiped out of his mind.

Burton, however, on waking on the banks of The River, had found his memory unimpaired. Somehow, X had succeeded in averting the erasure and in fooling his colleagues.

Burton reasoned also that X must have arranged it so that the Ethicals couldn't find him whenever they wished to. Burton had gone up-River then, looking for the others whom X had recruited. Just when and how they could help him, X wouldn't say, though he promised to reveal the time and the methods at a later time.

Something had gone wrong. X hadn't appeared for years, and the resurrections had suddenly stopped.

Then Burton had found out that the Peter Jairus Frigate and the Tau Cetan, who'd been with Burton from the beginning, were either Ethicals or the Ethicals' agents. Before Burton could seize them, the two had fled.

Burton could no longer hide his secret from his companions. Alice was shocked by the story, stunned. Later, she became furious. Why hadn't he told her the truth long ago? Burton had explained that he wanted to protect her. If she knew the truth, she might be subject to abduction and questioning and God only knew what else by the Ethicals.

Since that time, she'd been slowly burning. The repressed anger had now and then broken out, and the flames had scorched Burton. He, always willing to burn back, had quarreled with her. And though they'd always reconciled afterward, Alice knew that the day of parting had to come soon.

She should have made the break before signing on the *Rex*. But she also wanted to know the answers to the mysteries of the Riverworld. If she stayed behind, she would always regret not having gone on. So she had boarded with Richard, and here she was in their cabin wondering what to do next.

Also, she had to confess that there was more to her being here than the desire to reveal mysteries. For the first time in her life on this world, she had hot and cold running water and a comfortable toilet and bed and air-conditioning and a grand salon in which she could see movies and stage plays and hear music, classical and popular, played by orchestras which used the instruments known on Earth, not the clay and skin and bamboo substitutes used on the banks. There was also bridge and whist and other games. All these comforts of body and soul and others were hers. They would be hard to give up.

It was indeed a strange situation for a bishop's daughter born May 4, 1852, next to Westminster Abbey. Her father was not only the dean of Christ Church College but famous as the co-editor of Liddell and Scott's *Greek-English Lexicon*. Her mother was a beautiful and cultured woman who looked as if she were Spanish. Alice Pleasance Liddell came to Oxford when she was four and almost immediately made friends with the shy, stammering mathematician-clergyman with the offbeat sense of humor. Both lived in Tom Quad so that their meetings were frequent.

As the daughters of a bishop of royal and noble descent, she and her sisters had not been allowed to play with other children very often. They were educated principally by their governess, Miss Prickett, a woman who strove mightily to teach her girls but had not enough education herself. Nevertheless, Alice enjoyed all the advantages of a privileged Victorian childhood. John Ruskin was her drawing teacher. She often managed to eavesdrop on the conversations of her father's dinner guests: the Prince of Wales, Gladstone, Matthew Arnold, and many other notables and greats.

She was a pretty child, dark, her straight hair in bangs, her face a reflection of her quiet dreaming soul when she was pensive but bright and eager when stimulated, especially by Dodgson's wild stories. She read a lot and was largely self-educated.

She liked to play with her black cat, Dinah, and to tell her stories which were never as good as the reverend's. Her favorite song was "Star of Evening," which Dodgson was to satirize in *Alice* as the Mock Turtle's song, "Turtle Soup."

> *Soup of the evening, beautiful soup!*
> *Soup of the evening, beautiful soup!*

The real Alice's favorite section of the book, however, was that about the

Cheshire Cat. She loved cats, and even when she'd grown up she would occasionally talk to her pet as if it were human when no one else was around.

She'd grown up to be a good-looking woman with a splendid physique and something special about her, an indefinable misty air which had attracted Dodgson when she was a child and had also drawn Ruskin and others. To them she was the "child of pure unclouded brow and dreaming eyes of wonder."

Despite her adult attractiveness, she did not get married until she was twenty-eight, which made her an old maid in Victorian 1880. Her husband, Reginald Gervis Hargreaves of the estate of Cuffnells, near Lyndhurst, Hampshire, was educated at Eton and Christ Church, and became a justice of the peace, living a very quiet life with Alice and her three sons. He liked to read, especially French literature, to ride and hunt, and he had a huge arboretum which included Douglas pines and redwoods.

Despite certain inhibitions and awkwardness in the beginning, she had adjusted to the sexual act and came to desire it. She loved her husband, and she sorrowed deeply when he died in 1926.

But Burton she had loved with a passion far exceeding that for Reginald. No longer, she told herself.

She couldn't put up with his eternal restlessness, though it looked as if he would be staying in one place for many years now. But it was the place that was moving him. His rages, his eagerness to pick a quarrel, his intense jealousy, were becoming tiresome. The very traits which had attracted her because she had lacked them were now driving her away.

The greatest wedge was that he had kept to himself The Secret.

The trouble with leaving Richard at once was that she had no place to go. All the cabins were taken. Some were occupied by single men, but she did not intend to move in with a man she didn't love.

Richard would have scoffed at that. He claimed that all he wanted in a woman was beauty and affection. He also preferred blondes, but in her case he had waived this requirement. He would tell her to find some good-looking man with at least passable manners and live with him. No, he wouldn't. He would threaten to kill her if she left him. Or would he? Surely, he must be getting as tired of her as she was of him.

She sat down and smoked a cigarette, something she wouldn't have dreamed of doing on Earth, and she considered what to do. After a while, finding no answer, she left the cabin and went to the grand salon. There was always something pleasant or exciting there.

In the salon she walked around for a few minutes admiring the paintings and statuettes and listening to a piece by Liszt being played on the piano.

While she was feeling very lonely and hoping that someone would come up and break her mood, a woman approached her. She was about five feet tall, slim, long-legged, and had medium-sized conical breasts with up-tilted nipples thinly covered with a wispy cloth. Her features were beautiful despite her somewhat too long nose.

Exposing very white and even teeth, the blonde said, in Esperanto, "Hello, I'm Aphra Behn, one of His Majesty's pistoleers and ex-mistresses, though he still likes an occasional rerun. You're Alice Liddell, right? The woman of the fierce-looking ugly-handsome Welshman, Gwalchgwynn."

Alice acknowledged that she was right and asked immediately, "Are you the authoress of *Oroonoko?*"

Aphra smiled again. "Yes, and of several plays. It's nice to know that I was not unknown in the twentieth century. Do you play bridge? We're looking for a fourth."

"I haven't played for thirty-four years," Alice said. "But I loved it. If you don't mind some clumsiness at first . . ."

"Oh, we'll sharpen you up, though it may hurt some," Aphra said. She laughed and led Alice by her hand toward a table near a wall and below a huge painting. This depicted Theseus entering the heart of Minos' labyrinth where the Minotaur awaited him. Ariadne's thread was tied to the hero's enormous erection.

Aphra, seeing Alice's expression, grinned.

"Does give you a start when you first see it, doesn't it? Don't know if Theseus is going to kill the bullman with his sword or bugger him to death, what?"

"If he does the latter," Alice said, "he'll break the thread and won't be able to find his way back out to Ariadne."

"Lucky woman," Aphra said. "She can die still thinking he loves her, not knowing he plans to desert her at the first opportunity."

So this was Aphra Amis Behn, the novelist, poet, and dramatist whom London called the Incomparable Astrea, after the divine star maiden of classical Greek religion. Before she died in 1689 at the age of forty-nine, she had written a novel, *Oroonoko,* which was a sensation in her time and was reprinted in 1930, giving Alice a chance to read it before she died. The book had been very influential in the development of the novel, and Aphra's contemporaries rated her with Defoe when she was at her best. Her plays were bawdy and coarse but witty and had delighted the theatergoers. She was the first English woman to support herself entirely by writing, and she had also been a spy for Charles II during the war against the Dutch. Her behavior was scandalous, even for the Restoration period, but she was buried in Westminster Abbey, an honor denied the equally scandalous and far more famous Lord Byron.

Two men were waiting impatiently at the table. Aphra made the introductions, giving a slight biography of each.

The man at the west end of the table was Lazzaro Spallanzani, born A.D.

1729, died 1799. He had been one of the more well-known natural scientists of his time and was chiefly noted for his experiments with bats to determine how they could fly through total darkness. He'd discovered that they did so by use of a form of sonar, though that term wasn't known in his day. He was short, slim, dark, and obviously Italian though he spoke Esperanto.

The man who sat at the north end was Ladislas Podebrad, a Czech. He was of medium height (for the middle and late twentieth century), very broad, muscular, and thick-necked. His hair was yellow, and his eyes were cold and blue. The eyebrows were very thick and yellowish. His eaglish nose was large, and his massive chin was deeply clefted. Though his hands were broad—as big as a bear's, thought Alice, who tended to exaggerate— and the fingers were relatively short, he handled the cards like a Mississippi riverboat gambler.

Aphra commented that he'd been picked up only eight days ago and that he was an electromechanical engineer with a doctor's degree. She also said—and here Alice was suddenly very interested—that Podebrad had attracted John's attention when John saw him standing by the wreck of an airship on the left bank. After hearing Podebrad's story and his qualifications, John had invited him to come aboard as an engineer's mate in the engine room. The duraluminum keel and gondola of the semirigid dirigible had been cut up and put in a storage room in the *Rex*.

Podebrad didn't talk much, seeming to be one of those bridge players who was all intent on the game. But since Behn and Spallanzani chattered back and forth, Alice was emboldened to ask him some questions. He replied tersely, but gave no outward signs of being annoyed. This didn't mean that he wasn't; his face was stony throughout the playing.

Podebrad explained that he had been head of a state far far down-River called Nova Bohemujo, Esperanto for New Bohemia. He'd been qualified for the position since he'd also been head of a government post in Czechoslovakia and a prominent member of the Communist party. He no longer was a Communist, though, since that ideology was as useless and irrelevant as capitalism was here. Also, he'd been very attracted to the Church of the Second Chance, though he'd never joined.

He'd had a recurring dream that there were large deposits of iron and other minerals deep under the area of Nova Bohemujo. After much urging, he'd gotten his people to dig for them. This was a long and wearisome task and wore out many flint, chert, and wood tools, but his zeal had kept them at it. Besides, it gave them something to do.

"You must realize that I am not at all superstitious," Podebrad said in a basso profundo. "I despise oneiromancy, and I would have ignored this series of dreams, no matter how sustained and compelling they were. That is, under most circumstances I would have. It seemed to me that they were the expressions of my unconscious, a term I don't like to use, since I reject

Freudianism, but useful here to describe the phenomena I was experiencing. They were, at first, only the expressions of my wishes to find metal, or so I thought. Then I came to believe that there might be another explanation, though the first was really no explanation. Perhaps there was an affinity between metal and myself, some sort of earth current that put me in its circuit, that is, the metal was one pole and I the other so that I felt the flow of energy."

And he says he isn't superstitious, Alice thought. Or is he kidding me?

Richard, however, would have gone for that sort of rot. He believed that there was an affinity between himself and silver. When he'd suffered from ophthalmia in India, he'd placed silver coins on his eyes, and, when he had gout in his old age, he'd put them on his feet.

"Though I do not believe in dreams as manifestations of the unconscious, I do believe that they may be a medium for transmission of telepathy or other forms of extrasensory perception," Podebrad said. "Much experimentation was done with ESP in the Soviet Union. Whatever the reason, I felt strongly that there was metal deep under the surface of Nova Bohemujo. And there *was*. Iron, bauxite, cryolite, vanadium, platinum, tungsten, and other ores. All jumbled together, not in a natural strata. Evidently whoever re-formed this planet had piled the ores there during the process."

All this was said between bidding, of course. Podebrad talked as if he hadn't been interrupted, picking up exactly where he'd left off.

Podebrad had industrialized his state. His people had been armed with steel swords and fiberglass bows and firearms. He'd built two armored steamboats, neither nearly as large as the *Rex*.

"Not for conquest but for defense. The other states were jealous of our mineral wealth and would have liked to possess it, but they didn't dare attack. My ultimate object, however, was to build a large boat with screw propellers to travel to the headwaters of The River. I didn't know at that time that there were two giant boats already coming up The River. If I had known, I would have built my own vessel anyway.

"Eventually I fell in with some adventurers who proposed to get to the headwaters by means of an airship. Their idea intrigued me and soon after I made the blimp and set out in it. But a storm wrecked it. I and my crew got out alive, and then the *Rex* came along."

The game was over a few minutes later with Podebrad and Alice winners and Spallanzani angrily demanding why Podebrad had led with a diamond instead of a club. The Czech refused to tell him but said that he should be able to figure it out for himself. He congratulated Alice on her correct playing. Alice thanked him, but she still didn't know any more than Spallanzani how Podebrad had done it.

Before they parted, however, she said, "*Sinjorino* Behn forgot to say exactly when you were born and died on Earth."

He looked sharply at her.

"Perhaps that is because she doesn't know. Why do you want to know?"

"Oh, I'm just interested in that sort of thing."

He shrugged and said, "A.D. 1912 to 1980."

Alice hurried off to find Burton before she had to go on duty and learn to set bones and make plaster-of-paris casts. She caught him in the corridor on the way to their cabin. He was sweating, his dark skin looking like oiled bronze. He'd just finished two hours of stick-fighting and fencing and had half an hour before he fell in for drill.

On the way to the cabin, she told him about Podebrad. He asked her why she seemed so excited about the Czech.

"It's nonsense, that about his dream," she said. "I'll tell you what I think about it. I think he's an agent who got stranded and who knew where that deposit of ores was. He used the dream as an excuse to get his people to dig it up. Then he built the blimp and tried to get to the tower itself, not just the headwaters. He must have!"

"Oh, reeeally," Burton drawled in that infuriating manner. "What other slight evidence do you have, if it's even slight? After all, the chap didn't live past 1983."

"That's what *he* said! But how do we know that some agents . . . you've said so yourself . . . haven't changed their story? Anyway . . ."

She paused, her whole being radiating eagerness.

"Yaas?"

"You described the council of twelve. He looks like he might be the one called Thanabur or maybe the one called Loga!"

That rocked him. But after a few seconds, he said, "Describe this man again."

When he'd heard her out he shook his head.

"No. Both Loga and Thanabur had green eyes. Loga was red-headed, and Thanabur was brown-haired. This Podebrad has yellow hair and blue eyes. He may look much like them, but I suppose there are millions who do."

"But Richard! Hair color can be changed! He wasn't wearing those plastic lens that can change the eye color that Frigate told us about. But don't you think the Ethicals would have the means to change eye color without obvious aids?"

"It's possible. I'll take a look at the fellow."

After showering, he bustled down to the grand salon. Not finding Podebrad there he returned to the engine room. Later when he next met Alice, Burton said, "We'll have to see. He could be Thanabur or Loga. If one can be a chameleon, the other can. But it's been twenty-eight years since I saw them, and our meeting was very brief. I really can't say."

"Aren't you going to do anything about it?"

"I can't very well arrest him on John's boat! No. We'll just have to watch him, and if we get something to justify our suspicions, then we'll see what we can do.

"Remember Spruce the agent. When we caught him, he killed himself just by thinking a sort of code and released poison into his system from that little black ball in his brain. It'll be very tricky if we do act, and we can't until we're sure. Personally, I think it's just a coincidence. Now, Strubewell . . . there's someone we don't have any doubt about. Well, not much perhaps. After all, it's only a theory that anyone claiming to be post-1983 is an agent. It *is* possible that we just haven't met many."

"Well, I'll be playing bridge a lot with Podebrad, if I don't come a duffer. I'll watch him."

"Be very careful, Alice. If he is one of Them, he'll be very observant. In fact, you shouldn't have asked him about the dates. That may have put him on his guard. You should have found out from someone else."

"Can't you ever give me full credit?" she said, and she walked out.

9

LOGHU WAS NO LONGER THE KING'S FAVORITE.

King John had become so smitten with a very pretty redhead with large blue eyes whom he'd seen on the bank that he decided to stay in the area for a while. The boat was anchored by a large dock the locals had built long ago. After two days to make sure that the people here were as friendly as they pretended to be, John permitted shore leave. He didn't say anything to anybody at first about his sudden attack of irresistible lechery, but his behavior made that obvious.

Loghu didn't especially care that she had to leave the grand suite after John had talked the woman into going to bed with him. She wasn't in love with him. Besides, she was more than somewhat interested in one of the locals, a big dark Tokharian. Though he wasn't of her century, he was of her nation, and they had many things to talk about between lovemaking. However, she was humiliated that she had lasted such a short time with the monarch, and she was heard to mutter that she might just push John overboard some dark night. There *had* been, there *were* now, there *would be* many who would like to remove him from the living.

Burton stood guard duty the first night. The next, he moved into a hut with Alice near the dock. The people here, most of whom were Early Minoan Cretans, were hospitable and fun-loving. They danced and sang around the bonfires in the evening until their allotment of lichen alcohol was gone and then reeled to bed to sleep or couple or "pluralize," as Burton called it. He was happy to stay here for a few weeks anyway because he'd have a chance to add the language to his now long list. He mastered its basic grammar and vocabulary quickly since it was closely related to Phoenician and Hebrew. There were, however, many words which were non-Semitic, these having been borrowed from the aboriginals of Crete while the conquerors from the Middle East were assimilating them. They all spoke Esperanto, of course, though it deviated somewhat from the artificial tongue invented by Dr. Zamenhof.

John had no trouble getting his new mistress to agree to go to bed with him. But he had a problem. There was no cabin space for Loghu, and he couldn't throw her off the boat without a good reason. Autocratic though he was, he was able to override her rights. His crew would see to that. Remembreing the Magna Carta, he did not buck them, but he was undoubtedly trying to think of a way to get rid of Loghu which would seem justifiable.

On the fourth night of shore leave, while John was in his grand suite with Blue-eyes, and Burton was with Alice in their small but comfortable quarters, a helicopter dropped out of the night sky onto the landing deck of the *Rex*.

Burton would find out very much later that the raiders came from the airship *Parseval* and had been ordered to capture King John if they could or to kill him if they couldn't. All he knew then was that the gunfire on the *Rex* meant bad trouble. He put on a cloth around his waist and fastened it with the magnetic tabs inside the material. Then, grabbing a rapier and a fully loaded pistol from the table by the bed, he ran outside while Alice was still yelling to him.

He could hear men screaming and shouting in the midst of shots and then a great explosion apparently in the engine room. He ran as fast as he could toward the boat. There were lights on in the pilothouse; somebody was at the controls. Then the paddlewheels began to turn. The boat started moving backward, but Burton leaped onto the promenade of the boiler deck just before the lines tied to the pilings pulled them down and the dock collapsed.

A moment later, a stranger came down the stairs from the lowest story of the pilothouse. Burton emptied his pistol at him but missed. Cursing, he dropped the gun and proceeded toward the fellow. Then the slippery one showed up again with a rapier in his hand.

Never had Burton faced such a demon with the sword! No wonder. The tall thin demon was Cyrano de Bergerac! Playfully he introduced himself during a lull in the swordplay but Burton saw no such reason to waste breath. Both were slightly wounded—a good indication that they were evenly matched. Somebody shouted, Burton's attention was distracted and that was enough. The Frenchman drove his blade deep into Burton's thigh.

He fell to the deck, helpless. The agony came a few seconds later, making him clench his teeth to keep from screaming. De Bergerac was a gallant man. He made no effort to kill Burton, and, when one of his men appeared a moment after, de Bergerac told him not to shoot Burton.

The helicopter lifted off shortly thereafter as men shot at it from the deck. Before it had gotten a hundred feet, however, a naked white body appeared in the beam of a searchlight and then dropped into the darkness. Somebody had either leaped or been thrown from the craft. Burton guessed that it was King John.

Groaning, Burton wrapped the heavily bleeding wound in a cloth, tied its ends, and forced himself to hobble to the steps leading up to the pilothouse base. The *Rex* was drifting down-River, and there was nothing to do about it. John was hauled aboard moments later, unconscious, an arm and a leg broken.

Five miles downstream, the *Rex* beached, and, ten minutes later, the first of the men who'd run all the way along the bank, following the boat, came aboard.

Doctor Doyle set John's bones and administered Irish coffee for shock.

When John was fit enough to curse and rave, he did so. But he was glad to be alive, and the engine could be repaired with the precious aluminum wire in the storage room. That would take a month, though, and meanwhile the Clemens boat was slowly gaining on them.

Since twelve guards had been killed, there was a cabin for Loghu to move into. The king had to replace the dead men, but he seemed to be in no hurry to do so. After days of examining candidates and then putting some through mental and physical tests, he chose only two.

"There's no hurry," he said. "I want only the best. These locals are a scroungy lot."

One result of the raid was that John became fond of Burton, whom he gave the most credit for saving his life. He couldn't promote him over the heads of Burton's fellow marines, but he could make him a bodyguard. And he promised Burton to give him a commission whenever it was possible to do so. Burton and Alice moved into the cabin next to John's quarters.

Burton was displeased in one way because he liked to dance attendance to no man. However, it did give him an opportunity to be with Strubewell a lot and to study him. He listened carefully to the man's speech for traces of a foreign accent. If Strubewell was an agent, he had mastered American Midwestern.

Alice kept an intent eye and ear on Podebrad while playing bridge and during other social activities. Loghu liked one of the suspected agents, a huge man named Arthur Pal who claimed to have been a Hungarian electrical engineer, so she moved in with him after his mate left him. Burton's suspicions were increased when Loghu noted that Pal spent much time with Podebrad. Her efforts to trip him up on his story were fruitless, but Burton said that if enough time elapsed she was bound to do so. If the agents had a common story, they would have memorized it. However, they were (presumably) human and so would make mistakes. One contradiction would be enough.

Alice still had not been able to bring herself to force the split with Burton. She kept hoping that he would change his attitude toward her enough to justify staying with him. That their duties kept them apart most of the day helped ease matters. He seemed so glad to see her at the end of the day that she felt better, and she talked herself into believing that they would get back to their original passionate state. They were like an old married couple in many ways. They still had a certain fluctuating affection but were increasingly irritated by character traits they could have once easily overlooked.

In one sense, they were old though their youthful bodies had been restored. She had lived on Earth to be eighty-two and he to sixty-nine. ("Considering my sexual preferences, a significant age at which to die," Burton had once drawled.) A long life tended to ossify more than the arteries; it also ossified habits and attitudes. It made it much more difficult to adjust, to change one's self for the better. The impact of the resurrection and the Riverworld had shattered many people's beliefs and helped set them up for change. It had decalcified many, though in some the fragmentation was only slight, in others much more, and many had been unable to adjust at all.

Alice had suffered a metamorphosis in many respects, though her basic character remained. It was down there in the abysm of the soul, the deeps which make the spaces between the stars seem a mere step over a puddle. It was the same with Burton.

So Alice stayed with him, hoping what she knew was hopeless.

At times, she dreamed of finding Reginald again. But she also knew that that was even more hopeless. She would never go back to him whether he had remained the same or changed. It was doubtful that he had changed. He was a good man, but, like all the good, he had faults, some grave, and he was too stubborn to change.

The thing was that no caterpillar could ever effect a metamorphosis in another. The other, if it is to become a butterfly, must do it itself. The difference between man and caterpillar was that the insect was pre-programmed and the human had to re-program himself.

Thus the days passed for Alice, though there was much more to them than thinking such thoughts.

And then one day, when the *Rex* connected its batacitor and grail lines to a stone on the right bank, the stone failed to discharge.

10

SHOCK AND PANIC.

Fifteen years ago, the grailstones on the left bank had quit operation. Twenty-four hours later, they had resumed functioning. King John had been told by Clemens that the line had been severed by a great meteorite but that it had been reconnected and all damage restored in that amazingly short period. It must have been done by the Ethicals, though anybody in the area to witness the re-forming had been overcome by something—probably a gas—and slept through the whole project.

Now the question was: Would the line be repaired again?; the lesser question: What caused this disaster? Another meteorite? Or was it one more step downward in the breakdown of this world?

King John, though stunned, rallied swiftly. He sent his officers to calm down the crew, and he gave orders to serve everybody the mixture of lichen alcohol, water, and powdered irontree blooms called grog on the *Rex*.

After all were soaked enough in the drink that gives good cheer and courage, he ordered that the copper "feeder" cap be taken back into the boat. Then the *Rex* proceeded up-River in the shallows near the left bank. There was enough energy in the batacitor to keep the boat going until the next mealtime. When it was two hours to dusk, John commanded that it stop and the copper cap be attached to a stone.

As expected, the locals refused to "loan" a stone to the *Rex*. One of the steam machine guns loosed a stream of plastic bullets over the heads of the crowd on the bank, and it ran back panicked halfway across the plain. The two amphibian launches, once named *Firedragon I* and *II*, now *Eleanor* and *Henry*, rumbled onto shore and stood guard while the cap was placed over the stone. Within an hour, however, locals from stones as far away as a mile on each side gathered, including those whose grailstones were in the foothills. Whooping war cries, yelling, thousands of men and women charged the amphibians and the riverboat. At the same time, five hundred in boats attacked from the water.

Exploding shells and rockets from the *Rex* wiped out hundreds. The steam guns mowed down hundreds more. The marines and crew members lined along the railings shot rifles, pistols, and arrows, and launched small rockets from bazookas.

The bank and the waters around the *Rex* quickly became bloodied and strewn with corpses and pieces of corpses. The charge broke, but not before small and large rockets sent by the locals had done some damage and killed and wounded some of John's people.

Burton could still barely walk though wounds healed more quickly than they would have on Earth. He nevertheless dragged himself to the railing of the texas-deck promenade and fired a rifle with .48-caliber wooden bullets. He hit at least a third of his targets, which were on The River side. When all the boats, dugouts, canoes, war canoes, and sailing boats had been sunk, he struggled around to the other side to help.

He got there in time for the third and final charge. This had been preceded by much haranguing by the enemy officers, pounding of drums, and blowing of fishhorns, and then, with another yell, the locals ran toward the boat. By this time, the launches had exhausted their ammunition and retreated to the dock in the rear of the motherboat. However, the two fighter planes, the single-seater reconnaissance, the torpedo bomber, and the helicopter went up to add their fire.

Almost, a few locals reached the water. Then, the ranks wilting, they broke and fled. Shortly thereafter, the stones boomed and flashed, and the grails and the batacitor were recharged.

"God's teeth!" King John said, his eyes wild. "Today was bad enough! Tomorrow. . . ! God save us!"

He was right. Before dawn the next day, the hunger-mad right-bankers came in hordes. Every boat available, including many two-masters, was jammed to capacity with men and women. Behind them came another horde of swimmers. And when the sun rose, for as far as the eye could reach, The River was alive with vessels and swimmers. The front ranks, the boats, were met with all the rockets and arrows the defenders had. Nevertheless, most of the boats grounded, and from them leaped the right-bankers.

Caught between two forces, the *Rex* battled mightily. Its fire cleared space around the grailstones, and the amphibians, spouting flame, rolled on their trackless treads to the stone. While they kept off the raging defenders and attackers alike, the crane of the *Henry* swung the cap onto the stone.

The grailstones thundered, and immediately the cap was swung off by the crane, which then telescoped into the interior of the *Henry*.

After the launches had returned to the boat, John ordered that the anchor be taken up. "And then full power ahead!"

It was easier commanded than carried out.

The press of vessels around the *Rex* was so great that it could move only very slowly. While the paddlewheels dug into the water, and the prow crushed into pieces the large sailing boats and ground the smaller between them, the right-bankers bombarded it. Men and women managed to clamber onto the promenade of the boiler deck, though they didn't stay there long.

Finally, the *Rex* broke loose and headed for the other shore. There it swung into the weaker current near the bank and forged up-River. Across the stream, the battle was still raging.

At noon, John had to decide whether or not to recharge. After a minute of deliberation, he ordered the boat to anchor by a big dock.

"We'll let them kill each other," he said. "We have plenty of smoked and dried food to keep us going through tomorrow. The day after, we'll recharge. By then the slaughter should be over."

The right bank was a strange sight indeed. They had gotten so used to seeing its throngs, noisy, chattering, laughing, that the unpeopled land was eerie. On this side, except for a very few wise or timid persons who'd elected not to try to fill their bellies at the expense of the left-bankers, not a soul was to be seen. The huts and the longhouses and the big state log buildings were tenantless, and so were the plains and the foothills. Since no animals, birds, insects or reptiles existed on this planet, only the wind rustling the leaves of the few trees on the plains made any sound.

By then, the warring peoples across the stream had exhausted their gunpowder, and only occasionally could the *Rex*-ites hear a very low murmur, the diluted and compressed sound of people voicing their fury, hunger, and fear, their pain and their deaths.

The casualties on the *Rex* from both days were thirty dead and sixty wounded, twenty seriously, though it might be said that any wound was taken seriously by the sufferers. The corpses were cast in weighted fishskin bags and into the middle of The River after a brief ceremony. The bags were only to spare the feelings of the survivors since the bags would be ripped open and the flesh devoured by the fish before they reached the bottom.

Along the left bank the waters were thick with corpses, bumping into each other while the eating fish thrashed the bloodied waters. For a month, the logjam of bodies made The River hideous. Everywhere, apparently, the fighting had taken place, and it would be a long time before the drifting corpses disappeared. Meanwhile, the fish ravened, and the colossal riverdragonfish came up from the depths and took the bloating dead whole in their mouths until their stomachs were crammed. And when they had digested and eliminated these, they rose again to feed and to digest and to eliminate.

"It's Armageddon, the Apocalypse," Burton said to Alice, and he groaned.

Alice wept more than once, and she had nightmares. Burton comforted her so much that she felt that they were close again.

The afternoon of the next day, the *Rex* ventured across The River to recharge. But instead of going on, it went back to the right bank. It was necessary to make gunpowder and to repair damages. That took a month, during which time Burton completely recovered from his wound.

After the boat resumed its journey, some of its crew were tasked with making a count of the survivors in various areas picked at random. The result: an estimate that nearly half the population must have been killed, if the fighting had occurred on the same scale everywhere. Seventeen and a half billion people had died within twenty-four hours.

It was a long time before gaiety came back to the riverboat, and the people on the bank behaved like ghosts. Even worse than the effect of the slaughter was the dread thought: What if the remaining grailstone line quits?

Now, thought Burton, was the time to question the suspected agents. But if they were cornered, they might kill themselves even if no resurrection awaited them. And there was also the restraint that the post-1983 people might be innocent.

He would wait. He could do nothing else but wait.

Meanwhile, Loghu was subtly questioning her cabinmate, and Alice, though not subtle, was doing her best with Podebrad. And Burton was waiting for Strubewell to make a slip.

Several days after the voyage had started again, John decided that he would do some recruiting. He stopped the *Rex* during the noontime meal and went ashore to make it known that he had empty berths to fill.

Burton, as Sergeant Gwalchgwynn, had the duty with others of wandering through the crowd looking for possible assassins. When he came across an obvious early paleolithic, a squat massive-boned fellow who looked like a pre-Generalized Mongolian, and started to talk to him, he forgot his job for a while. Ngangchungding didn't mind giving him a quick lesson in the fundamentals of his native speech, one which Burton had never encountered before. Then Burton, speaking Esperanto, tried to get him to sign up on the *Rex*. Not only would he be a desirable marine, he would give Burton the opportunity to learn his language. Ngangchungding refused his offer. He was, he said a Nichirenite, a member of that Buddhist discipline which stressed pacifism as strongly as its chief rival, the Church of the Second Chance. Though disappointed, Burton gave him a cigarette to show that there were no hard feelings, and he went back to King John's table.

John was interviewing a Caucasian whose back was partially blocked from Burton's view by a tall, skinny-legged, long-armed, broad-shouldered Negro. Burton walked by them to place himself behind John.

He heard the white man say, "I am Peter Jairus Frigate."

Burton whirled, stared, glaring and then he leaped at Frigate. Frigate went down under him, Burton's hands around his throat.

"I'll kill you!" Burton shouted.

Something struck him on the back of the head.

11

WHEN HE REGAINED HIS SENSES, HE SAW THE NEGRO AND THE FOUR MEN who'd been behind him struggling with John's bodyguards. The monarch had leaped on top of the table, and, red-faced, was shouting orders. There was some confusion for a minute before everybody settled down. Frigate, coughing, had gotten to his feet. Burton pulled himself up, feeling pain in the back of his head. Evidently, he'd been hit with the knobkerrie the black had carried suspended from a thong on his belt. It lay on the grass now.

Though not entirely clear-headed, Burton realized that he had, somehow, erred. This man looked much like the Frigate he knew, and his voice was similar. But neither his voice nor his features were quite the same, and he wasn't as tall. Yet . . . the same name?

"I apologize, *Sinjoro* Frigate," he said. "I thought . . . you looked so much like a man whom I have good reason to loathe . . . he did me a terrible injury . . . never mind. I am truly sorry, and if I may make amends . . ."

What the devil, he thought. Or perhaps it should be, Which the devil?

Though this was not *his* Frigate, he couldn't help looking around for Monat.

"You almost scared the piss out of me," the fellow said. "But, well, all right. I accept. Besides, I think you've paid for your error. Umslopogaas can hit hard."

The black said, "I only tapped him to discourage him."

"Which you did," Burton said, and he laughed, though it hurt his head.

"You and your friends were fortunate you weren't slain on the spot!" John bellowed. He got down from the table and sat down. "Now, what is the difficulty?"

Burton explained again, secretly elated since under the circumstances the "almost" Frigate couldn't reveal to John that Burton was using an assumed name. John got assurances from Frigate and his four companions that they held no resentment against Burton and then ordered his men to release them. Before continuing the interviews, he insisted that Burton give him an account of why he had attacked Frigate. Burton made up a story which seemed to satisfy the monarch.

He said to Frigate, "How do you explain this startling resemblance?"

"I can't," Frigate said, shrugging. "I've had this happen before. Not the attack, I mean. I mean running across people who think they've seen me before, and I don't have a commonplace face. If my father had been a traveling salesman, I could explain it. But he wasn't. He was an electrical and civil engineer and seldom got out of Peoria."

Frigate didn't seem to have any superior enlistment qualifications. He was almost six feet tall and muscular but not especially so. He claimed to be a good archer, but there were hundreds of thousands of bowmen available to John. He would have dismissed him if Frigate had not mentioned that he'd arrived in an area a hundred miles up-River in a balloon. And he'd seen a huge dirigible. John knew that had to be the *Parseval*. He was also interested in the balloon story.

Frigate said that he and his companions had been journeying up-River with the intention of getting to the headwaters. They'd gotten tired of the slow rate of travel in their sailboat, and when they came to a place where metal was available, they'd talked its chief of state into building them a blimp.

"Ah!" John said. "What was this ruler's name?"

Frigate looked puzzled. "He was a Czech named Ladislas Podebrad."

John laughed until the tears came. When he'd finished, he said, "That is a good one. It just so happens that this Podebrad is one of my engineers now."

"Yeah?" one of Frigate's companions said. "We have a score to settle with him."

The speaker was about five feet ten inches high. He had a lean muscular body and dark hair and eyes. His face was strong but handsome and distinctive-looking. He wore a cowboy's ten-gallon hat and high-heeled boots, though his only other clothing was a white kiltcloth.

"Tom Mix at your service, Your Majesty," he said in a Texas drawl.

He puffed on his cigarette and added, "I'm a specialist in the rope and the boomerang, Sire, and I was once a well-known movie star, if you know what that is."

John turned to Strubewell. "Have you ever heard of him?"

"I've read about him," Strubewell said. "He was long before my time, but he was very famous in the twenties and thirties. He was a star of what they called horse operas."

Burton wondered if it was likely that an agent would know that.

"We sometimes make movies on the *Rex*," John said, smiling. "But we don't have horses, as you know."

"Do I ever!"

The monarch asked Frigate more about the adventure. The American said that at the same time they'd sighted the dirigible, they'd sprung a leak in an apparatus used to heat the hydrogen in the envelope. While trying to cover the leak in the pipe with some quick-setting glue, they'd vented gas from the bag so they could drop quickly into thicker and warmer air and thus open the ports of the gondola.

The leak had been fixed, but a wind started blowing them back and the batteries supplying fresh hydrogen had become dead. They decided to land. When they heard that John had sent a launch ahead to this place to announce that he was recruiting, they'd sailed down here as fast as they could.

"What were you on Earth?"

"A lot of things, like most people. In my middle age and old age, a writer of science-fiction and detective stories. I wasn't exactly obscure, but I was never near as well known as him."

He pointed at a medium-sized but muscular man with curly hair and a handsome Irish-looking face.

"He's Jack London, a great early twentieth-century writer."

"I'm not too fond of writers," John said. "I've had some on my boat, and they've generally caused a lot of trouble. However . . . who is the Negro who knocked my sergeant on the head without my permission?"

"Umslopogaas, a Swazi, a native of South Africa of the nineteenth century. He is a great warrior, especially proficient with his axe, which he calls Woodpecker. He also is notable as providing the model for the great fictional Zulu hero of the same name created by another writer, H. Rider Haggard."

"And he?"

John pointed at a brown-skinned black-haired man with a big nose. He stood a little over five feet and wore a large green cloth wrapped in turban fashion.

"That is Nur ed-Din el-Musafir, a much-traveled Iberian Moor, Your Majesty. He lived in your time and is a Sufi. He also happened to have met Your Majesty at your court in London."

John said, "What?" and stood up. He looked closely at the little man, then shut his eyes. When he opened them, he said, "Yes, I remember him well!"

The monarch got up and strode around the table, his arms open, speaking the English of his time rapidly and smiling. The others were astonished to see him embrace the little man and kiss him on both cheeks.

"Jeeze, another Frenchy!" Mix said, but he was grinning.

After the two had gabbled for some time, John said, "All I have to know is that Nur el-Musafir has traveled far with you and still regards you as his friends. Strubewell, you sign them up and give them instructions. Sergeant Gwalchgwynn, you assign them their cabins. Well, my good friend and mentor, we will talk after I have completed the interviews."

On the way down the corridor to their quarters, they ran into Loghu. She stopped, turned pale, then red, and screaming, "Peter, you bastard!" she hurled herself at Frigate. He went down with her hands clutching his throat. Laughing, the black and Mix pulled her off of him.

"You sure got a way with people," Mix said to Frigate.

"Another case of mistaken identity," Burton said. He explained to Loghu what had happened.

After he'd quit coughing and feeling his finger-marked neck, Frigate said, "I don't know who this other Frigate was, but he sure must not be likable."

Reluctantly, Loghu apologized. She was not fully convinced that this Frigate wasn't her former lover.

Mix muttered, "She can grab me any time she wants to, but not around the neck."

Loghu overheard him. She said, "If your whacker is as big as your hat, I might just grab it."

Surprisingly, Mix blushed. When she had hip-swayed away, he said, "Too bold and brassy for me."

Two days later, they were living together.

Burton was not content to admit that the resemblance of the two Frigates was just a coincidence. Whenever he had a chance, he talked to the fellow, delving into his background. What startled him was the discovery that this Frigate, like the other, had been a student of his, Burton's, life.

The American, in his turn, had been watching Burton, though covertly. Every once in a while, Burton caught him staring at him. One night, Frigate cornered him in the grand salon. After looking around to make sure their conversation wasn't overheard, the American said, without preamble and in English, "I'm familiar with the various portraits of Richard Francis Burton. I even had a big blowup of him when he was fifty on the wall in front of my desk. So I think I could recognize him without his mustachios and his forked beard."

"Yaas?"

"I recall well a photograph of him taken when he was about thirty. He had only a mustache then, though it was very thick. If I mentally remove the lip-hair . . ."

"Yaas?"

"Burton looks remarkably like a certain Dark-Ages Welshman I know. The name he claims is Gwalchgwynn, which, translated into English, is *white hawk*. Gwalchgwynn is an early form of the Welsh name which became better known much later as Gawain. And Gawain was the knight who, in the earlier King Arthur cycles, was first to seek the Holy Grail. The metal cornucopias we call grails look remarkably like the tower that's supposed to be in the middle of the north polar sea—from what I've heard. You might say it's the Big Grail."

"Very interesting," Burton said after he'd sipped on his grog. "Another coincidence."

Frigate looked steadily at him, disconcerting him a trifle. The devil take him. The fellow looked enough like the other to be his brother. Perhaps he was. Perhaps both were agents, and this one was playing with him as the other had.

"Burton would know all about the Arthurian cycles and the earlier folk tales on which they were based. It would be just like him, if he assumed a disguise—and he was famous on Earth for assuming many—to take the name of Gwalchgwynn. He would know that it signified a seeker after the Holy Grail, but he wouldn't expect anyone else to."

"I'm not so dense that I can't see that you think I'm that Burton fellow. But I never heard of him, and I don't care to have you pursue this matter even if it amuses you so much. I am not amused."

He lifted the glass to his lips and drank.

"Nur told me when he was visited by the Ethical, the Ethical told him that one of the men he'd picked was Captain Sir Richard Francis Burton, the nineteenth-century explorer."

Burton was able to control himself enough to keep from spitting the drink out.

Slowly, he put the glass down on the bar.

"Nur?"

"You know him. Mr. Burton, the others are waiting in the stage-prop room. Just to show you how sure I am that you're Burton, I'll reveal something. Mix and London used to go under assumed names. But they recently decided to hell with it. Now, Mr. Burton, would you care to go with me there?"

Burton considered. Could Frigate and his companions be agents? Were they waiting to seize and question him, turning the tables on him?

He looked around the crowded and noisy salon. When he saw Kazz, he said, "I'll go with you if you insist on this nonsense. But I'll take my good friend the Neanderthal with me. And we'll be armed."

When Burton entered the prop room ten minutes later, he was accompanied also by Alice and Loghu.

When Mix saw Loghu, his jaw dropped in astonishment.

"You in on this, too?"

12

THEY HAD AGREED NEVER TO TALK ABOUT THE ETHICAL OR ANYTHING connected with him in their cabins. These might be bugged. Their next meeting was at a table where they played poker. Present were Burton, Alice, Frigate, Nur, Mix, and London. Loghu and Umslopogaas were on duty.

When Burton had heard Nur's and Mix's story of their visits from X, he had been convinced that they were indeed recruits of the Ethical. Nevertheless, he had listened to what each had to say in detail before he had admitted his real identity. Then he had told his story, holding back nothing.

Now he was saying, "See you and raise you ten. No, I don't think we should plant eavesdropping devices in the cabins of any of the suspects. We might learn something valuable. But if they find one, then they'll know that X's agents, we could be called that, are on to them. It's too dangerous."

"I agree," the little Moor said. "Do the rest of you?"

Even Mix, who'd proposed planting the bugs, nodded. However, he said, "What about Podebrad? I run into him now and then, and all he does is say howdy to me and then pass on grinning like a parson who's just found out his girlfriend ain't pregnant. It galls me. I'd like to tear into the bastard."

"Me, too," London said. "He figures he's going to get away scot-free after making suckers of us."

"Attacking him would only get you thrown off the boat," Nur said. "Besides, he is tremendously strong. I believe that he would tear you apart while you were tearing into him."

"I can take him!" Mix and London said at the same time.

"You've bloody good reason for revenge," Burton said. "But it's out, for the time being anyway. Surely you can see that?"

"But why'd he say he was taking us along on the blimp and then desert us like we had B.O.?"

Nur ed-Din said, "I've thought about that. The only reasonable explanation is that he somehow suspected that we were X's men. That would be one more bit of evidence that he is an Ethical agent."

"I think he's just a goddamn sadist!" London said.

"No."

Burton said, "If he suspects you four, then you'll have to be on guard. The rest of us will, too. I didn't think of what Nur said or I'd not have suggested that we meet in the salon."

"It's too late to worry about that," Alice said. "Anyway, he isn't going to do anything, if he is an agent, until he gets to the headwaters. Any more than we are."

Burton won the pot with three jacks and two tens. Alice dealt. Burton thought that Nur must be concentrating on other matters than poker. The Moor won about half the time, and Burton suspected that he could rake in the chips even more often if he cared to. Somehow, the little man seemed to be able to tell what his opponents had in their hand just by looking at their faces.

"We might as well enjoy the ride," Frigate said.

Burton looked at him from lowered lids. The fellow had the same adulation for him that the other Frigate had or had pretended to have. Whenever he got the chance, he would ply Burton with questions, most of them about periods in his life which Burton's biographers had only been able to speculate about. But, also like the other, he would question attitudes and beliefs which Burton held dear. His attitude toward women and the colored races, for instance, and his belief in telepathy. Burton had too often had to explain that what he had believed on Earth did not necessarily hold here. He had seen too much and experienced too much. He had changed in many respects.

Now he thought it was a good time to delve into the matter of the pseudo-Frigate.

"There has to be a very good reason for the so-called coincidence."

"I've been pondering that, too," the American said. "Fortunately, I was an avid science-fiction reader and writer in that field. So I have a certain flexibility of imagination, which you'll need if you're going to bear with me, because I believe that the Frigate you've known by no coincidence at all is my brother James, dead at the ripe old age of one year!

"Now, consider the children who died on Earth. One reason, the best, is that if they were raised here, they would jam the planet. There wouldn't be enough living space here. In fact, the population of children deceased before five would be the largest segment of the entire population by far.

"So what would the Ethicals do with them? They'd resurrect them on another planet, perhaps one like this, perhaps not. Maybe it'd take two planets to hold them comfortably.

"Anyway, let's assume that this has happened. Unless," he lifted a finger, "unless for some reason they haven't been resurrected as yet. Maybe they're to be raised here after we're gone. Who knows?

"I don't. But I can speculate. Say that the infants were incarnated on another planet. It couldn't be done with the entire population at once because there would have to be adults to take care of them. And that would crowd a planet the size of Earth. So maybe they're incarnated at a certain rate, that is, so many infants within a certain time. These are raised to adulthood, and then they become the nurses, the teachers, the foster parents of more infants. And so on. Or maybe it's all done at once on more than one planet. I doubt that, though. The energy involved in planet re-forming would be enormous. On the other hand, they may use planets which don't have to be re-formed."

"Keep dealing," London said. "If you don't people'll wonder what the hell we're talking about!"

"I can open," Mix said.

They were silent except for announcing their play for a minute. Then Frigate said, "If what I propose were true, well, let me put it this way. Ah

. . . I was the eldest child in my family. The oldest alive, that is. My older brother, James, died at one. I was born six months later. Now . . . ah . . . he would be resurrected. And when he grew up, he became an agent for the Ethicals.

"He was planted here on Resurrection Day. He was assigned to watch Burton. Why would he be assigned? Because the Ethicals knew that, somehow, Burton had awakened in that vast chamber of floating bodies before Resurrection Day, before he was supposed to awake. They must have figured that it was no accident, that . . . uh . . . somebody awakened him on purpose. Well, we don't have to speculate on that. We know that's what the Council of Ethicals told Burton when they caught him. He was supposed to have his memory of that erased, but X arranged it so that he kept it.

"Anyway, the Ethicals were suspicious. So they put this pseudo-Frigate, well, actually he's a real Frigate, on Dick's trail. My brother was to keep an eye on him and report anything suspicious. But like everybody in The Valley, he got caught with his kilt down."

"I'll take two cards," Burton said. "That's very intriguing, Peter. It seems a wild concept, but it may just be true. However, if your brother was an agent, then *what* was Monat the Tau Cetan or Arcturan or whatever he is? Certainly, he'd have to be an agent, a strange one true, but nevertheless . . ."

"Perhaps he's an Ethical!" Alice said.

Burton, who didn't like to be interrupted, glared.

"I was just going to say that. But if Monat is an agent, I don't think he's an Ethical, otherwise he'd have been in the Council . . . no, by Allah, he wouldn't have been! If I'd have seen him there, I'd have known that he was one of 'em! And he wouldn't have been able to stay with me. Though why he stuck to me, I don't know.

"However, Monat's presence means that there is more than one species . . . genus . . . zoological family . . . extra-Terrestrials . . . involved in this."

"I'll take one card," Frigate said. "As I was about to say . . ."

"Pardon me," London said. "But how could Peter's brother know about Burton?"

"I suppose that the children are educated, probably better than they'd be on Earth. And maybe, just maybe, my brother knew I was his brother. How do we know what incredibly vast and minute knowledge the Ethicals have? Look at the photo of Burton which he found in the kilt of that agent, Agneau. It was taken when Dick was twenty-eight and a subaltern in the East India Army. Doesn't that prove that the Ethicals were on Earth in 1848? Who knows how long they've been walking the streets of Earth taking data? Don't ask me for what purpose."

"Why would James take your name?" Nur said.

"Well, I was a rabid Burton fan. I even wrote a novel about him. Maybe it pleased James' sense of humor. I have one. My whole family is known for . . . an odd sense of humor. And so it struck him funny to be his brother, to pretend to be the Peter that he never knew. Maybe he could vicariously relive the life he'd been denied on Earth. Maybe he thought that if he ran into someone who'd known the Frigate family, he could pass himself off as me. Maybe all these reasons are true. Whatever . . . I'm sure he punched out Sharkko, the crooked publisher, to avenge me, which shows that he knew much about my life on Earth."

Alice said, "But what about the story that agent, Spruce, told? He said he was from the seventy-second century A.D., and he said something about a chronoscope, something which could look back in time."

"Spruce may have been lying," Burton said.

"Anyway," Frigate said, "I don't believe there could be a chronoscope or such a thing as time-travel in any form. Well, maybe I shouldn't say that. We're all time-traveling. Forward, the only way there is."

"What nobody has said," Nur said, "is that somebody had to resurrect the children. It may or may not have been people from the seventy-second century. More probably, it was Monat's people who did it. Note also that it was Monat who did most of the questioning of Spruce. He may have been, in a sense, coaching Spruce."

"Why?" Alice said.

That was one question nobody could answer unless the Ethical's story was true. By now, his recruits thought that he might be as big a liar as his colleagues.

Nur closed that round with the speculation that the agents who'd gotten on the boat early in its voyage had told their post-1983 story and were stuck with it. Agents who'd gotten on later knew that the story might be suspect, so they'd avoided it. For instance, the huge Gaul named Megalosos—his name meant "Great"—claimed that he'd lived about Caesar's time. His saying so, however, didn't make it so. It seems he found Podebrad congenial, though how anyone could was beyond Nur. He could be an agent, too.

SECTION 4

On the *Not For Hire:*
New Recruits and Clemens' Nightmares

13

DE MARBOT'S EYES PROVED THAT THE RESURRECTION MACHINERY DID NOT always work perfectly.

Jean Baptiste Antoine Marcelin, Baron de Marbot, had been born in 1782 with brown eyes. Not until long after Resurrection Day did he find out that they had changed color. That was when a woman called him Blue-eyes.

"*Sacre bleu!* Is it true?"

He hastened to borrow a mica mirror which had recently been brought in a trading boat—mica was rare—and he saw his face for the first time in ten years. It was a merry face with its roundness, its snub nose, its ever-ready smile, its twinkling eyes. Not at all unhandsome.

But the eyes were a light *blue*.

"*Merde!*"

Then he reverted to Esperanto.

"If I ever get within sword range of the abominable abominations who did this to me. . . !"

He returned fuming to the woman who lived with him, and he repeated his threat.

"But you don't have a sword," she said.

"Must you take me so literally? Never mind. I will get one someday; there must be iron somewhere in this stony planet."

That night he dreamed of a giant bird with rusty feathers and vulture's beak which ate rocks and the droppings of which were steel pellets. But there were no birds at all on this world, and if there had been there would have been no *oiseau de fer*.

Now he had metal weapons, a saber, a cutlass, an épée, a stiletto, a long knife, an axe, a spear, pistols, and a rifle. He was the brigadier general of the marines, and he was very ambitious to be full general. But he loathed politics, and he had neither interest nor ability in the dishonorable game of intrigue. Besides, only by the death of Ely S. Parker could he be general of the marines of the *Not For Hire,* and that would have saddened him. He loved the jolly Seneca Indian.

Almost all the postpaleolithics aboard were over six feet, some of them huge. The paleolithics had small men among them, but these, with their massive bones and muscles, did not have to be so tall. De Marbot was the pygmy among them, only five feet four inches high, but Sam Clemens liked him and admired his feistiness and courage. Sam also liked to hear stories of de Marbot's campaigns and to have people under him who had once been generals, admirals, and statesmen. "Humility is good for them, builds their character," Sam said. "The Frenchy is a first-rate commander, and it amuses me to see him ordering those big apes around."

De Marbot was certainly experienced and capable. After joining the republican army of France when he was seventeen, he rose rapidly in rank to aide-de-camp to Marshal Augereau, commanding the VII Corps in the war against Prussia and Russia from 1806 to 1807. He fought under Lannes and Masséna in the Peninsular War, and he'd gone through the Russian campaign in the War of 1812 and the terrible retreat from Moscow, and, among others, the German campaign in 1813. He'd been wounded eleven times, severely at Hanau and Leipzig. When Napoleon returned from his exile at Elba, he promoted de Marbot to general of brigade, and de Marbot was wounded at the bloody battle of Waterloo. De Marbot was exiled by the Bourbon king, but he returned to his native land in 1817. After serving under the July monarchy at the siege of Antwerp, he was rewarded some years later by being made a lieutenant general. From 1835 to 1840, he was in the Algerian expeditions, and at the age of sixty was wounded for the last time. He retired after the fall of King Louis Philippe in 1848. He wrote his memoirs, which so delighted Arthur Conan Doyle that he used him as the basis of his fictional character, Brigadier Gerard. The main difference between the literary and the real-life character was that de Marbot was intelligent and perceptive, whereas Gerard, though gallant, was not very bright.

When he was seventy-two years old, the brave soldier of Napoleon died in bed in Paris.

It was a measure of Clemens' affection for him that he had told him about the Mysterious Stranger, the renegade Ethical.

Today the riverboat was docked while Clemens interviewed volunteers for a post aboard. The hideous events after the right-bank stones had failed were two months behind the crew, and The River was now free of the stench and jampack of rotting bodies.

De Marbot, clad in a duraluminum helmet topped by a roach of glue-stiffened fish-leather strips and a duraluminum cuirass, looking like the popular conception of a Trojan warrior, walked up and down the long line of candidates. His job was to pre-interview them. In this way, he could sometimes eliminate the unfit and so save his captain time and work.

Near the middle of the line he saw four men who seemed to know each other well. He stopped by the first, a tall muscular dark man with huge hands. His color and very wavy hair could only mean that he was a quadroon, and he was.

At de Marbot's polite inquiry, he said that his name was Thomas Million Turpin. He'd been born in Georgia sometime around 1873—he wasn't sure just when—but his parents had moved to St. Louis, Missouri, when he was young. His father operated the Silver Dollar, a tavern in the red-light district. In his youth Tom and his brother Charles had purchased a share of the Big Onion Mine near Searchlight, Nebraska, and worked it, but, failing to find gold after two years, had roamed the west for a while before returning to St. Louis.

Turpin had settled down in the District and worked as a bouncer and piano player, among other things. By 1899 he was the most important man in the area, controlling the music, liquor, and gambling. His Rosebud Cafe, the center of his little empire, was famous throughout the nation. Downstairs it was a tavern-restaurant and upstairs a "hotel," a whorehouse.

Turpin, however, was more than a big-time political boss. He was, according to his own statement, a great piano player, though he admitted he wasn't quite as good as Louis Chauvin. A frontiersman in syncopated music, he'd been known as the father of ragtime in St. Louis, and his "Harlem Rag," published in 1897, was the first ragtime piece published by a Negro. He'd written the famous "St. Louis Rag" for the opening of the world fair there, but that had been postponed. He died in 1922, and since he'd been on the Riverworld had wandered up and down.

"I hear there's a piano on your boat," he said, grinning. "I'd sure like to get my hands on them ivories."

"There are ten pianos," de Marbot said. "Here. Take this."

He handed Turpin a wand of wood six inches long and incised with the initials: M.T.

"When you get to the table, give this to the captain."

Sam would be happy. He loved ragtime, and he once had said that he couldn't get enough players of popular music on his boat. Moreover, Turpin looked big and capable. He had to be to have bossed the rough black red-light district.

The man behind him was a wild-looking Chinese named Tai-Peng. He was about five feet ten inches tall and had large glowing green eyes and a demonic face. His black hair hung to his waist, and three irontree blooms were stuck in its crown. He claimed in a loud shrill voice to have been a great swordsman, lover, and poet in his time, which was that of the T'ang dynasty in the eighth century A.D.

"I was one of the Six Idlers of the Bamboo Stream and also of the Eight Immortals of the Wine Cup. I can compose poetry on the spot in my native Turkish, in Chinese, in Korean, in English, in French, and in Esperanto. When it comes to swordplay, I am as quick as a hummingbird and as deadly as a viper."

De Marbot laughed and said he didn't choose the recruits. But he gave the Chinese a wand and moved on to the man behind Tai-Peng.

This was a short man, though still taller than de Marbot, dark-skinned, black-eyed, fat, and with a bulging Buddha's belly. His eyelids were slightly epicanthic, and his nose was aquiline. His clefted chin was massive. He, he said, was Ah Qaaq, and he came from the eastern coast of a land which de Marbot would call Mexico. His people had called the area in which they lived the Land of Rain. He didn't know exactly when he lived according to the Christian calendar, but from his talks with a scholarly man it must have been around 100 B.C. His native tongue was Mayan; he was a citizen of the people that later cultures had called Olmec.

"Ah, yes," de Marbot said. "I have heard talk of the Olmecs. We have some very learned men at the captain's table."

De Marbot understood that the "Olmecs" had founded the first civilization in Mesoamerica and that all others in pre-Columbian times had derived from it, the later Mayas, the Toltecs, the Aztecs, what have you. The man, if he was an ancient Mayan, did not have the artificially flattened head and the squint-eyes so favored by that people. But on reflection de Marbot realized that these, of course, would have been rectified by the Ethicals.

"You're that rarity, a fat man," de Marbot said. "We of the *Not For Hire* lead an extremely active life, no room for indolents and overeaters, and we also require that the candidate have something special to qualify him."

Ah Qaaq said in a high voice, though not as high as the Chinese's, "The fat cat may look soft, but it is very strong and very quick. Let me show you."

He took the handle of his flint-headed axe, a piece of oak eighteen inches long and two inches thick, and he snapped it as if it were a sugarstick. Then he picked up the head and let the Frenchman heft it.

"About ten pounds, that one, I'd say," de Marbot said.

"Watch!"

Ah Qaaq took the axehead and hurled it as if it were a baseball. Eyes wide, de Marbot watched it soar high and far before it struck the grass.

"*Mon Dieu!* No one but the mighty Joe Miller could throw that as far! I congratulage you, *sinjoro*. Here. Take this."

"I am also an excellent archer and axeman," Ah Qaaq said quietly. "You won't regret taking me aboard."

The man behind the Olmec was exactly his height and had a squat Herculean physique. He even looked like Ah Qaaq with his eaglish nose and rounded clefted chin. But he had no fat, and though he was almost as dark, he was no Amerindian. His name, he said, was Gilgamesh.

"I have arm-wrestled Ah Qaaq," Gilgamesh said. "Neither of us can defeat the other. I am also a great axeman and archer."

"Very good! Well, my captain will be pleased with your tales of Sumeria, of which I'm sure you have plenty. And he will also be pleased to have a king and a god aboard. Kings he's met, though he's not been too happy with most of them. Gods, well, that's a different story. The captain has never met a god before! Here. Take this!"

He moved on, and when he was out of sight and earshot of the Sumerian—if he was one—laughed until he rolled on the grass. After a while he got up, wiped off the tears, and resumed his interviewing.

The four were accepted with six others. When they marched up the gangplank onto the boiler deck, they saw Monat the extra-Terrestrial standing by the railing, his keen eyes sweeping over them. They were startled, but de Marbot told them to go on. He would explain all about the strange creature later on.

The recruits did not meet Monat that evening as planned. Two women quarreled about a man and started shooting at each other. Before the argument was settled, one woman was badly wounded and the other had jumped off the boat, her grail in one hand and a box of possessions in the other. The man decided to leave also since he preferred the woman who'd done the shooting. The boat was stopped, and he was let off. Sam was so upset that he called off the introductions in the grand salon until the next day.

Sometime that night, Monat Grrautut disappeared.

No one had heard a cry. No one had seen anything suspicious. The only clue was a bloodstain on the aft railing of the A deck promenade, and that might have been an oversight by the clean-up squads after the battles over the left-bank stones.

Clemens suspected that one of the four new recruits might have been responsible. These, however, claimed steadfastly that they were asleep in their bunks, and no one had any evidence to refute them.

While Sam pondered the case and wished he had Sherlock Holmes aboard, the *Not For Hire* forged ahead. Three days after Monat's disappearance, Cyrano de Bergerac flagged the boat down. Sam cursed when he saw him. He'd hoped that they would pass Cyrano during the night, but there he was, and at least fifty of the crew had also seen him.

The Frenchman came aboard smiling and quickly kissing his male friends on the cheeks and his female friends on the mouth lingeringly. When he came into the control room, he cried, "Captain! What a tale I have!"

Clemens thought sourly that that could be said of any dog.

14

A MAN AND A WOMAN LAY IN BED. THEIR SKINS TOUCHED; THEIR DREAMS were lightyears apart.

Sam Clemens was dreaming again of that day when he had killed Erik Bloodaxe. Rather, when he had set in motion other men, one of whom had put a spear into the Norseman's belly.

Sam had wanted the buried meteorite for its nickel-steel. Without it, he could not build the great paddlewheeled boat he envisioned so often. Now, in this dream, he talked to Lothar von Richthofen of what must be done. Joe Miller was not present, having been treacherously captured by the man who had once been king of England. An invading fleet was sailing from down-River to seize the grave of the fallen star. King John was up-River, readying a fleet to sail down and grab the site of the buried treasure of nickel-steel. Sam's army was between the two and weaker than either one. His would be ground to meal between the millstones. There was no chance for victory except by making an alliance with John. Also, if Joe Miller was to get out alive, Sam would have to make a deal with his captor, King John.

But Erik Bloodaxe, Sam's partner, had refused to consider the alliance. Besides, Erik hated Joe Miller, who was the only human he had ever feared—if you could call Joe a human. Bloodaxe said that his men and Sam's would make a stand and would smash the two invaders in a glorious victory. This was foolish boasting, though the Norseman may have believed what he said.

Erik Bloodaxe was the son of Harald Haarfager (Harold Finehair), the Norwegian who'd united, for the first time, all of Norway and whose conquests had led to mass migrations to England and to Iceland. When Harald died circa A.D. 918, Erik became king. But Erik wasn't popular. Even in a day of harsh and cruel monarchs, he led the pack. His half-brother, Haakon, then fifteen years old, had been reared in the court of King Athelstan of England since he was one year old. Supported by English troops, he raised a Norwegian army against his brother. Erik fled to Northumbria in England, where he was given its kingship by Athelstan, but he didn't last long. According to the Norse chroniclers, he died in A.D. 954 in southern England while making a great raid there. The old English tradition had it that he was expelled from Northumbria and was killed during a battle at Stainmore.

Erik had told Clemens that the former account was the true one.

Clemens had joined the Norseman because Erik owned a very rare steel axe and was looking for the source of ore from which the axe had been made. Clemens hoped that there'd be enough ore to make a large paddlewheeled steamboat in which he could go to the headwaters of The River. Erik didn't think much of Sam but took him in as a member of his crew because of Joe Miller. Erik didn't like Joe, but he knew that the titanthrop was a very valuable asset in battle. And then Joe had been made a hostage by King John. Desperate, fearful that Joe would be killed by King John and that he would lose the meteorite, Sam had discussed the situation with Lothar, the younger brother of "The Red Baron." He had made his proposal. They should kill Bloodaxe and his Viking bodyguards. After that, they could talk to John, who would see the advantage of teaming up with Clemens' force. Together, the two might be a match for von Radowitz' forces from down-River.

Sam further strengthened his rationalizations with the thought that Bloodaxe probably intended to kill him after their enemies had been defeated. A showdown was inevitable.

Lothar von Richthofen agreed. It wasn't treachery if you attacked a traitor. Besides, it was the only logical thing to do. If Bloodaxe was a true friend, then the case would be different. But the Norseman was as trustworthy as a rattlesnake with a toothache.

And so the foul deed had been done.

Yet, even though it was justified by all counts, the deed *was* foul. Sam had never gotten over his guilt. After all, he could have walked away from the meteorite, given up his dream.

With Lothar and some picked men, he had approached the hut in which Bloodaxe and a woman were humping away. The fight lasted a minute, the Norse guards being taken by surprise by a larger force. The Viking king, naked, holding his great axe, had dashed out. Lothar had pinned him to the wall of the hut with the spear.

Sam had been about to vomit, but he thought that at least the deed was all over. Then a hand had clamped on his ankle, causing him almost to faint with terror. He had looked down, and there was the dying Bloodaxe, holding him with a grip like an eagle's.

"*Bikkja!*" the Norseman had said, weakly but clearly.

That meant *bitch,* a word he often used to indicate his contempt for Clemens, whom he considered effeminate. "Droppings of Ratatosk," he continued. In other words, crap of the giant squirrel, Ratatosk, that raced around the branches of the world-tree, Yggdrasill, the cosmic ash which bound together earth, the abode of the gods, and hell.

And then Bloodaxe had prophesied, saying that Clemens *would* build his great boat. He would pilot it up The River. But its building and its voyage would be grief and sorrow for Clemens with little of the joy he anticipated. And when Clemens at long last neared the headwaters of The River, he would find that Bloodaxe would be waiting for him.

Sam remembered clearly the dying man's speech. It came up now again from the shadowy figure that held his foot from a deep narrow hole in the ground. Eyes in the vague black mass in the earth burned into Clemens'.

"I will find you! I will be waiting on a distant boat, and I will kill you. And you will never get to the end of The River nor storm the gates of Valhalla!"

Even when the hand had slackened, Sam had been too cold with horror to move away. Death rattled in the throat of the sinister shadow, and still Sam was frozen on the outside, though vibrating inside.

"I wait!"

Those were Erik Bloodaxe's last words, echoing yet in his dreams down the years.

Sam had scoffed at the prophecy—later on. No one could see into the future. That was superstitious rot. Bloodaxe might be up-River, but, if he was, it was due to chance alone. There was a fifty-fifty probability that he was down-River. Moreover, even if the Norseman was waiting for revenge, he wasn't likely to have an opportunity to wreak it. The boat only made three stops a day, except for some occasional shore leaves of a week or so. Very probably Bloodaxe would be standing on the bank when the riverboat traveled by. Run or paddle or sail though he might, Erik could not catch up with the swift vessel.

Believing this did not, however, keep Bloodaxe out of Sam's nightmares. Perhaps this was because, deep within him, Sam knew that he was guilty of murder. Therefore, he should be punished.

In one of those sudden shifts of scene the Supervisor of Dreams so slickly contrives, Sam found himself in a hut. It was night, and rain and lightning and thunder were like a cat-o'-nine-tails against the back of darkness. The flashes in the sky faintly illumined the interior of the hut. A shadowy figure squatted near him. The figure was cloaked; a huge dome on its shoulders covered its head.

"What's the occasion for this unexpected visit?" Sam said, repeating the question he'd asked during the Mysterious Stranger's second visit.

"The Sphinx and I are playing draw poker," the Stranger said. "Would you like to sit in?"

Sam awoke. The luminous digits of the chronometer on the wall across the cabin read 03:33. *What I tell you three times is true*. Gwenafra, beside him, groaned. She muttered something about "Richard." Was she dreaming about Richard Burton? Though she had only been about seven when she had known him, and had been with him for only a year, she still talked of him. Her child's love for him had survived.

There was no sound now except for Gwenafra's breathing and the far-off chuff-chuff of the great paddlewheels. Their cycling sent slight vibrations throughout the ship. When he had his hand on the duraluminum frame of the bed, he could feel the faint waves. The four wheels turned by the colossal electrical motors were driving the vessel toward his goal.

Out there, on both banks, people were sleeping. Night lay over this hemisphere, and an estimated 8.75 billion were abed, dreaming. What were their shadowy visions? Some would be of Earth; some, of this world.

Was the ex-caveman turning restlessly in his sleep, moaning, dreaming of a sabertooth prowling outside the fire in the entrance? Joe Miller often dreamed of mammoths, those hairy curving-tusked leviathans of his time, food to stuff his capacious belly and skin to make tents and ivory to make props for the tents and teeth to make enormous necklaces. He also dreamed of his totem, his ancestor, the giant cave bear; the massive shaggy figure came to him at night and advised him on matters that troubled him. And he dreamed sometimes of being beat with clubs on the soles of his feet by enemies. Joe's eight hundred pounds plus his bipedal posture caused flat feet. He could not walk all day like the Homo sapiens pygmies; he had to sit down and ease his aching feet.

Joe also had nocturnal emissions when dreaming of a female of his kind. Joe was sleeping with his present mate, a six-foot seven-inch beauty, a Kassubian, a Slavic speaker of the third century A.D. She loved Joe's massiveness and hairiness and the grotesque nose and the gargantuan penis and most of all his essentially gentle soul. And she may have gotten a perverse pleasure from making love to a not-quite-human being. Joe loved her, too, but that didn't keep him from dreaming amorously of his Terrestrial wife and any number of other females of his tribe. Or, like humans everywhere, of a mate constructed by the Master of Dreams, an ideal living only in the unconscious.

"Every man is a moon and has a dark side which he never shows to anybody."

So Sam Clemens had written. How true. But the Master of Dreams, that master of ceremonies of bizarre circuses, trotted out his caged beasts and trapeze artists and tight-rope walkers and side-show freaks every night.

In last night's dream, he, Samuel Langhorne Clemens, had been locked in a room with an enormous machine on the back of which rode his alter ego, Mark Twain. The machine was a monstrous and weird creature, squat, round-backed, a cockroach with a thousand legs and a thousand teeth. The teeth in the oblong mouth were bottles of patent medicine, "snake oil." The legs were metal rods with round feet on the bottoms of which were letters from the alphabet. It advanced toward him, teeth clinking together while the legs squeaked and squealed from lack of oil. Mark Twain, seated in a gold-plated diamond-encrusted howdah on its back, pulled levers to direct it. Mark Twain was an old man with bushy white hair and a white bushy mustache. He wore an all-white suit. He grinned and then glared at Sam and jerked at the levers and steered his machine this way and that, trying to cut off Sam's attempts to escape.

Sam was only eighteen, his famous mustache not yet grown. He clutched the handle of a carpetbag in one hand.

Round and round the room Sam fled, while the machine clinked and squeaked as it spun around and ran toward him and then backed up. Mark Twain kept yelling things at Sam, such as: *"Here's a paige from your own book, Sam,"* and *"Your publisher sends you his regards, Sam, and asks for more money!"*

Sam, squealing like the machine, was a mouse trapped by a mechanical cat. No matter how fast he ran, how he spun, whirled, and leaped, he was inevitably going to be caught.

Suddenly, ripples passed over the metal shell of the monster. It stopped, and it groaned. A clicking issued from its mouth; it squatted, the legs bending. From an orifice in its rear spurted a stream of green paper. They were thousand-dollar bills, and they piled against the wall and then began to flow over the machine. The pile grew and grew and then fell into the howdah, where Mark Twain was screaming at the machine that it was sick, sick, sick.

Fascinated, Sam crept forward, keeping a wary eye on the machine. He picked up one of the bills. "At last," he thought, "at long lust."

The paper in his hand became human feces.

Now he saw that all the bills had suddenly turned to feces.

But a door had opened in the hitherto unbroken wall of the room.

H. H. Rogers stuck his head through. He was the rich man who'd aided Sam during his troubles, even though Sam had excoriated the big oil trusts. Sam ran toward him, yelling, "Help! Help!"

Rogers stepped into the room. He wore nothing except red longjohns, the rear flap of which hung unbuttoned. On his chest in gold letters was the legend: IN STANDARD OIL WE TRUST; ALL OTHERS, GOD.

"You've saved me, Henry!" Sam gasped.

Rogers turned his back for a minute, exposing the sign on his buttocks: PUT IN A DOLLAR AND PULL THE LEVER.

Rogers, frowning, said, "Just a minute." He reached behind him and pulled out a document.

"Sign here, and I'll let you out."

"I haven't got a pen!" Sam said. Behind him, the machine was beginning to move again. He couldn't see it, but he knew that it was creeping up on him. Beyond Rogers, through the door, Sam could see a beautiful garden. A lion and a lamb sat side by side, and Livy was standing just behind them. She smiled at him. She wore nothing, and she was holding a huge parasol over her head. Faces peeked from behind flowers and bushes. One of them was Susy, his favorite daughter. But what was she doing? Something he knew he wouldn't like. Was that a man's bare foot sticking out from the bush behind which Susy was hiding?

"I don't have a pen," Sam said again.

"I'll take your shadow for collateral," Rogers said.

"I already sold it," Sam said. He groaned as the door swung shut behind Rogers.

And that had been the end of that nightmare.

Where now were his wife Livy, Clara, Jean, and Susy, his daughters? What dreams were they dreaming? Did he figure in them? If so, as what? Where was Orion, his brother? Inept bumbling ne'er-do-well optimistic Orion. Sam had loved him. And where was his brother Henry, poor Henry, burned so badly when the paddlewheeler *Pennsylvania* blew up, lingering for six excruciatingly painful days in the makeshift hospital in Memphis. Sam had been with him, had suffered with him, and then had seen him carried off to the room where the undoubtedly dying were taken.

Resurrection has restored Orion's charred skin, but it would never heal his interior wounds. Just as it had failed to heal Sam's.

And where was the poor old whiskey-sodden tramp who had died when the Hannibal jail caught fire? Sam had been ten then, had been awakened out of sleep by the fire bells. He had run down to the jail and seen the man, clinging to the bars, screaming, blackly silhouetted against the bright red flames. The town marshal could not be found, and he had the only keys to the cell door. A group had tried to batter the oaken doors down and had failed.

Some hours before the marshal had picked up the bum, Sam had given the bum some matches to light his pipe. It was one of these that must have set fire to the straw bed in the cell. Sam knew that he was responsible for the tramp's terrible death. If he had not felt sorry for him and gone home to get the matches for him, the man would not have died. An act of charity, a moment of sympathy, had caused him to be burned to death.

And where was Nina, his granddaughter? She was born after he'd died, but he had learned about her from a man who'd read her death notice in the *Los Angeles Times* of January 18, 1966.

RITES PENDING FOR NINA CLEMENS,
LAST DESCENDANT OF MARK TWAIN

The fellow had a very good memory, but his interest in Mark Twain had helped him to record the heading in his mind.

"She was fifty-five years old and was found dead late Sunday in a motel room at 20-something-or-other North Highland Avenue. Her room was strewn with bottles of pills and liquor. There wasn't any note and an autopsy was ordered to find out the exact cause of her death. I never saw the report.

"She'd died across the street from her luxurious three-bedroom penthouse in the Highland Towers. Her friends said she often checked in there for the weekend when she was tired of being alone. The paper said she'd been alone most of her life. She'd used the name of Clemens after she divorced an artist by the name of Rutgers. She had been married to him briefly in, ah, 1935, I think. The paper said she was the daughter of Clara Grabrilowitsch, your only daughter. It meant that she was your only *surviving* daughter. Clara married a Jacques Samoussoud after her first husband died. In 1935, I think. She was a devout Christian Scientist, you know."

"No, I didn't know!" Sam said.

His informant, knowing that Sam loathed Christian Science, that he had once written a defamatory book about Mary Baker Eddy, had grinned.

"Do you suppose she was getting back at you?"

"Spare me your psychological analyses," Sam had said. "Clara worshiped me. All my children did."

"Anyway, Clara died in 1962, not long after she'd authorized publication of your unpublished *Letters to the Earth*."

"*That* was printed?" Sam said. "What was the reaction?"

"It sold well. But it was pretty mild stuff, you know. No one was outraged or thought it was blasphemous. Oh, yes, your *1601*, uncensored, was also printed. When I was young, it could be obtained only through private presses. But by the late 1960s, it was sold to the general public."

Sam had shaken his head. "You mean children could buy it?"

"No, but a lot of them read it."

"How things must've changed!"

"Anything, well, almost anything, went. Let's see. The article said that your granddaughter was an amateur artist, singer, and actress. She was also a shutterbug—a person who liked to take photographs—she took dozens of pictures every week of friends, bartenders, and waiters. Even strangers on the street.

"She was writing an autobiography, *A Life Alone*, which title tells you a lot about her. Poor thing. Her friends said the book was 'generally confused' but parts of it showed some of your genius."

"I always said that Livy and I were too highstrung to have children."

"Well, she wasn't suffering from lack of money. She inherited some trust funds from her mother, about $800,000, I believe. Money from the sale of your books. When she died, she was worth one and a half million dollars. Yet, she was unhappy and lonely.

"Oh, yes. Her body was taken to Elmira, New York . . . *for burial in a family plot near the famed grandfather whose name she bore.*"

"I can't be blamed for her character," Sam had said. "Clara and Ossip can take credit for that."

The informant shrugged and said, "You and your wife formed the characters of your children, Clara included."

"Yes, but my character was formed by my parents. And theirs by theirs," Sam had said. "Do we go back to Adam and Eve to fix the responsibility? No, because God formed their temperaments when he created them. There is but one being who bears the ultimate responsibility."

"I'm a free-willer myself," the man had said.

"Listen," Sam had said. *"When the first living atom found itself afloat on the great Laurentian sea, the first act of that first atom led to the second act of that first atom, and so on down through the succeeding ages of all life until, if the steps could be traced, it would be shown that the first act of that first atom has led inevitably to the act of my standing in my kilt at this instant, talking to you.* That's from my *What Is Man?* slightly paraphrased. What do you think of that?"

"It's bullshit."

"You say that because you have been determined to do so. You could not have said anything else."

"You're a sorry case, Mr. Clemens, if you don't mind my saying so."

"I do. But you can't help saying that. Listen, what was your profession?"

The man looked surprised. "What's that got to do with it? I was a realtor. I was also on the school board for many years."

"Let me quote myself again," Sam had said. *"In the first place, God made idiots. This was for practice. Then he made School Boards."*

Sam chuckled now at the memory of the man's expression.

He sat up. Gwen slept on. He turned on the nightlight and saw that she was smiling slightly. She looked innocent, childlike, yet the full lips and the full curves of the breast, almost entirely exposed, excited him. He reached out to awake her but changed his mind. Instead, he put on his kilt and a cloth for a cape and his visored high-peaked fish-leather cap. He picked up a cigar and left the room closing the door softly. The corridor was warm and bright. At the far end, the door was locked; two armed guards stood by it. Two also stood at the near end by the elevator doors. He lit a cigar and walked toward the elevator. He chatted for a minute with the guards and then entered the cage.

He punched the P button. The doors slid shut, but not before he saw a guard starting to phone to the pilothouse that La Bosso (The Boss) was coming up. The cage rose from the D or hangar deck, where the officers' quarters were, through the two narrow round rooms below the pilothouse, and then to the top chamber. There was a brief wait while the third-watch exec checked out the cage with closed-circuit TV. Then the doors slid open, and Sam entered the pilothouse or control room.

"It's all right boys," he said. "Just me, enjoying insomnia."

There were three others there. The night pilot, smoking a big cigar, eyeing the dials lackadaisically. He was Akande Erin, a massive Dahomeyan who had spent thirty years operating a jungle riverboat. The most outrageous liar Sam had ever known, and he had met the world's best. Third-mate Calvin Cregar, a Scot who had put in forty years on an Australian coastal steamer. Ensign Diego Santiago of the marines, a seventeenth-century Venezuelan.

"Just came to look around," Sam said. "Carry on."

The sky was unclouded, blazing as if that great arsonist, God, had set it afire. The Valley was broad here, and the light fell softly, showing dimly the buildings and boats on both banks. Beyond them was a darker darkness. A few sentinel fires made eyes in the night. Otherwise, the world seemed asleep. The hills rose dark with trees, the giant irontrees, a thousand feet high, spiring up from the others. Beyond, the mountains loomed blackly. Faint starlight sparked on the waves.

Sam went through the door to stand on the port walk that ringed the exterior of the pilothouse. The wind was cool but not yet cold. It ran fingers through his bushy hair. Standing on the deck, he felt like a living part, an organ, of the vessel. It was spanking along, paddlewheels churning, its flags flapping, brave as a tiger, huge and sleek as a sperm whale, beautiful as a woman, heading always against the current, its goal the Axis Mundi, the Navel of the World, the dark tower. He felt roots grow from his feet, tendrils that spread through the hull, extended from the hull, dropped through the black waters, touched by the monsters of the deep, plunged into the muck three miles below, grew laterally up through the earth, spread out, shooting with the speed of thought, growing vines which erupted from the earth, stabbed into the flesh of every living human being on this world, spiraled upward through the roofs of the huts, rocketed toward the skies, veined space with the shoots which wrapped themselves around every planet on which lived animal life and sentients, enveloped and penetrated these, and then shot exploring tentacles toward the blackness where no matter was, where only God existed.

In that moment, Sam Clemens was, if not one with the universe, at least integral with it. And for a moment he believed in God.

And at that moment Samuel Clemens and Mark Twain inhabited the same flesh, merged, became one.

Then the thrilling vision exploded, contracted, dwindled, shot back into him.

He laughed. For several seconds he had known an ecstasy that surpassed even sexual intercourse, up to that moment the supreme feeling in his, and humanity's, lot, disappointing as it often was.

Now he was within himself again, and the universe was outside.

He returned to the control room. Erin, the black pilot, looking up at him, said, "You have been visited by the spirits."

"Do I look that peculiar?" Sam said. "Yes, I have."

"What did they say?"

"That I am nothing and everything. I once heard the village idiot say the same thing."

SECTION 5

Burton's Soliloquy

15

LATE AT NIGHT, WHILE THE EXCEPTIONALLY THICK AND HIGH FOG shrouded even the pilothouse, Burton prowled.

Unable to sleep, he roamed here and there with no place to go in mind— except that of getting away from himself.

"Damn me! Always trying to outrun my own self! If I had the wits of a cow, I'd stay and wrestle with him. But he can outrun, outwrestle me, the Jacob to my angel. Yet . . . I am Jacob also. I have a broken cog, not a broken thigh, I am an automaton Jacob, a mechanical angel, a robot devil. The ladder to heaven still leans against its window, but I can't find it again.

"Destiny is happenchance. No, not that. I make my own. Not I, though. That thing which drives me, the devil that rides me. It waits grinning in the dark corner, and when I've reached my hand out to grab the prize, it leaps out and snatches it away from me.

"My ungovernable temper. The thing that cheats me and laughs and gibbers and runs away to hide and to emerge another day.

"Ah, Richard Francis Burton, Ruffian Dick, Nigger Dick, as they used to call me in India. They! The mediocrities, the robots running on the tracks of Victoria's railroad . . . they had no interest in the native except to lay the women and eat good food and drink good drink and make a fortune if they could. They couldn't even speak the native language after thirty years in the greatest gem in the queen's crown. A gem, hah! A stinking pesthole! Cholera and its sisters! The black plague and its brothers! Hindus and Moslems laughing behind pukka Sahib's back! The English couldn't even fuck well. The women laughed at them and went to their black lovers for satisfaction after Sahib had gone home.

"I warned the government two years before it happened, the Sepoy Mutiny, and they laughed at me! Me, the only man in India who knew the Hindu, the Moslem!"

He paused on the top landing of the grand staircase. Light blazed out, and the sound of revelry tore through the mists without moving them. No curtain there to be moved by a breath.

"Arrgh! Damn them! They laugh and flirt, and doom waits for them. The world is falling apart. The rider on the black camel waits for them around the next bend of The River. Fools! And I, a fool also.

"And on this Narrboot, this great vessel of fools, men and women sleep who in their waking hours plot against me, plot against all natives of Earth. No. We're all native to this universe. Citizens of the cosmos. I spit over the railing. Into the mists. The River flows below. It receives that part of me which will never return except in another form of water. H_2O. Hell doubled over. That's a strange thought. But aren't all thoughts strangers? Don't they drift along like bottles enclosing messages cast away by that Great Castaway into the sea. And if they chance to lodge in the mind, my mind, I think that I originated them. Or is there a magnetism between certain souls and certain thoughts, and only those with the peculiar field of the thinkers are drawn to the thinkers? And then the individual reshapes them to fit his own character and thinks proudly—if he thinks at all in any sense more than a cow does—that he originated them? Flotsam and jetsam, my thoughts, and I the reef.

"Podebrad! What are you dreaming of? That tower? Your home? Or are you a secret one or just a Czech engineer? Or both?

"Fourteen years I've been on this riverboat, and the boat has been driving its paddlewheels up-River for thirty-three. Now I'm captain of the marines of that exalted bastard and regal asshole, King John. Living proof that I can govern my temper.

"Another year and we arrive at Virolando. There the *Rex* stops for a while, and we talk to La Viro, La Fondinto, the pope of the poopery of the Church of the Second Chance. Second chance, my sainted aunt's arse! Those who gave it to us don't have a chance now. Caught in their own trap! Hoisted by their own petard, which is French for 'little fart.' As Mix says, we don't have the chance of a fart in a windstorm.

"Out there on the banks. The sleeping billions. Where is Edward, my beloved brother? A brilliant man, and that gang of thugs beat his brains in, and he never spoke another word for forty years. You shouldn't have gone tiger hunting that day, Edward. The tiger was the Hindu who saw his chance to beat and rob a hated Englishman. Though they'd been doing it to their own people, too.

"But does it matter now, Edward? You've had your terrible injury healed, and you've been talking as of yore. Perhaps not now, though. Lazarus! Your body rots. No Jesus for you. No 'Arise!'

"And mother! Where is she! The silly woman who talked my grandfather into willing her vicious brother, his son, a good part of his fortune. Grandpa changed his mind and was on his way to see his solicitor to arrange that I get that money. And he dropped dead before he got to the solicitor, and my uncle threw the fortune away in French gambling halls. And so I could not buy myself a decent commission in the regular army, and I could not finance my explorations as they should have been and so I never became what I should have been.

"Speke! The unspeakable Speke! You cheated me out of finding the true source of the Nile, you incompetent sneak, you piece of dung from a sick camel! You sneaked back to England after promising you'd not announce our discoveries until I got there, and you lied about me. You paid; you put a bullet into yourself. Your conscience finally got to you. How I wept. I loved you Speke, though I hated you. How I wept!

"But if I chance across you now—what? Would you run? Surely you'd not have the perverted courage to hold out your hand for me to shake. Judas! Would I kiss you as Jesus kissed the traitor? Judas! No, I'd kick your arse halfway up a mountain!

"Sickness, the iron talons of African disease, gripped me. But I'd have recovered, and I'd have discovered the headwaters of the Nile! Not Speke, not hyena, not jackal Speke! My apologies, Brother Hyena and Sister Jackal. You're only animals and useful in the scheme of things. Speke wasn't worthy to kiss your foul arseholes.

"But how I wept!

"The headwaters of the Nile. The headwaters of The River. Having failed to get to one, will I fail to get to the other?

"My mother never showed any of us, me, Edward, Maria, any affection. She might as well have been our governess. No. Our nannies showed us more love, gave us more time, than she did.

"A man is what his mother makes him.

"No! There is something in the soul that rises above the lack of love, that drives me on and on toward . . . what?

"Father, if I may call you that. No. Not father. Begetter. You wheezing selfish humorless hypochondriac. You forever self-exile and traveler. Where was our home? A dozen foreign lands. You went here and there seeking the health which you thought you didn't have. And we dragged along in your wake. Ignorant women our nannies and drunken Irish clergymen our tutors. Wheeze away, damn you! But no more. You've been cured by the unknowns who made this world. Have you? Haven't you found some excuse to cozen yourself into hypochondria? It's your soul, not your lungs, that has asthma.

"By Lake Tanganyika, Ujiji, the sickness seized me in demon fingers. In my delirium I saw myself, mocking, gibing, jeering, leering at me. That other Burton which mocks at the world but mostly at me.

"It couldn't stop me, though, I went on . . . no . . . not then. Speke went on, and he . . . he . . . hee, hee! I laugh, though it startles the revelers and wakes the sleeping. Laugh, Burton, laugh, you Pagliacci! That silly-arse Yank, Frigate, tells me that it was I who became known as the great explorer and your treachery became infamous. I, I, not you, you Unspeakable! I have been vindicated, not you.

"My misfortune began with my not being a Frenchman. I wouldn't have had to fight against English prejudice, English rigidity, English stupidity. I . . . but I wasn't born a Frenchman, though I am descended from a bastard of the Louis XIII. The Sun-King. Blood will tell.

"What bloody nonsense! Burton blood, not the Sun-King's, will tell.

"I traveled, restless-footed, everywhere. But *Omne solum forti patria. Every region is a strong man's home*. It was I who was the first European to enter the holy and forbidden city of Harar and come alive out of that Ethiopian hellhole. It was I who made a pilgrimage as Mirza Abdulla Bushiri to Mecca and wrote the most famous, detailed, and true book about it and who could have been torn to pieces if I'd been found out. It was I who discovered Lake Tanganyika. It was I who wrote the first manual of the use of the bayonet for the British army. It was I . . .

"Why recount to myself these vainglories? It's not what a man's done that counts, it's what he's going to do.

"Ayesha! Ayesha! My Persian beauty, my first true love! I would've renounced the world, my British citizenship, I would have become a Persian and lived with you until I died. You were most foully murdered, Ayesha! I avenged you, I slew the poisoner with my own hands, choked the life from him and buried his body in the desert. Where are you, Ayesha?

"Somewhere. And if we met again—what? That ravening love is now a dead lion.

"Isabel. My wife. The woman . . . did I ever love her? Affection I had. Not the great love I had for Ayesha and still have for Alice. 'Pay, pack, and follow' I told her whenever I left for a journey, and she did so, as obediently and as uncomplaining as a slave. I was her hero, her god, she said, and she set herself a list of rules for the perfect wife. But when I became old and bitter, a neglected failure, she became my nurse, my keeper, my cager, my prison guard.

"What if I should see her again, this woman who said that she could never love another man on Earth or in Heaven? Not that this world is Heaven. What would I do, say, 'Hello, Isabel. It's been a long time'?

"No, I'd run like the veriest coward. Hide. Yet . . .

"And here's the entrance to the engine room. Is Podebrad on duty tonight? What if he is? I cannot confront him until we get to the headwaters.

"There goes a figure, dim in the mists. Is it an agent of the Ethicals? Or X, the renegade, skulking in the fog? He is always here now, there then, as elusive as the concept of time and eternity, nothingness and something-ness.

"Who goes there?" I should shout. But he—she—it is gone.

"While I was in that transition between sleeping and waking, between death and resurrection, I saw God. 'You owe for the flesh,' He said, that bearded old gentleman in the garments of 1890, and in another dream He said, 'Pay up.'

"Pay what? What is the price?

"I didn't ask for the flesh, I didn't petition to be born. Flesh, life, should be gratis.

"I should have detained Him. I should have asked him if a man does have free will or are all his actions, his nonactions, too, determined. Written down in the world's Bradshaw, so-and-so will arrive at such-a-place at 10:32 A.M. and will depart at 10:40 on track 12. If I am a train on His railway, then I am not responsible for anything I do. Evil and good are not my doing. In fact, there is no evil and good. Without free will, they don't exist.

"But He won't be detained. And if He were, would I understand his explanation of death and immortality, of determinism and indeterminism, of determinacy and indeterminacy?

"The human mind cannot grasp these. But if it can't, it's God's fault—if there is a God.

"When I was surveying the Sind area in India, I became a Sufi, a Master Sufi. But watching them in the Sind and in Egypt and seeing them end by proclaiming themselves to be God, I concluded that extreme mysticism was closely allied to madness.

"Nur ed-Din el-Musafir, who is a Sufi, says that I do not understand. One, there are fake or deluded Sufis, degenerates of that great discipline. Two, when a Sufi says that he is God, he does not mean that literally. He is saying that he has become one with God, though not God.

"Great God! I will penetrate to His heart, to the heart of the Mystery and the mysteries. I am a living sword, but I have been attacking with my edge, not with my point. The point is the most deadly, not the edge. I will be from now on the point.

"Yet, if I'm to find my way through the magic labyrinth, I must have a thread to follow to the great beast that lives in its heart. Where is that thread? No Ariadne. I will be myself the thread and Ariadne and Theseus, Just as . . . why didn't I think of this before?—I am the labyrinth.

"Not quite true. What *is?* It's always *not quite.* But in human, and divine, affairs, a near-hit is sometimes as good as a direct hit. The larger the exploding shell, the less it matters that it doesn't strike the bull's eye.

"Yet a sword is no good unless it's well balanced. It has been said of me, I have the wide-reading Frigate for authority, that some have said that I was one in whom Nature ran riot, that I had not one but thirty splendid talents. But I had no sense of balance or of direction either. That I was an orchestra without a director, a fine ship with only one flaw: no compass. As I've said of myself, a blaze of light without focus.

"If I couldn't do something first, I wouldn't do it.

"That it's the abnormal, the perverse and the savage, in men, not the divine in their nature, that fascinate me.

"That, though I was deeply learned, I never understood that wisdom had little to do with knowledge and literature and nothing to do with learning.

"They were wrong! If they were once right, no more!"

Burton prowled on and on, looking for he knew not what. He passed down a dim corridor and paused by a door. Within should be Loghu, unless she was dancing in the grand salon, and Frigate. They were together again, having gone through two or three lovers in fourteen years. She had not been able to tolerate him for a long time, but then he'd won her over—though it might be the other Frigate whom she still loved—and now they shared the same quarters. Once more.

He went on, seeing a shadowy figure faintly outlined in the light over the exit. X? Another sufferer from insomnia? Himself?

He stood outside the texas and watched the guards pacing back and forth. Watchman, what of the night? Well, what of it?

On he walked. Where have you been? From walking to and fro, not over this giant world but on this pygmy cosmos of a riverboat.

Alice was in his cabin again, having left him a little less than fourteen years ago and having returned twice. This time, they would be together forever. Perhaps. But he was glad that she was back.

He emerged on the landing deck and looked up at the dim light emanating from the control room. Its big clock boomed fourteen strokes. Two A.M.

Time for Burton to go back to bed and try to storm the citadel of sleep again.

He looked up at the stars, and, while doing so, a cold wind swept down from the north and cleared the upper deck of the mists—momentarily. Somewhere northward was the tower in the cold and gray mists. In it were, or had been, the Ethicals, the entities who thought they had a right to raise the dead without their permission.

Did they hold the keys to the mysteries? Not all mysteries, of course. The mystery of being itself, of creation, of space and infinity, time and eternity would never be solved.

Or would they?

Was there somewhere, in the tower or deep underground, a machine which converted the metaphysical into the physical? Man could handle the physical, and if he didn't know the true nature of the beyond-matter, what of it? He didn't know the *true* nature of electricity, either, but he had enslaved it for his own purposes.

He shook his fist at the north, and he went to bed.

SECTION 6

On the *Not For Hire:* The Thread of Reason

16

AT FIRST, SAMUEL CLEMENS HAD TENDED TO AVOID CYRANO DE Bergerac as much as possible. The very perceptive Frenchman quickly detected that but seemed not to resent it. If he did, he was successfully hiding his reaction. He was always smiling and laughing, always polite but not cold. He acted as if Clemens liked him and had no reason not to.

After a while—several years—Sam began to warm up to the man who'd been Sam's Terrestrial wife's lover. They had much in common: a keen interest in people and in mechanical devices, a taste for literature, an abiding devotion to the study of history, a hatred for hypocrisy and self-righteousness, a loathing for the malevolent aspects of religions, and a deep agnosticism. Though Cyrano was not, like Sam, from Missouri, he shared with him a "show me" attitude.

Moreover, Cyrano was an adornment at any party but did not try to dominate the conversation.

So it was that one day Sam talked to his other self, Mark Twain, about his feelings for de Bergerac in the privacy of his suite. The result was that Sam now saw—though he'd always known deep within him—that he'd been very unfair to Cyrano. It wasn't the fellow's fault that Livy had fallen in love with him and had refused to leave him for her ex-husband after she'd found him. Nor, really, was it Livy's fault. She could only do what her inborm temperament and predetermined circumstances forced her to do. And Sam had been acting as his inborn character, his "watermark," and circumstances forced him to do. Now, as a result of another aspect of his character rising from the depths, plus the inevitable push of events, he had changed his attitude toward Cyrano. After all, he was a good fellow, and he'd learned to shower regularly, to keep his fingernails clean, and to quit urinating in corners at the end of corridors.

Whether Sam really believed that he was an automaton whose acts were programmed, Sam did not know himself. Sometimes, he thought that his belief in determinism was only an excuse to escape his guilt about certain matters. If this were true, then he was exercising free will in making up the explanation that he wasn't responsible for anything, good or bad, that he did. On the other hand, one aspect of determinism was that it gave humans the illusion that they had free will.

In either case, Sam welcomed Cyrano into his company and forgave him for what really didn't need forgiving.

So now, today, Cyrano was one of the group invited by Sam to talk about some puzzling features of what Sam called "The Case of X." The others were Gwenafra (Sam's cabinmate), Joe Miller, de Marbot, and John Johnston. The latter was huge, over six feet two and weighing 260 pounds without an ounce of excess fat. His head and chest were auburn-haired; he had extraordinarily long arms and hands that looked as large as the paws of a grizzly bear. The blue-gray eyes were often cold or dreamy but they could be warm enough when he was with trusted friends. Born about 1828 in New Jersey and of Scotch descent, he had gone to the West to trap the mountains in 1843. There he had become a legend even among the legendary mountain men, though it took some years before he became famous. When a wandering party of young unblooded Crow braves killed his Flathead Indian wife and unborn baby, Johnston swore a vendetta against the Crows. He killed so many of them that the Crows sent out twenty young men to track him down and kill him, and they were not to return to their tribe until the deed was done. One after the other got to him but were instead slain by Johnston. He cut out their livers and ate them raw, the blood dripping onto his red beard. It was these exploits that earned him the sobriquets of "Liver Eater" and "Crow Killer." But the Crows were a fine tribe, dignified, honorable, and mighty warriors. So one day Johnston decided to call off the feud, and, having informed them of his decision, became their good friend. He was also a chief of the Shoshoni.

He died in 1900 at the Veterans' Hospital in Los Angeles and was buried in the crowded cemetery there. But in the 1970s, a group who knew that he could never rest there, not the man who became vexed if his nearest neighbor was within fifty miles, had his bones taken to a mountainside in Colorado and reburied there.

"Liver Eating" Johnston had mentioned several times on the boat that he'd never been forced to kill a white man (while on Earth), not even a Frenchy. This remark had made de Marbot and Cyrano a little uneasy at first, but they had come to like and admire the huge mountaineer.

After they'd had a few drinks and some cigarettes and cigars and chatted idly, Sam brought up the subject he most wanted to talk about.

"I've been doing some thinking about the man who called himself Odysseus," he said. "You remember what I said about him? He came to our help when we were battling von Radowitz, and it was his archery that killed off the general and his officers. He claimed to be the historical Odysseus, the real man to whom the legends and fairy tales were attached later and whose exploits furnished Homer with the materials for his *Odyssey*."

"I never knew him," Johnston said, "but I'll take yer word fur it."

"Yes. Well, he said that he also had been contacted by an Ethical and sent down-River to help us. After the battle he hung around for a while, but when he went up-River on a trading expedition, he disappeared. Dropped out of sight like he'd fallen through a trapdoor.

"What makes him particularly important is that he had a strange tale to tell about the Ethical. Now, the one that talked to me, X, the Mysterious Stranger, was a man. At least, his voice was certainly a male's, though I suppose it could have been disguised. Anyway. Odysseus told me that his Ethical was a *woman!*"

Sam puffed out green smoke and looked at the brass arabesques on the ceiling as if they were hieroglyphs that held answers to his questions.

"Now, what could that mean?"

Gwenafra said, "That he was either telling the truth or lying."

"Right! Give that pretty woman there a big cigar! Either there are two Ethicals who have become renegades or the self-named Odysseus was a liar. If a liar, then he would have to be my Ethical, X. Personally, I think he was mine, yours, too, Cyrano and John, and I think he was lying. Otherwise, why didn't X tell us that there were two of his kind and that one was a woman? That would have been very important. I know he didn't have much time to talk to us because the other Ethicals were hot on his trail, breathing down his neck. But surely that item of information was one he wouldn't have neglected to impart."

"Why would he lie?" de Marbot said.

"Because . . ." Here Sam pointed his cigar at the arabesques. "He knew that we might get caught by the other Ethicals. And they might get from us this false information. Then they'd be confused and even more alarmed. What? Two traitors in their midst? Holy smoke! And if they put us to some sort of lie-detector, they'd see that we weren't lying. After all, we believed what Odysseus told us. What X told us, I should say. It was just his way of confusing the issue still further! There! What do you think of that?"

There was a short silence, then Cyrano said. "But if that is true, we have seen the Ethical! And we know what he looks like!"

"Not necessarily true," Gwenafra said. "He surely must have numerous aids for disguise."

"Undoubtedly," Cyrano said. "But can he change his height and his physique? Hair and eye color perhaps and some other things. But not . . ."

"I think we may take it that he's short and has a very muscular body," Clemens said. "But so have several billion other men. What we've done is to eliminate the possibility that there's a female Ethical who's also a renegade. At least, I believe so."

"Mought be," Johnston said, "that he was an agent who found out that we'd been contacted by X, and he was trying to confuse us."

"I don't think so," Sam said. "If he was an agent who'd known that much, we'd have had the Ethicals on us faster than a wardman would sell his mother to gain a few votes. No. That Odysseus was Mr. X."

"But," Gwenafra said, "that . . . that takes us deeper than that. What about Gulbirra's description of Barry Thorn? He resembled Odysseus in some respects. Could he have been X? And what about that so-called German, Stern, who tried to kill Firebrass? What was he? If he was an agent, he would've been Firebrass' colleague. After all, we think Firebrass was an agent, and he was blown up by X so that he couldn't get into the tower ahead of him. Firebrass lied to us when he told us he was one of X's recruits. He . . ."

"No," Cyrano said. "I mean, yes. He seems to have been an agent of the other Ethicals. But if he knew so much about us, why didn't he inform the Ethicals and bring them down on our necks?"

"Because," Sam said, "for some reason, he couldn't tell the Ethicals. I think that was because about then the big troubles started in the tower. Why or how, I don't know. But it seems to me that about the time Odysseus disappeared, rather, X vanished, that the whole project of the Ethicals went shebang. We didn't notice it at the time, but it was shortly thereafter that the resurrections ceased. It wasn't until the *Not For Hire* was some distance on its way that we began getting reports that the resurrections had stopped. When we were in Parolando, we noticed it but thought it was just a local phenomenon."

"Hmm," Cyrano said. "I wonder if that Hermann Göring fellow, the missionary killed by Hacking's men, was resurrected? He was a strange one, that."

"He was a troublemaker, that one," Sam said. "Anyway, maybe Firebrass did tell the Ethicals that he'd gotten hold of some of X's recruits. But the Ethicals told him they wouldn't do anything about it for a while. Firebrass was to learn all he could from us before they moved in. He would also tell them if he saw anybody who looked like X so they could jump him then and there. Who knows? But . . . I wonder if Firebrass planted any bugs on us so he'd know when X came to visit us again. Only, he never did."

Cyrano said, "I believe that he, X, got stranded after he, as Odysseus, left us."

"Then why didn't he rejoin us as Odysseus?"

Cyrano shrugged.

"Because he missed the *Not For Hire*," Sam snapped. "We went by him during the night. But he'd heard that Firebrass was building a dirigible to go straight to the tower. That would be even better for him than the *Not For Hire*. But as Odysseus, an ancient Hellene, he wouldn't be qualified for a post on the airship. So he became Barry Thorn, a much-experienced Canadian aeronaut."

"But I," Cyrano said, "was of the seventeenth century, yet I was a pilot on the *Parseval*. And John de Greystock was of a much earlier time, yet he was made captain of the blimp."

"Despite that," Sam said, "X would have a much better chance to get on the *Parseval* if he had experience. Only . . . I wonder where he got it? Why would an Ethical know all about a dirigible?"

"If you live a very long time or are immortal, perhaps you learn everything about everything in order to pass the time," Gwenafra said.

SECTION 7

Göring's Past

17

HERMANN GÖRING WOKE UP SWEATING AND GROANING. *"JA, MEIN Führer! Ja, mein Führer! Ja, mein Führer! Ja, ja, ja!"*

The screaming face faded. The black gunsmoke pouring in through the shattered windows and broken walls vanished. The windows and walls disappeared. The bass Russian artillery which had been counterpointing der Führer's alto soprano became muted, then withdrew, roaring sullenly. The droning which had been a counter-counterpoint to the madman's screech dwindled and died. That noise, he was vaguely aware, had been from the motors of the American and British bombers.

The darkness of the nightmare was succeeded by the Riverworld's night.

It was comforting and peaceful, though. Hermann lay on his back on the bamboo bed and touched the warm arm of Kren. She stirred and muttered something. Perhaps she was talking to someone in her dreams. She would not be distressed or bewildered or horrified. Her dreams were always pleasant. She was a Riverchild, dead on Earth at or around the age of six. She remembered nothing of her native planet. Her earliest memory, and that was vague, was waking in this valley, her parents gone, everything she'd known gone.

Hermann warmed himself with the touch and with pleasant memories of their years together. Then he got up, dressed in the body-covering early-morning outfit, and stepped outside. He was on a platform of bamboo. Ahead and behind on the same level as his hut were many others. Above was another level of dwellings, and there was another above that. Below were three levels. All were continuous bridges stretching for as far as he could see to the south and terminating far to the north. The supports were usually tall thin spires of rock or irontrees; each length of bridge was seldom less than one hundred and fifty feet or more than three hundred. Where extra support was needed, pylons of oak or mortared stone had been placed.

The Valley here was thirty miles wide. The River widened to form a lake ten miles broad and forty miles long. The mountains were no higher than six thousand feet, fortunately for the inhabitants, since The Valley here was far up in the northern hemisphere and they needed all the daylight possible. At the west end of the lake, the mountains curved into The River itself. Here the waters boiled through a high narrow passage. In the warmer hours of the afternoon, the easterly wind pushed through the strait at an estimated fifteen miles an hour. It then lost some of its force, but it was carried up by the peculiar topography, causing updrafts of which the inhabitants took advantage.

Everywhere on the land, towers of rock, tall columns bearing many carved figures, rose. Between many of these were multilevels spans. These were of wood: bamboo, pine, oak, yew. At intervals, depending upon the weight the spans could bear, were huts. Gliders and folded balloon envelopes were stored on top of many of the broader spires.

Drums were beating; fishbone horns, wailing. People began appearing in the doorways of the huts, stretching, yawning. The day was officially beginning. The sun had just shown its top. The temperature would rise to 60 F in the heavens, 30 F short of the zenith of the tropics. At the end of fifteen hours, the sun plunged below the mountains, and in nine hours would rise again. The length of its sojourn in the skies almost made up for the weakness of its oblique rays.

With two grails in the net attached to his back, Hermann climbed down the fifty feet to the ground. Kren had no duties today and so would sleep in. Later she would come down, pick up her grail from the storage shed near the stone, and eat a belated breakfast.

As he walked along he greeted those he knew, and in the population of 248,000, he could call ten thousand by their first names. The scarcity of paper in The Valley had forced a reliance on, and development of, memory, though on Earth his own memory had been phenomenal. The greetings were in the truncated, collapsed Esperanto dialect of Vivolando.

"*Bon ten, eskop.*" ("Good morning, Bishop.")

"*Tre bon ten a vi, Fenikso. Pass ess via.*" ("A very good morning to you, Phoenix. Peace be yours.")

He was formal and stately then, but a few seconds later he stopped a group to tell them a joke.

Hermann Göring at this time was happy. Yet he had not always been so. His tale was long, shot with gaiety and peace here and there but in general sad and stormy and by no means always edifying.

His Terrestrial biography went thus:

Born at Rosenheim, Bavaria, Germany, on January 12, 1893. His father was a colonial official, in fact, the first governor of German Southwest Africa. At the age of three months, Göring was parted from his parents, who went to Haiti for three years, where his father was the German consul general. This long separation from his mother at such a tender age had a very bad effect on Hermann. The pain and loneliness of this period never entirely left him. Moreover, when he became aware at an early age that his mother was having an affair with his godfather, he felt great contempt, mingled with rage, for her. He managed, however, to restrain any overt manifestations of his feelings. His father he treated with a silent contempt, though he was seldom openly insulting to him. But when his father was buried, Hermann wept.

At the age of ten he became very sick with a glandular disease. In 1915, a month after his father's death, he became a lieutenant in the 112th Prinz Wilhelm Infantry Regiment. At this time the blue-eyed, blond, slender, and passably good-looking officer was a very popular person. He loved to dance and drink and in general was much fun. His godfather, a Jew converted to Christianity, gave him money to help him financially.

Shortly after World War I started, a painful arthritis in his knees hospitalized him. Eager to get into action, he left the hospital and became an observer in the plane of a friend, Lörzer. For three weeks he was unofficially absent without leave from the army. Though he was judged unfit to serve in the infantry because of his physical incapacity, Göring joined the Luftwaffe. His vigorous and unorthodox language amused the Crown Prince, who was commanding the 25th Field Air Detachment of the Fifth Army. In the autumn of 1915 he went through the Freiburg Aviation School, easily qualifying as a pilot. In November 1916 he was shot down, badly hurt, and was out of action for six months. Despite this, he flew again. His rise was rapid since he was not only an excellent officer and flier but an outstanding organizer.

In 1917 Hermann received the *Ordre Pour le Mérite* (the German equivalent of the Victoria Cross) in acknowledgment of his leadership qualities and for having shot down fifteen enemy planes. He was also given the Golden Airman's Medal. On July 7, 1918, he was made commander of *Geschwader 1*, its commander Richthofen having been killed after eighty victories. Göring's great interest in technical details and problems of equipment made him a natural for his position as commander. His deep knowledge of all aspects of aerial warfare was to stand him in good stead in later years.

By the time Germany surrendered, he had thirty enemy planes to his credit. But this did not do him any good during the period immediately following the end of the war. Aces were a drug on the market.

In 1920, after some time barnstorming in Denmark and Sweden, he became flight chief of the Svenska Lufttrafik in Stockholm, Sweden. Here he met Karin von Kantznow, sister-in-law of the Swedish explorer Count von Rosen. He married her, though she was a divorcée and mother of an eight-year-old boy. He was a good husband to her until she died. Despite his later career in an organization distinguished for gross immorality, he was faithful to her and to his second wife. Sexually, he was a puritan. He was also a political puritan. Once having given his loyalty, he did not withdraw it.

It was a wonder that he ever amounted to anything. Though he dreamed much of advancement to high positions and wealth, he drifted. Without any guiding light, he allowed chance people and events to carry him along.

It was his fortune, or misfortune, that he met Adolf Hitler.

During the abortive Putsch of 1923, in Munich, Göring was wounded. He escaped the police for a while by taking refuge in the home of Frau Ilse Ballin, wife of a Jewish merchant. Göring did not forget this debt. He aided her during the persecution of the Jews after Hitler became head of the German state, and he arranged for her and her family to flee to England.

Breaking his word of honor that he would not escape after his arrest, he fled to Austria. Here the badly infected wound hospitalized him, forcing him to take morphine for the pain. Sick and penniless, his virility affected by various operations, he became mentally depressed. At the same time, his wife's health, never good, was getting worse.

Now a drug addict, he went to Sweden, where he spent six months in a sanitorium. Discharged as cured, he returned to his wife. All seemed hopeless, yet, having hit the bottom, his spirits rose, and he began to fight. This was typical of him. Somehow, from somewhere, he gathered his energy to fight when all seemed lost.

On returning to Germany, he rejoined Hitler, whom he believed to be the only man who could make Germany great again. Karin died in Sweden in October 1931. He was with Hitler in Berlin then, meeting Hindenburg, who had decided that Hitler would become his successor as head of the state. Göring always felt guilty because he had chosen to be with Hitler instead of with Karin when she was dying. Her death drove him back to morphine for a while. Then he met Emmy Sonnemann, an actress, and married her.

Though he had great talents as an organizer, Göring was inclined to be sentimental. He also had a hot temper which allowed his tongue to run away with him. During the trial of the men charged with burning the Reichstag building, Göring made wild accusations. Dimitrov, the Bulgarian Communist, coolly exposed the illegal methods and illogicality of the charges against him. Göring's failure to control the trials spoiled their propagandistic effect and demolished the false facade of the Nazis' propaganda machine.

Despite this, Göring was given the job of forming the Reich's new air force. He was no longer the slender ace, having put on much weight. But his double personality had won him two new titles, *Der Dicke* (The Fatty) and *Der Eiserne* (The Man of Iron). His rheumatism was giving him pains in the legs and making him take drugs (chiefly paracodeine).

He was not a scholar or a writer, but he did dictate a book, *Germany Reborn,* which was published in London. He had a passion for the works of George Bernard Shaw and could quote long passages from them. He also was familiar with the German classics, Goethe, Schiller, the Schlegels, *et al.* His love of paintings was well known. He had a fondness for detective stories and for mechanical toys and gadgets.

By now he dreamed of a Göring dynasty, one which would last a thousand years and forever impress his name in history. It was highly probable that Hitler would have no child, and he had named Göring as his successor. This dream was shattered when his only child, a girl, Edda, was born. Emmy was not going to have any more children, and it was unthinkable to him to divorce her and take a wife who might produce sons. Though he must have been intensely disappointed, he did not reveal it. He loved Edda, and she loved him to the end of her life.

Another aspect of his puzzling persona was demonstrated when he visited Italy on a diplomatic mission. The King and the Crown Prince took him on a deer hunt. The three stood on a high platform while hundreds of deer were herded past them. The royalty slaughtered them, the King killing one hundred and thirteen. Göring was so disgusted that he refused to shoot at all.

Nor did he want to invade Czechoslovakia and Austria, and he especially objected to the invasion of Poland. Thought of war depressed him; he had been in low spirits at the idea just before both World War I and II. Nevertheless, he went along with his beloved leader in this matter, just as he had not protested publicly against the persecution of the Jews. But at his wife's request, he saved dozens of Jews from imprisonment.

In 1939 Hitler promoted Hermann to Field Marshal and made him Economic Minister of the Reich. As Air Minister of the Luftwaffe he was also its commander-in-chief. He tried to get a stratobomber built which would attain a twenty-mile altitude and fly to America, but he did not succeed.

Despite his high positions, he had a tendency to turn away from realities.

In 1939 he told the German public, "If any enemy bomber reaches the Ruhr, my name is not Hermann Göring. You can call me Meier." ("Meier" was a folk-joke name, indicating a mythical character who bumbled and numbskulled his way through life.)

After a while, Göring was often called Meier by the Nazi Party bigwigs and by the public. But the affectionate feeling implicit in *Der Dicke* was missing in Meier. The British and American bombers were making a shambles of Germany. The Luftwaffe had failed to soften England for invasion, and now it was failing to turn back the hordes of metal birds dropping deadly eggs onto the Reich. Hitler blamed Göring for both, though it was Hitler's decision to bomb the English cities instead of first wiping out the Royal Air Force bases that was responsible for the Germans' plight. Just as Hitler's decision to attack neutral Russia before England was laid low was ultimately the cause of Germany's downfall.

As it was, Hitler had wanted to invade Sweden, too, when Norway was taken. But, Göring, loving Sweden, had threatened to resign if Sweden was attacked. He had also pleaded the advantages of a neutral Sweden to Hitler.

His health had been getting worse before the war. During the great conflicts, his sicknesses and his lessening prestige made him turn to drugs. He was anxious, nervous, and given to melancholia, on the skids, out of control, and no way to stop the descent. And his beloved country was heading toward the Götterdämmerung which horrified him but which, in a strange way, gratified Hitler.

With the Allies advancing across Germany on all fronts, Göring thought that it was time for him to take over the government. Der Führer, instead, stripped him of all his titles and positions and expelled him from the Nazi Party. His worst enemy, Martin Bormann, ordered his arrest.

Near the end of the war, while trying to flee the Russians, he was taken into custody by an Army lieutenant, ironically, a Jew. During his trial at Nuremberg, he defended himself but with a lack of conviction. Despite what Hitler had done, he defended him, too, loyal to the end.

The verdict was inevitable. He was sentenced to be hanged. The day before his execution, October 15, 1946, he swallowed one of the cyanide capsules he had hidden in his cell and died. He was cremated, and the ashes were, according to one story, flung onto a refuse heap in Dachau. Another, with more authority, says that the ashes were dropped onto a muddy country road outside Munich.

That should have been the end. Göring was glad to die, glad to be rid of his sicknesses of body and soul, of the consciousness of his great failure, and of the stigma as a Nazi war criminal. The only thing he regretted about dying was that his Emma and little Edda would be left unprotected.

18

BUT IT WAS NOT THE END. LIKE IT OR NOT, HE HAD BEEN RESURRECTED on this planet. He was young in body again, a slender youth. How or why, he did not know. He was rid of his rheumatism, his swollen lymph glands, and the dependency on paracodeine.

He resolved to set out to look for Emma and Edda. Also, to find Karin. How he would be able to have both his wives was something he did not care to contemplate. The search would be long enough for thinking about this.

He never found them.

The old Hermann Göring, the highly ambitious and unscrupulous opportunist, still lived in him. He did many things of which he became deeply ashamed and remorseful when, after many adventures and much wandering,* he was converted to the Church of the Second Chance. This happened suddenly and dramatically, much like the conversion of Saul of Tarsus on the road to Damascus, and it took place in the small and sovereign state of Tamoancan. This was composed chiefly of tenth-century Nahuatl-speaking Mexicans and twentieth-century Navahos. Hermann lived in the newcomers' hall until he was thoroughly grounded in the tenets and disciplines of the Church.

He moved out then into a recently abandoned hut. After a while, a woman named Chopilotl was living with him. She, too, was a Chancer, but she insisted that they keep in their hut a soapstone idol. It was a hideous figure about thirty centimeters high, addressed as Xochiquetzal, the divine patroness of sexual love and childbirth. Chopilotl's adoration of the goddess signified her passion for passion. She demanded that Hermann and she make love in front of the idol in the light of torches flanking it. Hermann did not mind that, but he did tire of the frequency of her insistence.

Also, it seemed to him that she shouldn't be allowed to worship a pagan divinity. He went to his bishop, a Navaho who had been a Mormon on Earth.

"Yes, I know she has that statue," Bishop Ch'agii said. "The Church doesn't countenance idolatry or polytheism, Hermann. You know that. But it does permit its members to keep idols, provided that the owner fully realizes that it is only a symbol. Admittedly, this is dangerous, since the worshiper too easily takes the symbol for the reality. This failing wasn't confined to the primitives, you know. Even the so-called civilized peoples were sucked into this psychological trap.

"Chopilotl is rather literal-minded, but she's a good person. If we got too stubborn about her idiosyncracy and demanded that she cast the idol out,

---

*See *To Your Scattered Bodies Go* for the details.

she might backslide into a genuine polytheism. What we are doing might be called theological weaning. You have seen how many idols there are around here, haven't you? Most of them at one time had a multitude of worshipers. But we have gradually detached the religionists from them, achieving this through a patient and gentle instruction. Now the stone gods have become only *objets d'art* to most of their former worshipers.

"In time, Chopilotl will come to regard her goddess as such. I'm banking on you to assist her to get over her present regrettable attitude."

"You mean, give her a theological goose?" Hermann said.

The bishop looked surprised, then he laughed. "I had my Ph.D. at the University of Chicago," he said. "I do sound stuffy, don't I? Have a drink, my son, and tell me more about yourself."

At the end of a year, Hermann was baptised with many other naked shivering teeth-chattering neophytes. Afterward, he toweled off a woman while she dried him. Then all donned body-covering cloths, and the bishop hung around the neck of each a cord from which was suspended the spiral vertebra bone of a hornfish. They were not titled priests; each was simply called *Instruisto,* Teacher.

Hermann felt as if he were a fraud. Who was he to be instructing others, and acting, in effect, as a priest? He was not even sure that his belief in God or in the Church was sincere. No, that was not right. He was sincere—most of the time.

"The doubts are about yourself," the bishop said. "You think you can't live up to the ideals. You think you aren't worthy. You have to get over that, Hermann. Everybody has the potentiality of being worthy, which leads to salvation. You have it; I have it; all God's children have it," and he laughed.

"Watch two tendencies in yourself, son. Sometimes you are arrogant, thinking you are better than others. More often you are humble. Too humble. I might even say, sickeningly humble. That is another form of arrogance. True humility is knowing your true place in the cosmic scale.

"I'm still learning. And I pray that I may live long enough to be rid of all self-deceit. Meanwhile, you and I can't spend all our time in exploring ourselves. We must also work among the people. Monasticism, retreat from the world, reclusivism, that's a lot of crap. So where would you like to go? Up-River or down?"

"I really hate to leave this place," Hermann said. "I've been happy here. For the first time in a long time, I feel as if I'm part of a family."

"Your family lives from one end of The River to the other," Ch'agii said. "It contains many unpleasant relatives, true. But what family doesn't? It's your job to aid them to become right-thinking. And that is the second stage. The first is getting people to admit that they are wrong-thinking."

"That's the trouble," Hermann said. "I don't think I'm beyond the first stage myself."

"If I believed that, I would not have permitted you to graduate. Which is it? Up or down?"

"Down," Hermann said.

Ch'agii raised his eyebrows. "Good. But the neophyte usually chooses to go up-River. They've heard that La Viro is somewhere in that direction. And they thirst to visit him, to walk and talk with him."

"That is why I choose the other direction," Hermann said. "I am not worthy."

The bishop sighed, and he said, "Sometimes I regret we are forbidden any violence whatsoever. Right now, I would like to kick you in the ass.

"Very well, go down, my pale Moses. But I charge that you give a message to the bishop of whatever area you settle down in. Tell him or her that Bishop Ch'agii sends his love. And also tell the bishop this. *Some birds think they are worms.*"

"What does that mean?"

"I hope you find out some day," Ch'agii said. He waved his right hand, three fingers extended, blessing. Then he hugged Hermann and kissed him on the lips. "Go, my son, and may your *ka* become an *akh*."

"May our *akh*s fly side by side," Hermann said formally. He left the hut with tears running down his cheeks. He had always been a sentimentalist. But he told himself that he was weeping because he loved the little dark sententious man. The distinction between sentiment and love had been drilled into him in the seminary. So, this was love he felt. Or was it?

As the bishop had said in a lecture, his students would not really know the difference between the two until they had much practice dealing with them. Even then, if they didn't have intelligence, they wouldn't be able to separate one from the other.

The raft on which he was to travel had been built by himself and the seven who were to accompany him. One of these was Chopilotl. Hermann stopped at the hut to pick up her and his few belongings. She was outside with two neighbor women, hoisting the idol onto a wooden sled.

"You're not thinking about taking that thing along?" he said to her.

"Of course I am," she said. "It would be like leaving my *ka* behind if I did not take her. And she is not just a *thing*. She is Xochiquetzal."

"She's just a symbol, need I remind you for the hundredth time," he said, scowling.

"Then I need my symbol. It would be bad luck to abandon her. She would be very angry."

He was frustrated and anxious. This was the first day of his mission, and he was contronted with a situation he wasn't sure he could handle properly.

"*Consider thy latter end, my son, and be wise,*" the bishop had said in a lecture, quoting *Ecclesiastes*.

He had to act so that the final result of this particular event would be the right one.

"It's this way, Chopilotl," he said. "It's all right, at least, not bad, keeping this idol in this country. The people here understand. But people elsewhere won't. We're missionaries, dedicated to converting others to what we believe to be the true religion. We have authority behind us, the teachings of La Viro, who received his revelations from one of the makers of this world.

"But how can we convince anybody if one of us is an idolater? A worshiper of a stone statue? Not a very pretty one, I might add, though that is really irrelevant.

"People will mock us. They'll say we're ignorant heathen, superstitious. And we'd be sinning grievously because we'd give people an entirely wrong picture of the Church."

"Tell them that she is just a symbol," Chopilotl said, sullenly.

His voice rose. "I told you they wouldn't understand! Besides, it'd be a lie. It's obvious that this thing is much more to you than just a symbol."

"Would you throw away your spiral bone?"

"That's different. It's a sign of my belief, a badge of my membership. I don't worship it."

She flashed white teeth in a sardonic dark face.

"You throw it away, and I'll abandon my beloved."

"Nonsense!" he said. "You know I can't do that! You're being unreasonable, you bitch."

"Your face is getting red," she said. "Where is your loving understanding?"

He breathed deeply and said, "Very well. Bring that *thing* along."

He walked away.

She said, "Aren't you going to help me drag it?"

He stopped and turned. "And be an accessory to blasphemy?"

"If you've agreed that it can come with us, then you're already an accessory."

She wasn't stupid—except in that one respect and that was emotional stupidity. Smiling a little, he resumed walking away. On reaching the raft, he told the others what to expect.

"Why do you allow this, brother?" Fleiskaz said. He was a huge red-haired man whose native language was primitive Germanic. This was one of the tongues of central Europe of the second millennium B.C. From it had originated twentieth-century Norwegian, Swedish, Danish, Icelandic, German, Dutch, and English. His nickname had been Wulfaz, meaning Wolf, because he was such a fear-inspiring warrior.

But on the Riverworld, when he'd converted to the Church, he'd renamed himself Fleiskaz. This, in his natal language, meant "a piece of torn flesh." No one knew why he'd adopted that, but it might have been because he thought of himself as a piece of the good flesh living in an evil body. This piece, torn from the old body, had the potentiality to grow into a complete new body, spiritually speaking, a thoroughly good body.

"Just bear with me," Hermann said to Fleiskaz. "The whole matter will be settled before we have put fifty meters between us and the shore."

They sat around, smoking and talking, watching Chopilotl pull the sled with its stone burden. By the time she had crossed the wide plain, she was scarlet-faced, sweating, and panting. She swore at Hermann, finished by telling him that he would be sleeping by himself for a long time.

"This woman doesn't set a good example, brother," Fleiskaz said.

"Be patient, brother," Hermann said quietly.

The raft was butting into the bank, held from drifting by an anchor, a small boulder at the end of a fish-leather cable. Chopilotl asked those aboard the raft to help her haul the sled onto it. They smiled but did not move. Cursing under her breath, she got it onto the raft. Hermann surprised everybody by helping her scoot it off and rolling it to the middle of the raft.

They up-anchored and shoved off then, waving at the crowd assembled on the bank to wish them bon voyage. A single mast was set forward. The square sail was hoisted, and the braces slanted to drive them toward the middle of The River. Here the current and the wind speeded them, and they set the sail to get the full benefit of the breeze. Brother Fleiskaz was at the rudder.

Chopilotl retired to the tent close to the mast to sulk.

Hermann gently rolled the idol to the starboard edge of the raft. The others looked at him questioningly. Grinning, he held his finger to his lips. Chopilotl was not aware of what was going on, but when the idol was at the edge, its weight tipped the raft slightly. Feeling the tilt, she looked out from the tent. And she screamed.

By then Hermann had the statue upright.

"I am doing this for your good and for the good of the Church!" he shouted at her.

He pushed on the monstrous head as Chopilotl, shrieking, ran toward him. The idol toppled over into the water and sank beneath the surface.

Later, his companions told him that she had hit him on the side of the head with her grail.

He did regain enough of his senses to see her, buoyed by her grail, swimming toward the shore. Bessa, Fleiskaz's woman, was swimming after Hermann's grail, which Chopilotl had tossed overboard.

"Violence begets violence," Bessa said as she handed him the cylinder.

"Thanks for rescuing it," he said. He sat down again to nurse a painful head and aching conscience. It was obvious what her remark implied. By dumping the idol, he had committed violence. He had no right to deprive Chopilotl of it. Even if he had had the right, he should not have exercised it.

She had to be shown her error and then the example had to ferment in her mind until it boiled over onto her spirit. All he had done was to anger her so much that she became violent. And she would probably get somebody to carve another idol for her.

He certainly had not started out well.

That led to other thoughts of her. Why had he wooed her? She was pretty; she exuded sexuality. But she was an Indian, and he had felt a certain repugnance about coupling with a colored woman. Had he made her his woman because he wanted to prove to himself that he was not prejudiced against coloreds? Was it this unworthy motive that had compelled him?

If she had been a black, a kinky-haired blubber-lipped African, would he have even considered mating? To be truthful, no. And now that he remembered it, he had looked for a Jewish woman. But there were only two in the area that he knew of, and these were already taken. Besides, they had lived in the times of Ahab and Augustus and were as dark as Yemenite Arabs, squat, big-nosed, superstitious, and violence-prone. Anyway, they had not been Chancers. But, come to think of it, Chopilotl was also superstitious and violence-prone.

However, being a Church-member indicated that she had potentiality for spiritual advancement.

He steered his mind back to something which it wanted to avoid.

He had searched for a Jewish woman and had taken the Indian woman in order to salve his conscience. To demonstrate to himself that he had progressed spiritually.

Had he advanced? Well, he had not loved her but he had been fond of her. Once the initial dislike of physical contact with her had been overcome, he had not experienced anything but passion during their lovemaking.

However, during their infrequent but stormy quarrels, he had wanted to hurl racial insults at her.

True advancement, true love, would come when he did not have to restrain himself from voicing such pejoratives. There would be no inhibitions about such because he would not think of them.

You have a long way to go, Hermann, he told himself.

And if he did, then why had the bishop accepted him as a missionary? Surely Ch'agii must have seen that he was far from ready.

19

By the time, many years later, that Göring was near the state of Parolando, none of the original crew of people he'd set out with were with him. They'd been killed or had stopped at various areas to carry out their missionary activities there. When Göring was several thousand miles from Parolando, he began hearing rumors of the great falling star, the meteorite, that had struck down-River. It was said that its impact had killed hundreds of thousands directly or indirectly, and wrecked the valley for over sixty miles each way. As soon as the area had been safe to enter, however, many groups had moved in, eager to get the nickel-steel of the meteorite. After a savage struggle, two bands had been triumphant. These had then allied and now held the site.

Among other rumors was that the meteorite had been mined and was being used to build a giant boat and that two famous men were directing the operations. One was the American writer, Sam Clemens. The other was King John of England, the brother of Richard the Lion-Hearted.

Hermann did not know why, but the gossip made his heart jump. It seemed to him that the land which held the fallen star was his goal and had been all along, though he hadn't known it until now.

At the end of a long voyage, he arrived at Parolando. The rumors were true. Sam Clemens and King John, nicknamed "Lackland," were co-rulers of the land which sat above the treasure of the meteorite. By this time, large amounts of the metal had been mined, and the area looked like a mini-Ruhr. In it were many steel furnaces, rolling mills, and nitric-acid factories, and bauxite and cryolite were being processed to make aluminum. The ores from which aluminum was made, however, were to be found in another state. And there was trouble over that.

Soul City was a state twenty-six miles down-River from Parolando. It sat on large deposits of cryolite, bauxite, and cinnabar, and small deposits of platinum. Clemens and John needed these, but the two rulers of Soul City, Elwood Hacking and Milton Firebrass, were driving hard bargains. Moreover, it was evident that they would like to get their hands on the nickel and steel of the meteorite.

Hermann paid little attention to the local politics. His primary mission was to convert people to the doctrines of the Church of Second Chance. His secondary mission, he decided after a while, was to stop the building of the great metal paddlewheeler. Clemens and John had become obsessed with the vessel. To build it, they were willing to turn Parolando into an industrial desolation, to strip the land of all vegetation except the invulnerable irontrees. They were polluting the air with the smoke and stink from the factories.

Worse, they were polluting their *kas*, and that made their business Hermann Göring's. The Church maintained that humanity had been resurrected so that it could have another opportunity to save its *kas*. It had also been given youth and freedom from disease and want so that it could concentrate on salvation.

About a week after his arrival at Parolando, Hermann and some other missionaries held a large meeting. This was in the evening just after dusk. Scores of great bonfires were arranged around a platform lit by torches. Hermann and the local bishop were on the platform with a dozen of the more distinguished members of their organization. There was a crowd of about three thousand, composed of a small minority of converts and a majority who came to be entertained. The latter brought their bottles of alcohol and a tendency to heckle.

After the band finished playing a hymn, said to have been composed by La Viro himself, the bishop gave a short prayer. He then introduced Hermann. Boos here and there followed the mention of his name. Evidently some in the crowd had lived during his time, though it was possible they just didn't like Chancers.

Hermann held up his hands until silence had fallen, and then he spoke in Esperanto.

"Brothers and sisters! Hear me out with the same love with which I speak to you. The Hermann Göring before you is not the man of the same name who lived on Earth. He abhors that man, that evil being.

"Yet, that I stand here before you today, a new man, reborn, testifies that evil can be overcome. A person can change for the better. I have paid for what I did. Paid in the only coin worth anything. Paid with guilt and shame and self-hate. Paid with a vow to kill off the old self, bury it, and go forth as a new man.

"But I'm not here to impress you with what a wretch I was. I'm here to tell you about the Church of the Second Chance. How it came into being, what its credo is, what its tenets.

"Now, I know that those of you who were raised in Judaeo-Christian and Moslem countries, and those Orientals who encountered Christian or Moslem visitors or occupiers of their country, are expecting an appeal to faith.

"No! By the Lord among us, I will not do that! The Church doesn't ask you to believe on faith only. The Church brings—not faith—but *knowledge!* Not faith, I say. *Knowledge!*

"The Church does not ask you to believe in things as they should be or perhaps will be some day. The Church asks you to consider facts and then to act as the facts require. It asks you to believe only in the believable.

"Consider this. Beyond any dispute, we were all born on Earth and we died there. Is there anyone among you who would contradict that?

"No? Then consider this. Man is born to sorrow and evil as the sparks fly upward. Can any of you, remembering your life on Earth and here deny that?

"Whatever the religion on Earth, it promised something that just was not true. The evidence of that is that we are not in Hell or Heaven. Nor are we going through reincarnations, except in a limited sense that we are given new bodies and new life if we die.

"The first resurrection was a tremendous, an almost shattering, shock. No one, religionist, agnostic, or atheist, was in the state he believed he'd be in after the end of Terrestrial existence.

"Yet, here we are, like it or not. Nor is escape from this world possible, as it was on Earth. If you are killed or kill yourself, you rise the next day. Can anyone deny this?"

"No, but I sure as hell don't like it!" a man shouted. There was a general laugh, and Hermann looked at the man who had made the remark. He was Sam Clemens himself, standing in the middle of the crowd on a chair on a platform erected for this occasion.

"Please, brother Clemens, do me the courtesy of not interrupting," Hermann said. "Very well. So far, facts only. Now, can anyone deny that this world is not a natural one? I do not mean by that that this planet itself, the sun, the stars, are artificial. This planet was created by God. But The River and The Valley are not natural. Nor is the resurrection a supernatural event."

"How do you know that?" a woman yelled. "Now you're getting away from facts. You're slipping into surmise."

"That isn't all he's slipping into!" a man shouted.

Hermann waited for the laughter to subside.

"Sister, I can prove to you that the resurrection is not something worked *directly* by God. It was and is performed by people like us. They may not be Terrestrials. They undoubtedly are superior in wisdom and science. But they look much like us. And some of us have talked face to face with them!"

Uproar. Not because the crowd had not heard this before, though not in just these terms. The unbelievers just wanted to have some fun, to relieve tension.

Hermann took a drink of water and by the time he'd put the cup down, he had comparative silence.

"This world and these resurrections, if not made with human hands, have been brought about by hands that are human in appearance. There are two men who can testify to this. For all I know, there may be many others. One of these is an Englishman named Richard Francis Burton. He was not unknown on Earth during his time, in fact, he was famous. He lived from 1821 to 1890, and he was an explorer, anthropologist, innovator, author, and linguist extraordinaire. Perhaps some of you have heard of him? If so, please raise your hands.

"Ah, I count at least forty, among them your consul, Samuel Clemens."

Clemens did not seem to like what he was hearing. He was scowling and chewing frantically on the end of his cigar.

Göring proceeded to recount his experiences with Burton, stressing what Burton had told him. The crowd was caught; there was scarcely a sound. This was something new, something no Chancer missionary had ever spoken of.

"Burton called this mysterious being the Ethical. Now, according to Burton, the Ethical who talked to him did not agree with his fellows. Apparently, there is dissension even among beings whom we could account as gods. Dispute or discord in Olympus, if I may draw such a parallel. Though I do not think that the so-called Ethicals are gods, angels, or demons. They are human beings like us but advanced to a higher ethical plane. What their disagreement is, I frankly do not know. Perhaps it is about the means used to achieve a goal.

"But! The *goal* is the same! Have no doubt of that. And what is that goal? First, let me tell you of the other witness.

"Again, to be frank . . ."

"I thought you were Hermann!" a man shouted.

"Call me Meier," Göring said, but he did not pause to explain the joke.

"About a year after Resurrection Day, he, the witness, was sitting in a hut on a ledge on a very high foothill in a land far to the north of here. He has a natal name, Jacques Gillot, but we of the Church usually refer to him as La Viro. The Man, in English. We also call him La Fondinto, the Founder. He had been a very religious man on Earth during all his long life. But now his faith was smashed, totally discredited. He was bewildered, very troubled.

"This man had always tried to lead a virtuous life according to the teachings of his church, which spoke for God. He did not think that he was a *good* man. After all, Jesus Himself had said that *no* man was good, including Himself.

"But, relatively speaking, Jacques Gillot was good. He was not perfect; he had lied but only so he would not hurt another's feelings, never to escape the consequences of his own deeds. He had never said anything behind a person's back he wouldn't say to his face. He had never been unfaithful to his wife. He had given his wife and children an intense interest and love without spoiling them. He had never turned a person away from his table because of social position, political preference, race, or religion. He had been unjust a number of times, but that was from hastiness and ignorance, and he had always apologized and determined to repair these faults. He had been robbed and betrayed but had left vengeance up to God. However, he wouldn't let anyone walk over him without a fight.

"And he had died with his sins forgiven and the rites administered.

"So what was he doing here, rubbing elbows with politicians, back-stabbers, child-beaters, dishonest businessmen, unethical lawyers, rapacious doctors, adulterers, rapists, thieves, murderers, torturers, terror-ists, hypocrites, cheaters, word-breakers, parasites, the mean, the grasp-ing, the vicious, the unfeeling?

"As he sat in that hut just below the mountain, as the rain beat and the wind howled and the lightning exploded and the thunder boomed like the footsteps of an angry god, he pondered on the seeming injustice. And he reluctantly came to this conclusion. In the eyes of Someone, capital S, he was not much better than those others.

"It didn't make him feel any better to reflect that everybody else was in his state. When a man's sinking in a boat, knowing that everybody else aboard is going to drown doesn't bring much joy.

"But what could he do about it? He didn't even know what he was supposed to do.

"At this moment, as he stared into the small fire, he heard a knock on the door. He stood up and seized his spear. Then, as now, evil men roamed, looking for easy prey. He had nothing worth stealing, but there were men who liked to kill for the twisted pleasure it gave them.

"He called out in his native tongue, 'Who is it?'

"'No one you know,' a man said. He spoke in Quebecan French but with a foreign accent. 'No one who means you harm either. You won't need that spear.'

"This astonished La Viro. The door and windows were closed. No one could see within.

"He unbarred the door. A lightning flash glowed behind the stranger, revealing a cloaked and hooded man of medium stature. La Viro stepped back; the stranger entered; La Viro closed the door. The man threw back his hood. Now the fire showed a white man with red hair, blue eyes, and handsome features. Under the cloak he wore a tight-fitting seamless suit of silvery material. From a silver cord around his neck hung a gold helix.

"The clothes were enough to tell La Viro that this was no Riverdweller. The man looked like an angel and might be one. After all, the Bible said that angels looked just like men. At least, that was what the priests had told him. The angels who had visited the daughters of men in the days of the patriarchs, the angels who rescued Lot, and the angel who wrestled with Jacob, passed for men.

"But the Bible and the priests who had read it to him had been wrong about many things.

"Looking at the stranger, La Viro was in awe. At the same time, he felt delighted. Why would an angel honor him, of all people, with a visit?

"Then he realized that Satan was also an angel, that the demons were all fallen angels.

"Which was he?

"Or was he neither? After all, La Viro, despite his lack of formal education and his humble station, was not unintelligent. It seemed to him that a third alternative existed. At that, he felt easier though still far from comfortable.

"After asking permission, the stranger sat down. La Viro hesitated, then he, too, sat down on a chair. They looked at each other for a moment. The stranger church-steepled his fingers and frowned as if trying to think how best to start. This was strange, since he knew what he wanted and should have had time to prepare for this visit.

"La Viro offered him a drink of alcohol. The stranger said he would take tea instead. La Viro busied himself with pouring the powder into the water and stirring it. The stranger was silent until he thanked La Viro for the tea. After taking a sip, he said, 'Jacques Gillot, who I am and where I come from and why I am here would take all night and all day if I told all in detail.

"'What little I can tell you will be the truth—in a form which you can understand at this stage. I am one of a group which has prepared this planet for you whom we resurrected. There are other planets re-formed for other Terrestrials, but that is not at present your concern. Some are being used now. Some are waiting to be used.

"'This world is for those who need a second chance. What is the second chance? What was the first chance? By now you must have accepted the fact that your religion, in fact, none of the Earthly religions, truly knew what the afterlife would be. All made guesses and then established these as articles of faith. Though, in a sense, some were near the mark, if you accept their revelations as symbolic.'

"And then the visitor said that his kind called themselves the Ethicals, though they had other names for themselves. They were on a higher plane of ethical development than most Earthlings. Notice that he said *most*. This indicates that there have been some of us who have achieved the same level as the Ethicals.

"The visitor said that his people were not the first Ethicals, not by any means. The first were an ancient species, nonhumans, who originated on a planet older than Earth.

"These were individuals who had deliberately retarded themselves, kept themselves in the flesh, as it were, instead of Going On. And when they saw that there was one species, also nonhuman, which was capable of carrying on The Work, they showed this species how to do it. And they passed on.

"The visitor called this species the Ancients. Yet, in comparison with those who had been their mentors, they were very young.

"Now, this is what the visitor said the Ethicals had learned from the Ancients. The Creator, God, the One Spirit, call it what you will, forms all. It is the universe; the universe is it. But its body is formed of two essences. One is matter; the other, for lack of a better word, is nonmatter.

"We all know what matter is. Philosophers and scientists have tried to define it exactly but have failed. Yet everyone *knows* what matter is. We directly experience it.

"But what about this nonmatter? What is it?"

20

"A VACUUM!" A WAG SHOUTED. "THE INSIDE OF YOUR HEAD!"

Clemens stood up and bellowed, "Quiet, there! Let the man speak his piece." And then with a grin, "Even if he makes no sense!"

"Thank you, Mr. Clemens," Göring said. "A perfect vacuum is the absolute absence of matter. A learned man once told me that there is no such thing as a perfect vacuum. It does not exist except as a concept. Even a vacuum is matter.

"Nonmatter is what the old religions of Earth spoke of as the soul. But the definitions of the soul were always vague, very abstract. The peoples of ancient and classical times, and their unliterate ancestors, thought of it as a shadowy thing, a ghostly entity reflecting palely the matter to which it had been attached before death.

"Later, more sophisticated peoples thought of it as an invisible entity, also attached to the body. But it could be refleshed after death, given a new and immortal body. Some Oriental religions thought of it as something which would be reabsorbed into the Godhead after numerous trials on Earth, after a good karma had been achieved.

"All these had some truth in them; they saw parts of the total truth.

"But we are not concerned with such philosophical probings. What we need are facts. The fact is that every living creature, from the simplest to the most complex, has its nonmatter twin. Even an amoeba has its nonmatter twin.

"But I don't want to get into confusing issues or too much detail. Not at this time.

"The visitor said, 'Nonmatter is indestructible. That means that your body on Earth had its indestructible nonmatter twin.'

"At this point, La Viro, who had said nothing before, interrupted.

"'How many twins does a living creature have? I mean, a man changes in appearance. He gets older, he loses an eye or a leg. He gets a diseased liver. Is this nonmatter image like a series of photographs made of a man? If so, how often is the photograph made? Every second, once a month? What happens to the old photographs, the old images?'

"The visitor smiled, and he said, 'The image, as you call it, is indestructible. But it records the changes in the physical body it's attached to.'

"'Then what happens?' La Viro said. 'Wouldn't images of the rotting corpse be produced?'

"As I told you," Göring said, "La Viro was illiterate and he had never been to a big city. But he was not stupid.

"'No,' the visitor said. 'Forget for the moment about all matter and nonmatter except that composing humankind. The rest is irrelevant for our purposes. First, though, let's give this entity which you call a soul another name. *Soul* has too many incorrect meanings for humans, too many verbal reverberations, too many contradictory definitions.

"Speak the word *soul,* and unbelievers will automatically become deaf to what follows. Those who believe in souls will always hear you through the mental constructs which they formed on Earth. Let us call this nonmatter twin the . . . ah . . . *ka*. That is an old Egyptian word for one of the several souls in their religion. Except for the Egyptians, it will have no special connotation or denotation. And they can adapt to it.'

"From which," Göring said, "we know that the visitor knows something about Terrestrial history. Also, he could speak Canadian French, which means that he had studied much to prepare himself for this interview. Just as that Ethical who talked to Burton had learned English.

"'Now,' the visitor said, 'we have the *ka*. As far as we know, it forms at the moment of conception, the union of sperm and egg. The *ka* changes in correspondence with the change in the body.

"'The difference in the body and the *ka* at the moment of the body's death is this. During life, the body projects an aura. This is invisible to the naked eye—except in the case of a favored few—and floats above the head of the living person. It can be detected through an instrument. Seen through this device, the aura seems to be a globe of many colors and hues, whirling, swelling, contracting, shifting colors, extending arms, collapsing them. A wild and wonderful thing the beauty of which has to be seen to be appreciated. We call it the *wathan*.

"'A person loses the *wathan* or *ka* at the moment of death, which is when the body is beyond revivification. Where does the *ka* go? As seen through our device, let's call it a kascope, it usually drifts off at once, carried by what etheric wind we don't know. Sometimes it remains attached to a locality, why we can't guess. But eventually it cuts loose and drifts off.

"'The universe is filled with these, yet they can never increase enough to occupy all of space. They can intersect, pass through each other, an unlimited number can occupy the same space.

"'We assume that the *ka* is unconscious though it contains the intelligence and memory of the dead person. So the *ka* wanders through eternity and infinity, a vessel for the mental potentiality of the living person. A frozen soul, if you will.

"'When a dead person's body is duplicated, the *ka* reattaches itself to that body. No matter how far away it might be from the body in spatial terms, it flashes back at the first second of life of that duplicated body. There is an affinity between the two that knows no bounds. But when the reunion takes place, the *ka* has no memory of the interval between the moment of death of the first body and the first moment of consciousness of the second or duplicate body.

"'However, some have said that it is possible that the *ka* is fully conscious during its bodiless periods. Evidence for this theory was lent by a certain phenomenon of afterlife which was well documented, I understand, in the 1970's. As I remember the accounts a significant number of men and women who were legally dead were revivified. They testified that while dead they had experienced out-of-body flights, had watched relatives grieve and had been yanked back into life. Whether or not the *ka* does have a memory during these times, we are concerned only with its incarnations, its enfleshed states.'

"La Viro was both stunned and ecstatic. But he interrupted again, it seeming to be a human function, a built-in compulsion, to interrupt."

Göring paused, then said, "As I know only too well."

There was some laughter.

"'Pardon me,' La Viro said. 'How do you make this duplicate body?'

"He looked down at his own body and thought of how it had been dust and now was whole again.

"'We have instruments which can detect and scan the *ka*,' the visitor said. 'These can determine the nature of and location of each non-matter molecule. From then on, it is a matter of energy-matter conversion.'

"'Can you duplicate any *ka* at any stage?' La Viro said. 'I mean, what if a man died at eighty? Could you duplicate his *ka* at the age of twenty?'

"'No. The *ka* of the eighty-year-old is the only one existing. Then, while the mind is unconscious, the body made from the records is regenerated to the twenty-year-old state. All defects are corrected. A recording of that body is made and destroyed. For the first resurrection on the surface of this planet, another energy-matter conversion is made. During this process, the bodies are unconscious.'

"'What if you made two duplicates?' La Viro asked. 'At the same time? To which would the *ka* be attached?'

"'Presumably, to the first that was revivified,' the visitor said. 'No matter how synchronized the new resurrections, there would still be at least a microsecond difference. Our machines cannot cut it so close that there is an absolutely simultaneous revivifying. Besides, that experiment would not be done. It would be evil. Unethical.'

"'Yes,' La Viro said, 'but what if it were done?'

"'The body without a *ka* would develop its own, I suppose. And though the second body is the duplicate of the first in the beginning, it would soon become another person. Its different environment, different experiences, would differentiate it from the first. In time, though it would always look like the first, it would become another person.

"'But we are getting into minutiae. The important thing is this. Most disembodied *kas* go forever without consciousness. At least, we hope so. It would be hell to be imprisoned in an intangible body, without control of it, without communication with others, yet aware of it all. The inevitable result would be the torments of the damned. It is too horrible to contemplate.

"'Anyway, nobody who's been resurrected remembers the interval between death and the second life.'

"And so," Göring said, "La Viro was told that out of the billions who died on Earth, only a minute fraction was not part of that wandering horde of *kas*. A few went *out*. Disappeared. The visitor did not know where and why. The Ancients had only told the Ethicals that these few had *gone on*. They had united with the Creator or were at least keeping company with It.

"The visitor said that he could see that La Viro had many questions. He would answer a few, but they would be confined to the center of this subject. How did the Ethicals know that a few *kas* had gone on? How could every one of the billions of *kas* be numbered, be kept track of?

"'You must have some awareness of the vast powers of our science and technology,' the visitor said. 'Even the forces that shaped this world and brought you back to life are beyond your imagination. But what you experience here is only a small part of what is available to us. I tell you that we have counted every *ka* that came into being on Earth. It took over a hundred years to do it, but it was done.

"'You see, it is science that has brought about what was thought to be possible only to the supernatural. The mind of humankind has done what the Creator did not intend to do Itself. Because, I suppose, the Creator knew that sentient beings would do it. Indeed, it is possible that sentiency is the *ka* of God.

"'Let me detour a little myself, though it is not really an irrelevancy. You seem to regard me as, if not a god, at least a cousin to one. I can hear you breathing hard, smell the fright in your sweat, see the awe in your face. Be not afraid. It is true that I am ethically advanced beyond you. But I am not proud because of that. You could catch up with me. Even, perhaps, overtake and pass me.

"'I have powers at my fingertips which make the science of your day look like an ape's. But I am no more intelligent than the most intelligent of Riverdwellers. I can make mistakes and errors.

"'Also, keep this in mind. When—or if—you go out to preach, stress this always. He who climbs up may slip back. In other words, beware of regression. You do not know the word? Then, beware of backsliding. Not until the *ka* has winged its way outward forever is it safe from regression. Who lives in flesh lives in danger.

"'That advice applies to me as well as to you.'

"At this point, La Viro reached toward his visitor. He felt an urge to touch the man, to assure himself that he was indeed flesh and blood.

"The visitor recoiled and cried, 'Do not do that!'

"La Viro withdrew his hand, but his injured feelings showed. His visitor said, 'I am sorry, sorrier than you can imagine, but please do not touch me. I will say no more of this. But when you have gotten to the point where I may embrace you, then you will understand.'

"And so, my brothers and sisters," Göring said, "the visitor proceeded to tell La Viro why he should found this new religion. The name of our organization was La Viro's idea, nor did the visitor compel La Viro to found it. He merely asked that he should do so. But he must have known his man, for La Viro said he would do as his visitor asked.

"The principles of the Church of the Second Chance and the techniques for enfleshing them are not tonight's subject. It will take too long to propound and defend them. That is for tomorrow night's meeting.

"At the end, La Viro asked the Ethical why he had chosen him, of all people, to become the founder of the Church.

"'I am an ignorant half-breed,' La Viro said. 'I was raised in the deep Canadian forest. My father was a white trapper, and my mother was an Indian. Both were looked down upon by the British who ruled our land. My mother was almost an outcast in her own tribe because she married a white man. My father was scorned as a squawman, a dirty Frenchie, by the English he worked for.

"'When I was fourteen, very large for my age, I became a lumberjack. At twenty an accident lamed me, and I spent the rest of my life cooking for the lumber camps. My wife was also half-Indian, and she brought in money by washing clothes. We had seven children, four of whom died young, and the others were ashamed of their parents. Yet we sacrificed for them and gave them love and a devout upbringing. My two sons went to Montreal to work and then were killed in France fighting for the English, who despised them. My daughter became a whore and died of a disease—or so I heard. My wife died of a broken heart.

"'I don't tell you this because I ask for sympathy. I just want you to know who and what I am. How can you ask me to go out and preach when I could not convince my own children that my beliefs were right? And when my own wife died cursing God? How can I go out and talk to men who were scholars and statesmen and priests?'

"The visitor smiled and said, 'Your *wathan* tells me that you can.'

"The visitor stood up. He lifted the silver cord from around his neck and past his head, and he placed it around La Viro's neck. The golden helix now lay on La Viro's chest.

"'This is yours, Jacques Gillot. Do not dishonor it. Farewell. I may or may not see you again on this world.'

"La Viro said, 'No! Wait! I have so many questions!'

"'You know enough,' the visitor said. 'God bless you.'

"He was gone. The rain and thunder and lightning were still making a tumult. Gillot went out a moment later. He could see no sign of the visitor, and after searching the stormy skies he returned to his hut. There he sat until dawn came up with the thunder of the grailstones. Then he went down to the plains to tell his story. As he had expected, those to whom he told his story thought he was crazy. But in time there were those who came to believe him."

SECTION 8

The Fabulous Riverboats Arrive at Virolando

21

OVER THIRTY-THREE YEARS AGO, HE HAD ARRIVED IN VIROLANDO. IT WAS his intention to stay only long enough to talk a few times to La Viro, if he were permitted to do so. Then he would go wherever the Church sent him. But La Viro had asked him to settle there, though he had not said why or how long he could remain. After a year there, Göring had adopted the Esperanto name of Fenikso (Phoenix).

Those had been the happiest years of his lives. Nor was there any reason to think he would not spend many more here.

This day would be much like the others, but its sameness was enjoyable and little varieties would garnish it.

After breakfast, he climbed up to a large building built on top of a rock spire on the left bank. Here he lectured his seminary students until a half-hour before noon. He went down swiftly to the ground and joined Kren at a grailstone. Afterward, they went up to another spire and strapped themselves into hang-gliders and launched themselves from the edge of the spire, six hundred feet above the ground.

The air above Virolando glittered with thousands of gliders which slanted up and down, turned, dipped, rose, swooped, danced. Hermann felt like a bird, no, a free spirit. It was an illusion of freedom, all freedom was illusion, but it was the best.

His glider was bright-red, painted so in memory of the squadron he had led after Manfred von Richthofen had died. Scarlet was also the symbol for the blood of the martyrs of the Church. There were many such in the skies, mingling their color with white, black, yellow, orange, green, blue, and purple craft. This land was blessed in having hematite and other ores from which pigments could be made. It was blessed in many things.

Hermann sped above and below the bridges holding houses, spanning the gap between the spires. He passed closely to the wooden and stone pylons, sometimes too closely. It was sinful to risk his life, but he could not resist it. The old thrill of flight on Earth had returned, doubling in ecstasy. There was no motor roaring in his ears, no fumes of oil in his nostrils, no sensation of being enclosed.

Sometimes he sailed by a balloon and waved at the people in the wickerwork baskets beneath them. During his holidays, he and Kren would board a balloon, rise to a height of a thousand meters, and let the wind carry them down The Valley. On long holidays, they would float for a whole day, talking, eating, making love in the cramped quarters while they rode without a bump, without a touch of the wind, since the balloon rode at the same speed as it did.

Venting the hydrogen at dusk, they would land on the bank, pack the collapsed envelope in the basket, and take a boat back upstream next day.

After half an hour, Hermann swooped down along The River, veered, and came down running on the bank. With hundreds of others, he disassembled the glider, and then walked with a cumbersome bundle on his back to the spire from which he had jumped.

A messenger wearing a chaplet of red and yellow blooms stopped him. "Brother Fenikso, La Viro wishes to see you."

"Thank you," Hermann said, but a small shock traveled through him. Had the chief bishop decided that the time had come to send him out?

The Man waited for him in his private quarters in the red-and-black-stone temple. Hermann was ushered through the high-ceilinged rooms to a small chamber, and the oaken door was closed behind him. The room was simply furnished: a big flat-topped desk; several large chairs of fishskin leather; some small ones of bamboo; two cots; a table with pitchers of water and some flavored alcohol, cups, boxes of cigars, cigarettes, lighters, and matches; a chamberpot; two grails; pegs in the walls from which hung cloths; a table beside a mica mirror on the wall; another table holding the lipsticks, small scissors, and combs which the grails occasionally provided. There were several rugs of bamboo fiber and one star-shaped fishskin on the floor. Four torches burned, their ends thrust into wall-holders. The private door in the outside wall was open now, letting in the air and sunlight. Vents in the ceiling gave additional ventilation.

La Viro rose as Hermann entered. He was huge, about six feet six inches high, and very dark. His nose was the beak of a giant eagle.

"Welcome, Fenikso," he said in a deep voice. "Sit down. Would you like a drink, a cigar?"

"No, thank you, Jacques," Hermann said. He sat down in the easy chair indicated.

The chief bishop resumed his seat. "You've heard about this giant metal boat coming up-River, of course? The drums say it's about eight hundred kilometers from the southern border. That means it will reach our border in about two days.

"You have told me all you know about this man Clemens and his partner, John Lackland. You did not know what happened after you were killed, of course. But apparently those two succeeded in repelling their enemies and in building their boat. They are going to pass through our territory soon. From what I hear, they are not warlike, and so we need fear no trouble. After all, they are dependent upon cooperation from those who own the grailstones along The River. They have the power to take what they want, but they don't use it unless they have to. However, I have heard some disturbing reports about the behavior of some of the crew when the boat has stopped for—what is it called?—shore leave. There have been some ugly incidents, mostly to do with drunkenness and women."

"Pardon me, Jacques. That does not sound like the type of people Clemens would have on board. He was obsessed, and he did some things which he should not have done to get that boat built. But he isn't, or at least wasn't, one to condone such behavior."

"In all these years, who knows how he's changed? For one thing, the name of this boat is not what you told me it would be. Instead of the *Not For Hire* it is *Rex Grandissimus*."

"That is strange. That sounds more like a name which King John would pick."

"From what you tell me of this John, he may have killed Clemens and taken over the boat. Whatever the truth, I want you to meet the boat at the border."

"Me?"

"You knew the men who built the boat. I want you to get aboard it at the border. You will find out what the situation is, what kind of people live on it. Also, you will estimate its military potential."

Hermann looked surprised.

"Now, Fenikso, you have told me of the story which this giant long-nosed man—Joe Miller?—told Clemens and which Clemens told others. If it be true, there is a great tower in the middle of the sea at the north pole. These men mean to enter it if they can. I think their intent is evil."

"Evil?"

"Because that tower is obviously the work of the Ethicals. These boat people wish to penetrate that tower, to discover its secrets, perhaps to take captive or even kill the Ethicals."

"You do not know that," Hermann said.

"No, but it is reasonable to suppose that."

"I never heard Clemens say that he wanted power. He just wanted to get to the headwaters."

"What he says publicly and what privately may be two different things."

"Really, Jacques," Hermann said. "What do we care what they do even if they should manage to get to the tower? Surely you do not think that their puny machines and weapons can do anything to harm the Ethicals? Humans would be as worms to them. Anyway, what can we do about them? We may not use force to stop them."

The bishop leaned forward, his huge brown hands gripping the edge of the desk. He stared at Hermann as if to peel him, layer by layer, and see what formed the center.

"There is something wrong in this world, grievously wrong! First, the little resurrections have stopped. This seems to have happened shortly after your last resurrection. You remember the consternation that this news caused?"

Hermann nodded and said, "I suffered much from anxiety myself. I was in a panic of doubt and despair."

"So was I. But, as archbishop, I had to reassure my flock. However, I had no facts to use as a basis for hope. It was possible that we had been given the time we needed. All who were going to achieve Going On had done so. The rest would also die, and their *kas* would roam the universe, forever beyond redemption.

"But I did not think so. For one thing, I knew that I was not ready to Go On. I have a way to go, perhaps a long one, before I have done that.

"Yet, would the Ethical have picked me to found the Church if I were not a strong candidate for Going On?

"Or, and you can imagine my agony at this thought, had I failed? Had I been appointed to show others the way to salvation and yet I had to remain behind? Like Moses who led the Hebrews to the promised land but was forbidden to go down into it himself?"

"Oh, no!" Hermann murmured. "That could not be!"

"It could be," Viro said. "I am only a man, not a god. For a while, I even thought about resigning. Perhaps I had allowed myself to ignore my own ethical progress because I was too busy running the affairs of the Church. I had become arrogant; my power had corrupted me in a subtle way. I would let the bishops elect a new chief. I would change my name and go down The River as a missionary.

"No, do not protest. I was seriously considering that. But then I told myself that I would be betraying the trust given by the Ethicals. And perhaps there was another explanation for this terrible event.

"Meanwhile, I had to make some sort of public explanation. You know what it was; you were among the first to hear it."

Hermann nodded. He had been entrusted to carry the message for two thousand miles below Virolando. That had meant being absent from his beloved country for over a year. But he had been glad to do it for La Viro and the Church. The message was: Be not afraid. Have faith. The last days are not here. The trial is not over. We are in an interim which will not last forever. Someday, the dead will arise again. That is promised. Those who made this world and gave you the chance to be immortal cannot fail you. The interim is a test. Be not afraid. Believe.

Many had asked Hermann what the "test" was. He could only reply that he did not know. Perhaps La Viro had learned what it was from the Ethicals. Perhaps to reveal the purpose of the test would be to defeat its end.

Some had not accepted this. Bitterly denouncing the Church, they had left it. The majority, however, had remained. Surprisingly, many new converts had been made. These had come in through fear, fear that perhaps there really was a second chance to attain immortality and now their time to do it was short. This was not a rational attitude, since La Viro had said that the resurrections would come again. But they were taking no chances of losing their chance.

Though fear did not make a long-term believer, it caused a step toward the right direction. Perhaps true faith would follow.

"The only statement in my message which was not strictly true," La Viro said, "was that about the interim being a test. I had no direct authority, that is, no direct message from the visitor, that such was the case. But, in a sense, my statement was not a pious lie. The stopping of the resurrections is a test. A test of courage and belief. It does indeed try all of us.

"At that time, I thought that it was being done for some good purpose by the Ethicals. And it may well be that that is so. But the visitor did tell me that he and his fellows were no more than human despite the superpowers available to them. They could make mistakes and errors. Which means that they are not invulnerable. Accidents can happen to them. And enemies could do harm to them."

Hermann sat straight up. "What enemies?"

"I cannot know their identity—if indeed there are any. Consider this. This subhuman, no, I will not call him that, since he is human, despite his strange appearance. This giant, Joe Miller, and the Egyptians got to the polar sea despite great odds. Also, others had preceded them. For all we know, others may have followed the Egyptians. *How do we know that some of these may not have gotten into the tower? And there did something terrible, perhaps without meaning to do so?"*

"I find it hard to believe that the Ethicals would not have invulnerable defenses," Göring said.

"Ah!" La Viro said, holding up a finger. "You forget the ominous significance of the tunnel and the rope which Miller's party found. Somebody bored the hole in the mountains and set the rope there. The question is, who and why?"

"Perhaps it was one of the second-order Ethicals, a renegade agent," Hermann said. "After all, the visitor told you that regression was possible even to him. If it is possible to his kind, think how much more likely it is for an agent."

La Viro was horrified. "I . . . I should have thought of that! But it is so . . . unthinkable . . . so perilous!"

"Perilous?"

"Yes. The agents have to be more advanced than we, yet even they . . . wait."

La Viro closed his eyes, holding up his right hand with the thumb and index finger forming an O. Hermann said nothing. La Viro was mentally reciting the acceptance formula, a technique used by the Church, invented by La Viro himself. At the end of two minutes, La Viro opened his eyes and smiled.

"If it should be, we must face all its implications and be ready," he said. *"Reality be Thine . . . and ours.*

"However, back to the main reason I sent for you. I want you to get on that boat and observe everything you can. Find out the disposition of the captain, this King John, and his crew. Determine if they are a threat to the Ethicals. By this, I mean, do they have devices and weapons which might conceivably allow them to get into the Tower."

La Viro frowned and said, "It is time that we took a hand in this matter."

"You surely do not mean that we may use violence?"

"No, not to people. But nonviolence and passive resistance apply only to persons. Hermann, if necessary, we will sink that boat! But we will only do it as a last and regrettable measure. And we will do it only if we can be sure that no one will be harmed."

"I . . . I don't know," Hermann said. "It seems to me that, if we do that, we lack faith in the Ethicals. They should be able to handle anything that mere men can bring against them."

"You have fallen into the trap the Church continually warns against, the trap of which you have warned many yourself. The Ethicals are not gods. There is only one God."

Hermann stood up. "Very well. I will leave immediately."

"You are pale, Fenikso. Don't be so frightened. It may not be necessary to destroy that boat. In any event, we will do it only if we are one hundred percent sure that no one will be injured or killed."

"It is not that which frightens me," Hermann said. "What does is that a part of me is eager to get into the intrigue, thrilled with the idea of sinking that boat. It's the old Hermann Göring, still alive down there, though I thought I had put him away forever."

22

THE *REX GRANDISSIMUS* WAS INDEED A BEAUTIFUL AND AWING VESSEL. She plowed speedily in the middle of The River, towering whitely, her great black smokestacks lofty, her two giant paddlewheels churning. From atop the pole above the pilothouse, her flag whipped, showing wavily three golden lions on a scarlet field.

Hermann Göring, waiting on the deck of a three-masted schooner, raised his eyebrows. The banner was certainly not the scarlet phoenix on blue which Clemens had planned.

The sky was freckled with hang-gliders swooping above the great riverboat. The River itself was crowded with vessels of all kinds, officials, and sightseers.

Now the boat was slowing, its captain having interpreted correctly the meaning of the rockets fired from Göring's schooner. Besides, the other craft were forming an obstacle beyond which he could not go without smashing them.

Finally, it stopped, its wheels turning just enough to match the current.

As the schooner came alongside, its captain yelled through a riverdragon-fish horn at the *Rex*. A man on the lowest deck hurried to a phone on a bulkhead and talked to the pilothouse. In a moment, a man leaned out of the pilothouse, holding an instrument with a horn. His voice blared from it, startling Hermann. The device must amplify sounds electrically, he thought.

"Come aboard!" the man said in Esperanto.

Though the captain was at least fifty-five feet above the water, and a hundred feet away horizontally, Hermann recognized him. The tawny hair, broad shoulders, and oval face were those of John Lackland, ex-King of England, Lord of Ireland, etc., etc. In a few minutes Hermann had boarded the *Rex* and was accompanied by two heavily armed officers via a small elevator to the top deck of the pilothouse. On the way he said, "What happened to Sam Clemens?"

The men looked surprised. One said, "How did you know about him?"

"Gossip travels faster than your boat," Hermann said. This was true, and if he had not exactly told the truth, he also had not lied.

They entered the control room. John was standing by the pilot's chair and looking outward. He turned at the sound of the elevator closing. He was five feet five inches tall, a good-looking virile-seeming man with wide-set blue eyes. He wore a black uniform which he probably never put on except to impress locals. The black jacket, trousers, and boots were of riverdragon-leather. Gold buttons adorned the jacket, and a golden lion's head roared soundlessly from above the visor of the cap. Hermann wondered where he had gotten the gold, an extremely rare item. Probably, he'd taken it from some poor wretch.

His chest was bare. Tawny hair, a shade or two darker than that on his head, curled thickly over the V of the jacket top.

One of the officers who'd escorted him snapped a salute. "The emissary of Virolando, Sire!"

So, Hermann thought, it was *sire*, not *sir*.

It was evident that John did not recognize his visitor. He surprised Hermann by walking to him, smiling, and holding out his hand. Hermann took it. Why not? He was not here to revenge himself. He had a duty to perform.

"Welcome aboard," John said. "I am the captain, John Lackland. Though, as you see, I have no land I do have something even more valuable, this vessel."

He laughed and added, "I was once the King of England and Ireland, if that means anything to you."

"I am Brother Fenikso, a sub-bishop in the Church of the Second Chance and a secretary to La Viro. In his name I welcome you to Virolando. And, yes, Your Majesty, I have read about you. I was born in the twentieth century in Bavaria."

John's thick tawny eyebrows went up. "I've heard much of La Viro, of course, and we were told that he lived not too far up-River."

John introduced the others, none of whom Hermann knew except the first mate, Augustus Strubewell. He was an American, very large, blond, and handsome. He crushed Hermann's hand and said, "Welcome, Bishop." He didn't seem to recognize him either. Göring shrugged mental shoulders. After all, he hadn't been in Parolando long, and that was over thirty-three years ago.

"Would you like a drink?" John said.

Hermann said, "No, thank you. I hope you will let me stay aboard, Captain. I am here to escort you to our capital. We welcome you in peace and love and hope that you come in the same spirit. La Viro wishes to meet you and to extend his blessing. Perhaps you would like to stay awhile and stretch your legs on shore. In fact, you may stay here as long as you wish."

"I am not, as you see, a member of your congregation," John said, accepting a cup of bourbon from an orderly. "But I have a high regard for the Church. It's had a highly civilizing influence along The River. Which is more than I can say for the church to which I once belonged. It has made our voyage much easier, since it has reduced militancy. However, not many people would care to attack us anyway."

"I'm glad to hear that," Hermann said. He decided it would be best not to mention what John had done in Parolando. Perhaps the man had changed. He would give him the benefit of the doubt.

The captain made arrangements for Göring's quarters. His cabin would be in the texas, a long structure which was an extension of the room just below the pilothouse and which was on the extreme forward starboard side of the landing deck. The top officers were cabined in this.

John asked about his Terrestrial life. Göring replied that the past wasn't worth talking about. What mattered was the present.

John said, "Well, perhaps, but the present is the sum of the past. If you won't talk about yourself, would you tell me of Virolando?"

It was a legitimate question, though Göring wondered if John wished to find out the state's military potential. He wouldn't tell him that it did not have any. Let him find out for himself. He did make it clear, however, that no one of the *Rex* would be allowed to bring arms ashore.

"If this were any other place, I wouldn't abide by that rule," John said, smiling. "But I'm sure we'll be safe in the heart of the Church."

"This land is, as far as I know, unique," Hermann said. "It's topography and its citizens are remarkable. The first you can see for yourself," and he waved at the rock spires.

"It's a columnar country indeed," John said. "But what makes the citizens so different?"

"The great majority of them are Rivertads. When the first resurrection occurred, this area was filled with children who had died between the ages of five and seven. There were about twenty to every adult. Nowhere else that I've heard of has had that proportion. The children seemed to be from many places and times, of many nations and races. They had one thing in common, though. They were frightened. But, fortunately, the adults were mostly from peaceful and progressive countries, Scandinavia, Iceland, and Switzerland of the twentieth century. The area wasn't subjected to the vicious struggles for power that occurred elsewhere. The strait to the west cuts off the titanthrops who lived there. The peoples immediately westward down-River were of the same kind as those here. Thus, the adults could give full time to taking care of the children.

"Then La Viro announced that he had spoken to one of the mysterious beings who had made this world. He would have been received as all prophets have been in the beginning of their careers. With rejection by all but a few. But La Viro had something substantial, something beyond words and his conviction. He had solid visible proof. It was something which no one else had, which had to be the product of the Ethicals.

"This was The Gift, as it's generally called. You'll see it in the Temple. A golden helix. And so he made his home here.

"The children were brought up with discipline and love, and it was they who built this culture you see all about you."

John said, "If the citizens are as beautiful in spirit as their country is to the sight, then they must be angels."

"They're human," Göring said, "and so this is no Utopia, no Paradise. I believe, however, that you will not find any other place which has so many truly friendly, open, generous, and loving persons. It is a very pleasant place to live in, if you have a kindred spirit."

"Perhaps this would be a good place for a long shore leave," John said. "Besides, the motors need rewiring, and that takes time."

"How long you stay here depends upon you," Göring said.

John looked sharply at him.

Göring smiled. Was John considering how he could take advantage of the Virolanders? Or was he merely thinking that he could relax here, not have to worry about his boat being seized?

At this moment, a man entered the control room. He was about six feet high, deeply sun-bronzed, wide-shouldered, and barrel-chested. His straight hair was very black. Thick black eyebrows shaded large fierce black eyes. His face was as strong as any Göring had ever seen. The man radiated an aura which in Göring's childhood would have been called "animal magnetism."

John, catching sight of him said, "Ah, Gwalchgwynn, the captain of my marines. You must meet him. He is a capital fellow, a superb swordsman and pistol shot, a great poker player. He is a Welshman descended from kings on both sides of his family, if what he says is true."

Göring felt as if his blood had deserted his heart.

He murmured, "Burton!"

23

NO ONE SEEMED TO HAVE HEARD HIM.

From Burton's shocked expression, quickly masked, Göring knew that he had recognized him. When Göring was introduced to him as Brother Fenikso, La Viro's emissary and a sub-bishop, Burton bowed. He drawled, "Your Reverence," and he smiled mockingly.

"The Church has no such titles, Captain," Göring said. Burton knew that, of course. He was just being sarcastic.

That didn't matter. What did matter was that Burton seemed to have no desire to reveal that Fenikso was in reality Göring. He wasn't doing it to help Göring because he liked him, however. If he gave Göring's natal name, then Göring would reveal Burton's. And Burton must have much more at stake than he, Göring, had. Actually, Göring had no strong reason to be pseudonymous. He just wanted to avoid having to explain why he was now a member of the Church. It was a long story and took much time, and many just refused to believe that his conversion had been sincere.

King John was charming to his visitor. He must have completely failed to recognize the man whose head he'd once savagely struck with a pistol butt. Göring wanted it to stay that way. If John still believed that he could rape and rob the locals, he would be on guard if he knew that a victim of the past was present. If he thought Fenikso was just a simple innocent bishop, he might not be so careful to hide his intentions.

Of course, it might be that John's nature had changed for the better. Would Burton serve him if it hadn't?

Yes, he might if he wanted strongly to get to the headwaters.

But perhaps John was no longer a human hyena. Not that Göring meant to give the hyenas a bad name.

Wait and find out.

John invited the bishop to tour the boat. Göring accepted gladly. He'd been through it in Parolando before it was quite finished and so, even after so many years, knew its layout well. But now he could see it fully furnished and armed. He'd give a complete report to La Viro. His chief could then determine if it would be possible to sink the boat if it was necessary to do so. Göring didn't really take La Viro's statements about this seriously. He was sure that it couldn't be done without some bloodshed. However, he'd keep his counsel until asked for it.

Burton disappeared shortly after the tour began. He reappeared behind them ten minutes later and quietly rejoined them. This was just before they went into the grand salon. On entering, Göring saw the American, Peter Jairus Frigate, and the Englishwoman, Alice Hargreaves, playing billiards. He was shocked, and he stuttered for a moment replying to one of John's questions. The memory of what he'd done to them, especially to the woman, smote him with guilt.

Now his identity would be out. John would remember him. Strubewell would, too. And John would be deeply distrustful of him.

Göring wished now that he'd given his old name as soon as he met John. But who would have thought that, out of over thirty-five or -six billion people, one whom he'd known too well would be on this boat? And who would have imagined that not one but three such would be aboard?

Gott! Were there others? Where was that Neanderthal, Kazz, who worshipped Burton? The Arcturan who also claimed to be from Tau Ceti? The Tokharian, Loghu? The Jew, Ruach?

Like most of the many people in the salon, they looked up when the party entered. Even the black man playing the ragtime piece, "Kitten on the Keys," on the piano stopped, his fingers poised.

Strubewell loudly asked for silence and attention and got it. He introduced Brother Fenikso, La Viro's emissary, and said that Fenikso would be traveling with them to Aglejo. He was to be treated with every courtesy but at this time was not to be approached. His Majesty was taking him for a tour of the *Rex*.

The piano playing and the conversation started up again. Frigate and Hargreaves stared at him for a minute longer, then returned to their game. They did not seem to recognize him. Well, Göring thought, it has been nearly sixty years since we last saw each other. They didn't have his near-perfect recall. Still, their experiences with him had been so harrowing that he would have thought they'd never forget his face. Besides, Frigate, on Earth, had seen many photographs of him as a young man, which should reinforce his memory.

No, they wouldn't have forgotten. What had happened was that Burton had gotten to them during his absence from the tour. He'd told them to act as if they'd never seen him before.

Why?

To spare him guilt, their silence saying, in effect, "We forgive you now that you've changed. Let it be as if we're meeting for the first time"?

That didn't seem likely unless Burton's character had also changed. The true reason probably was that Göring, if revealed, would then reveal Burton. And for all he knew, Frigate and Hargreaves were under false names.

He didn't have much time to think about this matter. King John, playing the gracious host, insisted on showing him almost everything in the *Rex*. He also introduced him to many people, a large number of whom had been famous, infamous, or well known in their time. John, during the many years of travel up The River, had had a chance to pick up such notables. Which meant that he must have had to kick off those not so famous to make room for the famous.

Göring was not as impressed as John had expected him to be. As one who'd been the second-in-command of the German empire and thus had met many of the world's greats, Göring was not easily awed or bamboozled. Even more, his experiences with the greats and the near-greats on both worlds had made him well aware that the public image and the person behind the facade were often pathetically or disgustingly dissimilar.

The one who'd impressed him most on the Riverworld was a man who, on Earth, would have been thought a complete nonentity and failure by almost anybody. That was Jacques Gillot, La Viro, La Fondinto.

During his Terrestrial existence, however, the person who'd awed him the most, in fact, overpowered him, enslaved him by force of personality alone, had been Adolf Hitler. Only once had he stood up to his Führer during the many times he'd known the Führer was wrong, and then he'd quickly backed down. Now, in the retrospect of many years on the Riverworld and the knowledge he'd gained as a Second Chancer, he had no respect at all for the madman. Nor did he have any respect for the Göring of that time. Indeed, he loathed him.

But, he wasn't so full of self-hatred that he considered himself past salvation. To think thus was to put himself into a special class, to be criminally proud, to be full of hubris, to possess a peculiar form of self-righteousness.

However, there was also the danger of having all these prides because you didn't have them. To be proud because you were humble.

This was a Christian sin, though also counted as such in some other religions. La Viro, who'd been a stoutly devout Catholic all his Terrestrial life, had never even heard of such a sin then. His priest had never mentioned it during his long sleep-inducing sermons. Gillot had conceived of this old but little-publicized sin himself after he'd come to this planet.

Though Göring recognized before the end of the war that Hitler was crazy, he'd still remained loyal to him. Loyalty was one of Göring's virtues, though in him it was so resistant to reason that it became a fault. Unlike most of the others at the Nuremberg trial, Göring had refused to renounce and denounce his chief.

Now, he wished he'd had the courage to stand up to his leader even though it might have meant his downfall much earlier than it occurred and perhaps even his death. If only he could do it all over . . .

But as La Viro had told him, "You are doing it all over again now, every day. The circumstances differ, that's all."

The third person who'd made the greatest impression on him was Richard Francis Burton. Göring didn't doubt that Burton, if he'd been in Göring's place, would not have hesitated in saying to Hitler, "No!" or "You are wrong!" How then, had Burton managed to keep from being thrown off the *Rex* in all these years? King John was a tyrant, arrogant, intolerant of those who argued with him.

Had John changed? Had Burton also changed? And then the changes had been enough so that each man could get along with the other?

John said, "Over there, playing draw poker, are the seven pilots of my air force. Come, I'll introduce you."

Göring was startled when Werner Voss stood up to shake hands with him. He had met him once, but Voss obviously didn't recognize him.

Göring was a fine pilot, but he would readily admit that he could never equal Voss. Voss had scored his first victories, two Allied planes, in November 1916. On September 23, 1917, shortly after his twentieth birthday, Voss was shot down after a lone-wolf battle against seven of Britain's best fighter pilots. In less than a year, during which he'd flown against the enemy, he'd scored forty-eight kills, enough to make him the fourth-ranking ace of the Imperial German Air Service. And in that short time he'd been removed several times from the front for administrative or other duties. It was not a coincidence that this happened when he was getting close to the score of Manfred von Richthofen. The baron had great influence, nor was Voss the only one whom von Richthofen had managed to withdraw from action for a while. Karl Schaefer and Karl Allmenröder, hotshot pilots, had been similarly manipulated.

Voss was a first lieutenant of the air force, the second-ranker, John explained. The captain was Kenji Okabe, one of Japan's great aces. The grinning little brown man bowed to Göring, who bowed back. Göring had never heard of him because Germany had not gotten much news from its ally during World War II. His record must have been impressive, though, for John to give him a higher rank than the great Voss. Or perhaps Okabe had joined the airmen before Voss and therefore had greater seniority.

The other aviators, the two fighter-plane replacement pilots, the pilots of the torpedo bomber and of the helicopter, were unknown to Göring.

Göring would have loved to have talked with Voss about the old days of World War I. Sighing, he followed John up a staircase to the C or hurricane deck. At the end of the tour, they went back to the grand salon for iced drinks. Göring took only one drink. John, he noted, downed two in a short time. His face got red, but his speech remained unslurred. He asked Göring many questions about La Viro. Göring answered truthfully. What was there to hide?

Could the bishop give John any indication about whether or not La Viro would give permission for the boat to put in for extended repairs?

"I can't speak for La Viro," Göring said. "But I believe that he'll say yes. After all, you are potential converts to the Church."

King John grinned and said, "By God's teeth, I don't care how many of my crew you hook after we sink Clemens' boat! Perhaps you don't know that Clemens tried to slaughter me and my good men so that he could have the boat for himself and his swinish followers. May God strike the polecat with lightning! But I and my brave men foiled him and almost succeeded in killing him! And we took the boat up The River while he stood on the bank raving and ranting and shaking his fist at us. I laughed then, thinking that that was the last time I'd ever see him. I was mistaken."

Göring said, "Do you have any idea how close Clemens is to you?"

"I'd estimate that it will be only a few days behind," John said, "after we get our motor rewinding done. We were also delayed for a long time because of the damage done by the raiders."

"Then that means. . . ?"

Göring did not like to put his thought into words.

John grinned savagely. "Yes, that means that we will *fight!*"

It was evident to Göring that John meant to use this wide and long lake for his stand. It would give him plenty of room for maneuvering. He didn't think it would be wise to mention this at this time.

John began cursing out Clemens as a lying, traitorous, bloodthirsty, rapacious monster. He was a hellbent criminal, and John was his innocent victim.

Göring wasn't fooled. Having known both Clemens and John, he was sure that John was the liar, the traitor, and the rapacious. He wondered how those who'd been in on the hijacking had managed to keep the truth from those who joined the crew afterward.

Göring said, "Your Majesty, it's been a very long, arduous, and dangerous voyage. Your casualty rate must have been high. How many of your original crew are left?"

John narrowed his eyes. "That's a strange question. Why do you ask it?"

Göring shrugged and said, "It's not important. It's just that I was curious. There are so many savage peoples on The River, and I'm sure that many have tried to take the boat away from you. After all, it . . ."

"Is a treasure worth far more than its weight in diamonds?" John said, smiling. "Yes. It is. By God's backside, I could tell you tales of the mighty battles we've had to keep the *Rex* from falling into enemy hands. The truth is that, of the fifty who left Parolando, only two are still on the boat. Myself and Augustus Strubewell."

Which might mean, Göring thought, that John had managed that no loosemouth would tell new recruits the truth. A push in the dark of a rainstorm, a splash no one could hear. A quarrel provoked by John or Strubewell and the discharge of the crewman for incompetence or insubordination. There were many ways to kill and many excuses for throwing a man or woman off the boat. And accident and warfare and desertion would take care of the others.

Now Göring realized another reason why Burton might have kept silent about his identity. If John recognized Göring, he'd know that Göring would know that he was lying. And he just might cause an "accident" to Göring before the boat got to Aglejo. Thus, no bad report about John would get to La Viro.

Perhaps, Göring thought, he was being too suspicious. He didn't really think so.

24

THEY HAD LEFT THE GRAND SALON AND GONE TO THE ROOM AT THE BOW end of the texas. This was semicircular and walled with shatterproof glass. The elevator shaft that went through the room above and to the pilothouse formed part of the rear wall. Here there were chairs and tables, several sofas, and a small bar. As in most places on the boat, music was piped in from a central station. But it could be turned off. After some conversation about the rewinding, which would take two months at least, Göring steered the talk toward the forthcoming battle. He wanted to say, "What good will it do to fight? What purpose could it serve? Why must all these people on your boat and Clemens' risk death and mutilation and terrible pain just because of something that happened many decades ago?

"I think that you and Clemens are both mad. Why don't you two call this off? After all, Clemens has his own boat now. What could he do with two boats? Which he isn't going to have, anyway, because one boat is going to be destroyed, and I suspect it'll be yours, Your Majesty. Knowing the size and potentiality of Clemens' boat, there's little doubt."

What he said was, "Perhaps it won't be necessary to fight Clemens. After all these years, could he still thirst for revenge? Do you want vengeance because he tried to kill you? Can't you forgive him? The passage of time often cools hot passions and allows cool reason to reign. Perhaps . . ."

John shrugged broad heavy shoulders and raised his hands, palms upward.

"Believe me, Brother Fenikso, I would thank God if Clemens had regained his mind and become a man of peace. I am not warlike. All I want is fellowship for everyone. I would lift my hand against none if none would lift their hand against me."

"I am indeed happy to hear that," Göring said. "And I know that La Viro will be very happy to act as intermediary so that any disputes between you two may be settled amicably. La Viro, all of us here, are eager to avoid bloodshed and to establish good will, love, if possible, between you and Clemens."

John frowned.

"I doubt that that demon-possessed bloody-minded creature will agree even to a meeting . . . unless it is to kill me."

"We can only do our best to arrange a meeting."

"What troubles me, what makes me think that Clemens will always hate me, is that his wife, his ex-wife rather, was accidentally killed during the battle for the boat. Though they'd parted, he still loved her. And he will hold me responsible for her death."

"But this happened before the resurrections stopped," Göring said. "She would have been translated elsewhere."

"That doesn't matter. He'll probably never see her again, so she is as good as dead to him. Anyway, she was dead to him before she died. As you may know, she was in love with that big-nosed Frenchman, de Bergerac."

John laughed loudly.

"The Frenchman was one of the raiders. I kicked him in the back of the head when I escaped from the chopper. It was also de Bergerac who ran his épée through the thigh of Captain Gwalchgwynn. He's the only man who's ever defeated Gwalchgwynn in swordplay. Gwalchgwynn claims that he was distracted, otherwise de Bergerac never would have gotten through his guard. Gwalchgwynn would not like it if Clemens and I made peace. He too thirsts for revenge."

Hermann wondered if Gwalchgwynn—Burton—did indeed feel this way, but when he looked around, the Englishman was gone.

At that moment, two crewmen entered carrying small kegs of watered alcohol. Göring recognized one of the men. Was this boat loaded with old acquaintances?

He was good-looking, of medium height, and with a slim but wiry physique. His short hair was almost sandy, and his eyes were hazel. His name was James McParlan, and he'd entered Parolando the day after Hermann's arrival. Hermann had talked to him about the Church of the Second Chance and found him polite but resistant.

What strengthened Hermann's memory of him was that McParlan had been the Pinkerton detective who'd infiltrated and eventually destroyed the Molly Maguires in the early 1870s. The Molly Maguires was a secret terrorist organization of Irish coal miners in the Pennsylvania counties of Schuylkill, Carbon, Columbia, and Luzerne. Göring, a twentieth-century German, would probably never have heard of it if he hadn't been an ardent student of the Sherlock Holmes stories. He'd read that the fictional Scowrers, Vermissa, and McMurdo of A. Conan Doyle's Holmes novel, *The Valley of Fear*, were based, respectively, on the real Molly Maguires, the Pennsylvania coal counties, and McParlan. That had led him to read Alan Pinkerton's book on McParlan's exploits, *The Molly Maguires*.

In October 1873 McParlan, under the name of James McKenna, succeeded in insinuating himself into the secret society. The young detective was in grave danger many times, but he slipped through safely by his courage, aggressiveness, and quick wits. After three years in this perilous disguise, he exposed the inner workings of the Maguires and the identities of its members. The chief terrorists were hanged; the power of the Molly Maguires was broken. And the mine owners continued for many decades to treat the miners as if they were serfs.

McParlan, going by Hermann on the way out, glanced at him. His face was expressionless. Yet Hermann believed that McParlan had recognized him. The eyes had flicked away too quickly. Moreover, the fellow was a trained detective, and he'd once told Göring that he never forgot a face.

Was it the discipline of a marine on duty which had prevented McParlan from reintroducing himself? Or was it for another reason?

Burton entered and joined the party. After a few minutes he went into the toilet by the elevator. Hermann excused himself and followed him in. Burton was at the far end of the urinal, and no one was near him. Hermann came up to his side and, while urinating, spoke in German in a low voice.

"Thanks for not telling your commander my natal name."

"I didn't do it for love of you," Burton said.

Burton dropped his kilt, turned, and went to a washbasin. Hermann quickly followed him. Under cover of the gushing faucets, he said, "I am not the Göring you knew."

"P'raps not. I fancy I don't like either of you."

Hermann burned to explain the difference of the two, but he dared not take the time. He hurried back to the observation room.

John was waiting to tell him the party was going to step out onto the deck. They would have a more open view of the lake, which the boat was just entering.

Ahead, for as far as they could see, rock spires of various heights and many shapes rose from the surface of the water. These were mostly rose-colored, but there were also black, brown, purple, green, scarlet, orange, and blue rocks. About one in twenty was striped horizontally in red, green, white, and blue, the stripes being of different widths.

Hermann told them then that at the western end of the lake the mountains curved in and formed a narrow strait about two hundred feet wide and between smooth vertical walls seven thousand feet high. The force of the current was so strong that no manual- or wind-driven vessel could go against it. The traffic by boat was all one-way, down-River, and there was little of that.

However, some travelers had long ago cut out a narrow path on the southern cliff. This was about five hundred feet above the strait and went a mile and a half to the end of the strait. So there was some foot traffic.

"Just beyond the strait is a rather narrow valley, though The River there is a mile wide. There are grailstones there, but no one lives there. I suppose because of the current, which is so strong it precludes fishing or sailing anywhere but through the straits. Then, too, The Valley gets little sunshine. There is, though, a sort of bay about a half-mile up where boats may anchor.

"A few miles above the bay, The Valley widens considerably. There begins the land of the enormous-nosed hairy giants, the titanthrops or ogres. From what I've heard, so many of these have been killed that half the population is now your ordinary-sized human."

Göring paused, knowing that what he would say would, or should, be vastly interesting to the others.

"It's estimated that it's *only* twenty thousand miles from the strait to the headwaters of The River."

He was trying to give John the idea that it might be better to keep on going. If the headwaters were so close, why should he stop here to fight? Especially, since he was likely to be defeated. Why not go to the headwaters and from there launch the expedition toward the misty tower?

John said, "Indeed."

If he had taken the bait, he gave no sign of having done so. He seemed interested only in the strait and the immediate area beyond it.

After some questions from John about these, Hermann understood what John was considering. The bay would be an excellent place for the rewinding. The strait would be near ideal for waiting for the *Not For Hire*. If the *Rex* could catch it while it was coming through the strait, it could loose some torpedoes in the passage. These would have to be remotely controlled, though, since the strait curved at least three times.

Also, if John docked in the bay, he would keep his crew from the pacifistic influence of the Second Chancers.

Göring's speculations on John's thinking was right. After a day's visit with La Viro, John up-anchored the *Rex* and took it through the strait. It anchored again at the bay, and a floating anchored dock was built from the shore to the vessel. From time to time, King John and some of his officers, or just his officers, would come in a launch to Aglejo. Though invited to stay overnight or longer, they never did so.

John assured La Viro that he was not going to venture out onto the lake for a battle.

La Viro pleaded with him to negotiate for an honorable peace with La Viro as intermediary.

John refused during the first two meetings with La Viro. Then, on the third, he surprised La Viro and Göring by agreeing.

"But I think it will be a waste of time and effort," John said. "Clemens is a monomaniac. I'm sure he thinks of only two things. Getting his boat back and killing me."

La Viro was happy that John was at least willing to make the effort. Hermann was not so happy. What John said and what John did were often not the same.

Despite La Viro's urgings, John refused to permit missionaries to talk to his crew about the Church. He had set up armed guards at the end of the cliff-path to insure that the missionaries didn't come over it. His excuse, of course, was that he didn't want to be attacked by Clemens' marines. La Viro told John that he had no right to prevent nonhostiles from crossing over. John replied that he had signed no agreement with anyone concerning passage on the path. He held it, and that made him the determiner of the rights.

Three months passed. Hermann waited for his chance to get Burton and Frigate to one side when they came to Aglejo. Their visits were very infrequent and when they did come in he could never get them alone.

One morning, Hermann was summoned to the Temple. La Viro gave him the news, which had just come via the relay drums. The *Not For Hire* would be at Aglejo in two weeks. Göring was to meet it at the same place he'd boarded the *Rex*.

Even though Clemens had not been friendly when Hermann had known him in Parolando, he hadn't been murderous. When Göring went up to the pilothouse, he was surprised to feel happy at seeing Clemens and the gigantic titanthrop, Joe Miller. Moreover, the American recognized him within four seconds of their introduction. Miller claimed to have known him within a second by his odor.

"Although," Miller said, "you don't thmell ekthactly as you uthed to. You thmell better than then."

"Perhaps it's the odor of sanctity," Hermann said and laughed.

Clemens grinned, and said, "Virtue and vice have their own chemistries? Well, why not? How do I smell after these forty years of travel, Joe?"

"Thomething like old panther pithth," Joe said.

It wasn't quite like old friends meeting after a long absence. But Göring felt that, for some reason, they were as pleased to see him as he was them. Perhaps it was a perverted kind of nostalgia. Or guilt may have played some part in it. They may have felt responsible for what had happened to him at Parolando. They shouldn't, of course, since Clemens had done his best to make him leave the state before something violent happened to him.

They told him in brief outline what had occurred since they'd last seen him. And he described his experiences since then.

They went down to the grand salon to get a drink and to introduce him to various notables. Cyrano de Bergerac was called down from the flight deck, where he'd been fencing.

The Frenchman remembered him, though not well. Clemens described again what Hermann had been doing, and then de Bergerac recalled the lecture Göring had given.

Time had certainly worked some changes with Clemens and de Bergerac, Hermann thought. The American seemed to have shed his great dislike for the Frenchman, to have forgiven him because he had taken Olivia Clemens as his mate. The two now were on easy terms, chatting, joking, laughing.

There came a time when the good time had to end. Hermann said, "I suppose you've heard that King John's boat came to Aglejo three months ago? And that it's waiting for you just beyond the strait at the western end of the lake?"

Clemens swore and said, "We've known that we were closing the gap between us fast. But no, we didn't know that he'd stopped running!"

Hermann described what had happened since he'd boarded the *Rex*.

"La Viro still hopes that you and John will be able to forgive each other. He says that after this long a time, it doesn't matter whose fault it was in the beginning. he says . . ."

Clemens' face was red and grim.

"It's easy enough for him to talk of forgiveness!" he said loudly. "Well, let him talk from now until doomsday about forgiveness, and I won't stop him! A sermon never hurt anybody, and it's often beneficial—if you need a nap.

"But I haven't come this far after all the hardships and heartaches and treacheries and griefs just to pat John on the head and tell him what a good boy he is beneath all that rottenness and then kiss and make up.

"'Here, John, you worked hard to get my boat and to keep it from all those thieving rascals that tried to take your hard-earned Riverboat away from you. What the hell, John, I loathed, despised, and detested you, but that was a long time ago. I don't carry a grudge long; I'm a good-hearted sap.'

"The hell I am!" Clemens roared. "I'm going to sink his boat, the boat I once loved so much! I wouldn't have it now! He's dishonored it, made it into crap, stunk it up! I'll sink it, get it out of sight. And one way or another, I'm ridding this world of John Lackland. When I'm done with him, his name'll be John Lacklife!"

"We were hoping," Hermann said, "that after all these years, two generations as they used to be counted, that your hatred had cooled, perhaps entirely died. That . . ."

"Well, sure, it did," Clemens said with a sarcastic tone. "There were minutes, days, weeks, even months, even a year now and then, that I didn't think of John. But when I tired of this eternal travel on The River, when I longed to go ashore and stay ashore and get the racket of the paddlewheels out of my ears and the never-ending routine, the three-times-a-day stop to recharge grails and batacitor, the always-going-on arguments to settle and the ever-recurring administrative details to manage and my heart stopping every once in a while when I saw a face that looked like my beloved Livy or Susy or Jean or Clara only to find out that she was none of them . . . Well, then when I tired and almost gave up, almost said, 'Here, Cyrano, you take over the captainship. I'm going ashore and get some rest and have a good time, and forget about this monstrous beauty and you take it on up The River and don't bring it back,' then I remembered John and what he'd done to me and what I was going to do to him. And then I'd gather my forces together, and I'd cry, 'Forward, onward, excelsior! Keep going until we've caught up with Evil John and sent him to the bottom of The River!' And that, the thought of my duty and my dearest desire, to make John squeal before I wrung his neck, is what's kept me going for, as you describe it, two generations!"

Hermann could only say, "It grieves me to hear that."

It was useless to say any more about that subject.

25

BURTON, SUFFERING AGAIN FROM HIS CURSED INSOMNIA, LEFT HIS CABIN quietly. Alice slept undisturbed. He went down the dimly lit corridor, out of the texas, and onto the landing deck of the *Rex*. The fog was building up below the railing of the B deck. The A deck was entirely shrouded. Directly above, the sky blazed brightly, but to the west clouds were swiftly moving toward the boat. On both sides of The Valley the mountains cut off much of the sky. Though the *Rex* was anchored in a small bay two miles up from the strait, The Valley had broadened only a little here. It was a cold place, gloomy, despondency-making. John had had a difficult time keeping up morale here.

Burton yawned, stretched, and thought about lighting up a cigarette or perhaps a cigar. Damn his sleeplessness! In sixty years on this world, he should have learned how to overcome the affliction which had lasted fifty years on Earth. (He'd been nineteen when the terrible affliction had struck him.)

Techniques to combat it had been offered aplenty to him. The Hindus had a dozen; the Moslems, another dozen. Several of the savage tribes of Tanganyika had their sure-fire remedies. And on this world, he'd tried a score or more. Nur el-Musafir, the Sufi, had taught him a technique which had seemed more efficacious than any he'd ever learned. But after three years, slowly, inching in night by night, Old Devil Insomnia had secured a good beachhead again. For some time, he'd been lucky if he got a good sleep two out of seven nights.

Nur had said, "You could conquer insomnia if you knew what was causing it. You could strike at the source."

"Yaas," Burton had replied. "If I knew what and where the source was, I could get my hands on it, I'd be able to conquer more than insomnia. I could conquer the world."

"First, you'd have to conquer yourself," the Moor had said. "But when you did that, you'd find out that it wasn't worthwhile ruling the world."

The two guards by the rear entrance to the texas were walking in the semidarkness of the landing deck, wheeling, marching to the middle of the deck, each solemnly presenting his rifle to the other's, wheeling, then striding back to the edge of the landing deck, wheeling, and so on.

During this four-hour watch, Tom Mix and Grapshink were on guard duty. Burton didn't hesitate to talk to them, since there were two guards at the front of the texas, two in the pilothouse, and many more at different parts of the boat. Ever since the raid by Clemens' men, John had set up night sentinels all over the boat.

Burton chatted for a while with Grapshink, a native Amerind, in his own tongue, Burton having taken the trouble to learn it. Tom Mix joined them, and he told them a dirty joke. They laughed, but afterward Burton said he'd heard a different version of it in the Ethiopian city of Harar. Grapshink confessed that he'd heard another version, too, when he was on Earth. This would have been about 30,000 B.C.

Burton told the two he'd be going on to check the other guards. He walked down the stairs to the B or main deck and went toward the stern. As he passed a diffused light in the fog, he saw something moving out of the corner of his left eye. Before he could turn toward it, he was struck on the head.

Some time later, he awoke on his back, staring upward into the fog. Sirens were wailing, some very near him. The back of his head hurt him very much. He felt the bump, winced, and his fingers came away sticky. When he struggled to his feet, swaying, dizzy, he saw that the lights were on all over the boat. People ran past him calling out. One stopped by him. Alice.

She cried out, "What happened?"

"I don't know," he said, "except that someone coshed me."

He started toward the bow but had to stop to steady himself with a hand against the wall.

"Here," she said, "I'll help you get to the sick bay."

"Sick bay be damned! Help me to the pilothouse. I have to report to the king."

"You're crazy," she said. "You may have a concussion or a fractured skull. You shouldn't even be walking. You should be on a stretcher."

He growled, "Nonsense," and started to walk. She made him put his arm around her shoulder so she could half-support him. They started again toward the bow. He heard the anchors being pulled up, the chains rattling in the holes. They passed people manning the steam machine guns and the rocket tubes.

Alice called out to a man, "What happened?"

"I don't know! Somebody said the big launch was stolen. The thieves took it up The River."

Burton thought that if that was true, he'd been slugged by someone posted to insure that the thieves weren't surprised.

The "thieves," he was sure, had been crew members. He didn't think that anybody could slip aboard unnoticed. The sonars, radar, and infrared detectors were operating at night and had been ever since the raid. Their operators dared not fall asleep. The last one who'd done that, ten years ago, had been thrown off the boat into The River two minutes after being caught.

Arriving at the pilothouse, Burton had to wait a few minutes before the busy king could speak to him. Burton reported what had happened to him. John wasn't at all sympathetic; he was beside himself with rage, cursing, giving orders, stomping around.

Finally, he said, "Go to sick bay, Gwalchgwynn. If the doctor says you're unfit for duty, Demugts will take over. There isn't much the marines can do now, anyway."

Burton said, "Yes, Sire," and he went to the C deck hospital.

Doctor Doyle x-rayed his skull, cleansed the wound on his head, bandaged it, and ordered him to lie down for a while.

"There's neither concussion or fracture. All you need is some rest."

Burton did so. Shortly thereafter, Strubewell's voice came over the loudspeakers. Twelve people were missing, seven men, five women.

John took over then, apparently too enraged to allow his first mate to call out the names of the missing. His voice shaking, he denounced the twelve as "treacherous dogs, mutinous swine, scurvy stinking polecats, cowardly jackals, yellow-bellied hyenas."

"Quite a menagerie," Burton said to Alice.

He listened to the roll call. All were suspected agents, all having claimed to have lived past 1983.

John thought they had deserted because they were afraid to fight.

If he weren't too furious to think straight, John would have remembered that the twelve had shown their courage in many battles.

Burton knew why they had fled. They wanted to get to the tower as quickly as possible, and they didn't want to be in a fight which they regarded as totally unnecessary. So they had stolen the launch and were now racing up-River as fast as possible. Undoubtedly, they were hoping that John wouldn't go after them, that he'd be too concerned with Clemens.

In fact, John had been worried that the *Not For Hire* might come up through the strait while the *Rex* was chasing after the launch. However, the guards on the path above the strait had a transceiver, and they would report instantly if the *Hire* moved toward the channel. Still, if the *Rex* was too far up The River, it couldn't get back in time to block the *Hire*.

Despite this, John was taking his chances. He was not going to allow the deserters to get away with the launch. He needed it for the coming battle. And he wanted desperately to catch and punish the twelve.

In the old days on Earth, he would have tortured them. He probably would like to put them to rack and wheel and fire now, but he knew that his crew, most of them anyway, wouldn't tolerate such barbarisms. They would permit the twelve to be shot, though they wouldn't relish the deed, because discipline did have to be maintained. Moreover, stealing the launch had compounded the felony.

Suddenly, Burton groaned. Alice said, "What's the matter, dear?"

"Nothing," he said. "Just a twinge."

Since there were other nurses around, he couldn't tell her that it had just occurred to him that Strubewell had stayed aboard. Why? Why hadn't he gone with the other agents?

And Podebrad! Podebrad, the Czech engineer, the chief suspect. His name wasn't on the list.

One more question to add to the dozens he would ask an agent someday. Perhaps he should not wait until *someday*. Why not go to John now and tell him the truth? John would have Strubewell and Podebrad into the brig and put them to the question with a speed unhampered by legalities and red tape.

No. It couldn't be done now. John wouldn't have the time to do this. He'd have to wait until after the battle. Besides, the two would just commit suicide.

Or would they?

Now that there were no resurrections, would an agent kill himself?

He might, Burton thought. Just because the Valleydwellers weren't resurrected was no proof that agents weren't. They could rise again somewhere else, in the vast underground chambers or in the tower.

Burton didn't believe this. If the agents were resurrected elsewhere, they wouldn't have hesitated to board the suicide express. They wouldn't now be traveling via paddlewheeler to get to the tower.

If he and Strubewell and Podebrad survived the battle, he was going to catch them unawares, knock them out before they could transmit the mental code which would release the poison in the little black balls in their forebrains, and then hypnotize them as they came out of unconsciousness.

That was satisfying to visualize. But in the meantime, why had the twelve taken off and the two stayed?

Had Strubewell and Podebrad remained on the boat so they could sabotage it if it looked as if John were going to catch the twelve?

That seemed the only explanation. In which case, Burton must go to John to expose them.

But would John believe him? Wouldn't he think that the blow on Burton's head had deranged him?

He might, but he'd have to be convinced when Burton brought in Alice, Kazz, Loghu, Frigate, Nur, Mix, London, and Umslopogaas as witnesses.

By then, however, Strubewell and Podebrad might find out about what was going on and flee. Worse, they might blow up the boat or whatever they were planning on doing.

Burton wiggled his finger at Alice. When she came, he told her softly to take a message to Nur el-Musafir. Nur was to station one or more of their group with Podebrad in the boiler room and Strubewell in the pilothouse. If either did something suspicious, something which could threaten the boat, he was to be clubbed on the head at once. If that wasn't possible, he was to be shot or stabbed.

Alice's eyes widened.

"Why?"

"I'll explain later!" he said fiercely. "Go while there's still time!"

Nur would figure out what the orders meant. And he'd see that they were somehow carried out. It wasn't going to be easy to get someone into the boiler room and the pilothouse. At the moment, everybody had his or her station. To leave it for any reason without authorization was a serious crime. Nur would have to think fast and cleverly to send somebody to watch the two.

And then Burton said, "I've got it!"

He picked up the sick-bay phone and called the pilothouse. The phone operator there was going to call Strubewell, but Burton insisted that he speak to the king instead. John was very annoyed, but he did as Burton requested and went down to the observation room. There he flicked a switch which made it impossible for their conversation to be listened to on the pilothouse line unless the line had been bugged.

"Sire," Burton said, "I've been thinking. How do we know that the deserters haven't planted a bomb on the boat? Then, if it looks as if we're going to catch them, they transmit a coded message to the receiver, and the explosives are set off."

After a short silence, John said, his voice a trifle high, "Do you think that's a possibility?"

"If I can think of it, then why shouldn't the deserters?"

"I'll start a search at once. If you're up to it, you join it."

John hung up. A minute later, Strubewell's voice bellowed over the loudspeakers. He gave orders that every inch of the vessel was to be examined for bombs. The officers were to organize parties at once. Strubewell laid out who was responsible for which area and told them to get going.

Burton smiled. It hadn't been necessary to reveal anything to John, and Podebrad and Strubewell would find themselves directing a search for the very bombs they may have hidden.

26

BURTON STARTED OUT THE DOOR. SINCE HE HADN'T BEEN ORDERED TO any area, he considered himself a free agent. He'd go to the boiler or A deck and inspect the engine room and the ammunition rooms.

Just as he started down the steps to B deck, he heard pistol shots and shouting. They seemed to come from below, so he hurried down, wincing with pain every time his foot hit a step. When he got to A deck he saw a crowd halfway down the boat by the railing. He walked to it, made his way through the people, and looked down at the object of attention.

It was an oiler named James McKenna. He was lying on his side, a pistol near his open hand. A tomahawk was firmly wedged in the side of his skull.

A huge Iroquoian, Dojiji, stepped forward, stooped, and wrenched the tomahawk loose.

"He shot at me and missed," he said.

King John should have issued orders by word of mouth, not by the loudspeaker system. Then McKenna might have been caught while in the act of pressing the ten pounds of plastic explosive against the hull in a dark corner of the engine room. It really made no difference, however. McKenna had walked away from the alcove the moment he'd heard the search order. He had been cool, and his bearing was nonchalant. But an electrician's mate had seen him and challenged him, and McKenna had shot him. He had run then and shot and killed a man and a woman on his way to the railing deck outside. A search party, running toward him, had shot at him and failed to hit him. He'd wounded one of them but had missed Dojiji. Now McKenna lay dead, unable to tell them why he had tried to blow up the boat.

King John came down to look at the bomb. The clock was attached by wires to the fuse and the shapeless mass of plastic. Its hand indicated 10.20 minutes to go.

"There's enough to blow a hole in the hull bigger than the starboard side itself," a bomb expert said cheerfully. "Shall I remove it, Sire?"

"Yes. At once," King John said coolly. "One thing, though. This doesn't have a receiver radio, too, does it?"

"No, Your Majesty."

John had frowned. He said, "Very strange. I just don't understand this. Why should the deserters leave one of their number behind to set the time clock when they could far easier have blown it with a wireless frequency? McKenna could have been with them. They'd not have to put one of their own in danger. It doesn't make sense."

Burton was with the group of officers accompanying John. He said nothing. Why bother to enlighten him, if indeed what he had to offer was enlightening?

McKenna had shown up immediately after the raid from the *Parseval*, and he'd volunteered to replace one of the men killed in it. It seemed evident to Burton, or at least a strong possibility, that McKenna had been dropped off from a plane or via parachute or glider from the airship *Parseval*. What did the twentieth-century call such people? The . . . "fifth column" . . . that was it. Clemens had planted this man for the day when the *Not For Hire* caught up with the *Rex*. He'd been ordered to blow up the boat when that day came.

What Burton didn't understand was why Clemens had told McKenna to wait until then. Why hadn't McKenna blown the boat at the first opportunity? Why wait for forty years? Especially since it was very likely that McKenna, after living with the *Rex*ites for so many years, might have found himself sympathetic with them? He'd be isolated from his fellows on the *Not For Hire* and almost inevitably, and subtly, his loyalties would transfer from those who d become a distant memory to those he lived intimately with for a long time.

Or had Clemens not considered that?

That wasn't probable. As anyone who'd read his works knew, Clemens was a master psychologist.

It was possible that Clemens had given McKenna orders not to destroy the *Rex* unless it was absolutely necessary.

King John gestured at the corpse and said, "Throw that filth into The River."

It was done. Burton would have liked to find an excuse to have the body taken to the morgue. There he could open up the skull and inspect the cerebrum for a tiny black ball. Too late. McKenna would be opened up only by the fish.

Whatever had happened, it was over for McKenna. And though the one bomb had been found, the search continued for more. At last, it was called off. There was no secretly planted explosive device in the vessel or outside it. Divers had gone over every inch of the exterior of the hull.

Burton thought that the deserters, if they'd had their wits about them, would have made provisions to sink the craft before leaving. Then neither it nor the airplanes could have pursued them. But they were agents, loathing violence though able to deal with it if the situation required.

There had been only one way to make sure that McKenna was an agent of the Ethicals or an agent of Clemens'.

One thing was certain. Podebrad and Strubewell were not saboteurs.

But why had they stayed aboard?

He thought about the problem, puzzling over it a while, then said, "Hah!"

They were volunteers. They'd elected to remain with the boat because there was someone or someones on the *Not For Hire* whom they wanted to make contact with. He or she or they might be enemies or friends, but the two had their reasons for wanting to get hold of the person or persons. So, they'd made the very risky decision to stay with the *Rex* through the battle. If the *Rex* won, which it might, though the odds now seemed against it, then the two, if they survived, would be able to get to whoever it was that was on Clemens' boat.

But . . . how would the two know that the whoever was on the *Not For Hire?*

They might have some secret method of communication. Just what, Burton couldn't imagine.

He got to thinking about the agents who'd deserted. Did they know about the boats in the cave on the shore of the polar sea and the door at the base of the tower?

He hoped that they hadn't heard Paheri's tale. As far as he knew, only he and Alice, Frigate, Loghu, Nur, London, Mix, Kazz, and Umslopogaas knew about the ancient Egyptian's discovery. That is, they were the only ones on the boat who had. There would be others, perhaps many many people, who had heard Paheri's tale first-hand and then second-, third- and fourth-hand.

However, for all he knew, X was among the deserters. Which meant that the agents would know about the hidden entrance, too.

Not necessarily. X might be posing as a friendly agent. He'd fled with them but planned to use them to get him to the tower. And then he'd see that they, like Akhenaton and the other Egyptians of his party, were rendered unconscious or dead.

Or perhaps . . . Podebrad and Strubewell somehow knew that X was on the *Not For Hire.*

But . . . either one of the two could be X.

Burton shrugged. He'd just have to let events take their course until he saw a chance to influence them. Then he'd pounce like an owl on a mouse.

That wasn't a good simile. The agents and the Ethicals were potentially more like tigers.

It didn't make any difference to him. He was going to attack when he had to.

Again, he considered telling King John everything. Thus, he'd insure that the captured agents would not be executed on the spot. Of course, the agent would have to be knocked out before he could commit suicide. But with twelve to seize, fourteen if Strubewell and Podebrad were included, surely at least one would be unconscious . . . well, he'd wait a little more. He might not have to divulge anything to John.

The boat had stopped to anchor again while the scuba divers had inspected the hull. It had then resumed its up-River course at top speed. But it put into shore again to hook up the metal cap to a grailstone. Dawn came; the stones thundered and lightninged. The cap was swung back into the boat, and it sped after the deserters once more. Shortly after breakfast, the motors of three planes were warmed up. Then Voss and Okabe took off in their biplane fighters and the torpedo-bomber roared out of the swung-open stern section from the launch dock.

The pilots would be able to spot the launch within an hour or two. What would happen after that was up to them, within the limits of John's orders. He did not want the launch sunk or badly damaged because he needed it in the expected battle. The planes could fire on the launch and keep it from continuing up-River, if possible. They must delay it until the *Rex* could catch up with it.

An hour and twenty-two minutes after flyoff, Okabe reported in. The launch was sighted, and he'd tried to talk to the deserters by radio. He'd gotten no reply. The three planes would swing down over the boat in single file and fire machine guns at it. Not for long, however, since the lead bullets were too valuable, too needed for the fight against the *Not For Hire*. If a few bursts didn't make the deserters surrender or turn down-River or abandon the launch, then bombs would be dropped near the vessel.

Okabe also reported that the launch was several miles past the point where The Valley suddenly widened out. This was the area to which the launch had gone two months ago during the rewinding. Its crew had talked to many of the titanthrops, in Esperanto, of course, in an effort to recruit about forty as marines. King John had envisioned closing in with the *Not For Hire* and sending the forty ogres over in the van of the boarders. Two score like Joe Miller would wipe the decks of Clemens' boat clean in short order. Nor would the mighty Miller be able to withstand the onslaught of so many of his fellows.

Much to John's disgust and disappointment, his men had discovered that every titanthrop interviewed was a member of the Church of the Second Chance. They refused to fight and in fact tried to convert the crew.

It was probable that there were titanthrops who had not succumbed to the preachings of the missionaries. But there wasn't time to look for them.

Now the airplanes lowered toward the launch while the people on shore, part of them average-sized Homo sapiens, part veritable Brobdingnags, lined the banks to watch these machines.

Suddenly, Okabe said, "The launch is heading for the right bank!"

He dived but not to fire. He couldn't have hit the launch without also hitting many locals, and he was under orders not to anger them in any way if he could help it. John didn't want to go through a hostile area after the *Rex* had sunk the *Not For Hire*.

"The deserters are jumping out of the launch and wading to the bank!" Okabe said. "The launch is drifting with the current!"

John cursed and then ordered the torpedo-bomber to land on The River. Its gunner must board the launch and bring it back to the *Rex*. And he must do it quickly before some local decided to swim out and appropriate the launch for himself.

"The deserters are mingled with the crowds," Okabe said. "I imagine they'll head for the hills after we've left."

"God's teeth!" John said. "We'll never be able to find them!"

Burton, in the pilothouse at this time, made no comment. He knew that the agents would later steal a sailboat and continue up-River. The *Rex* would overtake it, if the *Rex* wasn't sunk or too damaged to continue.

A few minutes after the launch was reberthed in the *Rex* and the two fighters had landed, a light on the pilothouse radio glowed orange. The operator's eyes widened, and he was so astonished he couldn't speak for a moment. For thirty years he and his fellow operators had waited for this to happen, though they'd not really expected it would.

At last the operator got the words out.

"Sire, Sire! The Clemens frequency!"

The frequency which the *Not For Hire* used was, of course, known. It could have been changed by Clemens, though even then the radio of the *Rex* would have scanned the spectrum until it had located it. But apparently Clemens had never seen any reason to shift to another wavelength. The few times that the *Rex* had received transmission from the *Not For Hire*, the message had been scrambled.

Not now. The message was not for the *Parseval* or the airplanes or launches of the *Not For Hire*. It was in nonscrambled Esperanto and meant for the *Rex*.

The speaker was not Sam Clemens himself. He was John Byron, Clemens' chief executive officer. And he wished to talk to, not King John, but his chief officer.

John, who'd gone down to his quarters for sleep or dalliance with his current cabinmate, or both, was summoned. Strubewell did not dare to talk to Byron until his commander authorized it. John was at first determined to talk directly to Clemens. But Clemens, through Byron, refused to do that nor would he say why.

John replied, through his first mate, that there would be no communication at all then. But, after a minute, while the radio hissed and crackled, Byron said that he had a message to deliver, a "proposition." His commander dared not speak to John face to face, as it were. Clemens was afraid that he'd lose his temper and cuss out King John as no one else in the universe had ever been cussed out before. And that included Jehovah's denunciation of Satan before He hurled him headlong from Heaven.

Clemens had a sporting offer to make John. However, it was necessary, as John should now understand, that it be transmitted via intermediaries. After waiting half an hour to make Clemens swear and fume and fret, John replied via Strubewell.

Burton was again in the pilothouse and heard everything from the beginning. He was staggered when Clemens' "proposition" was put forth.

John heard it all out, then replied that he'd have to talk about this to Werner Voss and Kenji Okabe, his top fighter pilots. He couldn't order them to accept these conditions. And, by the way, who were Clemens' two pilots?

Byron said that they were William Barker, a Canadian, and Georges Guynemer, a Frenchman. Both were famous aces of World War I.

There was more identification of the pilots. Their histories were expanded upon. John called Voss and Okabe to the pilothouse, and he told them what had happened.

They were astounded. But after they'd recovered, they talked to each other.

And then Okabe said, "Sire, we have been flying for twenty years for you. It's mostly been dull work though occasionally dangerous. We've been waiting for this moment; we've known that it would happen. We won't be facing fellow nationals or former allies, though I understand that my country was an ally of England and France in World War I.

"We will do this. We look forward to it."

Burton thought, what are we? King Arthur's knights? Idiots? Or both?

Nevertheless, part of him approved deeply and was very excited.

27

THE *NOT FOR HIRE* HAD BEEN ANCHORED NEAR THE RIGHT BANK A FEW miles up from the entrance to the lake. Göring was taken to Aglejo by the launch *Post No Bills*. Clemens sent his apologies to La Viro for not coming to meet him at once. Unfortunately, he said, a previous engagement had held him up. But late tomorrow or possibly the day after, he would come to the temple.

Göring had begged Clemens to make overtures of peace to King John. Clemens, as Hermann had expected, had refused to do so.

"The final act of this drama has been too long delayed. The damn intermission was forty years long. Now nothing is going to stop its being staged."

"This isn't a theater," Hermann said. "Real blood will be shed. Real pain will be felt. The deaths won't be faked. And for what?"

"For what matters," Clemens said. "I don't want to talk about it any more."

He puffed angrily on his big green cigar. Göring silently blessed him with the three-fingered gesture of the Church and left the pilothouse.

All day long the boat had been readied. The thick duraluminum plates with the small portholes were secured over the windows. Thick duraluminum doors were secured to the exterior entrances of the corridors and passageways. The ammunition was checked. The steam machine guns were fired for a few rounds. The elevation and vertical and horizontal movement machines of the 88-millimeter cannons were tested. Rockets were placed in the launching tubes, and the machinery for bringing more from the bowels of the A deck was checked. The one cannon using compressed air was tested. The airplanes were taken up for a wringout after being fully armed. The launches were also armed. The radar, sonar, and infrared detectors were given a checkout. The boarding bridges were extended and withdrawn.

Every station conducted a dozen drills.

After the batacitor and the grails were charged at evening, the *Not For Hire* went for a five-mile circular cruise, and more drills were conducted. Radar swept the lake and reported that the *Rex* was not within its range.

Before the crew went to bed, Clemens talked to almost all the crew in the grand salon. His short almost entirely serious speech went out over the loudspeakers to those on duty.

"We've had a fantastically long ride up The River, the longest river in the universe, perhaps. We've had ups and downs, our tragedies, our pains, our boredoms, our comedies, our cowardly deeds, our heroic. We've faced death many times. We've seen those we loved die, though we've been somewhat recompensed for this by also seeing those we hated die.

"It's been a long long ride. We've gone 7,200,020 miles. That's about half of the estimated 14,500,000 miles of The River. It's been a long voyage. But if we'd walked it, we'd still be walking. We would've walked only about 127,500 miles, leaving more than 7,000,000 miles to go.

"Everybody who signed on knew before signing what the ride on the greatest and most luxurious vessel in the world would cost him. He and she were made aware of the price of the ticket. This ride is paid for at the end, not the beginning.

"I know each of you well, as well as one human being can know another. You were all hand-picked, and you've all justified my judgment. You've gone through many tests and passed them with flying marks. So I have complete confidence that you'll pass the final, the hardest, test tomorrow.

"I'm making this sound like an arithmetic examination in high school or like the speech a football coach gives before his team goes out to play. I'm sorry about that. This test, this game, is deadly, and some of you alive today won't be by tomorrow's end. But you knew the price when you signed up, and none should think of welshing.

"But after tomorrow is over . . ."

He paused to look around. Joe Miller, sitting on a huge chair on the podium, looked sad, and tears were trickling down his craggy cheeks.

Little de Marbot leaped up then and raised his glass of liquor and cried, "Three cheers for our commander and a toast to him!"

Everybody huzzaed loudly. After they had drunk, tall big-nosed rapier-thin de Bergerac stood up and said, "And a toast to victory! Not to mention death and damnation to John Lackland!"

Sam stayed up late that night. He paced back and forth for a while in the pilothouse. Though the boat was anchored, there was a full watch in the room. The *Not For Hire* could up-anchor and paddlewheel into the lake at top speed within three minutes. If John should try a night attack despite his promises not to, Sam's vessel would be ready for it.

The pilothouse watch said little. Sam left them with a good night and walked for a few minutes on top of the flight deck. Ashore, many fires blazed. The Virolanders knew what was coming tomorrow, and they were too excited, too apprehensive, to get to sleep at their customary time. Earlier, La Viro himself had appeared on the bank in a fishing boat and requested permission to board. Clemens had told him, through a bullhorn, that he was certainly glad to meet him. But he could not discuss anything until after tomorrow. Sorry. That was the way it had to be.

The big dark man with the lugubrious features had departed, though not before blessing Sam. Sam felt ashamed.

Now Sam walked the length of every deck on both sides to test the alertness of the sentries. He was happy with the results, and he decided it was foolish to spend any more time prowling the boat. Besides, Gwenafra would be expecting him to come to bed. She'd probably want to make love, too, because one or both of them might not be alive after tomorrow. He didn't feel like it at the moment, but she had some irresistible ways of arousing his spirits, among other things.

He was right. She did insist on it, but when his lack of enthusiasm became obvious, and she couldn't generate any, she quit. Nor did she reproach him. She only asked that he hold her tight and that he talk to her. It was seldom that Sam didn't have time to talk, so they spent at least two hours in conversation.

Shortly before they drifted into sleep, Gwenafra said, "I wonder if Burton could be on the *Rex*? Wouldn't that be funny if he were? I mean, peculiar, not laughable. It would also be horrible."

"You've never gotten over your little-girl crush on him, have you?" Sam said. "He must have been something. To you, anyway."

"No, I haven't," she said, "though I couldn't be sure, of course, that I'd like him now. Still, what if he were one of King John's men, and we killed him? I'd feel terrible. Or what if someone *you* loved were on the *Rex*?"

"It's just not very probable," he said. "I'm not going to worry about it."

But he did. Long after Gwenafra was breathing the easy breath of the deep sleeper, he lay awake. What if Livy were on the *Rex*? No, she wouldn't be. After all, it was one of John's men who'd killed her in Parolando. She'd never come aboard his boat. Not, that is, unless she wanted to kill him for revenge. No, she wouldn't do that. She was too gentle for that, even though she'd fight fiercely in defense of her loved ones. But revenge? No.

Clara? Jean? Susy? Could one of them be on the *Rex*? The chances were very very low that they could be. Yet . . . the mathematically improbable sometimes happened. And a missile fired from his boat might kill her. And she'd be lost forever to him since there were no more resurrections.

Almost, almost, he rose from bed and went to the pilothouse and had the radio operator send a message to the *Rex*. A message that he would like to make peace, to call off the battle and the hatred and lust for revenge.

Almost.

John would never agree anyway.

How did he, Sam, know that he wouldn't unless he tested him?

No. John was incorrigible. As stubborn as his enemy, Sam Clemens.

"I'm sick," Sam said.

After a while, he slid into sleep.

Erik Bloodaxe pursued him with his double-headed axe. Sam ran as he had run in so many nightmares about this terrible Norseman. Behind him, Erik screamed, "*Bikkja!* Droppings of Ratatosk! I told you I'd wait for you near the headwaters of The River! Die, you rotten backstabber! Die!"

Sam awoke moaning, sweating, his heart pounding.

What irony, what poetic justice, what retribution if Erik should happen to be on the *Rex*.

Gwenafra murmured something. Sam patted her bare back and said, softly, "Sleep, little innocent. You never had to murder anyone, and I hope you never will."

But, in a way, wasn't she being called on to commit murder tomorrow?

"This is too much," he said. "I must sleep. I must be in top physical and mental condition tomorrow. Otherwise . . . an error on my part . . . fatigue . . . who knows?"

But the *Not For Hire* was too much larger than the *Rex*, too much more heavily armored and armed, not to win.

He must sleep.

He sat up suddenly, staring. Sirens were wailing. And from the intercom on the wall, Third Mate Cregar shouted, "Captain! Captain! Wake up! Wake up!"

Clemens rolled out of bed and crossed to the intercom. He said, "Yes, what is it?"

John was making a sneak attack? The rotten son of a bitch!

"The infrared operators report that seven people have gone overboard, Captain! Deserters, it looks like!"

So . . . his little speech about everybody having passed the test, about their proven courage, had been wrong. Some men and women had lost their bravery. Or, he thought, had come to their senses. And they'd taken off. Just as he had when the War Between the States had started. After two weeks in the Confederate volunteer irregulars in Missouri, after that innocent passerby had been shot by one of his comrades, he had deserted and gone west.

He didn't really blame the seven. He couldn't allow anyone to know that he felt that way, of course. He'd have to put on a stern face, rave and rant a little, curse the rats and so on. For the sake of discipline and morale, he must.

He had no sooner stepped into the elevator to go up to the pilothouse than the revelation came.

The seven were not cowards. They were agents.

They had no reason to stay aboard and perhaps be killed. They had a higher duty than to Clemens and the *Not For Hire*.

He walked into the pilothouse. The lights were on all over the vessel. Several searchlights showed some men and women carrying grails on the bank. They were running as if their deepest fears had been embodied and were about to seize them.

"Shall we fire on them?" Cregar said.

"No," Sam said. "We might hit some of the locals. Let them go. We can always pick them up after the battle."

The seven would undoubtedly take sanctuary in the temple. La Viro wouldn't turn them over to Clemens.

Sam ordered Cregar to make a roll call. When the missing seven were identified, Sam looked at the list of names on the message screen. Four men and three women. All had claimed to have lived after 1983. His suspicions about this claim were valid. But it was too late to do anything about it.

No. Just now he couldn't act. But after the battle he would find some way to abduct the seven and to question them. They knew enough to clear up at least half of the mysteries that perplexed him. Perhaps they knew enough to clear up all.

He spoke to Cregar.

"Turn off the sirens. Tell the crew that it's a false alarm, to go back to sleep. Good night."

It wasn't a good night, though. He woke up many times, and he had some frightening nightmares.

SECTION 9

The First and Last Dogfight on the Riverworld

28

Hɪɢʜ ɴᴏᴏɴ ɪɴ ᴛʜᴇ ᴠᴀʟʟᴇʏ ᴏꜰ Vɪʀᴏʟᴀɴᴅᴏ.

For thirty years, the sky beneath the zenith sun had been a kaleidoscope of multicolored gliders and balloons. Today, the blue was as unflecked as a baby's eye. The River, which was always streaked with boats, with white, red, black, green, violet, purple, orange, and yellow sails, was today a solid green-blue.

The drums beat along both banks. *Stay away from the air and the water and keep away from the banks.*

Despite this, multitudes crowded the left bank. The majority, however, were on the spires or the bridges among the spires. They were eager to see the battle, their curiosity overriding their fear. No amount of exhortations by La Viro to stay on the hills could keep them away from this spectacle. They ignored the wardens who tried to press them back to a safe distance. Not having experienced anything like twentieth-century weapons, or, indeed, any weapons more advanced than those of 1 ᴀ.ᴅ., they had no idea of what would happen. Few of them had seen violence on even a small scale. And so the innocents flocked to the plains or climbed the spires.

La Viro, on his knees in the temple, prayed.

Hermann Göring, having failed to console him, went up a ladder to the top of a rock tower. Though he hated this viciousness, he intended to watch it. And, he had to admit to himself, he was as excited as a child awaiting the first act of a circus. It was deplorable; he had a long way to go before the old Göring was completely destroyed. But he could not stay away from the battle and its bloodshed. No doubt, he would regret this bitterly. But then nothing like this had ever happened before on the Riverworld. Nor would it happen again.

He was not going to miss it. In fact, for a moment, he longed to be flying one of the airplanes.

Yes, he had a long way to go. Meanwhile, he might as well enjoy this as much as he could. He was willing to pay for it with soul-suffering afterward.

The giant boats, the *Not For Hire* and the *Rex Grandissimus,* plowed through the waters, headed for each other. They were at this time separated by six miles. The agreement was that when they were five miles apart, they would stop. Unless, that is, the air battle was over before then. After that, everything went, no holds barred, may the best boat win.

Sam Clemens paced the deck of the pilothouse. For an hour, he had been checking all stations and had been rehearsing the battle plan. The crew assigned to the SW were in A deck now, waiting. When the signal came, they would bring up the SW and mount it behind the thick steel shield which had once protected the fore steam machine gun. This had been removed, and the platform which had held the gun was ready for the SW.

The steam-gun crew had been startled when the orders had come down to remove it. They had asked questions which were not answered. Rumors flew through the boat from prow to stern, from deck to deck. Why had the captain made this strange move? What was going on?

Meanwhile, Clemens had talked three times to William Fermor, the marine lieutenant guarding the SW crew. Sam had impressed on him the importance of his duty.

"I am still worried about John's agents," he said. "I know that everybody has been triple-cleared. But that doesn't mean much. Any saboteur sent by John will be as full of duplicity as a Missouri barnyard is of crap. I want everybody who comes near the SW room checked."

"What could they do?" Fermor said, referring to the SW men. "None of them are armed. I even looked under their kilts to make sure they're not concealing anything there. They did not like that, I tell you. They feel that they should be trusted."

"They should understand the necessity," Clemens said.

The control-room chronometer indicated 11:30. Clemens looked out on the rear port. The flight deck was ready. The airplanes had been brought up on the elevators, and one was now mounted on the steam catapult at the far end of the deck. There were two, the only single-seaters to survive the long voyage, and these had been wrecked and repaired several times.

Both original single-seaters, monoplanes, had been destroyed, one in battle, one in an accident. The two replacements, constructed from parts from the storage rooms, were biplanes with in-line alcohol-burning motors capable of pulling them at 150 miles per hour at ground-level. Originally, they had been fueled by synthetic gasoline, but the supply of this had long ago run out. Twin belt-fed .50-caliber machine guns were on the nose just ahead of the open cockpit. They were capable of firing lead bullets from the brass cartridges at five hundred rounds a minute. The ammunition had been stored through the voyage for just such an event as today's. Several days ago, the cartridges had been refilled with new charges and each had been rechecked for exact length, width, and straightness to insure against their jamming the guns.

Sam checked the chronometer again and then went down the elevator to the flight deck. A small jeep carried him to the planes, where the flight crew, the reserve pilots, and two chief pilots waited.

Both craft were painted white, and on the rudder and on the underside of the lower wings of each was painted a scarlet phoenix.

One bore on its sides a red stork in flight. Just below the cockpit were letters in black. *Vieux Charles*. Old Charlie. Georges Guynemer's nickname for the planes he had flown during World War I.

On each side of the cockpit of the other plane was the head of a black and barking dog.

Both airmen were dressed in white palefish leather. Their knee-length boots were trimmed with red, as were their jodphurs. Their jackets bore a scarlet phoenix on the left breast. The flier's leather helmets were topped by a tiny spike, the tip of a hornfish horn. Their goggles were edged with scarlet. Their gloves were white, but the gauntlets were red. They were standing by Old Charlie, talking earnestly with each other, when Clemens got out of the jeep. As he approached them, they snapped to a salute.

Clemens was silent for a moment, eyeing them. Though the exploits of the two men had happened after he had died, he was thoroughly conversant with them.

Georges Guynemer was a thin man of medium height with burning black eyes and a face of almost feminine beauty. At all times, or, at least, outside of his cabin, he was as taut as a violin string or a guy wire. This was the man whom the French had called "the Ace of Aces." There were others, Nungesser, Dorme, and Fonck, who had shot more Boches out of the sky. But then they saw more action, since Georges' career had been ended relatively early.

The Frenchman was one of those natural fliers who automatically became part of the machine, an airborne centaur. He was also an excellent mechanic and technician, as careful in checking out his airplane and weapons or devising improvements as the famous Mannock and Rickenbacker. During the Great War, he had seemed to exist for nothing but flying and air-fighting. As far as was then known, he had nothing to do with women as lovers. His only confidante was his sister, Yvonne. He was a master of aerobatics but seldom used this talent in the air. He roared into battle using "the thrust direct," as the French fencers called it. He was as wild and uncautious as his English counterpart, the great Albert Ball. Like him, he loved to fly alone and, when he encountered a group of the enemy, no matter how large it was, he attacked.

It was seldom that he did not return with his Nieuport or Spad full of bullet holes.

This was not the way to live a long life in a war in which the average life of a pilot was three weeks. Yet he managed fifty-three victories before he himself fell.

One of his comrades wrote that when Guynemer got into the cockpit to take off, "the look on his face was appalling. The glances of his eyes were like blows."

Yet this was the man who had been rejected by the French ground services as being unfit for duty. He was frail and easily caught cold, coughed much, and was unable to relax in the boisterous conviviality of his mates after the day's fighting was done. He looked like a consumptive and probably was.

But the French loved him, and on that black day of April 11, 1917, when he died, the whole nation went into mourning. For a generation afterward, the French schoolchildren were taught the legend that he had flown so high that the angels would not let him come back to Earth.

The truth, as known in those days, was that he had been alone as usual, and, somehow, a much lesser flier, a Lieutenant Wissemann, had shot him down. The plane had crashed into mud which was being churned by the shells of a great artillery duel. Before the thousands of explosions were done, Guynemer and his machine were blown to bits, mixed with mire, and completely disintegrated. Flesh and bone and metal became, not dust, but mud.

On the Riverworld, Georges had himself cleared up the mystery. While darting in and out of the clouds, hoping to surprise a Boche, or a dozen Boches—it made no difference to him—he had started to cough. The rackings got worse, and, suddenly, blood poured out of his mouth, running down his leather fur-lined *combinaison*. His fears that he had tuberculosis were now justified. But he could do nothing about it.

Even as his vitality drained away and his eyesight faded, he saw a German fighter plane approaching. Though dying, or believing that he was dying, he turned toward the enemy. His machine guns chattered, but his deadly marksmanship had deserted him. The German zoomed upward, and Guynemer turned Old Charlie tightly to follow him. For a moment, he lost him. Then bullets pierced his windshield from behind. And then . . . unconsciousness.

He awoke naked upon the Riverbank.

Now he did not suffer from the white plague, and his flesh had filled out a little. But his intensity was still with him, though not as much as in 1917. He shared a cabin with a woman who now sat crying in it.

William George Barker, a Canadian, was a natural flier who had performed the amazing feat of soloing after only one hour of instruction.

On October 27, 1918, as major of the No. 201 Squadron of the RAF, he was flying alone in the new Sopwith Snipe. At twenty thousand feet over the Marmal Forest, he shot down a two-seater observation plane. One of its crew saved himself by parachuting. Barker was interested and perhaps a little angered when he saw this. Parachutes were forbidden to the Allied fliers.

Suddenly, a Fokker appeared, and a bullet entered his right thigh. His Snipe went into a spin, but he pulled it out, only to find himself surrounded by fifteen Fokkers. Two of these he hammered with bullets and drove away. Another, hit within a range of ten yards, flamed out. But Barker was wounded again, this time in the left leg.

He lost consciousness, regaining it just in time to bring his plane out of another spin. From twelve to fifteen Fokkers were around him. At less than five yards, he shot the tail off of one, only to have his left elbow shattered by a bullet from a Spandau machine gun.

Once more, he fainted, came to his senses, and found himself in the midst of about twelve Germans. Smoke was pouring from the Snipe. Believing that he was on fire and so doomed, he determined to ram one of the Boches. Just as the two planes were about to collide, he changed his mind. Firing, he sent the other craft up in flames.

Diving away, he reached the British lines, crashing near an observation balloon but alive.

This was Barker's last flight, reckoned by all authorities as the greatest one-man aerial battle of WWI against overwhelming odds. Barker was in a coma for two weeks, and when he awoke the war was over. He was given the Victoria Cross for this exploit, but for a long time he had to use canes to walk and an arm-sling. Despite his crippling pain, he returned to flying, and helped organize the Royal Canadian Air Force. In partnership with the great ace William Bishop, he established the first large Canadian airline.

He died in 1930, while making a test flight of a new plane which crashed for no determinable reason. His official score was fifty enemy aircraft, though other records tallied it as fifty-three.

Guynemer also claimed fifty-three.

Clemens shook the hands of the two men.

"I'm against dueling, as you well know," he said. "I ridiculed the notion in my books, and I've talked to you many times of how I loathed the old Southron wickedness of settling disputes by killing. Though I suppose that anybody that's foolish enough to believe in that kind of arbitration ought to be killed.

"Now, I wouldn't have objected to this aerial duel at all if I knew that you'd be dead today and alive the next, as in the old days. But this is for real. I did have reservations, as Sitting Bull said to Custer, but you two seemed so eager, like warhorses hearing a trumpet call, that I saw no reason to turn down John's offer.

"Still, I wonder what's behind this. Bad John may be planning something treacherous. I gave my consent because I talked to one of his officers, men I knew or knew of, and they're honest honorable men. Though what men like William Goffe and Peder Tordenskjöld are doing on that boat, serving under that evil man, I can't imagine. He must have changed his ways, though I refuse to believe that he has changed the inner man.

"In any event, they assured me that everything was on the up and up. Their two men plan to leave the boat at the same time you do. Their planes will carry only machine guns, no rockets."

Barker said, "We've gone over all this, Sam. We think you're—we're—in the right. After all, John did steal your boat and he tried to kill you. And we know he's an evil man. Besides . . ."

"Besides, you two can't resist the chance to get into action again," Sam said. "You're suffering from nostalgia. You've forgotten how brutal and bloody those times were, haven't you?"

Guynemer said impatiently, "If they were not evil, they would not be on the *Rex*. Besides, we would be cowards if we did not accept their challenge."

Barker said. "We have to warm up the motors."

Sam Clemens said, "Well, I shouldn't even be talking like this. So long, boys. And good luck. May the best men win, and I'm sure you'll be the best!"

He shook hands again and walked to one side. This was both brave and foolish, he thought, but he had given his consent. The last-minute resumming up of the situation was due to his nervousness. He shouldn't have said anything. But, to tell the truth, he was looking forward to this. It was like the jousts of the knights of old. He hated those knights, since, historically, they were oppressors and bleeders of the peasants and the lower classes and rather murderous to their own class. A filthy bloody-minded bunch in reality. However, there was the reality, and there was the myth. Myth always put blinders on men, and perhaps there was something good to be said for myth. The ideal was the light; the real, the shadow.

Here were two exceptionally capable and courageous men, going to fight to the death in a prearranged duel. For what reason? Neither had to prove himself; they had done that long ago when the proving meant something.

What was it? Machismo? Definitely not.

Whatever their motive, they were secretly pleasing Clemens. For one thing, if they could down John's fliers, then they could go on to strafe the *Rex*. Of course, if they lost, then John's pilots would be raking the *Not For Hire*. He preferred not to think about that.

But the main source of pleasure was watching the combat. It was childish, or, at least, not mature. But like most men and many women, he enjoyed sport as a spectator. And this was a sporting event, however fatal for the participants. The Romans certainly knew what they were doing when they put on the gladiatorial combats.

Sam was startled when a trumpet call rang out. This was immediately followed by the stirring "Up in the Wild Blue," composed by Gioacchino Rossini for the boat's air force. The music, however, was electronically produced.

Barker, as commander, was the first to climb into the cockpit. The propeller turned slowly with a whine, then began whirling swiftly. Guynemer got into his plane. The people lining the edge of the flight deck and crowding the lower two rooms of the pilothouse cheered. Presently, the roar of the motor of Barker's fighter drowned out the huzzahs and hurrays.

Sam Clemens looked up at the control room. The executive officer, John Byron, stood at the stern port of the control room, ready to signal the captain. As soon as the chronometer indicated 12:00, he would drop a scarlet cloth from the port.

A woman burst from the crowd by the edge of the deck and threw bouquets of irontree blooms into the cockpits. Guynemer, looking through goggles, smiled and waved his bouquet. Barker raised his blooms as if to throw them out, then changed his mind.

Sam looked at his watch. The blood-colored cloth dropped. He turned and gestured that the catapult should be activated. There was a whoosh of steam and Barker's machine, released, was hurtling forward. Fifty feet before reaching the edge of the deck, it lifted.

The Frenchman's plane soared up eighty seconds later.

The crowd spread out over the flight deck as Clemens hurried to the pilot-house. From the control room he would climb a ladder through a hatch on the top of the structure. A chair and table were bolted down there, waiting for him. While he watched the dogfight he would drink bourbon and smoke a fresh cigar.

Nevertheless, he could not keep from worrying about King John. It was inevitable as a belch after beer that John was planning some sort of trickery.

29

THE *REX GRANDISSIMUS* WAS IN THE MIDDLE OF THE LAKE, ITS NOSE pointed into the wind, its paddlewheels rotating to drive it at ten miles per hour. This, added to the five-mph headwind, gave the airplanes a fifteen-mph wind to climb into during takeoff.

King John, clad in a blue kilt, scarlet cape, and black jackboots, was on the flight deck. He was talking to the two pilots while the deck crew was readying the aircraft. These were dressed in black leather uniforms similar to those of the enemy fliers. Near them were the fighter craft, being readied. These were also biplanes, though the noses were blunter than their counterparts. The wings and fuselage of one plane were covered with a blue-and-silver checkerboard pattern, on which were imposed the three golden lions of King John. Its crimson nose bore a white skull and crossbones. The second machine was white with the three lions on the wings and rudder. On both sides and the underside of the cockpit was a red ball, the rising sun of Japan, Okabe's sign.

Out of several hundred candidates interviewed in the past seven years, John had picked two to fly for this long-expected day. Kenji Okabe was a short husky slim man who radiated determination. Yet, most of the time he was congenial, interested in others besides himself. At this time, he looked grim.

Voss, with Barker, was distinguished as having fought the two greatest one-man stands against superior forces in the aerial history of World War I.

On September 23, 1917, Voss, a destroyer of forty-eight Allied aircraft, was flying alone in one of the new Fokker triplanes when he encountered seven S.E.S. fighters of the RVC Squadron No. 56. Their pilots were among Britain's finest fighter pilots. Five were aces, McCudden, Rhys-Davids, and Cecil Lewis being the best-known. Their leader, McCudden, immediately led his men into a circling attack. Voss was seemingly doomed to be shot down at once, the target of fourteen machine guns. But Voss flew his plane as if it were a gyrfalcon. Twice, just as McCudden had Voss in his sights, Voss went into a quick flat half-spin, a maneuver which none of the British had ever seen before. Performing outrageous yet perfectly control-led tricks, and also riddling some of their planes, Voss eluded the seven. But he could not break through the circle. Then Rhys-Davids, a superb marksman, kept him in his sights long enough to empty a drum of .50-caliber bullets from his Lewises into him. Voss's plane fell, not without the regrets of the British. If it had been possible, they would have preferred to have brought him down alive. He was the finest fighter pilot they had ever seen.

Voss was of partly Jewish descent. Though he had encountered some prejudice in the German air force, his splendid flying abilities and determination had brought him recognition which he deserved. He had even served for a while under Richthofen, the so-called Red Baron, who had made him a flight leader and assigned him to fly top cover in the formation.

Kenji Okabe, the captain of King John's air force, had been, during World War II, a noncommissioned officer, Naval Aviation Pilot First Class. He was one of his country's greatest fighter pilots, and he'd set the Navy's all-time record when, over Rabaul, the Bismarck Archipelago, he'd shot down seven American planes in one day. But while attacking a bomber over Bougainville, the Solomon Islands, he was surprised by an American plane diving from a high altitude. It shot off one of the wings of the Zero and set it on fire. Burning, Okabe fell.

John chatted with his two finest pilots for a few minutes. Then he shook Voss's hand and returned Okabe's bow, and the two got into the cockpits. Five thousand feet altitude, at a point halfway between the two boats, a spire with an onion-shaped top, was the agreed rendezvous.

The four biplanes spiraled upward. On reaching the designated height, as indicated by the altimeters, they straightened out. None of them thought of cheating, since they were honorable men. Nor had John suggested to his pilots that they go even higher to get the advantage. He knew them too well.

Now they headed toward each other. The sun was on the right of Voss and Okabe; on the left of Barker and Guynemer. All four would have preferred to have the sun to their backs and in their opponents' eyes. That was the classic method of attack. Hide in ambush in sun or cloud, then, after spotting the victim below, dive down, taking him by surprise.

The airplanes reached the stipulated five thousand feet. The two pairs, with two miles between them, headed straight for each other at a combined three hundred miles an hour. Perhaps five thousand people were watching the last aerial dogfight of Terrestrials.

Werner Voss headed straight for Bill Barker; Georges Guynemer and Kenji Okabe, for each other.

It was a coolly near-suicidal maneuver. Keep the machine dead-on a collision course. Hold the fire until within 1700 feet. Press the trigger button on the joystick. Loose about ten rounds. Hope that the burst would hit a propeller, knock it out of line a little, perhaps pierce an oil line or electrical wires. Maybe even skim the cowl, pierce the windshield and hit the pilot.

Then, at the last possible second, roll and turn away to the right. If there was a miscalculation, if the other pilot did not turn but continued on his course, smash!

Guynemer's blazing black eyes looked out of his goggles and through the ring-sight just ahead of the windscreen. The white plane was edge-on, seemingly flattened out. The whirling propeller gave a clear view of the other man; his teeth showed whitely in the sun. Then, the plane was huge, swelling at a speed that would have frightened most men. The Frenchman pressed the button. At the same time, the muzzle of the gun of his opponent shot red.

The two airplanes rolled simultaneously, and their wheels almost collided. Both brought their craft up and around in a turn so tight that the blood drained from their heads.

For a second, as he circled, Guynemer had the checkerboard machine in his sights. But he did not waste any bullets. It was gone too quickly.

Barker and Okabe crossed, almost hitting each other, so close they saw each other's faces.

It was a mad scramble now, each climbing with all the power of his motor, at an angle just short of a stall. Their motors sang with the labor.

Then Okabe slid off, dropping, and as his sight crossed Guynemer, he triggered a burst of four bullets.

The Frenchman ducked involuntarily as a hole was punched in his windscreen. Banking, he followed Okabe down, hoping to get on his tail. The plane displaying the red ball had taken a chance and almost succeeded. But now he was lower than Guynemer, and he must pay.

The Japanese came back up in a tight loop which almost stood the plane on its tail. It fell back, and Okabe, upside down, fired as Guynemer came into his sights again. The Frenchman was rolling then. Bullets stitched across the fuselage, just missing him. His fuel tank was hit, but it was self-sealing, a feature he didn't have in his old Spad. Okabe straightened the plane out and climbed again. Guynemer curved his machine around, sped up, hung it on its nose for several seconds, and loosed four bullets. One shot through the cockpit, burning the Japanese's hand on the stick. Grunting with pain, Okabe snatched his hand away. His plane fell off to the right, out of control for a moment.

Guynemer had fallen into a spin, though he brought it out quickly.

The Frenchman and the German were, without planning it, for a few seconds side by side, both climbing. Then Guynemer banked toward Voss, and, to prevent a collision, Voss also banked. Instead of turning *away*, as Guynemer had expected, Voss turned toward him but went down instead of up.

Voss' wingtip missed Guynemer's tail elevator by a half-inch.

The German drove down and then up in a loop, a maneuver not recommended when the enemy was on your tail. At its top, he rolled over and then dived.

Guynemer had thought, when Checkerboard turned into him, that it was all over. Quickly recovering, no time for thought about narrow escapes here, he started to climb, looking over his shoulder. For a moment he could not see Checkerboard. Then both it and Barker's machine flashed by him. His friend was behind Checkerboard, having somehow gotten on his tail. Checkerboard went into a barrel roll, lost speed in the maneuver, and then did a flat half-spin. Voss was quick as a cat at the controls. Suddenly, he was pointed in the opposite direction. Barker's plane shot by him, their wingtips almost touching.

Guynemer had no time for further looking except for the plane with the red ball. Now the fellow was behind him but below, climbing as fast as he but still unable to decrease the distance between them. His foe was about seven hundred feet, Guynemer estimated. Close enough to reach him with his fire but too distant for accurate shooting in the air.

Nevertheless, Red Ball did give him a burst. Holes walked across Guynemer's right wing as he raised it to turn. Red Ball also turned, jockeying his machine so that he could zero in on the man in the cockpit. Guynemer pushed in on the throttle until it was flat against the panel. If only his motor had more power than Red Ball's, he could pull away slowly even in this steep climb. But there was no use wishing. They were evenly matched in this respect.

He pulled the stick back with a smooth savagery. He decreased the angle of his climb, thus allowing Red Ball to narrow the gap between them. But Guynemer could not curve up and over onto his back without more power. To try that without flattening out his inclination to the horizon would send his ship into a stall. For about thirty seconds, he had to take a chance that his enemy's fire would miss vital parts of his target.

Okabe closed up, wondering why *Vieux Charles* had slowed down. By now he assumed that its pilot was Guynemer. Like all airmen, he knew Guynemer's history well. For some moments after seeing the name, he had felt strange. What was he doing up here trying to kill the famous Frenchie, to shoot down *Old Charlie*?

Okabe looked through the sight. When he came within fifty yards, he would shoot. Now, now he was in range. He depressed the button on top of the joystick; his craft shook as the machine gun spat. He wasn't close enough to see if he had hit, but he doubted it. And now the white ship emblazoned with the red stork was pulling its nose up. Now, it was standing on its tail, and now, it had flipped over and was shooting at him.

But Okabe had kicked rudder and pushed the stick. At this altitude, the plane did not respond as swiftly as in straight flight. But it performed the half-roll and then he was diving away. He looked back and saw that Old Charlie was coming out of the dive in the opposite direction.

He turned steeply and headed toward it, hoping to catch it before it could get above him.

Voss, finding the plane marked with the dog's head behind him, had little time to determine which maneuver might shake it off his tail. He doubted that any conventional aerobatics would do it. This man would just perform the same or would hang back a little and pounce on him when he came out of it.

Savagely, he yanked the throttle half-back.

Barker was surprised to come so close so suddenly. But he did not stop to think. Checkerboard was in his sight; the range was fifty yards and becoming less. Then the helmet of the pilot was inside the ring of his sight. He pressed on the trigger button.

Checkerboard, as if reading his mind, suddenly increased power and at the same time half-rolled. Barker's bullets sped by where the head had been, scorching the bottom of the fuselage, knocking off the tail skid.

Immediately, the Canadian half-rolled. If he had to shoot while on his side, he would do so.

Checkerboard righted itself but continued into a half-roll to the right. Doghead followed it. Checkerboard regained horizontal attitude, and Doghead pressed on the trigger button again.

But Checkerboard slid on into a turning dive. He must be desperate, Barker thought. I can turn and dive as fast as he. He also thought that Checkerboard must be Voss. He had to be.

But Checkerboard pointed his nose up quickly, barrel-rolled, and fell down again. Barker refused to emulate the maneuver. He pushed on the stick, his thumb ready to press, sticking to Checkerboard as closely as a duckling to its mother.

Guynemer, coming out of the dive, was in Checkerboard's line of fire. And Voss, estimating in a flash the vectors of his plane and Old Charlie's, the wind and the range, let loose a burst. There were only six bullets fired, and Guynemer was gone by. But one struck the Frenchman in the thigh, penetrating it at a downward angle.

Barker did not know that Voss was shooting until he saw Georges throw up an arm and snap his head backward. Then he closed his thumb on the button, but Voss had zoomed up and into a flat half-spin, suicidally throwing his wings around so that Barker had to bank away to keep from collision.

But he was around, turning as swiftly as a leopard fearing a hamstringing by a wild dog. Voss had momentarily escaped him, though at a cost. Forced to dive again to regain speed before Barker could get to him, he was below him again.

Barker slid down toward him, looking around at the same time for Red Ball.

He saw it. It was headed for him from above, coming to aid its fellow, now that Guynemer was momentarily, perhaps permanently, *hors de combat.*

It was vital to abandon Voss for the moment. Barker turned his plane up, its nose pointed on the same plane and in the same direction as Okabe's. Collision course.

But having to climb put him at a disadvantage. The enemy did not have to stay at the same level, nor did he. He banked slightly, turning to the left. Barker banked to the left. Okabe rolled to the right and then flattened out the dive. Evidently, he was trying to circle around to get on his tail. The Canadian looked down on both sides. Guynemer was climbing away now. He wasn't so badly wounded he was out of the fight. And the German was heading toward the Frenchman, who was almost at the same level. He was underneath him, in a perfect position for Barker to attack him. Unfortunately, Barker was in the same situation as Voss with respect to Okabe.

Barker turned his plane while still climbing. Within about thirty seconds, Okabe would come screaming down and around and behind him.

To hell with Okabe. He was going to attack Voss anyway.

Barker's plane dived in a long curve.

The wings shook with the speed of the descent. He glanced at his speedometer. Two hundred and sixty miles per hour. At ten miles per hour more, the wings would be under an intolerable strain.

He glanced back. Okabe was following him now but not that closely. Probably his wings had about the same tolerance as his own plane. Barker flattened out a little, decreasing the rate of descent. This would allow Okabe to narrow the gap between him and Barker. But Barker wanted to come up on Voss at a speed which would give him time for a long burst.

Now Voss, seeing Barker diving, the only target himself, turned his machine toward the swooping nemesis. For a few seconds, they were on the same line, and the muzzles of Voss' guns spat flame. He was taking a long chance, the odds high against success, since the range was four hundred yards. But there was little else he could do.

If the plane had been miraculously hit, Barker himself was untouched. Now he banked away, altering slightly the curve. He throttled back, looking backward at the same time. Okabe was getting closer, but he was still too far away to use his weapon.

Barker's machine, the wind howling over the edge of the windscreen, came around and behind Voss. The German did not look back, but he would see Barker in his rear-view mirror.

Evidently, he had, since he half-rolled and dropped back and away. Barker performed the same maneuver, and then he saw that Guynemer was going to be in Voss' line of fire as Voss leveled out. For a second or two, Guynemer's plane would be broadside to Voss's guns. Twice, the Frenchman had been in the line of fire of Voss, both times by accident.

Barker still did not know whether or not his buddy had been hit. He and

Voss zoomed past Guynemer; the back of Voss' head was in Barker's sight, the range only fifty yards, and he was closing the gap.

A glance in the mirror. Okabe was behind him by about fifty yards. And he was coming up fast. So fast that he would have only some seconds to fire unless he throttled back. Which he would do, of course, unless he was very sure of his marksmanship.

Barker pressed the trigger. Holes danced down the length of the fuselage from the tail, passed over the pilot, whose head exploded in a gout of blood, and danced along the motor.

The spectators on the shore now saw a strange sight. There were three airplanes in a line, and then, suddenly, four. Guynemer had come up behind Okabe. He was not above, the best position, and he did not have the speed which Okabe had gained in his dive. But as Voss' skull disintegrated, as Barker's spine was severed and the top of his head removed, Guynemer fired three rounds. One struck Okabe in the small of his back from below, angling up, ricocheting off the backbone, moving out toward the front of the body, and rupturing the solar plexus.

After that, Guynemer's vision failed, and he dropped forward, shoving the stick down though not knowing it, while blood poured from his arm and his side. Two of Voss' bullets had found their mark.

The checkerboard plane spun in, just missing the top of a rock spire on the bank, crashing through level after level of the bamboo bridges, and smashed into a hut. Flame gouted from it, burning alcohol splashed over neighboring huts and the wind took the flames to other buildings.

The first of many fires that was to become a holocaust had started.

The plane marked with the dog's head smashed into a spire and fell burning along its length, breaking through levels of bridges and huts, scattering pieces of hot metal and flaming fuel for many yards around.

The machine marked with the red ball whirled like a corkscrew into the beach, struck scores of screaming spectators as they dashed for safety, plowed through scores more, and ended up against the great dance hall. The fire danced, too, leaping and whirling along the front and quickly enmeshing the entire structure in unquenchable scarlet and orange.

Old Charlie descended in a shallow steep dive, turning over just before impact. It struck the edge of the bank of The River, dug a trench through the grass-covered earth while it flamed, smashed five people fleeing for their lives, and stopped at the base of an irontree trunk.

Göring, pale and shaking, thought that nobody had proved anything except that courage and great skill were not guarantees of survival, that Dame Fortune plays an invisible hand, and that war is fatal to soldiers and civilians, belligerents and neutrals alike.

SECTION 10

Armageddon: The *Not For Hire* vs. the *Rex*

30

KING JOHN HAD JUMPED THE GUN.

Just before the four aviators formed their bucket brigade of death, he spoke into the microphone on the pilothouse control panel.

"Taishi!"

"Yes, Captain."

"Attack! And may God ride with you."

Fifteen minutes before, the huge hatch at the stern had opened. A large two-seater plane with folded wings had slipped down a runway into the water. Floating on its pontoons, it had waited while its wings were extended and locked. Then Sakanoue Taishi, sitting in the pilot's seat forward of the wings, had started the two motors. While Taishi watched the aerial battle from the open cockpit, he warmed up the motors. Behind the wings, in the gunner's station, stood Gabriel O'Herlihy.

Both were veterans, the Japanese of World War II, the Irish-Australian of the Korean police action. Taishi had flown torpedo bombers for the Imperial Navy and had met his end in the Battle of Leyte Gulf. O'Herlihy had been a machine-gunner for the infantry. Despite his lack of aerial experience, he had been chosen for this post because of his superb marksmanship. It was said he could play a machine gun like Harpo Marx played the harp.

Suddenly, though not unexpectedly, the captain had told Taishi to get into action as arranged. Taishi spoke through the intercom headphones, and O'Herlihy sat down. The Japanese revved the motors and they headed up-River into the wind. It was a long takeoff, since they were carrying ten rockets, each with a hundred-pound warhead, under the wings and a torpedo under the fuselage. This was electrically driven and carried seven hundred pounds of cordite in its head.

At last, the big craft left the surface. Taishi waited until they were fifty feet up and pressed the pontoon release button. The gear and the two large pontoons fell off, and the machine picked up speed.

O'Herlihy, looking back and upward, saw the four fighter planes fall and crash, but he did not tell Taishi. The pilot was too busy turning the machine toward the left bank, keeping it at a low altitude. He flew it between two rock spires just above the topmost wooden bridges. The plan was to skim across the top of the trees and, where possible, fly between the hills. Once they got close to the mountains, they would turn downwind. Still keeping close to the treetops, they would fly along the mountains. Then they would wheel right and shoot across the hills and come down just above the bamboo complexes. And they would strike at the *Not For Hire* which would be broadside to them.

Taishi knew that Clemens' radar had picked them up the moment they left The River. But he hoped to elude it until he appeared suddenly from behind the hills.

The noncom had been trying to get Sam Clemens' attention for a minute. The captain, however, seemed not to hear him. He was standing up by the chair now, a burning cigar in his mouth, his eyes filmed with tears. He was murmuring, over and over, "Georges! Bill!"

Joe Miller stood near him. The titanthrop was clad in battle armor, a steel helmet with a heavy wire basket over the face, a sausage-shaped extension to guard his nose, a chain-mail shirt, fishskin leather gloves, plastic loin protection, and aluminum thigh and shin guards. In his mammoth right hand was the shaft of a double-bladed steel axe-head weighing one hundred pounds.

Joe's eyes were moist also.

"They vath nithe guyth," he rumbled.

"Captain!" the noncom said. "Radar says a big plane has taken off from the *Rex*!"

Sam said, "What?"

"A two-motored plane, pontoon type, has taken off. Radar reports that it's heading for the north."

Sam came to full attention then. "North? Why the hell. . . ? Oh! It's going to swing around and try to catch us broadside!"

He yelled at the others to get below. In a minute he had scrambled down the ladder onto the bridge. He shouted at the executive officer, John Byron.

"Did you order the *Goose* to take off?"

Byron said, "Yes, sir. The moment radar spotted their torpedo plane leaving! *They* broke the agreement!"

"Good man," Sam said. He looked out the port window. The *Goose*, a big twin-motored torpedo plane, was past the boat, heading into the window. Even as he caught sight of it, it lifted, water falling from the white pontoons. A minute later, the two pontoons fell, struck The River, glanced upward and ahead, then fell, were caught by the current, and drifted away.

"Battle stations!" Clemens said.

Byron punched a button. Sirens began howling, but the crowd on the decks had already started toward its posts.

"Full speed ahead!"

Detweiller, sitting in the pilot's chair, pushed his two control sticks as far as they would go. The giant electrical motors began turning; the huge paddlewheels attached to them dug into the water. The boat almost seemed to leap forward.

"That's a smart trick old John's pulled," Clemens said. "Radio the *Goose* and tell them to come in on the *Rex*'s broadside."

Byron hastened to obey. Sam turned to de Marbot. The little fellow wore a coal-scuttle helmet of duraluminum, a chain-mail shirt and kilt, and leather jackboots. A leather belt held a holster in which a Mark IV pistol was couched and a scabbard in which a cutlass was sheathed.

"Tell your men to bring up the SW," he said. "On the double!"

The Frenchman punched a button which would put him on the intercom to the storage room.

"Is the enemy plane still on the radar?" he said to the operator.

"Not at the moment," Schindler replied. "It's behind the hills, too close to the mountains."

"It'll come hellbent for election right over the tops of the trees," Clemens said. "We won't have much time."

De Marbot gave a groan. Clemens looked at his pale face and said, "What is it?"

"I don't know," de Marbot said. "I heard something that sounded like an explosion! The line's dead! Nobody answers!"

Sam could feel himself turning gray. "Oh, my God! An explosion! Get down there, find out what's going on!"

Byron was by another intercom on the bulkhead. He said, "Station 25 reports an explosion in Station 26."

The Frenchman stepped into the elevator and was gone.

"Sir, there's the enemy plane!" the radar operator said. "On the port bank, just above the structures, coming in between those two rock spires."

Sam ran to the window and looked out. The sun flashed on the silver-and-blue-streaked nose of an aircraft.

"Coming like a bat out of hell!"

He gripped the ledge, forced himself to be calm, and turned. But Byron had sent word down. It wasn't needed, since the attacker was visible.

"Hold your fire until the attacker is five hundred yards distant," Byron said. "Then fire the rockets. Cannons and small arms, wait until it's within two hundred and fifty yards."

"I shouldn't have waited," Sam muttered. "I should have brought the laser out as soon as those boys took off. It could slice that plane in half before it launched the torpedo."

One more regret in a lifetime of regrets.

And just what in blue blazes happened down there?

"Here it cometh!" Joe Miller said.

The torpedo plane had dipped down past the bridges running along the edge of the hills. Now it was skimming the grass of the plains. Whoever the pilot was, he was handling his big heavy machine as if it were a one-seater fighter.

Events happened fast after that. The plane was going at least 150 miles per hour. Once it reached The River, it would have a mile to go to its target. But it would release the torpedo within six hundred feet. Closer, if the pilot was daring. The nearer the release, the less chance for the *Not For Hire* to evade the missile.

It would have been better if the boat were to turn prow-on and so present a smaller target. But to do this would cut the defense fire to a minimum.

Sam waited. The moment that the silvery weapon of destruction was loosed from its carrier, he would give the order to Detweiller to swing the boat around. The plane would be a lesser menace then. In any event, if it survived the hail of fire, it would be getting to hell out.

"Five hundred yards," Byron said, reading the radarscope over its operator's shoulder. He spoke into the intercom linked with the batteries. "Fire the rockets!"

Twenty silvery cone-tipped cylinders, spouting flame from their tails, sprang like cats at a feline convention after a lone mouse.

The pilot had the reflexes of a cat, too. Twelve rockets, smaller than those hurled at him, sprang from below his wings. The two flights met in three battings of an eye and went up in flame surrounded by smoke. Immediately after, the plane bored through the clouds. Now it was so close to The River that it seemed the waves would snap its bottom.

"Fire the second battery of rockets!" Byron yelled. "Fire cannons and small arms!"

Another flight of missiles arced out. The steam machine guns hosed a stream of .80-caliber plastic bullets. The 88-millimeter cannon on the port side bellowed, spouting flame and gray clouds. The marines, stationed between the heavy platforms, fired their rifles.

The long sharkish-looking torpedo dropped from the airplane at an altitude of a hundred feet, hit the water, skipped, sank. Now all that could be seen of it was its wake, boiling white.

"Hard aport!" Sam said.

Detweiller yanked back on the port stick. The monster wheels on the left side slowed, stopped, began churning water in the opposite direction. Slowly, the boat swung around.

Taishi, feeling the plane suddenly relieved of the weight of the torpedo, pulled back on the stick. Up rose the nose as the twin motors, on full power, lifted her to pass over the boat. Taishi leaned over the side of the cockpit, the wind hitting him full in the face. He could not see the torpedo, even though the water was clear, because he had passed it.

Ahead, the sun shone briefly on rockets, trailing smoke. Another launching! Heat-seekers, too.

If things had gone otherwise, Taishi would have skimmed the edge of the boat's flight deck, passed beyond it, swung around, and come back to strafe. O'Herlihy was standing up now, bracing himself with one hand against the edge of his cockpit, waiting until the plane assumed a level to swing his guns around. But O'Herlihy would never get a chance to use his twin .50-calibers.

The plane, Taishi, and O'Herlihy disappeared in a great cloud, pieces flying out of it almost immediately, metal, flesh, bone, and blood.

One of the motors fell in an arc, smashing into the flight deck near a cannon. It rolled across and dropped over the edge and fell onto the hurricane deck, crushing two men.

A crewman called for a fire-fighting squad.

Sam Clemens, looking out the port window, saw the explosion, saw a dark object out of the corner of his eye, felt the vibrations of the impact.

"What in hell was that?"

But he kept his eyes on the torpedo's wake, sinister as a shark's approach and even more swift.

If only the boat could spin around faster, spin around on a dime and give five cents' change.

This was a strange geometry, a deadly one. The torpedo was describing a straight line, the shortest distance between two points—in this case, anyway. The boat was describing a circle in order to avoid being at the end of the line drawn.

Sam gripped the ledge, bit through his cigar so savagely that its outer part fell off, but, not totally severed, swung down. Its glowing end burned his chin, causing him to yell with pain. But that was a few seconds later. While the torpedo scraped against the hull, he felt nothing except extreme anxiety.

Then it had gone on, headed toward the shore, and he clapped his hand to his neck, burned his hand, and dashed the cigar away.

"Straighten her out," he told Detweiller. "Resume former course, full speed ahead."

Byron, looking out of the starboard window, said, "The torpedo's half-submerged against the bank, Captain. Its motor is still pushing it, but it's stuck in the mud, tilting up."

"Let them worry about it," Sam said, referring to the people on the bank. "Oh! Oh!"

He stopped. For several minutes, he'd forgotten about the explosion near the SW room.

"Byron! Has Marbot reported yet?"

"No, sir."

The bulkhead intercom tootled. Byron answered it with Clemens close behind him.

"De Marbot here. Is the captain occupied?"

"I'm listening, Marc!" Sam said. "What's happened?"

"The laser has been blown up! It's totally destroyed! The entire guard, including Fermor, was killed, and so were four crewmen who came upon the scene. The guards were blown up; the crewmen were gunned down! Captain, there's a saboteur or saboteurs aboard!"

Sam groaned. For a moment, he thought he was going to faint. He steadied himself with a hand against the bulkhead.

Byron said, "Are you all right, sir?"

Byron looked as pale as Sam felt. But he showed no evidence of hysteria. Sam straightened up, took a deep breath, and said, "I'm okay. Son of a blazing bitch! I should have had twenty men guarding that! I should have brought it up sooner! Now our ace in the hole is gone! And John didn't have a chance with it! Never overlook the human factor, Byron!"

Byron said, "No, sir. I suggest . . ."

"That we send search parties looking for the bastard? Or bastards? They'll be back at their posts by now. Maybe. Maybe they're planning on wrecking the generators. Send some men down to the engine room to stand guard.

"And start checking the stations. See if anybody left his post for any reason whatever. There may be some innocents there, but we can't take any chances. Anybody who left his post, throw him into the brig! I don't care if it's an officer and he seems to have a good excuse. We can't fight John and worry about being stabbed in the back at the same time!"

"Aye, aye, sir!" Byron said, and he began calling the stations by number.

"Enemy vessel is five miles away, Captain," the chief radar operator called. "Traveling at fifty-five miles per hour."

The *Rex* had a top speed of forty-five miles per hour in still water and no headwinds. Aided by the current and the wind, it was going at a speed equal to the *Not For Hire*'s.

"Any indication of the *Goose?*" Sam said.

"Nothing sir."

Sam looked at the chronometer. The big plane should still be flying alongside the mountains, hugging the top of the trees, down below the forest whenever possible. But it would not be attacking the *Rex* by itself. Its orders were to wait until the *Rex* was engaged with the motherboat. Then, while John's crew was occupied with firing upon the enemy, the *Goose* would come roaring out across the trees, swoop down to The River, and make a run for the broadside of the *Rex*. If John had had any sense, he would have held back his own torpedo plane until the full-scale battle started.

But then John had hoped that the people on the *Not For Hire* would be so busy watching the aerial fight that they would be taken by surprise.

"Enemy vessel four miles away, Captain. Dead ahead."

Sam lit another cigar and asked the medic to put some salve on his chin-burn. Smollett did so, and then Clemens stood by the starboard port, watching the smoke clouds rising from the fires on the left bank about a quarter of a mile ahead. Flames were eating the bamboo, pine, and yew structures. Pieces lifted off the blaze, carried by the wind, and landed on the bridges and houses. People were scurrying around, carrying belongings out of burning houses or climbing down ladders before the fire got to them. Others had formed lines, dipping their grails and fired-clay buckets into The River, passing the containers along to the other end, where the water was thrown onto the fires at the bases. That was a hopeless procedure; there was nothing to do but let the fire go. Apparently half of the sightseers had decided to do that. They thronged to the plains, where there were a few buildings and continued to wait for the meeting of the boats.

"Before we're done, we'll have leveled Virolando," Sam said to no one in particular. "We won't be very popular here."

"Enemy is three miles away, sir."

Sam walked to the intercom, where Byron was still talking to the stations. Joe's huge bulk came up behind him, and Sam could smell the bourbon emanating from the enormous nose. The titanthrop always liked to take several belts before a fight. It wasn't that he needed Dutch courage, he explained. It was just for his stomach's sake. It quieted the "butterflies."

"Bethideth, Tham, I need lotth of enerchy. You thaid alcohol giveth enerchy. My body burnth it up like a motor burnth fuel. And I got a big body."

"Yeah, but a whole fifth?"

Byron looked at him. "So far, nobody's been away from his post."

"Vhat if they had to take a pithth?" Joe said. "I alvayth have to pithth a lot chuth before a fight. No matter how brave I am, and I am, I get tenthe. It ain't nervouthneth. Chuth tenthion."

"And of course all that booze doesn't have a thing to do with it," Sam said. "If I had a fifth in me, I wouldn't be able to get out of the toilet. In fact, I'd be lucky if I could find it."

"The vhiskey clearth my kidneyth. Clear kidneyth; clear head. My head, I mean, not the boat'th head."

"Both heads have a lot in common," Sam said. "The toilet's got pipes full of water, and you have water on the brain."

"You're chuth talking nathty becauthe you're nervouth," Joe said. He patted Sam on the shoulder with fingers the size of bananas.

"Don't get familiar with the captain," Sam said. But he felt better. Joe loved him, and he would always be at his side. Could anything bad happen to him while that monster was guarding him? Yes. The boat could be destroyed, Joe or no Joe.

31

THE *REX GRANDISSIMUS* WAS VISIBLE BY NOW, A WHITE INDISTINCT MASS moving toward him. As minutes passed, it became sharper. For a moment, Sam Clemens felt a pain in his breast. The *Rex* had been his first boat, his first love. He had fought to get the metal for it, killed, even slain one of his colleagues for it—where was Erik Bloodaxe now?—helped plan it down to the least bolt, and all that killing and battling and struggle had been negated when King John had stolen it. Now it was his greatest adversary. It was a pity to have to destroy that craft, one of the only two of its kind on the whole planet.

He hated John even more because he was forcing him to sink the beauty. Maybe, though, just maybe the *Rex* could be boarded and taken. Then both boats could sail on up The River to its headwaters.

Sam had always seesawed from deepest pessimism to wildest optimism.

"Two and a half miles now," the radar operator said.

"Any blips on the *Goose?*"

"No . . . yes, sir! Got some! It's three miles to the starboard, just above the hills!"

"Sir, the enemy vessel is turning to starboard," the radarman said.

Sam looked out the fore port. Sure enough, the *Rex* was swinging around. And as the *Not For Hire* plowed toward it, the *Rex* presented its stern.

"Vhat in hell'th he doing?"

"He can't be running away!" Sam said. "Whatever else the sneaky bastard is, he's not a coward. Besides, his men wouldn't let him. No, he's up to something devious."

"Perhaps," Detweiller said, "the *Rex* has some mechanical difficulty?"

"If it does, we can catch it," Sam said. "Radar, check its speed."

"Enemy vessel is making thirty-five miles per hour, due west, sir."

"Against the current and wind, that's top speed," Sam said. "There's nothing wrong with it. Nothing I can see, anyway. Why in blue jumping blazes are they running? They haven't got any place to hide."

Sam paused, rolling his eyes as if they were looking for an idea. He said, "Sonar! Do you pick up any foreign object! Say, something that could be a mine?"

"No, sir. All clear underwater except for some schools of fish."

"It'd be just like John to make some mines and scatter them in our path," Sam said. "I'd do it myself if the situations were reversed."

"Yeth, but he knowth ve have thonar."

"I'd try it anyway. Sparks, tell Anderson to hold off until we're engaged or until further orders."

The radio operator transmitted the message to the pilot of the *Goose*, Ian Anderson. He was a Scot who had flown a British torpedo-bomber during World War II. His gunner, Theodore Zaimis, was a Greek who had been a tail-gunner in an RAF Handley Page Halifax on its night raids over France and Germany in the same war.

Anderson reported that he understood. Radar followed the *Goose* as it maintained a more or less level course eastward.

As the sun slowly arced downward, the *Not For Hire* decreased the gap between it and the *Rex*.

"Maybe John doesn't know how fast this boat can go," Sam muttered as he paced back and forth. He looked at the crowds on both banks and on the spires and bridges. "Why do they stand around gawking? Don't they know rockets and shells are likely to be landing among them? That's the least John could have done, warn them!"

The great red-and-black stone temple came into view, loomed, then dwindled. Now the pursuer was only half a mile behind the pursued. Sam gave Detweiller orders to ease up on the speed.

"I don't know what he's up to. But I'm not going to run full speed into any trap."

"It looks as if he's heading for the strait," Detweiller said.

"I might have known that," Sam said.

The mountains were curving in, their arcs on both sides almost meeting a mile ahead. Here the black, white, and red-streaked walls formed straight-up-and-down precipices out of which The River boiled. The *Rex*, though it must be under full power, was only making twenty miles an hour. Its rate of progress would be even less if it entered the towering and dark passage.

"Do you really suppose John's going to take her to the other side?" Sam said. He pounded his left palm with his fist. "By thunder, that's it! He's going to wait for us on the other side, catch us when we come out!"

"You vouldn't be that thtupid, vould you?" Joe Miller said.

Sam ignored him. He strode to the radio operator. "Get me Anderson!"

The pilot of the *Goose* spoke with a broad Lowland Scots brogue. "Aye, we'll go over and see what this skurlie is doing, Captain. But it'll take some time to climb over the pass."

"Don't climb over the mountains; go *through* the pass," Sam said. "If you see your chance, attack!" Then to Byron, "Heard anything?"

A slight annoyance passed over Byron's face. "I'll tell you as soon as I do."

Sam laughed and said, "Sorry, John. But the idea of somebody planting explosives down there . . . well, it concerns me. Carry on."

"Here it is," Byron said as the warrant officer of Station 26 spoke. Sam swung around to stand by Byron.

"Ensign Santiago left about half an hour ago, sir," Schindler said. "He put me in charge, said he was suffering from nervous diarrhea and he wanted to clean himself out so he wouldn't disgrace himself. He said he'd be right back. He didn't show up until ten minutes later, but I didn't think much about it, sir, since he said he just couldn't stop.

"He looked like he'd just had a shower, sir, was dripping wet. He said he'd fouled himself and so had to take a quick shower. Then, just after we heard the general call to report by the numbers, he excused himself again. But he hasn't been back."

"Station 27, report!" Byron said. He turned his head to Sam. "He might not be the only one."

All thirty-five stations reported that no one else had been missing even for a minute.

"Well, he's either hiding some place or went overboard," Sam said.

"I doubt he could leave the boat without someone seeing him," Byron said.

Sam called de Marbot. "Get all your marines, *all*, to search for Santiago. If he resists, shoot him. But I would like to talk to him if possible."

Sam turned to Byron. "Santiago's been with us from the beginning. John must have planted him, though how John knew about the laser I don't know. We didn't even think of it until after he stole the boat. And how in God's name did Santiago find out about the laser? Even Queen Victoria's sex life wasn't a better secret."

"He's had plenty of time to dig around," Byron said. "He's a sly one. I never did trust the dago."

"I liked him," Sam said. "He was always congenial, very good at his duties, and a hell of a good poker player."

Santiago was a seventeenth-century Venezuelan sailor who had captained a warship for ten years. Shipwrecked off an unidentified Caribbean island, he was speared by Indians as he struggled onto a beach. However, this only hastened his death a little. Syphilis had almost finished tearing him apart anyway.

"Of course," Sam added, "he was awfully jealous of his women and he had his stupid Latin machismo. But after one of his women, a twentieth-century jukado expert, beat him up, he reconsidered his ways and treated the ladies as if they were worth their weight in gold."

There were more pressing things to consider than Santiago's ego. For one, how would John know that his agent had succeeded? John was unaware of the laser. He would have originally charged the Venezuelan with blowing up some vital part of the boat. That command had not been carried out, since the generators and electromechanical control centers were too well guarded.

Also, unless there was a spectacular explosion, how would John know that his agent had done his work? Was a system of signals worked out? If so, Santiago had not sent any.

Unless . . . he had a radio set hidden somewhere on the vessel. And it was on a frequency not used by . . .

Sam felt a faint vibration in the deck, one not accounted for by the thrusting of paddles into the water.

He walked to the stern port and looked out. Wisps of smoke were issuing from the starboard side, apparently coming from the hurricane deck.

Sam ran to the intercom and bellowed into it. "Stations 15 and 16! What happened?"

A calm female voice answered. "This is P.O. Anita Garibaldi, Station 17! There's been an explosion down here, sir! A bulkwall's been blown up! The wires in it have been severed!"

Detweiller swore. Sam whirled around. "What is it?"

"I've lost control," Detweiller said, but Sam already knew that. The wheels had slowed, and even as he looked out the stern window, he saw that they had stopped. Slowly, the nose of the boat was turning to port, and it was being carried back by the current.

Detweiller reached out and punched a button. A light by it glowed. He grabbed the sticks again. The wheels began rotating, picked up speed. The boat swung back to its original course.

"The backup system is working," Detweiller said.

Sam grinned a little though he did not feel joyous at all. "Santiago wouldn't know about that," he said. "It was John, though, that gave me the idea for installing it! Hoist by his own petard!"

He yelled into the intercom, keeping his finger on the all-stations button. "All right, you incompetent bungling blind microcephalic dingdongs! You could expand your brains a hundredfold, and they'd still rattle around in a gnat's ass!

"Find Santiago!"

"The strait's dead ahead, Captain," Detweiller said.

A shadow passed over, and twin motors roared. The *Goose* shot in front of them at an altitude of about two hundred feet. It was climbing between the dark walls, its searchlight stabbing ahead of it, dwindling in distance and darkness, then disappearing as it went around a long bend.

"Can we keep in radio contact with the *Goose*?" Sam said to the radio operator.

"It's possible, sir. The long waves can bounce around that bend to us."

Sam turned away but spun at an exclamation from the operator.

"Jesus! The pilot just said, 'We're hit! The starboard's motor is on fire! A rocket. . . !'"

He looked up with a pale strained face. "That's all, Captain."

Sam swore.

"John must've been waiting for it! He knew I'd sent it to find out what he was doing!"

Why hadn't he let Anderson do as he wished, fly over the mountains? Then he would have been out of range of the rockets or at least have had time to take evasive maneuvers. But no, John knew his ex-partner, knew how impatient he'd be. So he had waited, and now he had the torpedo plane out of the combat.

But the *Rex* wouldn't have been taken through the strait just to ambush the airplane. He . . .

De Marbot's voice crackled. "Captain! We just got Santiago! He'd been hiding behind a bulkwall section! He made a dash up a passageway and almost got to the deck railing! Johnston shot him through the head!"

"Give me the details later," Sam said. "Continue the search for other agents. Look . . ."

"Rockets!" Detweiller screamed.

32

SAM CLEMENS TURNED AROUND. SOMETHING SWIFT AND SILVERY FROM above struck the base of the pilothouse. The explosion was deafening; the deck shook. Another roar from above. The pilothouse vibrated. Smoke shrouded the windows on all sides for several seconds. Then the wind seized it and scattered it.

"What the hell!" Sam said over and over.

"It's from up there," Detweiller said. He released a control stick just long enough to point up and to his right.

"Get her away!" Sam yelled. "Downstream!"

The pilot had already applied full power. A cool one, that Detweiller.

Again, another flash of silver. Dozens of them. More explosions. A battery of rockets on the starboard disappeared in a thunder of fire and smoke. A direct hit from *whoever* was launching those missiles from *wherever*.

"Zigzag her!" Sam shouted.

There were three more direct hits. Other missiles plunged into the water on both sides and aft.

"Our radar's gone," Byron said. He ordered the rocket crews to fire back, using visual calculations.

"But where are they?" Sam said.

"Up on the cliff!" Byron and Detweiller said at the same time.

"Thee!" Joe said, pointing out the stern port.

While Byron was asking for reports on the damage and casualties, Sam looked along the titanthrop's massive finger. About five hundred feet up, where there had been an unbroken wall of rock, there was now an opening. An oblong, it was thirty feet long and seven feet high. Tiny faces looked out from behind launchers, and the sun glinted on the silver of missiles and tubes.

"Jumping Jesus H. Christ!"

John's men must have found a cave up on the face of the mountain, and they'd carried rockets and launchers to it. A shield of some sort, probably papier-mâché simulating a patch of lichen, had been placed over the opening. While his rocketeers waited inside it, John had fled up the strait.

"Suckered!" Sam said, and he groaned.

A minute passed as the boat churned down-River. Then, making him jump though he knew they were coming, about twelve large missiles sped from the opening, the interior of the cave lit up for a second by flames.

"Hard aport!" Sam yelled.

Only one of the rockets hit. A steam machine gun disappeared in a cloud, pieces of bodies and metal flying out from it. When the smoke cleared, there was a large hole where the platform, gun, and three men and two women had been.

For a moment, Sam was numbed throughout, unable to move or to think anything except: War is not my element. War is no rational man's element. I should have faced reality and given Byron the command. But no, my pride, my pride. John was wily, wily indeed, and he also had the great Dane, Tordenskjöld, as adviser.

Vaguely, he became aware that the boat was heading toward the bank.

Byron's voice, as if from a long distance, was saying, "Should I keep her on course, Captain?"

"Tham, Tham," Joe rumbled behind him. "Chethuth Chritht, ve're going to run into the bank!"

Sam forced himself to move, to speak.

"We won't stay on course. Head her down-River and get back in the middle."

There were bodies on the main deck. Youngblood, Czerny, and de Groot. And there was the upper part of the beautiful Anne Mathy, the former Hollywood star. She looked like a China doll which some sick child had mutilated.

He had seen corpses and blood before, and he wasn't any youngster playing Confederate soldier. There was no Wild West to run away to, leaving the Civil War to those with a taste for it. He couldn't desert now.

From fear he went to anger. The cup of bourbon that Joe—good old Joe!—handed him fueled his wrath. Damn John and his sneaky tricks! He'd send the man to hell, go with him if it was necessary.

He spoke to Byron. "Do you think we could blast those bastards out of that cave?"

The exec took a long look. "I think so. Of course, if their missile supply is exhausted, there's no use wasting ours on them."

"I don't see any in the tubes," Sam said. "But they might be keeping them out of sight, hoping we'll come back to attack. Let's go back and make sure. I don't want those hyenas laughing at us."

Byron raised his eyebrows. Evidently he thought it was foolish to risk more hits. He said, "Yes, sir," and went back to the intercom. Sam told Detweiller what he wanted. And while the *Not For Hire* turned again, the rocket crews readied for their mission.

Byron gave his report in a flat cool voice. Twenty dead. Thirty-two badly wounded. Eleven of the wounded could be patched up and returned to duty. One steam machine gun, one rocket battery, and one cannon were destroyed. The rockets and the cannon shells had blown up also, doing more damage than the missiles themselves. There were two large holes in the flight deck, and the cabins in the lowest tier of the pilothouse had been blown out. Enough of the structure of the base remained to ensure stability. This couldn't be guaranteed if another rocket hit the structure. Their firepower was reduced, but the boat's performance was not affected.

Worst of all, the radar antennas had been destroyed.

A lookout told Sam that new rockets were being put into the tubes by the men in the cave.

"Byron, start firing when I give the word!" Sam said.

The exec relayed the order to sight in on the opening. The boat was now eight hundred yards from the base of the cliff. Sam told Detweiller to spin it, presenting its starboard side. He should then let the current carry it away until the starboard cannon batteries had fired. These were one 88-millimeter cannon, much more accurate than the rockets, and the compressed air cannon.

At Sam's relayed order, the 88-millimeter belched fire, smoke, and thunder, and the other whooshed. One shell struck just above the opening; the other struck just below. No second round was necessary. The rockets in the cave must have been set off by the lower explosion. They went up in a cloud from which spewed fragments that could have been bodies.

When the smoke cleared, only some twisted metal could be seen.

"I think we can take it for granted they're wiped out," Sam said. He felt gratified. The enemy were not human beings. They were things that could kill him and had to be killed before they could do so.

"Take her back to the center about a quarter-mile from the pass," Sam said. "Byron, order the helicopter brought up."

"King John is using his, too," Byron said. He pointed at the opening. Sam saw it, hanging about two thousand feet up, a tiny machine framed in the dark gate of the strait.

"I don't want John to see what we're doing," he said. "Tell Petroski to get rid of it."

Sam called in de Marbot. The instructions took two minutes. De Marbot saluted and went off to carry out the plan.

Petroski, the copter pilot, warmed up the motor, and took off with his two machine-gunners. The fuselage was fitted with ten small heat-seeking missiles, some of which, it was hoped, would down the enemy machine while others would strike the *Rex*.

Sam watched it as it climbed slowly, burdened with its deadly load. It took a while to climb up above the altitude of the craft in the mouth of the pass. Sam asked the Frenchman how he was coming. De Marbot, in the stern, replied that both launches were almost filled with rockets. He could leave in a few minutes.

"I'll give the word when the coast is clear," Sam said.

Petroski's machine finally quit climbing. The other copter was still in its original position. When its pilot saw the big all-white chopper moving to get above it, he spun his machine around and fled.

The radar operator, now posted as lookout, said, "Enemy aircraft is moving at an estimated eighty-five miles per hour."

"Then it's faster than ours," Sam said. "It's not carrying near as much weight. Byron, tell de Marbot he can go ahead."

The huge hatch had been open for some time. The larger of the launches, *Post No Bills*, slid out of the water-filled compartment, kicking up a white wake. It turned and headed toward the shore. Close behind it came the *After You, Gascon*. Both were loaded with rockets, dismantled launching apparatus, and marines.

Petroski's voice came from the set. "The enemy has gone around the bend. I'm going up another two thousand feet before I go around."

While Sam waited for another report, he watched the launches. Their noses were against the low bank now, and men were jumping out of them into the water. They quickly waded ashore and began off-loading the weapons and equipment. Each man would then carry a forty-pound missile or part of a disassembled launcher.

"John must have sent men up first with tackles and ropes," Sam said. "Then he must have winched those heavy rockets from the deck of the *Rex*. It would've been at night, of course, so the Virolanders wouldn't see them. It must've been a hell of a job. Too bad we don't have time to place heavy rockets. But those light rockets can do plenty of damage if they hit the right places on the *Rex*."

He rubbed his hands and blew out a cloud of smoke from his cigar.

"There's nothing like turning the tables on old John. Using his own trap to trap him."

"If we have time," Byron said. "What if the *Rex* comes barreling out of the strait before our weapons are situated?"

"That could happen, but it ain't likely," Sam said, frowning. "Once John reenters the pass, he can only go straight ahead. There isn't room to turn around, even if he spins on one wheel. For all he knows, we might be waiting for him, just outside the exit, out of radar sight, and out of sonar detection, too. We could blast his ass off as he comes around."

"Maybe he could back up," Joe said.

"With two cannon and fifty rockets aiming at the pilothouse and four torpedoes at the hull?"

Sam snorted.

"Anyway, I'd like to see you trying to run that boat in reverse in that current with only thirty feet to spare on each side. Detweiller couldn't do it. Even *I* couldn't do it!"

They waited. Sam watched the long line of marines, each man loaded with a silvery cylinder or a piece of equipment. Presently, de Marbot reported by walkie-talkie.

"I've found the path."

"I see you waving your arm," Sam said. "It should take you about an hour to get to the cave. It's not so high up but the path must be a long one."

"We'll go as fast as possible," the Frenchman said. "But we can't go too fast if the trail is narrow."

"I trust your judgment."

"Petroski's speaking again," the operator said. Sam could hear the pilot before he got to the radio.

"We've dropped to the surface," Petroski said. "I decided to come in at the height of the control room. They'll pick us up on the radar as soon as we get around the last bend. But I'm counting on shaking them up, spoiling their aim. Six rockets for the pilothouse, six for the chopper, whether it's in the air or the flight deck."

Petroski sounded happy. He was a wild Pole who had flown for the RAF against Hitler. After the war, he had refused to live in communist Poland and so had emigrated to Canada and earned his living first as a bush pilot and later as a police copter pilot.

"Hot damn!" Petroski bellowed. "The boat's just outside the entrance! Its nose is pointed straight at me. Only a quarter-mile to go! Wish me luck!"

The roar of motor and vanes was heavy, but his excited voice rode above that.

"Fire six!" Two seconds. Then, "Dead on! Missed the control room but blew the smokestacks all to hell! Can't see through the smoke! Pulling up now! Flak all over the place! Can't see through the smoke! Oh, oh! There's the chopper, on the flight deck! I'll . . ."

The radio operator looked up at Sam.

"Sorry, Captain. It's dead."

Sam ground the end of his cigar to shreds on the set and cast it on the deck.

"A rocket must've got him."

"Probably."

The operator's eyes were moist. Petroski had been his good friend for ten years.

"We don't know if he got John's chopper or not," Sam said. He wiped his eyes with his knuckles. "Shit, I feel like ramming right on it, making him pay . . ."

Byron raised his eyebrows again at this unprofessional attitude.

"Yeah, I know," Sam said. "We'd fall into his trap. Forget it. And I know what else you're thinking. It would have been better to have retained our observation facilities, to put it in cold military language. Now John can keep an eye on us with his chopper, if Petroski didn't destroy it."

"We took a chance, and perhaps it paid off," Byron said. "Perhaps both the copter and the control room were hit. Petroski wouldn't have had enough time to make an accurate assessment."

Sam strode back and forth some more, puffing so hard the air-conditioning couldn't keep up with the clouds. Finally, he stopped, thrust his cigar out as if he was spearing an idea. Which, in a sense, he was.

"John isn't going to come back unless he knows where we are. So, he'll either scout with his chopper or a launch. In either case, we'll not fire on it. Byron, tell de Marbot to hold his fire if either leaves the strait. And to lie low.

"Detweiller, take her to a grailstone near the temple. We'll dock there and do some repairing."

"How come, Tham?"

"How come? So John's spies will see us there. Then, if he's going to attack, he'll know he won't be ambushed. In fact, he might think the rockets from the cliff did us so much damage we're badly hurt. And he'll know he can get through the strait before we could even get near him. Then it'll be the last deal, with us holding a royal flush. I hope."

"But, Tham," Joe said, "vhat if Petrothki did blow up the control room? And Bad Chohn vath killed? Maybe they ain't in no pothithyon to fight."

"I don't see anybody under a white flag and offering to surrender. We'll just retreat and hope that John will come out to do battle. In the meantime, we'll do a little scouting of our own. Byron, send the *Gascon* out. Tell Plunkett to go through the strait at top speed, take a quick look, and get to hell back here."

"May I offer a suggestion?" Byron said. "The *Gascon* has torpedos."

"No, by thunder! I'm not going to sacrifice any more good men on suicide missions! It's dangerous enough as it is, as the old bachelor said to the spinster who proposed marriage. They could be attacked by the chopper, though I think it's more than an even match for the *Gascon* there. In fact, if the chopper should chase the launch out, de Marbot should then fire on it. We'll have our information, and John will wonder what in hell happened to his chopper. He won't be able to resist sending a launch out to scout. We'll let the launch get back.

"In any event, John isn't going to come through until nightfall. I think."

Byron transmitted the messages. Presently, the whitely shining *Gascon* swung away from the bank and headed toward the strait. Its commander was the younger son of an Irish baron and had been a naval aide-de-camp to King George V and then an admiral. He was a veteran of the battles of Heligoland, Dogger Bank, and Jutland, and a recipient of the Grand Cross, the Order of Orange-Nassau of Holland, and the Russian Order of St. Stanislas, Second Class, with swords. He was also a distant relative of the great fantasy writer, Lord Dunsany, and, through Dunsany, of the famous English explorer, Richard Francis Burton.

"Sir," John Byron said, "I think we've overlooked something. The marines are still a long way from having their rockets set up. If the enemy helicopter or launch should pursue the *Gascon*, they won't be in any danger from de Marbot's fire. And they might well see his men on the mountain path. Then they would know we're setting up an ambush."

"Yeah, you're right," Sam said reluctantly. "Okay. Tell His Lordship to come back until de Marbot is situated. No use his wasting power circling around."

"Yes, sir," Byron said. He spoke on the radio to Plunkett, then turned swiftly on Sam. "Only . . . the admiral is not properly referred to as His Lordship. He is the younger son of a peer, which legally makes him a commoner. And since his father was a baron, the lowest in the rank of peers, he does not even have an honorary title."

"I was being facetious," Sam said. "Lord preserve me from British sticklers!"

The little Englishman looked as if he thought facetiousness had no place in the control room. He was probably right, Sam thought. But he had to kid around a little. It was the only way he could let off pressure. If he didn't, he'd blow his mental boiler sky-high. *See the pretty pieces flying through the air. Those are Sam Clemens.*

Byron was tough, unperturbed in any situation, as calm as a man who's sold his stock just before the market crashed.

The boat was still far out in the lake, though cutting at an angle toward the bank. Big black clouds were visible to the north. Smoke from the fires started by the fallen airplanes. There would be even more fires tomorrow—unless the rain quenched them. The locals certainly would have no love for either King John or himself. It was a good thing they were pacifists. Otherwise, they might be objecting violently when one of their grailstones was borrowed this evening by those whom they could only regard as killers and arsonists. The giant batacitor of the *Not For Hire* had to be recharged, even though it was far from empty, and the crew had to refill their grails. He did not think that the *Rex* would show during this time. It had the same needs.

Unless . . . unless John thought he could catch them sitting. It was possible he might try to do that. His motors had not used up all the energy stored; the *Rex* had not traveled all day. He could have many hours' electrical supply left.

No, John wouldn't attempt it. Not knowing that his enemy was radarless, he would think that the *Rex* would be detected the moment it showed its nose. And he'd have to cross three miles of lake to get to the *Not For Hire*. Before he could do that, the enormous hemispherical plate covering the grailstone could be swung aboard and stored and the boat well on its way to meet the *Rex*.

If only he had an aircraft left to tell him when John's boat was being recharged. If the *Rex* was connected to a grailstone near the inlet of the strait, the *Not For Hire* could be on it before it could get into action. No, John would think of that. He'd go far enough up The River so he'd have time to get ready. And he'd know that Sam Clemens would take the same precaution.

But if he would think of that, why not charge on through and catch John with his royal pants down?

If only he knew the topography, the width of The River on the other side of the mountain. But Plunkett would get the data needed.

Byron said, "Would you like to bury the dead now, sir?"

33

"HEH?" SAM SAID. "OH, YES, MIGHT AS WELL GET IT OVER WITH NOW. WE won't have time later. Are there enough marines left for the burial squad?"

"Exactly forty-two, sir," Byron said with some satisfaction at having anticipated his captain.

"Good. That's enough to bury everybody, including themselves. In fact, we'd better just use three rifles. We need to conserve all the powder we can."

The services were short. The bodies were laid out on the stern of the flight deck, wrapped in cloths, weighted with stones. Half the crew was assembled; the rest stayed on duty.

". . . for now we know that resurrection is possible, all having experienced its truth. Thus we consign your bodies to the deeps of The River in the hope that you will once again walk the face of this world or some other. For those who believe in God, may He bless you. So long!"

The rifle salute was given. One by one the bodies in fishskin bags were picked up and swung out into the air. Weighted with stones, they would sink to be eaten by the small and the big fish prowling, pressing, dark, thousands of feet below.

The *Not For Hire* put into the bank, and its anchors were dropped. Sam went ashore to face an intensely angry La Viro. The big dark hawk-faced man raged at the stupidity and cruelty of both parties. Sam listened stony-faced. This was no time for a wisecrack. But when La Viro demanded that he leave the area, Sam said, "There is no way to avoid this conflict. One of us must go down. Now, do I have your permission to use a grailstone?"

"No!" La Viro shouted. "No! You do not!"

"I am indeed sorry," Sam said. "But I am using one anyway. If you interfere, you and your people will be fired upon."

La Viro said nothing for a minute. Finally, his breathing became lighter and the redness faded from his skin. "Very well. We will not use force. You knew we wouldn't. All I can do is appeal to your humanity. That has failed. On your own head be the consequences."

"You don't understand," Sam said. "We have to get to the polar sea. Our mission is vital to this world. I can't explain why, but, believe me, it is."

He looked up at the sun. In an hour, it would touch the top of the western range.

At that moment, Hermann Göring joined the small group behind La Viro. He said something to his chief in a low voice. La Viro said loudly, "Very well. Evacuate them."

Göring turned and spoke in a trumpet voice. "You heard La Viro! We will go east and get away from this hellish conflict. Spread the word! Everybody east! Martin, you send up the signal balloon!"

Göring turned to Clemens.

"You can see now, or should be able to see, that I was right! I objected to the building of your boat because your purpose was evil! We weren't raised from the dead and put here to glorify ourselves or indulge in mindless sensuality, in hate, and in bloodshed! We . . ."

Sam turned away. Followed by Miller, Sam walked out on the floating dock and up the gangplank to the hurricane deck. Joe said, "Thon of a bitch, Tham. He really chewed you out."

"He's not even in the race," Sam said. "I've been eaten out by the best. You should have heard my mother. Or my wife. They could give him a thousand-word start and catch up in ten seconds flat. Forget him. What does he know? I'm doing this for him and all the rest of those mealy-mouthed Chancers. For everybody, whether they deserve it or not."

"Huh? I alvayth thought you vath doing it for yourthelf."

"Sometimes you get too smart-alecky," Sam said. "You don't talk to the captain like that."

"I chutht call them ath I thee them," Joe said. He was grinning. "Anyvay, I'm not talking to you like a deckhand to the captain. I'm talking to you ath your friend, Choe Miller."

John Byron spoke to them as they entered the control room. "Sir, de Marbot reports that the launchers are set up."

"Good. Tell him to get back down to the launch. And tell Plunkett he can go ahead now."

The *Gascon* responded immediately, heading for the strait. The tiny figures of the marines were dimly visible against the blue-black stone and green-black algae as they walked down the ledge cut upon the mountain's face. They would be using their flashlights before they reached the bottom. The *Post No Bills* was cutting along the bank for the stone to the west. The noise of machinist's mates aluminum-welding supports across the shattered base of the pilothouse came to him. Torches flared bluely as men cut away the wreck of the steam machine gun in the bow. Others busied themselves with rockets and a tube-battery to be set up in place of the gun. A party worked furiously to replace the radar antennas.

A half-hour passed. The chief medic reported that five of the wounded had died. Sam ordered that their bodies be taken out in a small boat and dropped in the center of The River. It was done without fanfare, since he did not want to lower the morale of the crew anymore. No, he wouldn't say service over them first. Let one of the medics do it.

Sam looked at the chronometer. "Plunkett should just about be at the exit of the strait."

"Then we should see him coming back out in about ten minutes," the exec said.

Sam looked at the marines halfway down the path. "You did give de Marbot orders that he and his men should flatten out on the ledge if John's chopper or his launch appears?"

"Of course," Byron said stiffly.

Sam looked at the bank. There were thousands of men and women there, moving slowly in a closely packed mass eastward. There wasn't much noise coming from them. Most were burdened with bundles of cloths, pots, vases, statuettes, chairs, fishing poles, carpenter tools, disassembled gliders, and, of course, their grails. They looked at the great boat as they went by, and many held up their hands, the three middle fingers extended in blessing. That made Sam feel guilty and furious. "That thyure ith a pretty balloon," Joe said.

The huge pear-shaped globe, painted a bright yellow, rose from a roofless building. It soared swiftly upward at an angle, carried east by the wind. At an estimated four thousand feet of altitude, the balloon was a small object. But it was not so small that Sam could not see the sudden blazing red flare.

"They blew it up!" he said. "That must be the real signal!"

Burning, visible on both sides of the lake and for many miles up and down The River, the balloon fell. In a few minutes, it plunged into the water.

"Well, at least we don't have to worry anymore about civilian casualties," Byron said.

"I don't know about that," Detweiller said. "It looks like La Viro and some others are staying behind."

That was true. But the group was walking back toward the temple.

Sam snorted and said, "They're probably going to pray for us!"

"The *Gascon's* in sight!" a watchman said.

There it was, the sun white upon her, her bow up as she poured on full power. And there, about five hundred feet almost directly above her, was the enemy helicopter. It was slewing around, tilting, so that its machine-gunners could fire downward.

"Byron, tell de Marbot to fire upon the chopper!" Sam said loudly, but at that moment the roar of discharging grailstones drowned his voice. When the thunder had subsided, he repeated the order.

"Enemy launch sighted!" the lookout said.

"What . . .?" Sam said. Now he too saw the red sharp-nosed bow and the curving armor-plated back and gun turrets of the original *Post No Bills*, stolen by King John. It was coming out of the towering gap.

A single rocket leaped from the opening in the face of the cliff. It flew straight, locked into the red-hot exhaust of the copter. It shone like a long line drawn against the black mountain with a flaming pencil. And then it and the chopper became a round ball of scarlet.

"There goes the last flying machine on this world," Sam said.

The ever-cool Byron said, "Better wait, sir, until the helicopter has hit The River. Otherwise, the rockets'll go for it. It's the hottest object out there."

The blazing main body and its satellites of metal pieces fell with what seemed an unnaturally slow pace. Then they struck the water and disappeared.

Byron spoke into the radio reserved for communication with de Marbot's walkie-talkie. "Direct one rocket volley at the enemy vessel."

"Jesus, sir!" the lookout said. "The *Rex* is coming out too!"

Byron looked once, and he punched the alarm button. Sirens began whooping. The crowd that had been standing on the flight deck quickly disappeared.

Sam forced himself to speak calmly though his heart was racing. "Drop the grail-connector. Telescope the crane."

Byron had already told the deckhands to cast off the lines. Detweiller sat waiting for his orders, his hands on the sticks.

Byron looked out the port. "Lines all clear, sir!"

"Back her out, pilot," Sam said.

Detweiller eased the sticks from neutral, pulling them toward him. The giant wheels began turning, and the vessel slid by the dock.

There was smoke all around the launch of the *Rex*. It was swept quickly away, revealing a blackened boat. It wasn't moving, so perhaps it had been badly damaged. But three inches of duraluminum armored it. It could take a hell of a lot of punishment. Maybe the crew was just stunned by the explosions.

Now the *Rex Grandissimus* was halfway out of the darkened strait. It shone whitely, then became pale as the sun slid all the way behind the mountains. Twilight fell on the lake. The sky darkened. The mass of closely packed stars and gas sheets in the sky began to glow as the sunlight faded. By the time complete night came, the light above would be as bright as a full moon on a cloudless Earth.

The two launches were smudges of paleness. The *Rex* was a greater whiteness, like an albino whale seen just before it burst through the surface of the sea.

So, old John *had* decided to attack while the *Not For Hire* was tied up for recharging. He was not turning back. He'd take his punishment whether he liked it or not.

How had John known that the boat was tied up? Easy to explain. Somewhere up on the mountain on a ledge above the mouth of the strait was a lone observer with a transceiver. That would also explain the readiness of the *Rex*'s defenses against Petroski's attack.

Sam spoke quietly to the pilot. Detweiller stopped the vessel, then turned her toward the *Rex* and applied full speed ahead. Byron said, "What should the *Post No Bills* do?"

Sam waited a moment to reply while he watched the arc traced by the rockets from the cave. But surprise was dead now. John knew that the missiles came from his now usurped cave. Before the rockets had gone halfway, flames spurted from the *Rex*, and trails of fire rose from it. The two packs met about fifty feet above the boat, and the roar rolled across The River. Smoke covered the vessel and was whisked away.

If the *Rex* had been hit, it could not be determined from this distance.

John's rockets would not have hit so many of his unless they, too, had heat-seekers in their noses. Which meant that the enemy did have some of the devices. Apparently, John had had some manufactured. But how many did he have? Whatever their number, some had been sacrificed to stop the attack.

A second covey darted from the cave. This time, they were met halfway, and a flame-centered cloud spread out to be swiftly dissipated. Almost before that happened, a third flight shot from the *Rex*. Its arc ended against the cliff. Some had hit the cave itself, though. Flame belched like gas from a dragon's mouth. Mark off thirty good men and women.

Now the leviathans headed toward each other. Sam could see one light in it, that from the control room. Like his boat, it was blacked-out except for the one illumination needed.

The lookout reported that the enemy launch had resumed motion.

"Neither of his launches originally had torpedo tubes," Sam said to Byron. "But John may have fitted them with tubes. I'm betting he has. Where is his other launch, by the way?"

A moment later, the lookout reported that it was now detected. It must have just emerged from the stern launching compartment.

The *Post No Bills* was cutting toward the *Rex*. It had two torpedoes set to go and four waiting.

The *Gascon* was racing toward the motherboat, under orders to get into her compartment and take on torpedoes. Sam doubted that it could be gotten aboard soon enough.

"There goes the smaller enemy launch, sir," the lookout said. "Headed toward the *Bills*."

Sam told Byron to order the *Gascon* to assist its sister boat.

Four rockets sprang from the *Rex*. An explosion announced the end of one curve. A moment later, Admiral Anderson spoke over the radio. "That bird knocked us silly, sir. But we're on our way again. No damage to the boat—that I know about."

The *Gascon,* firing rockets at the enemy launch, swung about it. Little spurts of flame showed that their machine guns were operating. The other enemy launch continued doggedly toward the *Bills,* shedding warheads and bullets alike. The distance between the two larger vessels, as estimated by the eye, was five hundred feet. Neither was loosing its rockets. Evidently they were waiting until they got within close range.

The *Gascon* was circling behind the enemy now. Plunkett's voice came. "I'm going to ram."

"Don't be a fool!" Sam shouted, in his fear bypassing Byron, who should have relayed the message.

"Is that an order, sir?" Plunkett said calmly. "The crew has left—at my orders, sir. I think that I can wreck the enemy's propellers."

"This is the captain!" Sam said. "I order you not to do that! I don't want you to kill yourself!"

There was no answer. The smaller of the two white objects crept upon the stern of the bigger. At least, it seemed to be moving slowly. Actually it was overtaking the slower craft at about fifteen miles an hour. Not much speed, but the weight of the heavy armor-plated boat gave it a fearful amount of energy.

"*Gascon* and enemy launch closed, sir," the lookout said.

"I can see that, hear it, too," Sam said, looking through his night glasses.

All motion of the *Gascon* had stopped completely except for its drift with the current. The other launch was slowing down. Now it had stopped.

"By Jesus!" Sam said. "He did it! Poor bastard!"

"Maybe he ain't hurt," Joe said. "He voud've been thtrapped in."

The *Post No Bills* was closing in. It came within perhaps a hundred feet of its target. Then it swung sharply away. Several seconds later, the enemy boat rose in water and flames and came down in pieces.

"He torpedoed it!" Sam yelled with exultation. "Good old Anderson! He torpedoed it!"

Byron said coolly, "Good show, that."

"NFH! Anderson! What are my orders?"

"Find out if Plunkett's all right," Sam said. "And if the *Gascon* is still serviceable. And pick up the men who jumped."

"Sir, the *Rex* is an estimated fifty-two hundred feet away," the lookout said.

"Okay, Admiral," Sam said to Byron. "You take over the cannons."

Byron said, "Yes, sir," and he turned to the intercom. Sam heard him giving orders to the fore port-cannon lieutenant, but his eyes were on the launches. If the *Gascon* was operable, it could be used to harass the *Rex* with its small rockets. There wasn't enough time to fit it with torpedoes.

Byron, standing by the intercom, was repeating the range as the gunnery lookout reported it.

"Forty-nine hundred. Forty-seven hundred. Forty-five hundred."

"That's going to be a hell of a shock to John," Sam said to Joe Miller. "He doesn't know we have cannons."

"Fire!"

Sam counted the seconds. Then he swore. The first shell had missed.

The second struck, apparently just by the waterline near the fore. But the *Rex* continued steadily toward its enemy.

"Bring her around so we can give them a broadside from the port," he told Detweiller.

Both cannons spoke now. Columns of smoke roiled out from the *Rex*. A large fire was burning on the flight deck. Still, the boat came on. And now it was close enough to launch its larger rockets.

"Enemy within twenty-six hundred feet," the gunnery lookout said.

"Are the big birds ready?" Sam said to Byron.

"Yes, sir, all."

"Tell the officers to fire as soon as the *Rex* does."

Byron relayed the order. He had no sooner quit speaking than Sam saw a multitude of flames on the *Rex*. The coveys met about 450 feet away, headlong in the air. The explosions deafened Sam.

Joe Miller said, "Chehuth Chritht!"

Suddenly, shells struck the *Rex*. The starboard wheelhousing went up in flames, and smoke covered the pilothouse. Immediately following, gouts of flame arose along the starboard side. The shell had touched off a rocket battery, and the detonation of that had set off others in a series.

"Hot damn!" Sam said.

The smoke around the pilothouse cleared, though not so swiftly. The wind had died down, and the *Rex* had lost considerable speed.

"It's turning its port side to us!" Sam said.

Another flight of missiles arose, this time from the opposite side. Again, the *Not For Hire's* countermissiles struck, and the result was a blast in midair that shook the boat. But no damage was done.

By then Sam could see that the *Rex* was in serious trouble. Its decks on the starboard were blazing here and there, and it was turning away from them.

For a moment he thought that the *Rex* was fleeing. But no. It continued to turn. It was describing a small circle.

"The starboard wheel is malfunctioning or destroyed," he said. "They can't maneuver."

That knowledge relaxed him somewhat. Now all he had to do was to get out of effective rocket range and blast the *Rex* out of the water with his 88-millimeter and compressed-air cannons.

He gave the orders to do so. Detweiller turned the boat to put the necessary distance between it and its victim.

"Well, we didn't do so badly," he said exultingly to Byron.

"Not so far, sir."

"It's practically over! Don't you ever give way to human emotion, man?"

"Not on duty," Byron said.

Joe Miller said, again, "Chehuth Chritht!"

"What's the matter?" Sam said, grabbing Joe's enormous arm.

The titanthrop, his eyes goggling, strangling noises coming from his open mouth, pointed up and out to the stern. Sam stepped in front of him to look, but he did not get there.

The explosion tore the bulletproof glass out of the frame of the rear window in a solid piece and slammed it against him.

34

THE MOUSE HAD SPRUNG THE TRAP ON THE CAT.

While the *Not For Hire* was still two days' journey away, the crew of the *Rex* had removed from storage the envelope of a small airship made from the intestinal linings of dragonfish over two years ago. The hydrogen-generating equipment was set up on shore, and the envelope was inflated within the bamboo and pine hangar built two weeks ago.

The *Azazel*, as John had christened it, was a semirigid airship. The envelope depended upon the pressure of gas to fill it out, but a metal keel was attached to it. The control cabin and the two motor gondolas, salvaged from the wreck of Podebrad's blimp, were fitted to the keel. The electrical and mechanical connections between control gondola and motor gondola and the elevators and rudder were attached. The fuel tanks were filled with methyl alcohol. The bomb and the torpedo were fitted to the release mechanisms halfway along the underpart of the ship.

The bombardier and the pilot got aboard the airship and took it up for a two-hour shakedown cruise. Everything worked well. And when the *Rex* left to do battle with the *Not For Hire*, the dirigible lifted to the desired height and began circling. Not until it became dark would it go through the high part of the strait.

As the *Rex* circled, imitating a crippled duck, the blimp was down-River behind the enemy vessel. It had come over the strait and then had turned right, cruising alongside, but not too near to, the mountains. Its black color would keep it from being visually observed by the enemy. There was a chance that the enemy radar would detect it. It was John's hope that it would be centered on the *Rex*. Clemens would think that the *Rex* had no more aircraft, so why make a radar sweep at a high altitude?

When the radar of the *Not For Hire* was destroyed, John was jubilant. Though his boat and crew had suffered terrible punishment, he danced with joy. Now the *Azazel* could creep up on the enemy, avoiding all but visual observation. And in this pale light, with the enemy's eyes only for the *Rex*, the airship had a good chance to get within striking distance.

The plan had worked out. The airship had hugged the mountains to the north, coming down to an altitude below the tops of the highest hills at times. It had gone east for some distance, then had eased out over the treetops to The River. And it had sped full power then, the bottom of its control gondola only a foot or so above the surface.

All was going well, and now the *Azazel* was behind the *Not For Hire*. Its bulk was shielded by the enemy boat, undetectable by its mother vessel's radar.

Burton, standing near John, heard him mutter, "By the Lord's loins! Now we'll see if the airship is swift enough to catch up with Sam's boat! My engineers had better be right! It would be ironic if, after all this work and planning, it was too slow!"

Salvoes from the enemy struck the *Rex* along the starboard decks. Burton felt stunned as the roar deafened him, shook the deck beneath him, and blew in a starboard port. The others looked as shocked as he felt. Immediately afterward, John was yelling at Strubewell to get the damage and casualty reports. At least, that is what his mouth must have been voicing. Strubewell understood. He spoke into the intercom, but it was difficult to hear him. Within a short time, he was able to get in some reports and to tell his captain. By then, Burton could hear well enough, though not as well as he would have liked to.

This had been the worst punishment suffered yet. There were huge holes in many places on all the decks. The explosions had not only punched these on the decks and in the hull, but corridors filled with people had been blown open. A number of rocket-launching mechanisms, loaded with missiles, had gone up, adding their explosions. Several steam machine-gun turrets were knocked off their foundations.

The starboard paddlebox or wheelhousing had been almost blown off by two shells. But the paddlewheel was still operating at one-hundred-percent efficiency.

"Clemens must have seen those shells hit the paddlebox," John said. "He could be fooled into thinking that he's crippled us. By Christ's cup, we'll make him think so!"

He gave the order to put the boat into a wide circle. The inner or starboard wheel was turned slowly while the outer or port wheel rotated under two-thirds power.

"He'll come arunning like a dog panting to finish off a wounded deer!" John said. He rubbed his hands and chuckled.

"Ay, he's bound toward us like a great beast out of *Revelation!*" John said. "But he doesn't know that there's an even more fearsome monster hot on his tail, about to vomit death and hellfire all over him! It's the vengeance of God!"

Burton felt disgusted. Was John actually equating himself with his Creator? Had his brains become a trifle addled from the shock of shells and rockets? Or had he always secretly felt that he and God were co-partners?

"They'll have to estimate distance with the eye, and in this light they won't do well," John said. "Their sonar isn't going to do any range calculation, either!"

The enemy would be getting more than return pulses from the beam directed at the *Rex.* The sonar operators were going to be confused. They'd see pulses from four different targets on their screens. Three would be from tiny remotely controlled boats circling in the lake, each emitting sound pulses of the same frequency as those of the enemy transmitter. The little vessels also contained noise generators which simulated the pounding of giant paddlewheels against the water.

Burton could see the upper structures of the *Not For Hire* silhouetted against the blazing stars and the shimmering gas sheets on the eastern horizon.

And then he saw a dark semicircle, the upper part of the *Azazel,* against the celestial illumination just above the *Not For Hire.*

"Fire your torpedo!" John said loudly. "Fire now, you fools!"

Peder Tordenskjöld, the chief gunnery officer, said, "Distances are deceiving now, sir. But the airship must've launched the torpedo already."

All glanced at the panel chronometer. The torpedo, if it hit, should do so within thirty seconds. That is, it would if the dirigible were as close to the boat as it seemed to be. The *Azazel* would have dropped the missile while it was only a few feet above The River. Lightened by the release of the heavy missile, it would have risen swiftly. Its speed would be increased also by the loss of weight. So, if it were now over, or almost over, the enemy, the torpedo should be about to strike.

The *Not For Hire* should be taking evasive action by now. Though the airship may not have been seen by the eye, the torpedo would be detected by the sonars of the enemy. Its location and speed would be instantly known, its shape and size indicated. The enemy would know that a torpedo was speeding toward its stern, as John inelegantly put it, "driving right up Sam Clemens' asshole."

John stopped. His face was a study in fury. "By God's teeth, how could it have missed at such close range?"

"It couldn't have," Strubewell said. "Maybe it malfunctioned. Didn't go off."

Whatever had happened, the enemy had escaped the torpedo. Behind it the semicircle of the *Azazel*, which had disappeared for a moment, rose again. The pilot and the bombardier would either have jumped out or be just about ready to jump. Their parachutes, equipped with a compressed-gas device, would unfold fully the moment they leaped clear of the gondola. Without that, they would not open before the two hit The River.

Burton estimated that the two men had to have left the semirigid by now. It would be set on automatic pilot now, and the clock in the release mechanism of the bomb would be ticking away. Another mechanism would be valving off hydrogen to lower the craft. When the bomb fell, the airship would be lightened and would rise. But not far. A few seconds afterward, if the explosion did not ignite the gas, a fourth mechanism would detonate a smaller bomb.

Burton looked out the port screen. The decks of the *Rex* were blazing in a dozen places from the shells and rockets. Firefighters, clad in insulation suits, were spraying the flames with water and foam. Within about two or three minutes, the fires would be extinguished.

Burton heard the captain say, "Hah!"

He turned. Everybody except the pilot was gazing out of the port screen. The sausage shape of the dirigible was directly above the *Not For Hire*. Its nose would soon touch the back of the pilothouse.

"Incredible!" Burton said.

"What?" the captain said.

"That no one on the boat has seen it yet."

"God is with me," John said. "Now, even if it is seen, it will be too late. It can't be shot down without imperiling the boat."

Tordenskjöld said, "Something happened to the torpedo release mechanism. It's malfunctioning. But when the bomb goes off, it'll set the torpedo off."

John spoke to the pilot. "Get ready to bring her around. When I give the word, head directly for the enemy."

The chief radio operator said, "The two launches are heading for us, sir."

"Surely they can see the *Azazel* now!" John said. "No, they haven't!"

"P'raps the *Not For Hire*'s radio is knocked out, too," Burton said.

"Then He is indeed on our side!" John said.

Burton grimaced.

A lookout said, "Sir! The enemy launches are approaching on the port sternside."

Radar reported that both launches were at a range of four hundred yards. They were separated from each other by one hundred and twenty feet.

"They're planning to take us in our starboard side when we're on the other side of our circle," Strubewell said. "They think the motherboat should be firing on us by then."

"I can see that," John said somewhat testily. "You'd think by now that they'd be trying to signal the *Hire*. The radio must be out, too, but surely they could send up flares."

"There goes one," Strubewell said, pointing at the bright bluewhite glare in the sky.

"Now they'll see the *Azazel!*" John cried.

It was about thirty feet above the flight deck of the enemy or at least it seemed to be. It was difficult to estimate at that distance. It was not up to the pilothouse yet. That was apparent, since if it had been, it would have collided with the structure.

Something dark and small dropped through the area of bright sky between the airship and the *Not For Hire*.

"There goes the bomb!" John cried.

Burton couldn't be sure, but it seemed to him that the bomb had fallen on the stern of the flight deck, perhaps at its edge. The bombardier must have set its timed automatic-release mechanism, and then he and the pilot had jumped. But the timing had not been right. The release should have been activated when it was in the middle of the deck. Or, better, as close to the pilothouse as possible.

The explosion wreathed the flight deck in flames and silhouetted the pilothouse and the tiny figures in it.

The airship soared upward, bending in the middle, its keel twisted by the blast. And its envelope burst into flames, the hydrogen in it one huge ball of fire.

"The torpedo!" John shouted. "The torpedo! Why didn't it fall?"

Perhaps it had, and it couldn't be seen from the *Rex*.

But it should have been set off by now.

Now Burton could see the dirigible drift down, flaming. Its forward part fell upon the stern of the *Not For Hire* and then slid off into The River through the great hole made by the forty-pound bomb. The *Not For Hire* plowed on, leaving the blazing and spreading-out envelope behind it. The stern was aflame, too, the wooden flight deck burning furiously.

John yelled, "God tear those two to pieces in the deepest pits of Hell! They're cowards! They should have waited a few seconds more!"

Burton thought that the pilot and the bombardier had been very brave indeed. They must have waited until what seemed to them to be the last possible second before being able to jump. Under such pressure, they couldn't be blamed for having made such a slight miscalculation. Nor was it their fault that the torpedo had not exploded. They'd made several trial runs with a dummy torpedo, and the release mechanism had worked then. Mechanical devices frequently malfunctioned, and it was their bad luck, and the bad luck of their comrades, that it had failed now.

However, the torpedo might still go off. Unless it had slid off the stern with the wreck.

John was not so unhappy when he saw that the blast had ripped off all of the two lower decks of the pilothouse structure except for two vertical supporting metal beams and the elevator shaft. And these were bending forward slowly under the weight of the control room.

Somehow, a few people in the room had survived. They were silhouetted against the holocaust on the rear of the flight deck.

"God's balls!" John said. "He has spared Clemens so that I may take him prisoner!"

He paused, then said, "They won't be able to steer! We have them in our hands!"

He spoke to the pilot.

"Bring us up along the enemy's port at pointblank range!"

The pilot looked wide-eyed at his captain, but he said, "Aye, aye, sir."

John spoke to Strubewell and Tordenskjöld then, telling them to ready the crew for broadsides first and then for boarding.

Burton hoped that he would be ordered to join his marines. They had been sitting deep within the hurricane deck, behind locked doors, waiting. During the entire battle, they had not been informed of anything. All they knew was that the boat had rocked and shaken from time to time, and thunder had roared outside their room. Doubtless, they were all keyed up, nervous, sweating, wondering when they would see action.

The *Rex* plowed The River in a furrow angling in toward the stricken vessel. The gap between the two swiftly shortened.

"Batteries B2, C2, and D2 will aim for the pilothouse top deck," John said.

Strubewell relayed the orders. Then he said, "Battery C2 doesn't reply, sir. Either the communication's cut or it's out of action."

"Tell C3 to aim for the pilothouse control room."

"You forget, sir. C3's definitely out of action. The last salvo got it, sir."

"B2 can do it then," John said.

He turned to Burton. His face looked purplish in the night-light. "Get to your men now, Captain," he said. "Be prepared to lead a boarding party from the midport side."

Burton saluted and sped down the spiral ladder. He got off at the hurricane deck and hurried down a corridor. His men and women were inside a large chamber outside the armory. Lieutenant Gaius Flaminius was outside the hatch with two guards. His face lit up when he saw Burton.

"We're going into action?"

"Yes," Burton said. "Very quickly. Get them out here into the corridor."

While Flaminius bawled orders, Burton stood at the corner of the two corridors. He would have to lead his force down the corridor going to the outside. They would have to wait there until the command came down to board the *Not For Hire*. Or, if the communication system wasn't working, he would have to judge for himself when to order the attack.

It was while the marines were being lined up in the corridor that the broadside from the *Not For Hire* struck. The explosions were deafening; they made Burton's ears ring. A bulkhead down the corridor bulged in. Smoke poured in from somewhere, setting everybody to coughing. There was another roar that shook the decks and deadened their ears even more.

Up on the bridge, John hung on to the railing and shuddered as the boat vibrated. At a range of only thirty feet, the portside rocket batteries of four decks of the *Rex* and the starboard rocket and cannon and steam gun batteries—those still in force—of the *Not For Hire* had poured fire into each other. Great pieces of the hull had flown spinning into the air. Entire batteries of rockets and their crews had disintegrated in flame and smoke. The two remaining cannons on Clemens' boat had been torn from their mounts as the shell supplies behind them were touched off by rockets. Two steam machine-gun turrets, one on each vessel, had caved in, opened as a can opens to a metal punch, then had been peeled apart as rockets or shells came in through the tears in the metal.

The great boats were wounded beasts, cut open, their insides exposed, bleeding heavily.

In addition, certain batteries on each craft had aimed volleys at the control rooms, the brains of the beasts. A number of missiles had shot by their marks, either splashing harmlessly into the water or striking elsewhere. A few plumped ashore, starting more fires. None had hit the pilothouses directly. How they could miss at that range was inexplicable, but this often happened in combat. Shots that should have gone astray did not, and dead-certain shots went awry.

The sharp nose of the *Not For Hire* turned, whether from design or accident, John could not know. Its prow sliced into the giant port wheelguard of the *Rex*, tearing it off, lifting its many tons up and off and precipitating it into The River. The prow continued on, crushing the paddles, bending the frame of the wheel, and then snapping off the massive wheelshaft. In the midst of the eardrum-shattering explosions, the screech of tearing metal, the screams of men and women, the roar of burning hydrogen, both boats stopped. The impact of the collision hurled everyone who wasn't strapped in to the deck. The prow crumpled in and up, and water poured in through several rents in the hull.

At the same time, the pilot house of the *Not For Hire* toppled forward. It seemed to those within it, Miller, Clemens, and Byron, the only ones left alive in the structure, that it fell slowly. But it did not, being attracted by gravity as fully as any other object. It crashed upon the foredeck of the hangar deck, and out of it hurled Clemens and Miller. Sam landed on top of the giant, whose own fall was softened somewhat by the padded and insulated uniform and helmet.

They lay there for several minutes dazed, bruised, deafened, bleeding, too numbed to realize that they were lucky to be alive.

35

SAM CLEMENS AND JOE MILLER CLIMBED DOWN THE LADDER LEADING from the hangar deck. The fire raged behind them. Then they were on the hurricane deck. Joe carried his colossal axe in one hand. He said, "You okay, Tham?"

Sam did not reply. He grabbed one of the titanthrop's fingers and pulled him on around the corner. A bullet struck the bulkhead, its plastic fragments whizzing around them. None hit flesh, however.

"The *Rex* is right alongside us!" Clemens said.

"Yeah, I thaw that," Joe said. "I think they're going to try to board uth."

"I can't control my boat!" Sam cried. He looked as if he were going to weep.

Joe seemed as calm and as impervious to destruction as a mountain. He patted Sam on the shoulder. "Don't vorry. The boat'll chutht drift athyore. It von't think. And ve'll knock Chohn and hith aththholeth thilly."

Then both were hurled to the deck. Sam lay for a while, groaning, unaware that the *Not For Hire* had ripped off a paddlebox and wheel of the *Rex*. During the firing that broke out as soon as the boats had come to a stop, he continued to lie with his face pressed against the cold hard deck. A hand reached down and grabbed his shoulder and picked him up by it. He yelled with agony.

"Thorry, Tham," Joe rumbled. "I forgot mythelf."

Sam held his one shoulder. "You dumbbell, I won't ever be able to use that arm again!"

"You egthaggerate ath uthual," Joe said. "You're alive vhen by all rightth you thyouldn't be. Tho am I. Tho get vith it, Tham. Ve got vork to do."

Clemens looked up at the flight deck. The flames had by now covered not only that but had reached down into the hangar deck. There was not much to burn, however. The barrels of methanol that were usually stored there had been taken to the lowest deck before the battle had started. Though the flaming hydrogen was hot, it would burn itself out quickly.

As he thought this, he saw the flight deck cave in on itself. From this angle, he could only see its edges sticking out. But the crash that went with the falling parts told him that at least half of the structure had collapsed. And flame gusted out, like a dragon breathing at him.

Joe leaped forward, yelling, "Chethuth Chritht!"

He picked up Sam and continued forward until he had reached the edge of the hurricane deck. Then he dropped Sam.

"Tham, I think I'm burned!"

"Turn around," Clemens said. On inspecting the back, he said, "You clown! The armor saved you. You may be a little hot under the collar, but you're not hurt."

Joe went back to get the axe he'd dropped. Sam looked at the bulk of the *Rex*. Its port side was against the starboard port prow of his boat. Grappling lines were being shot or hurled from both sides on all three of the lower decks, and the boarding bridges were already extended. The walkways and the ports and hatches, as far as he could see, were crowded with men and women. All were either firing at pointblank range or getting ready to attack as soon as the lines were secured. The boarding bridges would be manned in a very short time.

He did not have a gun. Fortunately, there were plenty on the decks, dropped from nerveless hands. He picked one up, checked its chambers, removed a bandolier from a corpse, put it on himself, and removed bullets from the belt to put in the pistol. Joe's form loomed up from around the corner, startling him. He did not reproach Joe for being so silent, since Joe was supposed not to make noise. But he had thought his heart would stop.

"Vhat'll ve do now, Tham?"

"Join our men and let them know we're still alive and kicking," Clemens said. "That'll recharge their morale."

They arrived just in time to see the last of a large group storm onto the hurricane deck from the *Rex*. Below them, however, John's men were forcing back the would-be boarders from the *Not For Hire*. In fact, John's men were boarding his—Sam's boat—on some of the bridges.

Sam leaned over and emptied his pistol into the rear-guard of the boarders below. Two men fell, one going down in the narrow gap between the two vessels. But one of the boarders, still on the *Rex*, looked up and then shot his own pistol. Sam ducked as the first bullet screamed by his ear. The other missiles shattered against the railing or the hull just below the railing.

Joe was going to look over the railing then, but Sam yelled at him that if he did he'd get his head blown off.

After waiting until he was sure that the boarding bridges below were empty, he looked over and down. The deck below was jammed with struggling, shouting people and was noisy with ringing metal. Sam told Joe what he wanted to do. Joe nodded, lifting his great proboscis up and down like a log floating in a rough sea.

They ran across the boarding bridge, Joe bellowing to the men there that he and the captain were coming.

On both sides of their group were a few of the *Rex* crew, rapidly backing away before the superior force. These broke on seeing the great head and shoulders of the titanthrop above the crowd of Clemens' men. They ran as fast as they could, some diving into hatches, others leaping over the railing or through the gaps and into The River.

"That thyure ath hell didn't take long, did it, Tham?"

"No," Sam said. "I wish it was always that easy. Okay, Joe, you give them the orders."

The titanthrop yelled at the top of his voice at the men. They had no trouble hearing him. Indeed, at least half of the people halfway down both boats on this side must have heard the thunder. In fact, on one deck below and opposite, the battlers stopped for a few seconds.

The men ahead of Joe cleared to one side. Joe proceeded to the nearest ladder, Sam immediately behind him, and the others following. They went down the ladder to the hurricane deck and along it until they came to the boarding bridges. Here the men spread out, forming lines of two abreast at each of the eight bridges.

Sam checked that everybody was ready. Attacking John's men from behind them, from their own boat, tickled him. They would be demoralized when the titanthrop swung that Brobdingnagian axe upon their heads from behind them.

"Okay, Joe!" Sam yelled. "Go get 'em!"

Joe, bellowing a war cry in his native language, ran across the metal strip. Sam came behind him. There was not room on the bridge for another person where Joe went. Besides, it was more discreet to stay behind him.

Things happened so swiftly that only in retrospect was Sam able to figure out what happened.

A great noise deafened him, and a shock traveled through the bridge and hurled him onto it. Almost immediately after, the far end of the bridge lifted up, bending as its hooks kept their hold on the railing, then tearing loose with a screech of metal.

Sam, clinging stunned to the edges of the bridge, both arms extended to their utmost, the fingers clinging to the edges, looked up.

Joe had dropped his enormous axe. It slid along the upward and sidewise tilting bridge and fell off into the gap between the boats.

Joe had not fallen, but now he was bellowing in wrath. Or was it fear? It didn't matter. He was bellowing because both his arms were caught about his body by a noose.

The other end of the rope was being tied to a railing on the deck above. The man who had lassoed Joe from the hangar deck wore a Western sombrero, white enough to gleam in the pale light. His teeth flashed briefly below the wide brim.

Then Joe had fallen off the bridge. But, instead of going straight down into the chasm between the vessels, he swung down and then slammed against the hull of the *Not For Hire.* Joe quit bellowing then. His head lolled to one side, and he hung like a giant fly caught in the strand of an even larger spider.

Sam cried out, "Joe! Joe!"

It seemed impossible that anything serious could happen to Joe Miller. He was so enormous, so muscular, so . . . invincible. A man the size of a cave lion or a Kodiak bear should not be . . . mortal . . . vulnerable.

He did not have much time for such thoughts.

The bridge continued to tilt upward as the *Rex* rolled over. Sam clamped his hands on the sides of the bridge, his head turned away from Joe now. He saw men and women on the other bridges lose their holds and, screaming, fall into the narrow well of darkness between the vessels.

How ironic that the fabulous Riverboat *Rex,* which he had built, should be responsible for killing its builder. What a joke that the first boat should catch him halfway between the second boat and itself. Suspended him like Mohammed between heaven and earth.

Then he had let loose, had slid backward down the bridge, fallen into the angle made by the vertical deck and the horizontal bulkhead, had scrambled up it, and was sliding face down on the hull. He was up on his feet somehow and running down toward The River. Then he was slipping and rolling down the curve and into The River.

He went down, down, struggling to get rid of his cuirass. His helmet had come loose sometime during the struggle. He was terrified now that he could not get the armor from his body in time to keep from being sucked on down by the sinking *Rex.* That colossal sinking body would make a great whirlpool which, when it collapsed, would take all jetsam and flotsam, all debris, inanimate or animate, deep down with it. And if he was heavily burdened by his armor and weapons, he'd go down, too. Even if he were unburdened, he might sink.

At last, his belt and the bandolier and his chain-mail shirt and the attached skirt were off. He rose then, his chest seeming to burst, the ancient horror of drowning threatening to tear apart his hammering heart, his ears ringing with a tolling from the deeps. He had to breathe but dared not. Down there was the mud, as black and as evil as and far deeper than the mud of the Mississippi, and around him was water, squeezing like an Iron Maiden made of putty, and above—how far away?—was air.

It was too dark to see anything. For all he knew, he was going deeper, headed in the blackness the wrong way. No, his ears would hurt if he were diving instead of ascending.

He could not hold out much longer. Not more than a few seconds. Then . . . the death that his Mississippi boyhood had made him fear more than any other. Except one. If he had to die, he would do it in water rather than in fire.

For half a second, or however swiftly such thoughts went, he visualized Erik Bloodaxe.

At least that nemesis would not get him. The Viking, as a prophet and a nemesis, an avenging human machine, was a failure. All those nightmares of all those years had been wasteful torture. That the man could see into the far future, in fact assure it, was a superstition.

All those people in Hannibal who had prophesied that he would hang had been twice wrong.

Strange how such amusing thoughts could flash through the mind of a man whose only thought should be on the blessed air. Or was he actually drowning, almost dead, had forgotten the horror of having to open his nostrils and gulp in water, was thinking dying thoughts, his body flaccid and sinking, his eyes glazed, mouth open as any finny denizen, a tiny flicker of electricity in some cells of his brain the only life left in him?

Then his head was in the air, and he was drinking in oxygen and glad, glad, glad because he was not dead.

His flailing hand touched a rope, moved back, felt it, seized it. He was hanging on to a rope the other end of which was tied on to a stanchion from the main deck of his boat. He was near the stern. A few more seconds, and he would have found the boat out of reach.

He was lucky that he had come across the line at once. The River pulled at him, forcing him to clutch the line as tightly as he had the bridge. The *Rex* was gone, but it was dragging along a broad and deep hollow, waters whirling and sinking. There was an even greater pull on him as the walls of the whirlpool collapsed.

What had sunk the *Rex*? A torpedo from the *Post No Bills*?

He looked up. He couldn't see Joe's body hanging from the rope. It could still be there, but the decks were set too far back for him to see Joe from the surface of The River. Was he still hanging? Or had the man who'd lassoed him cut the rope? If so, Joe might have fallen onto the deck below, a long hard fall but still better than plunging into the water. But he could be dead or dying already. That long swing inward, ending up against the metal bulkhead, could have smashed his ribs, caved in his skull.

Never mind Joe now. He had to save himself.

For some time, while the howling and blasting went on above, and occasionally a man or woman would topple over the railing and fall with a splash near him, he hung on to the line. When the sound of immediate battle died down rather suddenly, he started to climb up. It was not easy, since so much of his strength had been squeezed out of him. He finally got his feet against the hull and, leaning outward above the water, pulled himself up puffing and panting, his muscles hurting, until he was near the railing. He eased himself down until his face was against the hull, and he began hauling himself up by his arms alone. Now he wished that he had not avoided daily exercise so much. For several minutes, as he rested, unable to hitch himself up until he had regained his breath, he thought that his clenched hands would come apart. He would drop back into The River and all would be over.

Finally, he got one hand up to grip the upright to the railing. He got his other hand around it. The long painful pull began. Then it was over, and he had managed to throw one leg over the edge of the deck. Wheezing, he squirmed until he had half his body on the deck. Then he was able to roll onto the deck, to lie there face up while he tried to get all the air in the world inside his lungs.

After a while, his narrow chest quit rising and falling so hard, like a pair of worn-out blacksmith's bellows. He rolled around to look back and up alongside the decks. He still could not see Joe.

Perhaps he was too far away and the angle of sight was too oblique. He needed to get further away, which he could not do, or get upon the same deck.

For that moment, he had to get weapons. And he also had to get at least a kilt. During his struggle his magnetically attached cloths had come off. Naked I came into this world, and naked . . . nonsense. He was not leaving. Not yet.

He got unsteadily to his feet. Bodies and parts of bodies lay along the deck in both directions. The parts of bodies or legs stuck out from hatches. Weapons were everywhere. So were cloths.

Shivering from fatigue or fear or both, he stripped a body. The cloths he made into a long kilt and a short cape. A belt went around his waist, a bandolier, over his shoulder; a loaded pistol, into a holster; a cutlass, into his hand. He was armed, but that did not mean that he was ready for combat. He had had enough today to last him for the rest of his life, even if it were a thousand years long.

What he wanted to do was to get back to Joe. The two of them would round up or join a large body of men. And he would be secure again, or as secure as it was possible to be under the circumstances.

For a moment he thought about taking refuge inside a cabin. He could hole up and then come out when the people from the *Rex* had been cleared out.

It was a nice thought, one which anyone with a logical mind and common sense would have.

Down along the deck, something struck with a metallic clang. A man cursed softly; somebody else spoke just as quietly but harshly, a reprimand. Sam stopped, his shoulder pressed against the cold bulkhead. Near the prow, the shadowy figures of men were coming down the steps from the hurricane deck. There seemed to be about twenty.

He slid backward, his shoulder against the metal. His left hand felt behind him. When he touched the edge of the open hatch, he turned swiftly and went into it. He was in another unlit passageway which went straight to the hatch on the other side. This was open, showing a pale oblong lit only by starlight and a flickering from the burning flight deck. Sam decided to get to that side, and he started trotting. Then he stopped.

It was his duty to ascertain who the men were and what they were doing. He'd feel like a fool if they were his people. And if they weren't, he should determine what they were up to.

Of course, they would be looking into every open entrance before they went past it. He opened the door to a cabin and stepped inside, leaving the door partly open. From this angle, he could see them but they couldn't see him in the darkness. He had opened another cabin door across the corridor so he could take refuge in that if he had to. He did not want to be trapped.

There was, however, nothing he could do about his situation now. The first of the party had bounded through the opening, stopped against the side of the hatchway, where he was barely visible, and pointed a pistol. A second man also leaped in and hurled himself toward the other side of the hatchway, his pistol ready.

Sam did not fire. If they would only be content to look along the passageway. They were. After several seconds, one said, "All clear!"

Both left for the walkway, and figures began filing past the oblong. The fourth one went by, and Sam gasped. The profile against the indirect light of the stars was that of a short broad-shouldered man. The figure walked with John's gait. It had been thirty-three years since he had seen the ex-monarch, but he had forgotten little about him.

36

Rage overcame fear, a rage that was a compression of all the rages he'd felt on Earth and here. He did not even think about the consequences. At last! Here it was! Vengeance!

He stepped outside the cabin and went softly across the deck. Though he was so exuberant that he was almost dizzy, he still had not lost all discretion. He wasn't going to warn them so they could shoot him before he got to John.

The only bad part about this was that he'd have to shoot John in the back. The bastard would never know who had killed him. But you couldn't have everything. He desired passionately to call out John's name, identify himself, and then squeeze the trigger. But John's men would shoot him down the second they were aware of his presence.

Just as he reached the hatchway, hell exploded outside. There was a crash of gunfire that deafened him and made him pin himself against the bulkhead as if he were a two-legged butterfly. His fluttering heart was the wings.

More shooting. Cries and screams. A man reeled backward into the passageway. Sam leaped for the open door of the cabin, spun, shut it, then opened it again. He looked through the narrow opening in time to see others come into the passageway. One was the bulky form of John, no mistake about that, outlined briefly against the light.

Sam opened the door fully (thank God it was well oiled!), leaned out, and rapped John over the side of the head with his pistol barrel. John grunted and fell. Sam stooped, dropped the pistol on the chest of the fallen man, gripped him by his long hair, and pulled him into the cabin. Once the feet were past the entrance, he shut the door and pressed the locking button. Outside, the explosions of gunfire were loud, but nothing struck the door. Apparently, the snatching of their leader had happened so swiftly and in such confusion and dark that they had not yet noticed his absence. Perhaps, when they did, they would assume that he had been downed in the corridor.

Sam quivered with delight. He was in great danger, but at the moment that meant nothing. By the Providence that did not exist, events had worked out perfectly. Whatever he had suffered, it was worth it—well, almost worth it. To have his greatest enemy, the only person he had ever really hated, in his power! And in such strange circumstances! Even John, when he awoke, would not be more surprised than he. Truth *was* stranger than fiction, and he could go on quoting many more clichés.

He pressed the light switch plate with one hand, the pistol held in the other. The ceiling globes shed a flickering light. John groaned, and his eyelids fluttered. Sam tapped him not too lightly on the head again. He did not want to kill him or to damage his brain overly much. John had to have all his senses operating one hundred percent. Otherwise, he wouldn't appreciate to the fullest what had happened to him.

Sam opened the drawers of a chest attached to the bulkhead. He withdrew some of the thin semitransparent cloths used as brassieres. With these he tied John's hands together behind his back and then bound his feet together. Puffing and grunting, he dragged the unconscious man to a chair bolted to the deck. Managing to get the heavy body onto the chair, he tied John's hands to the rungs of the back. Then he went into the head, drank two cups of water from the faucet, and filled a third cup. As this was done, the faucet rattled, and the flow thinned to a trickle. The water pump had suddenly quit.

Sam returned to the main cabin and threw the water in John's face. John gasped, and his eyelids opened. For a minute, he did not seem to know where he was. Then, recognizing Samuel Clemens, his eyes opened fully, and he drew in his breath with a harsh noise as if he had been struck in the pit of his stomach. Where his skin was not covered with smoke, it became gray-blue.

"Yes, it's me, John."

Sam grinned widely.

"You can't believe it, can you? But you'll get used to the idea in a moment. Though you won't like getting used to it."

John croaked, "Water!"

Sam looked into the red-shot eyes. Despite his hatred, he felt sorry for John. Not sympathy, just pity. After all, he wouldn't let a rabid dog suffer, would he?

He shook his head. "The water is all gone."

"I'm dying of thirst," John said hoarsely.

Sam snarled, "Is that all you can think about after what you've done to me? After all these years?"

John said, "Satisfy my thirst, and I'll satisfy yours."

His skin had recovered its normal color, and his eyes looked steadily into Sam's. Knowing John, Sam could see what strategy the cunning fellow had already formulated. He would talk reasonably to his captor, would talk quietly and logically, would appeal to his humanity, and would, in the end, avoid execution.

The hell of it, Sam realized, was that John would succeed.

The anger was draining out of him now. The thirty-three years of vengeance fantasies were blown away like farts in a high wind.

What was left was a man who was basically Christian, though a howling atheist, to use a phrase applied to him by one of his Terrestrial enemies.

He should have shot John in the head the moment he had turned on the light. He should have known what would happen if he did not. But he could not kill a man who was unconscious. Not even King John, whose blood he had lusted for all these years and who had been tortured so ingeniously and so excruciatingly in his daydreams. Never in his night-time dreams. Then it was John who was about to do something to a paralyzed or hopelessly trapped Sam Clemens. Or, mostly, it was Erik Bloodaxe who was about to be revenged upon him.

Sam grimaced and went back into the head. As he suspected, the shower pipes contained enough water for several cupfuls. He drank one and filled a second. Returning to the cabin, he put the cup to his captive's lips and tilted it as the man drank. John smacked his lips and sighed.

"Another, please?"

"Another! Please?" Sam said loudly. "Are you crazy! I just gave you one so you'll be able to stand up to what I'm going to do to you!"

John smiled briefly. He was as undeceived as his captor.

Knowing that infuriated Sam so much that he almost became capable of doing what he had threatened. The anger ebbed swiftly, leaving him with the pistol upraised to strike.

John's smile faded, but only because he did not wish to push Sam too far.

"Why are you so sure of yourself, of me?" Sam said. "Do you think I wouldn't have blasted you out of the water, sunk you to hell, watched you drown, and shoved you away if you had tried to get aboard?"

"Of course," John said. "But that was in the heat of battle. You won't torture me, much as you'd like to do so. Nor will you shoot me in cold blood."

"But you'd do all that to me, wouldn't you, you heartless bastard?"

John smiled.

Sam started to reply, then closed his mouth. The uproar in the passageway had suddenly stopped. John also started to say something, but at a sign from Sam he stopped. Apparently, he knew that if he tried to yell, he would regret it. His enemy was not that soft.

Minutes passed. Sam stood by the door, his ear against it, one eye on John. Now he could hear the faint voices of men. These cabins were soundproofed, so there was no determining how far away the voices were. He went back to John and placed a cloth over his mouth, tying it tightly behind his head.

"Just in case," he said. "But if you do manage to shout for help, I'll be forced to shoot you. Remember that."

And I hope you do cry out, he thought.

He turned off the light, unlocked the door, and pushed it slowly out, holding the pistol in his other hand. It took a few seconds for his eyes to adjust to the darkness. There were more bodies than there had been before. He looked cautiously around the door and down the corridor. Still more bodies. It looked as if the fight had progressed down it to the other side and on out. The handgun firing had ceased sometime during the struggle. It was replaced by the ring of blade on blade. And the distant din was composed only of voices and metal clash. It seemed that both sides had run out of ammunition.

He did not see how the numerically smaller boarders could hold out for long against his own people. He'd wait a little while to make sure that it was safe to emerge with his prisoner.

But, wasn't he rationalizing? Wasn't it his duty to get out there and lead his people? Yes, it was. But what about his prisoner?

That was easy. He would lock John in the cabin with the key now hanging by the door. Then he'd look for his crew. It wouldn't be difficult to find it. A good part would be where the noise was.

He returned to the cabin, shut the door, and turned on the light. John looked curiously at him.

"It's just about over," Sam said. "Your crew's about cleaned out. I'm going now, but I'll be back soon. And sometime in the future you'll be on trial."

He paused. John's expression did not change. Gurgling sounds came from behind the gag. Evidently, he wanted to speak. But what could he say? Why waste time?

"I don't want it said that I am not fair or that I am too personally involved to be just," Sam said. "So, you'll get a trial. It won't be by your peers. How many kings are running loose out there or within easy call? But it'll have a jury of twelve good men and true. That's only a phrase, since the ladies'll be represented too.

"Anyway, you'll get a fair hearing, and you can pick your own defense lawyer. I'll abide by the verdict, I won't even act as judge. Whatever the jury says, I'll go along with it."

Mangled words came through the gag.

"You can have your say at the proper time," Sam said. "Meantime, you can sit here and meditate on your sins."

He closed and locked the door, hesitated, then unlocked it, reached in, and switched off the light. John would suffer more if he was in darkness.

He should have been jubilant. He was not. Somehow, in some way he could not define, his old enemy had triumphed.

Most things were disappointments, but this, this should have been one of the most enjoyable events in his life. His victory was as unappetizing as a steaming dog turd served under glass.

Where to hide the key? Ah, of course, in the first cabin with an unlocked door. That was three cabins down. He threw the key onto the floor and closed the door. Now to get to Joe. To do that, he would have to have a large number of men behind him.

He went down a corridor which ran longitudinally through the vessel. The lights were off, but he dared turn them on briefly. He ran down its length for a hundred feet, then stopped at another corridor. Here was a stairway that led up to the hurricane deck. After turning the lights off, he went up the steps, aided by a pale square at the top. Once on the hurricane deck, he trotted down the passageway to the starboard side. Noise came to him, but it seemed far off. He peered around the corner onto the walkway. Joe should be somewhere near.

"Why're you hanging around here, Joe? Don't you have anything to do?"

"I'm vaiting for a buth, Tham."

"A buss? Who'd kiss your ugly mug, Joe?"

"No, not a buthth vith two etheth, you nincompoop. A buth vith vone eth. Vith vheelth and a motor. How in hell vould I know, Tham? I never theen a buth. Get me down off of here before I get mad and tear you apart, you thap."

Thus went the imaginary conversation, modeled on so many previous ones. But there was no great bulk hanging helpless from a rope. There was a rope, severed at one end and noosed at the other, lying on the deck.

Sam smiled with joy. Joe was alive, unhurt! Joe was on the loose, undoubtedly tearing up the opposition.

He turned but stopped halfway. A bellow had come from out on The River. It was a deep cry, one which would have been attributed to a lion or a tiger if it had been heard on Earth. Sam knew better. He ran to a staircase and sped down it, taking two steps at a time, one hand sliding on the railing. On the main deck, he paused. He could not ignore the enemy. But the two fights he heard were far away, one at the prow and one at the stern. There was no gunfire, only the clang of blades against blades.

He ran to the railing and leaned out. "Joe! Where are you, Joe?"

"Tham! Here I am, Tham!"

"I can't see you, Joe!" Clemens called, peering into the darkness. There were objects floating out there, pieces of timber or bodies, unidentifiable flotsam. Though the boat had been drifting with the current, and the fires on the south bank were bright, the starboard side was now toward the dark northern bank. Starlight was not enough there.

"I can't thee you either, Tham!"

He looked on both sides and behind him to make sure no one was creeping up on him. On turning back to look outward, he called, "Can you get back to the boat?"

"No!" Joe bellowed. "But I'm floating! I got hold of a piethe of vood! My left arm'th broken, Tham!"

"I'll get you back, Joe! Hang on! I'll save you!"

He had no idea how he could help Joe but he was determined to find a way somehow. The thought that Joe might drown panicked him.

"Joe, are you still in armor?"

"No, you thilly athth. I'd be on the bottom, food for the fithyeth if I had all that iron on. I got rid of it after I fell in, though my broken arm almotht killed me. Chethuth! The pain! You ever been kicked in the ballth, Tham? Lithten, that ain't nothin' compared to trying to undrethth vith a broken arm."

"Okay, Joe!" Sam said, and he looked around nervously again. Somebody was running his way from the prow, pursued by two men. All were too far away for him to identify them. Behind them was stillness.

The group near the stern was still battling, though it seemed that it had thinned out somewhat.

"I got cut down by thomebody!" Joe bellowed. "And I got loothe then. I grabbed a fire akthe and cleaned up around me and chathed vhat vath left down to the main deck. And then damned if thomebody didn't knock me over the railing, chuth like that! He mutht have been a hell of a thtrong man, the aththole!"

Joe kept on talking, but Sam didn't hear him. He crouched by the railing, unable to decide what to do. Though the runners were much nearer now, and coming swiftly, they were still unidentifiable in the dark. He was in agony. In the confusion and haste, his own men might attack him.

He raised the pistol in his left hand, keeping the cutlass in his right. He could aim with either hand, though not well. At this range, though, he could not miss. But did he have to shoot?

The decision never had to be made. As he waited, eyes straining, finger tight on the trigger, he was lifted up and hurled over the railing.

For a minute or so, he was so stunned that he had no idea of what had happened. He knew he was in the water, choking, spitting, struggling. But how had he gotten there? And why?

He bumped into something. His hands felt cold flesh. A corpse. He shoved it away and slipped off the heavy bandolier.

Before him, but now about sixty feet away, was the vast boat. How had he gotten so far away from it? Had he been swimming? Or floating? It didn't matter. He was here, and the boat was there. He would swim back to it. This was the second time he'd been in The River. What I dip you in three times is true.

As he thrashed toward the vessel, he saw that the railing of the boiler deck was closer to the water than it should be. The boat was sinking!

Now he knew what had tossed him off the deck like a fly shrugged off by a horse. Except that he had no wings. It had been an explosion below the water line. In the boiler deck where ammunition was stored. And it would have been set off, of course, by John's men.

He had gone through too much. Even the imminent loss of his beautiful *Not For Hire*, which should have brought tearing pain and tears, did not affect him much. He was too tired and too desperate. Almost, he told himself, too tired to be desperate.

He swam toward the boat. His right hand came down hard on something. He cried out with pain, then reached out again. Wet slippery wood curved under his hand. Gasping with joy, he seized it and pulled himself forward. He didn't know what it was, a piece of canoe or dugout, but it was enough to buoy him.

Where was Joe?

He called out. There was no answer. He tried again and got the same silence.

Had the explosion gotten Joe? The detonation would have hurled a strong pressure wave through the water. Anyone near it would probably have been killed. But Joe wasn't close enough. Or was he? It must have been a hell of a blast.

Or perhaps Joe had just lost consciousness from the pain of his broken bone and slipped off into The River.

He called twice more. Someone shrieked from far away, a woman's voice. Some other poor soul floating in The River.

The boat was visibly settling down. There would be many compartments, large and small, with closed doors and hatches. There might even be enough enclosed air to keep the Riverboat afloat. Eventually, she would drift into shore; she could even be towed in by sailing ships or rowboats or both.

For such a deep-shaded pessimist, he was incredibly optimistic.

He wasn't going to make it. The prow of the vessel—it was drifting backward—slid by him. And now he saw the launch, the *Post No Bills*. It was moving very slowly, apparently looking for swimmers. Its searchlight probed across the waters, stopped, moved back, and centered on something. It was too far away for him even to see whatever the beam was on. The launch was also too distant to hear his cries.

Suddenly, he remembered King John. The man was bound and helpless in a locked cabin. He was doomed unless someone got to him. He couldn't cry out, and it was doubtful that anyone would be near enough to hear him, if he could be heard. And even then there was no key available. The lock could be shot off, but . . . why speculate? John was doomed. He would sit there not even knowing that the boat was going down. The water would flood the main deck, and he still wouldn't know. Those cabins were watertight. Not until the air suddenly became stuffy would he guess what had happened. Then he would struggle desperately, squirm, twist, writhe, calling out for help through the gag. The air would get fouler and fouler, and he would slowly choke to death.

His last moments would be horrible.

It was a scene which Sam would once have projected on his mind's screen with great pleasure.

Now he could only wish that he could get to the boat and rescue John. Not that he'd let him go scot-free. He'd see that he got that promised trial. But he did not wish John to suffer so or to die so terribly. He did not want anybody to go through that.

Yes, he was soft, John would have enjoyed thinking of him if he were in such a situation. No matter. He wasn't John, and he was glad of it.

He forgot about John as the launch started up again. It headed for the other side of the Riverboat and then had disappeared. Was Anderson now about to pick up the survivors from the stricken vessel? If he was, he'd have to help finish the last hold-outs from the *Rex*, the jackasses who didn't know when to quit. Maybe they would have sense enough now to surrender.

"Tham!"

The bellow came from behind him. He turned, keeping one arm halfway around the curving wood. "Joe! Where are you?"

"Over here, Tham! I paththed out! I chutht came to, Tham, but I don't think I can make it!"

"Hang on, Joe!" Clemens shouted. "I'll get to you! Keep yelling! I'll be there soon! Keep yelling so I'll know where you are!"

It wasn't easy to turn the big piece of flotsam and get going straight toward the bank. He had to hang on with one arm and paddle with the other. He kicked his feet, too. Now and then he had to stop to catch his breath. Then he would shout, "Joe! Where are you? Joe! Yell so I can hear you!"

Silence. Had Joe fainted again? If so, had he strapped himself to whatever was holding him up? He must have. Otherwise, he would have sunk when he passed out the first time. But maybe he'd been lying on something. Maybe . . .

Since he had to rest for a moment, anyway, he looked behind him. The boat had slid even further downstream. The River was creeping up along the walls of the main deck. In a short time, John's cabin would be under water.

He began pushing the wood toward the bank. The fires on shore illuminated the surface somewhat. Though he could see plenty of debris, he couldn't distinguish any as Joe Miller.

Now he could see that the people on shore were putting out in boats and canoes. Their torches burned brightly by the hundreds. Coming to the rescue, though why they should want to help the people who'd burned down a quarter of their buildings was incomprehensible.

No. They were doing for the destroyers what he would have done for John if he could have. And, actually, the Virolanders did not have cause to hate the Riverboat people as he had to hate John.

By then he understood that he had drifted in much closer to shore than he had thought. It was only about a half mile to the bank. The dark silhouettes of the rescue craft were coming swiftly, considering they were all being paddled or rowed. Not swiftly enough, though. He was getting cold. The water was warmer than the air, but it wasn't warm enough. About forty-five degrees Fahrenheit in this area if he remembered correctly.

The River had lost much heat while passing over the north pole, and it hadn't picked up much yet. He was suffering from intense fatigue, aided and abetted by the shock of combat and chilly water. It would be ironic if he perished before the rescuers got to him.

Just like life. Just like death.

It would have been nice to quit stroking and kicking. So easy to give up, drift, and let others do the work. But he had to find Joe. Besides, if he did quit exercising, he'd lose his body warmth that much quicker. It would be so comfortable . . . he shook his head, breathed deeply, and tried to urge his dead limbs into life.

Presently—or was it presently, how much time had elapsed?—there was a boat alongside him. Many torches burned on it. Strong arms were hoisting him up, and he was laid shivering on the deck. Warm thick cloths were laid over him. Hot coffee was being poured down him. He sat up and shivered as the cloths fell off and the air struck him.

"Joe!" he said. "Joe! Get Joe!"

"What's he saying?" someone said in Esperanto.

"He's speaking English," a woman said. "He says to get Joe."

A woman's face was next to his. She said, "Who's Joe?"

"My best friend," Sam said weakly. "And he's not even human. Maybe that accounts for it." He laughed tiredly. "Ho, ho, ho! Maybe that's it."

"Where is this Joe?" the woman said. She was a good-looker. The flaming torches showed a heart-shaped face, big eyes, a broad high forehead, a retroussé nose, wide full lips, a strong chin and jaw. Long yellow wavy hair.

What was he doing admiring a woman at this time? He should be thinking of . . . Gwenafra.

Vaguely, he felt ashamed that not once since the action had started had he worried about Gwenafra. Where was she? And why hadn't he thought about her? He really loved her.

"This Joe?" the woman said again.

"He's a titanthrop, an ape-man. A hairy giant with a gigantic schnozzola. He's out there, somewhere close. Save him!"

The woman stood up and said something in Esperanto. A man beyond her held a torch out and looked into the darkness. There were many other torches out there, but they didn't seem to help. The sky was clouding up swiftly, the starlight was being shut out.

He looked around his immediate area. He was sitting on the raised deck of a longboat. Below him, on each side, were about a dozen paddlers.

"There's something floating out there," the man with the torch said. "It looks bulky. Maybe it's this titanthrop."

The man had his back turned to Sam. He wore an Eskimo suit of white cloths over head, body, and feet. He wasn't tall, but his shoulders were very broad. And his voice sounded vaguely familiar. Somewhere, a long time before, Sam had heard that voice.

The man called out to nearby boats and told them what to look for. Presently, there was a shout. Sam looked at the source. Some men on another longboat were attempting to haul something huge out of the water.

"Joe!" he croaked.

The man in the white suit turned then. He was holding the flaming pine so that his face was fully illumined.

Sam saw his features clearly, the broad handsome face, the thick straw-colored eyebrows, the square massive jaw, the even white teeth. His grin was evil.

"Bloodaxe!"

"*Já,*" the man said. "*Eirikr Bloδφx.*" Then, in Esperanto, "I have waited a long long time for you, Sam Clemens."

Screaming, Sam rose and leaped from the boat.

The cold dark waters closed upon him. He went down, down, then straightened out and began swimming. How far could he go before he had to surface for air? Could he get away from his nemesis long enough to get aboard another boat? Surely the Virolanders would not permit Erik to kill him? That would be against their principles. But Erik would wait until he had a chance, and then he would strike.

Joe! Joe would protect him! Joe would do more than that. He would kill the Norseman.

Gasping, sputtering, Sam's head broke through into the air. Ahead was a boat filled with people. The torches showed their faces clearly. All were looking at him.

Behind came the splashing of a swimmer.

Sam turned around. Erik was only a few feet from him.

Sam yelled again, and once more he dived. If he could come up on the other side of that boat, if he could get aboard it before . . .

A hand closed around his ankle.

Sam turned and fought, but the Norseman was bigger and far stronger. Sam was helpless. He would be drowned out of sight of the others, and Erik could claim that he had just been trying to save the poor mad devil.

An arm came from behind him and hooked around his neck. Sam struggled like a fish caught in a net, but he knew that he was done for. After all this time, after all these narrow escapes, to die like this . . .

He awoke on the deck of the longboat, coughing and choking. Water gushed from his mouth and nose. Two strong warm arms held him.

He looked up. Erik Bloodaxe was still holding him.

"Don't kill me!" Sam said.

Erik was naked and wet. The water on his body glistened in the torchlight. It also fell upon a white object connected to a cord around Erik's neck.

It was the spiral bone of a hornfish, the symbol worn by members of the Church of the Second Chance.

37

TWO MEN HAD COME TO THE SAME CONCLUSION.

They'd had enough of this senseless bloodshed. Now they'd do something they would have done if each hadn't been so sure that the other was on the other boat. But, during the long struggle, neither had seen the other. The other had never been on the boat or had wisely left it before the battle or had been blown to bits or into the water.

Each believed that if he died, the great project was doomed to failure, though each visualized the failure differently.

They saw an opportunity to escape now. In the heat and confusion of the combat, no one would notice their desertion. Or, if anyone did, he'd not be able to do anything about it. They would leap into The River and swim to shore and continue their long long journey. Neither had his grail, one being locked up in the sunken *Rex* and the other inside a locked storage room of the *Not For Hire*. They would steal free grails from the Virolanders and go on up The River in a sailboat.

One man had doffed his armor and dropped his weapon on the deck and had grasped the railing to vault over it when the other spoke behind him. The first man whirled, stooping, and picked up his cutlass. Though he hadn't heard the voice of the other for forty years, he instantly recognized it.

When he slowly turned around, though, he did not recognize the face and body he identified with the voice.

The man who'd come from the hatchway behind him spoke in a language which, now, only two on this boat could understand. His tone was harsh.

"Yes, it's I, though much changed."

The man by the railing said, "Why did you do it? Why?"

"You would never understand why," the man in the doorway said. "You're evil. So were the others, even . . ."

"*Were!*" the man by the railing said.

"Yes. *Were.*"

"They're all dead then. I'd suspected as much."

He glanced at the helmet and cutlass on the deck. It was too bad that he hadn't been halted before he discarded them. His enemy had an advantage now. The man by the railing also knew that if he tried to leap over the railing or flip backward over it, the other was swift and skilled enough to skewer him with his weapon by throwing it.

"So," he said, "you plan on killing me, too. You've reached bottom; you're lost forever."

"I had to kill the Operator," the first man said emotionlessly.

"I couldn't even think of doing such evil," the man by the railing said.

"I am *not* evil!" the other cried. "It is you who . . ."

He struggled with himself, then got the words out.

"There is no use arguing."

The man by the railing said, "Is it too late even now for you to change your mind? You would be forgiven, you would be sent to the Gardenplanet for therapy. You could join me and the agents and work with us to get to the tower . . ."

"No," the first man said. "Don't be stupid."

He lifted his cutlass and advanced on the other, who assumed the on-guard position. The duel was short and savage and ended when the unarmored man, bleeding from a dozen slashes, fell with the other's point in his throat.

The killer dragged the body to the railing, lifted it up in his arms, kissed the mouth of the corpse, and dropped it into the water. Tears streamed down his cheeks; he shook with sobs.

SECTION 11

The Final Duel: Burton vs. Bergerac

38

THE EVENTS IMMEDIATELY FOLLOWING THE EXPLOSION IN THE BOILER deck set off by Burton's group were swift, confusing, and blurred. For some time, Burton was either chasing or being chased, attacking or retreating. Mostly, he was retreating, since the enemy usually outnumbered them. By the time that Burton's group was forced into the great room of an armory, it was larger than when it had started. Though it had lost eight, it had picked up enough so that it now counted thirteen men and ten women. For all he knew, these were the only survivors of the *Rex*.

Neither side had any ammunition left for their firearms. From now on it would be cold steel only. The enemy withdrew to rest and to get their wind back. They also had to confer. The entrance to the armory was two and a half men wide, and storming it would be very difficult.

Burton looked over the array of arms and decided to discard his cutlass for an épée. This was a sword with a triangular edgeless blade three feet long. Its guard was bell-shaped; from the slightly curving handle protruded two wooden stops for better gripping. Burton tried the temper of the blade by placing its point against a beam of wood and bending it. The blade formed an arc to within a foot of the shell and sprang back to a straight line when the pressure was released.

The armory stank much of sweat and blood and not a little of urine and feces. It was also surprisingly hot. He removed his armor except for his helmet, and he urged the others to emulate him, though he wouldn't order them to do it.

"When we get to the deck, we won't have time to shuck off our iron," he said. "We'll have to dive into The River the moment we get to the open deck. It'll be much easier taking off the armor now than when you're in The River."

One of the women was the lovely Aphra Behn, no longer so lovely. Gunpowder smoke grimed her face; sweat and blood had made streaks and splashes on the blackened skin; her eyes were red with powder and fatigue; one eye was twitching. She said, "The boat must be sinking. If we don't get out soon, we'll drown."

Though she looked hysterical, her voice was calm enough, considering the circumstances.

"Yaas, I know," Burton drawled. He considered for a minute. They were on the B deck, and the A deck was probably filled with water by now. It wouldn't be long before this deck would be awash.

He strode to the hatch and stuck his head around its corner. The lights were still on in the corridor. There was no reason why they should go out since they were being fed from the batacitor. This would operate even if it was under water.

There was no one alive in the corridor. The enemy must be hiding in the rooms nearby, waiting until the *Rexites* tried to sally out.

"I'm Captain Gwalchgwynn of the marines of the *Rex!*" he said loudly. "I'd like to talk to your commander!"

No one answered. He shouted his request again, then stepped out into the passageway. If anyone was just inside the open doors near the armory, he couldn't see them.

Had they gone to the two ends of the corridor and were waiting around the corners, hoping to surprise them?

It was then that he saw water flowing toward him. It was only a film, but it would soon be swelling.

He called to the guards at the hatchway. "Tell the others to come on out! The Clemensites have left!"

He didn't have to explain to his people what had happened. They saw the water, too.

"Save himself who can," he said. "Get to the shore as best you may. I'll be joining you later."

He led them to the railing and said good-bye and good luck before they plunged in.

"Dick," Aphra said, "Why are you staying?"

"I'm looking for Alice."

"If the boat sinks suddenly, you'll be trapped in it."

"I know."

He didn't wait for her to jump in but began his search at once. He ran down the passageways calling out her name, stopping now and then to listen for her voice. Having covered this deck, he climbed the grand staircase to the grand salon. This occupied one-fourth of the stern area of the hurricane deck as did the grand salon of the *Rex*. But it was much larger. It was ablaze with ceiling and chandelier lights, even though blasts had blown many out or apart. Despite the damage from the explosions and the few mutilated corpses, it was very impressive.

He stepped inside and looked around. Alice was not here unless she was behind the immensely long bar or under or behind the smashed grand pianos or billiards tables. There seemed to be no reason for him to stay, but he was held for a few seconds by the grandeur of this room. Like its counterpart on the *Rex*, it had known many years of laughter, wit, humor, flirting, intrigue, gambling often playful but sometimes desperate, trysts of love and hate, music composed and played by some of Earth's masters, drama and comedy high and low on the stages. And now . . . It was a shameful loss, something to be very much regretted.

He started to cross the salon but stopped. A man had entered the great doorway of the other end. He paused when he saw Burton. Then, smiling, he walked jauntily toward him. He was an inch or two taller than Burton, greyhound-thin, and had extraordinarily long arms. His skin was blackened with smoke, his nose was very large, and his chin was weak. Despite this, his smile made him look almost handsome.

His glossy black ringleted hair fell to his shoulders. He wore only a black kilt and red riverdragon-leather calf-high boots, and his right hand gripped the hilt of an épée.

Burton had a swiftly passing *déjà vu*, a feeling that this meeting had happened a long time ago and under just such circumstances. He *had* encountered the man before and he had been hoping he would again. The long-healed wound in his thigh seemed to burn at the memory.

The man halted when he was twenty-five feet from Burton. He spoke loudly in Esperanto. It had a trace of French and a smidgeon of American English intonation.

"Ah, *sinjoro*, it's you! The very talented, perhaps endowed-with-genius swordsman with whom I crossed blades during the raid upon your vessel so many years ago! I introduced myself then as a gentleman should. You surlily refused to identify yourself. Or perhaps you failed to do so because you thought that I wouldn't recognize your name. Now . . ."

Burton advanced one step, his sword hanging almost straight down from his hand. He spoke in Parisian French circa A.D. 1650.

"Eh, *monsieur*. I was not sure when you made your introduction that you were truly whom you said you were. I thought that perhaps you might be an impostor. I admit now that you are indeed either the great monomachist Savinien de Cyrano II de Bergerac or someone who could be Castor to his Pollux and is his match in swordsmanship."

Burton hesitated. He might as well give his true name now. It was no longer necessary to use a pseudonym.

"Know, *monsieur*, that I am Captain Richard Francis Burton of the marines of the *Rex Grandissimus*. On Earth I was knighted by Her Majesty, Queen Victoria of the British Empire. This was not for making a fortune in commerce but as acknowledgment of my explorations in the far parts of the Earth and my many services to both my country and humanity. Nor was I unknown among the swordsmen of my time, which was the nineteenth century."

"*Hélas*, you would not have been also known for being long-winded, would you?"

"No, nor for possessing a huge nose," Burton said.

The man's teeth shone whitely.

"Ah, yes, always the reference to the proboscis. Well, know, *monsieur*, though I was not honored by my sovereign, Louis XIII, I was dubbed a genius by a queen even greater than yours, by Mother Nature herself. I wrote some philosophical romances which I understand were being read centuries after I died. And, as you obviously are aware, I was not unknown among the great swordsmen of my time, which gave birth to the greatest swordsmen of any time."

The thin man smiled again, and Burton said, "Perhaps you would like to surrender your blade? I have no desire to kill you, *monsieur*."

"I was about to ask you to hand over your weapon, *monsieur*, and become my prisoner. But I see that you, like me, would then be unsatisfied as to which of us is the better at bladeplay. I have thought about you many times, Captain Burton, since I drove my rapier into your thigh. Of all the hundreds, perhaps thousands, that I have dueled with, you were the best. I am willing to admit that I do not know how our little passage in arms might have turned out if you had not been distracted. Rather, I should say that you might have held me off a little longer if it were not for that."

"We shall see," Burton said.

"Oh, yes, we shall see, if the boat does not sink too soon. Well, *monsieur*, I delayed my leavetaking to have one more drink to toast the souls of those brave men and women who died fighting today for this once-splendid vessel, the last of the great beauties of man's science and technology. *Quel dommage!* But some day I will compose an ode to it. In French, of course, since Esperanto is not a great poetic language and, if it were, would still not be equal to my native tongue.

"Let us have one drink so that we may toast together those we loved but who have passed on. There will be no more resurrections, my friend. They will always be dead from now on."

"P'raps," Burton said. "In any event, I will join you."

The many doors of the huge and long liquor cabinets behind the bar had been locked before the battle started. But the key was in a drawer below a cabinet, and de Bergerac went behind the bar and unbolted the drawer. He unlocked a cabinet and unshot the bar across a line of bottles and pulled one from the hole in which it was set.

"This bottle was made in Parolando," de Bergerac said, "and it has journeyed unscathed through many battles and much mishandling by various drunks. It is filled with a particularly good burgundy which has been offered from time to time in various grails and which was not then drunk but put into this bottle to be used for a festive occasion. This occasion is, I believe, festive, though in a rather gruesome spirit."

He opened another cabinet and unlocked the indented bar holding a line of lead-glass goblets and took two and set them on the bar.

His épée was on top of the bar. Burton placed his own on the bar near his right hand. The Frenchman poured the burgundy to the brim, and he lifted his. Burton did likewise.

"To the dear departed!" he said.

"To them," Burton said. Both downed a small amount.

"I am not one for drinking much," de Bergerac said. "Liquor reduces one to the level of the beast, and I like at all times to remember that I am a human being. But . . . this is indeed a special occasion. One more toast, my friend, and then we shall fall to it."

"To the solution of the mystery of this world," Burton said.

They drank again.

Cyrano put his goblet down.

"Now, Captain Burton of the defunct marines of the defunct *Rex*. I loathe war and I detest bloodshed, but I do my duty when it must be done. We are both fine fellows, and it would be a shame if one were to die to prove that he is better than the other. Gaining knowledge of the true state of affairs by dying is not recommended by anyone with good sense. Thus, I suggest that he who draws the first blood wins. And if, thanks be to the Creator, who doesn't exist, the first wound is not fatal, the winner will take the other prisoner. And we will then proceed with haste but in an honorable manner to get off this vessel before she sinks."

"Upon my honor, that is the way it shall be," Burton said.

"Good! *En garde!*"

They saluted and then assumed the classic épée on-guard positions, the left foot at right angles to the right foot and behind it, knees bent, the body turned sidewise to present as small a target as possible, the left arm raised with the upper arm parallel to the ground, the elbow bent so the lower arm was vertical and the hand wrist limp, the right arm lowered and the blade it held forming a straight extension of the arm. The round *coquille,* or bellguard, in this position, protected the forearm.

De Bergerac, saying loudly the French equivalent of "Hah!," lunged. He was almost blindingly swift, as Burton knew from the Frenchman's reputation and from his one duel with him. However, Burton was also exceedingly quick. And, having spent many years on Earth and here in practice, his reaction to any particular attack was automatic.

De Bergerac, without feinting, had thrust toward Burton's upper arm. Burton parried and then riposted, that is, counterattacked. De Bergerac parried this and then thrust over Burton's blade, but Burton attempted a stop thrust, using the bellguard of his épée to deflect his opponent's tip and at the same time (almost) driving his own point into de Bergerac's forearm.

But de Bergerac counterparried and then quickly thrust around Burton's bellguard at Burton's forearm again. This maneuver was called the "dig" or the "peck."

Burton deflected the point again, though the edge of the blade drove along his arm. It burned, but it did not draw blood.

Dueling with the foil or the épée was something like trying to thread a moving needle. The tip of the attacker's blade was the end of the thread; the defender's, the eye of the needle. The eye should be very small and in this situation was. But in a second or less the thread-end would become the eye as the defender attacked. Two great swordsmen presented to each other very small openings which instantly closed and then reopened as the tip moved about in a small circle.

In competitive foil dueling, the target was only that part of the ⊌pponent's body exclusive of the head, arms, and legs but including the groin. In deadly combat, however, the head and the entire body were a target. If, somehow, a big toe was open, it should be skewered, could it be done without exposing the attacker to his antagonist's point.

It was an axiom that the fencer with a perfect defense could not lose. What then if both duelers had a perfect defense? Was it a case of the irresistible meeting the immovable? No. Human beings were neither. One of the perfect defenders would tire before the other or perhaps something in the milieu was to the slight or even great advantage of one fencer. This could be something on the floor to cause slipping or, in this situation, some object, a piece of blasted furniture, a bottle, a corpse over which one might stumble. Or, as when de Bergerac had fought Burton during the raid, a shout from a third party might distract a dueler for a fraction of a second, just enough for the cat-swift and eagle-eyed opponent to drive his sword into the other.

Burton was thinking of this with the edge of his mind while the main part concentrated on the dance of blades. His opponent was taller than he and had a longer reach. This was not necessarily to Burton's disadvantage. If he got into close quarters where the Frenchman's longer reach did not matter, then Burton would have the advantage.

De Bergerac knew this, as he knew everything about fencing, and so he maintained the distance proper for his benefit.

Metal rang upon metal while the breaths of the two hissed. De Bergerac, maintaining his straight-arm position, concentrated his attacks upon Burton's wrist and forearm to keep himself out of range of Burton's weapon.

The Englishman used a bent-arm position to make slanting thrusts, to bind his foe's blade, to "envelop" it. The binds were pushed with his blade against the other to make it go from one side to another. The envelopments were continuous binds in which the point of his blade made complete circles.

Meanwhile, he studied the Frenchman for weaknesses, just as the Frenchman was studying him. He found none. He hoped that de Bergerac, who was also analyzing him, would fail to discover any flaws.

As in their first encounter, they had established a definite rhythm of thrust and parry, riposte and counterparry. Even the feints became part of the pattern, since neither was fooled and thus left an opening.

Both were waiting for the opening which would not close quickly enough. The sweat ran down de Bergerac's face, streaking it where the liquid cleaned off the gunpowder grime. The salty liquid kept running into Burton's eyes, stinging them. Then he would retreat swiftly and wipe off his forehead and eyes with the back of his free hand. Most of the time, the Frenchman took advantage of this break to mop his own forehead with a small cloth stuck between his waist and the upper end of his towel-kilt. These intervals kept getting more and more frequent, not only to wipe their faces but to recover their wind.

During one of these, Burton removed a breast-cloth from a dead woman to blot up the sweat. Then, watching de Bergerac to make sure that he wouldn't make a *flèche*, a running attack, he tied the cloth around his head. De Bergerac stooped down and tore off a breast-cloth from another corpse to make a headband for himself.

Burton's mouth was very dry. His tongue felt as if it were as large and hard as a cucumber. He croaked, "A momentary truce, *Monsieur* de Bergerac. Let's both drink something before we die of thirst."

"Agreed."

Burton walked behind the bar, but the pipes of the sinks were empty. He went to the cabinet which the Frenchman had opened and brought out a bottle of purple passion. He removed the plastic stopper with his teeth and spat it out. He offered de Bergerac the first drink, but it was refused. He drank deeply and then handed the bottle over the bar to de Bergerac. The liquid burned in his throat and warmed his chest and guts. It helped his thirst somewhat, but he would not be satisfied until he got water.

De Bergerac held the bottle up against the light.

"Ah! You have swallowed three ounces, my friend. I shall do the same to insure an equal amount of inebriation in myself. It would not do if I were to kill you because you were drunker than I. You would then complain of unfairness, and the question of who is the superior swordsman would still be unanswered."

Burton laughed in his curious fashion between his teeth.

De Bergerac started, then said, "You sound like a cat, my friend."

He drank and when he put the bottle down, he coughed, his eyes tearing.

"*Mordioux!* It is certainly not French wine! It is for the barbarians of the North—or Englishmen!"

"You have never tasted it?" Burton said. "Not during the long voyage . . . ?"

"I told you I drank very little. *Hélas!* Never in all my life have I dueled unless absolutely sober. And now I feel the blood singing, my strength beginning to return, though I know it is a falseness, the liquor lying to my senses. Never mind. If I am somewhat drunk and so my reflexes are slow and my judgment numbed, you will be in the same condition."

"That depends upon one's idiosyncratic reaction to alcohol," Burton said. "It may well be that I, who love strong liquor, may be more accustomed to its effects. Hence, I will have an advantage over you."

"We shall see," de Bergerac said, smiling. "Now, *monsieur,* will you please come out from behind that bar so we may resume our little debate?"

"Certainly," Burton said. He walked to the end of the bar and around it. Why not try *la flèche,* the running attack? But if his running glide missed or was parried, then he'd be off-balance, exposed to de Bergerac's point. Still, it was possible that he could close in and thus block the Frenchman's blade.

No. Would he consider such a move if he did not have three ounces of fifteen-percent-alcohol purple passion in his bloodstream? No. Forget it.

But what if he picked up the bottle and threw it at the same time he made the *flèche?* His opponent would have to duck, and this might throw him off his balance.

He stopped when he got opposite the wine bottle. He looked at it for a second while de Bergerac waited. Then, his left hand opened, and he sighed.

The Frenchman smiled, and he bowed a little.

"My compliments, *monsieur.* I was hoping that you would not succumb to temptation and try something dishonorable. This is a matter to be settled with the blade alone.

"I salute you for understanding this. And I salute you as the greatest duelist I've ever met, and I've met many of the best. It is so sad, so very sad, and utterly regrettable that this, the most magnificent of all duels, unsurpassed anywhere or anytime, should be seen by only us. What a pity! No, it is not a pity. It is a tragedy, a great loss to the world!"

Burton noted that the fellow's speech was slightly slurred. That was to be expected. But was the wily Frenchman exaggerating the effects of the alcohol to make Burton overconfident?

"I agree with you in principle," Burton said, "and I thank you for your compliments. I also must say that you're the greatest swordsman I've ever met. However, *monsieur,* you spoke a little while ago about my long-windedness. I believe that, though you may be my equal in swordplay, you are my superior in gabbiness."

The Frenchman smiled. "I am as facile with my tongue as with my sword. I gave as much pleasure to the reader of my books and the hearer of my voice as to the spectator of my fencing. I forgot that you are a reticent Anglo-Saxon, *monsieur.* So I will let my blade speak for me from now on."

"I'll bet you do," Burton said. *"En garde!"*

Their épées clashed again in thrust, in parry, in riposte, in counter-riposte. But each had perfect defense in keeping the proper distance, in the timing, in the calculation, in the decision, and in coordination.

Burton could feel the poisons of fatigue and booze and knew that they must be slowing him down and affecting his judgment. But certainly they were working with equal or greater effect on his foe.

And then, as Burton parried a thrust toward his left upper arm and riposted with his point at de Bergerac's belly, he saw something coming in the doorway by the grand staircase. He leaped far backward and shouted, "Stop!"

De Bergerac saw that Burton was looking past him. He jumped backward to be far enough away from Burton if he were trying to trick him. And he saw the water flowing in a thin layer through the doorway.

He said, breathing hard, "So! The boat has sunk to our deck, *Monsieur* Burton. We do not have long. We must make an end to this very quickly."

Burton felt very tired. His breathing was harsh. His ribs felt as if knives were pricking them.

He advanced on the Frenchman, intending to make a running glide. But it was de Bergerac who did so. He exploded, seeming to have summoned from somewhere in his narrow body a burst of energy. Perhaps he had spotted finally a weakness in Burton's defense. Or he thought he had. Or he believed that he was the faster now that weariness had slowed his opponent more than it had him.

Whatever his reasons, he miscalculated. Or he may have performed perfectly. But Burton suddenly knew, by de Bergerac's body language, certain subtle muscular actions, a slight squinching of the eyes, what the

Frenchman intended to do. He knew because he had been ready to do the same, and he'd had to suppress his body language, the signals, which would tell his foe his next move.

De Bergerac came at him in the running glide, a sliding thrust along the opponent's blade with a slight pressure. It was sometimes used to surprise and might have succeeded if Burton had not been ready, had not, in a sense, been looking into a mirror of himself preparing for the same maneuver.

The successful flash required surprise, speed, and mastery over the opponent's weapon. De Bergerac had the speed, but the surprise was missing, and so he lost the mastery.

A knowledgeable spectator would have said that de Bergerac had the advantage of control. He was more erect than Burton. His hand was higher, thus allowing the fort, the strong part of the blade from the bellguard to the middle, to contact and so master the feeble of Burton's épée, the weak part, that from the middle to the point.

But Burton brought up his fort and turned the blade and drove de Bergerac's down and then crossed over and up to run him through his left shoulder. De Bergerac's face and body turned gray where the powder smoke did not cover it, but he still did not drop his sword. Burton could have killed him then.

Swaying, in shock, de Bergerac yet managed a smile. "The first blood is yours, *monsieur*. You have won. I acknowledge you as the victor. Nor am I ashamed . . ."

Burton said, "Let me help you," and then someone shot off a pistol from the doorway.

De Bergerac pitched forward and fell heavily on his face. A wound in his back close to the lower spine showed where the bullet had entered.

Burton looked at the doorway.

Alice was standing in it, a smoking pistol in her hand.

"My God!" he cried. "You shouldn't have done that, Alice!"

She came running, the water splashing about her ankles.

Burton knelt down and turned the Frenchman over and then got down on his knees and put the man's head in his lap.

Alice stopped by him. "What's the matter? He is an enemy, isn't he?"

"Yes, but he had just surrendered. Do you know who he is? He's Cyrano de Bergerac!"

"Oh, my God!"

De Bergerac opened his eyes. He looked up at Alice. "You should have waited to find out the true situation, madame. But then . . . scarcely anyone ever does."

The water was rising swiftly, and the deck was rapidly tilting at an angle. At this rate, the water would soon be above de Bergerac's head.

He closed his eyes, then opened them again.

"Burton?"

Burton said, "Yes."

"Now I remember. What a . . . what fools . . . we've been. You must be the Burton whom Clemens spoke of . . . you . . . the Ethical picked you?"

"Yes," Burton said.

"Then . . . why did we fight? I . . . didn't remember . . . too late . . . we . . . should have gone to the tower . . . the tower . . . together. Now . . . I . . ."

Burton bent down to hear the fading voice. "What did you say?"

". . . hated war . . . stupidity . . ."

Burton thought that de Bergerac had died after that. But a moment later, the Frenchman murmured, "Constance!"

He sighed, and he was gone.

Burton wept.

SECTION 12

The Last 20,000 Miles

39

BURTON AND HARGREAVES, ALONG WITH THE OTHER SURVIVORS, HAD TO
face the wrath of La Viro. The tall dark man with the big nose raved and
ranted for an hour while he strode back and forth before the assembled
"criminals." They stood in front of the smoke-blackened temple, a huge
stone structure with incongruous architecture: a Greek portico and Ionian
columns with an onion-shaped roof topped by a gigantic carved stone spiral.
These features were symbols in the Church of the Second Chance, but,
nevertheless, Burton and others thought that the temple was ugly and
ludicrous-looking. Oddly enough, the bad taste of La Viro, its designer,
helped them endure his tirade. He was right in much of what he said, but
much else seemed foolish. However, they were dependent upon him for
grails, cloths, and housing. So they did not defend themselves but got some
relief from their anger by silently laughing at the hideous temple and the
man who'd built it

At last, La Viro tired of pointing out in vivid detail and imagery how
stupid, callous, brutal, murderous, and selfish they were. He threw up his
hands and said he was sick of the sight of them. He would retire to the
sanctum in the temple and pray for the *kas* of the Virolanders they'd killed.
And also, though they didn't deserve it, for the living and the dead culprits.

He turned the survivors over to Frato Fenikso, Brother Phoenix, once known as Hermann Göring.

Göring said, "You look like deservedly chastened children, and I hope you feel like it. But I don't have, at this moment, anyway, much hope for you. That's because of my anger at you. I'll get over it, and then I'll do my best to help you change for the better."

He led them to the rear of the temple where he gave each of them a free grail and enough cloths to keep them warm in the coldest temperatures.

"Anything else you need or want will be up to you to get it," Göring said. He dismissed them, but he called Burton aside.

"Have you heard that Samuel Clemens died of a heart attack?"

Burton nodded.

"Apparently, he thought that Frato Eriko still intended to settle an old score. After all he'd gone through during the battle, this was just too much, the straw that broke the camel's back or, in his case, broke his heart."

"I heard the story from Joe Miller this morning," Burton said.

"Yes. Well, unless somebody does something for the titanthrop, he's going to die of a broken heart, too. He really loved Clemens."

Göring asked Burton if he intended to go on to the headwaters. Burton replied that he had not come this far just to quit. He was going to set out for the tower as soon as possible.

"You'll have to build a sailboat. Certainly, Clemens' men won't allow you to go with them in the *Post No Bills*."

"I don't know about that," Burton said.

"And I suppose that if they refuse, you'll hijack the launch?"

Burton didn't answer.

"Is there no end to your violence?"

"I didn't say I would use force," Burton said. "I intend to talk to Anderson about the trip as soon as possible."

"Anderson was killed. I warn you, Burton, don't shed any more blood here!"

"I'll do all I can to avoid it. I don't like it any more than you do, really. Only, I am a realist."

The smaller launch, the *After You, Gascon*, had disappeared with all of its crew. No one knew what had happened to it, though some Virolando witnesses thought they'd seen it explode.

"If you really push it, you could get to the headwaters in about thirty days in the launch," Göring said. "But the agents of the Ethicals will get there before you do."

Burton was shocked.

"You *know* about them?"

"Yes. I talked to both Frigate and Miller last night, trying to help them through their grief. I knew more than you'd think and suspected even more. Correctly, as it turned out. Neither saw any reason to keep silent about the renegade Ethical. I told La Viro, and he's thinking hard about the whole business. It's been a great shock to him, though it hasn't affected his faith any."

"What about you?"

"I see no reason to change my faith. I never thought that the people responsible for this world were angels or demons. There are, though, many puzzling things about the two stories I've heard. What intrigues me the most, and also upsets me the most, is the mystery of what happened to the nonhuman on Clemens' boat, Monat I think was his name."

Burton said, "What? I haven't heard about that!"

Göring described what Miller had told him, and added, "And you say that his companion, the man called Frigate, also disappeared?"

"*That* Peter Jairus Frigate was an agent," Burton said. "He wasn't an exact double of the Frigate you talked to, but he resembled him closely. He may have been Frigate's brother."

"Perhaps when—or—if you get into the tower, you'll find out," Göring said.

"I'll find out sooner than that if I catch up with those agents in the launch," Burton said grimly.

After some more discussion, Burton left Göring. He had not told the German what the news about Monat and the pseudo-Frigate meant. The Ethical X, the Mysterious Stranger, the renegade, had been on the *Not For Hire*. And he had gotten rid of Monat about eight hours after they'd boarded the vessel. Why? Because Monat would recognize him. He would have been in disguise, but Monat would have known him sooner or later. Probably sooner. So he'd had to work fast, and he had done so. How, Burton didn't know.

X had been on Clemens' boat.

"Had he lived through the battle? If he had, then he was among the few survivors of the *Not For Hire* now in this immediate area.

Perhaps. He might have left at once and gone up-River or he might have gotten to the other bank.

Burton went back after Göring and asked him if he'd heard about any survivors on the other side of the lake or any who'd gone through on the cliffpath above the strait.

"No," Göring said. "If there had been any, they'd have been reported."

Burton tried not to show his excitement.

Göring, however, said, smiling, "You think that X is here, don't you? At hand but in disguise?"

"You're deucedly clever," Burton said. "Yes, I do, unless he's been killed. Strubewell and Podebrad were agents, I don't mind telling you that now, and they were killed. So perhaps X was also."

"Did anyone see Strubewell and Podebrad die?" Göring said. "I know Joe Miller thinks Strubewell was dead because he didn't see him get out of the pilothouse after it fell. But Strubewell could have gotten out later on. All we know about Podebrad is that he was seen no more after the vessels collided."

"I wish they were available," Burton said. "I'd get the truth out of them somehow. I believe, however, that they died. That you citizens haven't seen them goes a long way to prove that. As for X, well . . ."

He said so-long to Göring and walked to the partly burned dock at which the *Bills* was tied up. It looked like a monstrous black turtle. Its high rounded hull was the shell, and the long narrow prow was part of the head sticking out. The barrel of the steam machine gun projecting from the extreme front of the prow was the turtle's tongue; the steam gun poking out from the stern, the turtle's tail.

Burton had been told by one of its crew that it carried a large batacitor and could hold fifteen people comfortably and twenty with some inconvenience. It could go thirty-five miles per hour against a ten-mile-per-hour current and a ten-mile-per-hour wind. It had an armory of fifteen rifles and fifteen pistols using gunpowder-filled cartridges and ten compressed air rifles and many other weapons.

Joe Miller, his enormous arm in a plaster cast, several of the crew and some survivors of the *Not For Hire* were standing on the dock. Having had the new captain of the *Bills* described to him, Burton had no difficulty picking him out. Kimon was a short burly dark man with intense hazel eyes, an ancient Greek whose life Burton had studied in school and afterward. He's been a great general, naval commander, and statesman, one of the main builders of the Athenian empire after the Persian wars. He was born in 505 B.C., if Burton remembered correctly.

Kimon was a conservative who had favored alliance with Sparta and so ran counter to the policies of Pericles. His father was the famous Miltiades, the victor of the battle of Marathon, in which the Greeks turned back the hordes of Xerxes. Kimon served during the naval battle of Salamis in which the Athenians sank two hundred enemy vessels with a loss of only forty and forever broke the Persian naval power.

In 475 Kimon drove out the pirates of Skyros and then located and brought to Athens the bones of Theseus, the legendary founder of the Attic state and killer of the Minotaur of the labyrinth of Knossos. Kimon was one of the judges who gave Sophocles first prize for tragedy in the competitions held at Dionysia in 468.

In 450 Kimon led an expedition against Cyprus, where he died during the siege of Kitium. His bones were brought back to Athens and buried there.

He certainly looked alive now and very mean, too. Kimon and a number of Clemensites were arguing loudly. Burton, acting as if he were just another Virolander, stood with those listening in.

Apparently, the argument was about which of Clemens' people would go on up The River and also about seniority. In addition to the eleven crew members of the *Bills*, ten people from the *Not For Hire* had survived. Kimon was outranked by three of these, but he was insisting that he was the commander of the launch and anybody who went along on it would be his subordinate. Moreover, he would not allow more than eleven on the voyage, and he thought that the crew of the *Bills* should be these. But he was willing to take some from the motherboat if some of his crew didn't want to go on.

After a while, Kimon and the others went inside the launch. Nevertheless, their voices came out loudly through the open ports.

The titanthrop had not gone aboard. He stood in one spot, softly talking to himself. His eyes were red, and he looked as if he'd grieved much.

Burton introduced himself.

Joe Miller, speaking in a deep kettledrum voice in English said, "Yeth, I've heard about you, Mithter Burton. Tham told me about you. Vhen did you get here?"

Reluctantly, Burton said, "I was on the *Rex*."

"Vhat the hell vere you doing on that? You vere vone of the Ekth'th men, veren't you?"

"Yes," Burton said. "But I didn't know until yesterday that some of his recruits were on the *Not For Hire*. Though, to tell the truth, I suspected that some would be."

"Who told you?"

Cyrano de Bergerac."

Joe brightened. "Thyrano? He'th alive? I thought he died! Vhere ith he?"

"No, he was killed. But he recognized me, and he told me that Clemens and he had also been visited by the Ethical."

Burton thought it would be better not to tell Miller that it was his woman who'd slain de Bergerac.

The titanthrop looked as if he were struggling with himself. Then he stopped shaking, and he smiled slightly. His giant hand shot out.

"Here. Thyake. I don't hold it againtht you. Ve vath all thtupid. Ath Tham uthed to thay, it'th the fortuneth of var."

Burton's hand was enfolded, squeezed, not too hard, and then released. Burton said, "I don't think we should talk here. Too many people around. You come with me, and I'll introduce you to two who also know about the Ethical."

They went to the foothill behind the temple. Here Alice and others were building huts. Burton called her, Frigate, Nur, and Aphra Behn to one side. After introducing Miller, Burton asked him to tell everything relevant he knew about X and those who'd been recruited by him. It was a long tale, interrupted by many questions, and it was not finished until long after supper. Since the huts were not completed, the five slept on the portico of the temple under piles of cloths. After breakfast, they returned to their building. By late afternoon they had two huts finished. Miller went down to the launch for a while to check on what was going on. When he returned, Burton told his story. That had to be stopped for the funeral of the casualties whose bodies had not sunk. These, which had been preserved in alcohol until the ceremony, were laid out on wooden biers. Miller wept over Sam Clemens and his cabinmate, a huge redheaded ancient Cimmerian woman. After Burton, representing the *Rex*, and Kimon, representing the *Not For Hire*, had spoken a few words about their dead comrades, La Viro gave a short but passionate speech about the uselessness of their deaths. Then the bodies were put on a huge pyre and burned to ashes.

Not until the rains came at about six in the morning were the tales of Burton and his people finished.

"I vathn't going on up," Miller told them. "Vell, actually, I vath going up a little vay. Vhen I found thome of my own people, I vath going to thettle down vith them. Maybe. I'm not tho thyure I'd be happy vith them now. I've theen too much, traveled too much, become too thivilithed to be happy vith them, maybe.

"Anyvay, I'd given up going on to the tower. It didn't theem vorthvhile. But now I've met you, maybe I will go on. If I didn't, it vould make Tham'th death, the thufferingth and the deathth of all thothe people, in vain.

"Bethideth, I vant to find out who Ekth ith. If he'th been tricking uth, me and Tham veren't too thyure he vathn't, I'll tear him apart, thkin by thkin."

"Skin by skin?" Burton said. "What does that mean?"

"It'th chuth a thaying of my people. Do I have to ekthplain it?"

"How many of your crew also know about X?" Burton said.

"There'th the little Frenchman, Marthelin, altho known as Baron de Marbot. But Tham told him about Ekth. Tham thought he could trutht him. Then there'th that vildaththed Chinethe Tai-Peng, only hith real name ith Li Po. There'th hith black-aththed thidekick, Tom Turpin, he can really tickle the ivorieth. Ekth never recruited Tom, but Tai-Peng blabbed about it to Tom one night vhen he vath drunk, that Thelethtial thyould've died of thirrhothith of the liver yearth ago, tho ve thought ve'd better take him in. He'th a good man, anyvay. And then there'th Ely Parker, who vathn't recruited by Ekth either, but Tham knew him on Earth, or of him, and he told him becauthe he vath a good friend of Ulyththeth Eth. Grant and altho a general on Grant'th thtaff during the Thivil Var. He vath an engineer on the *Not For Hire*. He'th an American Indian, an Iroquois of the Theneca tribe. And then there'th the ancient Thumerian who callth himthelf Gilgameth."

"Gilgamesh?" Burton said.

"That'th vhat I thaid. Tham thaid he may or may not be the king of the Thumerian thity of Uruk who lived thometime in the firtht half of the third millenium B.C. It vathn't very likely ve'd run into anybody who knew the real Gilgameth, though you never know.

"And then there'th the ancient Mayan, Ah Qaaq. He'th awful thtrong, that ith, for a thyort-nothed perthon, he ith."

"Ah Qaaq," Burton said. "That'd be Mayan for *fire*."

"Yeth. But he ain't no ball of fire. He'th more like a butterball. Fat ath a pig. But he'th very thtrong, ath I thaid. And he can thyoot a bow further than anybody I ever thaw, ekthept mythelf, naturally. Even further than thome Old Thtone Acherth that vath on the boat. He'th got a muthtache tattooed on hith lip that maketh him look like a vildman from Borneo."

"Then Kimon and the other survivors don't know about X and the agents?" Burton said.

"If they did, I vould have thaid tho."

Nur el-Musafir said, "It's possible that some of them may be agents, however."

"I'd like to talk to all of the people you mentioned," Burton said. He paused, then said, "If all of us who know about the Ethical are to go on the *Bills*, then others will have to step aside. They'll have to give up their berth on the launch. Is there much chance of that?"

"Thyure," the titanthrop said. He looked down his enormous nose at Burton, and he smiled. His teeth were huge dull-white blocks. "Thyure. There'th a chanthe. About ath much ath an ithecube in a bonfire."

"Then," Burton said, "we'll have to seize the launch. Hijack it."

"I thought tho," Miller said. "Vhy ith it that from the beginning ve've had to do tho many unethical thingth to help the Ethical?"

40

THERE WERE ELEVEN IN THE GROUP. OF THESE, FIVE HAD BEEN RE-cruited directly by the renegade Ethical. These were Richard Francis Burton, Nur ed-Din el-Musafir, Tai-Peng, Gilgamesh, and Ah Qaaq. At least, they claimed to have been visited by X. Burton, however, could be sure only of himself. One or more might be agents or even Ethicals.

Joe Miller had been told about X by Samuel Clemens. Alice knew about him from Burton. Aphra Behn hadn't been informed until yesterday, but she wanted very much to accompany them on their expedition. De Marbot had heard from Clemens about the Stranger, and he had told Behn about him. Since the Frenchman and the Englishwoman had once been lovers and were again, the others agreed that she could come with them.

Ely Parker, the Seneca, also knew about X from Clemens, and he had wished to go with them. But he'd changed his mind.

"To hell with the Ethicals and the tower and all that," he said to Burton. "I'm going to stay here and try to raise the *Not For Hire*. It's sunk in only about forty feet of water. Once it's up and repaired, I'll take it down-River. I'm not really interested in dying just to prove something that can't be proved. The Ethicals don't want us sticking our noses in their business. I think that the breakdowns came about because we interfered. Piscator may have screwed things up in the tower. And Podebrad told Sam that the people he left behind in Nova Bohemujo may have been responsible for the failure of the right-bank line. He said that before he left on the blimp some of his officers wanted to dig deep around a grailstone and see if they could tap into it to get a continuous source of power. He warned them not to, and before he took off he got them to promise they wouldn't monkey around with it. He said that what might have happened was that they broke their promise and somehow broke the circuit.

"If that happened, the area around it would've been blown up. There'd be a hole big enough to make a new lake on the right side of The River. The explosion could've wiped out Nova Bohemujo on that side. That's where the mineral deposits were, and if what Podebrad said was true, then that's the end of the mines and the New Bohemians.

"Anyway, I just don't like meddling around with the Ethicals. I'm no coward. Anyone who knows me'll tell you that. But I just don't think it's right to mess around with things we know nothing about."

In addition, Burton thought, you'd like to be captain of the riverboat and live the good and high life.

"You won't get much help from the locals," Burton said.

He gestured at the banks and the stream, which were crowded with people in boats or getting ready to shove off.

"This area will be near-emptied within a month. La Viro is sending almost everybody down-River to restore the faith of the Chancers, to correct deviations from their theology, and to make new converts. The breakdowns have shaken the faith of many."

"Yeah," Parker said, his broad brown face twisted with a sardonic smile. "Yeah. La Viro himself is shaken. I understand he's spending a lot of time on his knees praying. He doesn't look so sure of himself now."

Burton didn't try to argue the Seneca into going on with him. He did wish Parker luck before walking away, though he wasn't going to have any. The *Not For Hire* was going to stay where it was until the current nudged it off the ledge and it sank to the bottom, three thousand feet down.

When the *Post No Bills* sank or wore out, its end would be the end of the age of advanced technology on the Riverworld. What few metal tools and weapons existed would wear out. And then the Valleydwellers would be lucky if they had stone artifacts. The entire planet would be in the Wood Age.

The news about Podebrad's story was certainly interesting. Whether or not the Nova Bohemujo had brought about the line breakdown, Podebrad had been an agent or an Ethical. Only one of them could have known where the metal deposits were in that state. Only one of them could have known that trying to tap the power of the line could result in a catastrophe.

But Podebrad, or whatever his real name was, was dead.

Burton wondered if he could have been X.

Hearing a familiar voice hail him, he stopped and turned around. Hermann Göring, thinner than before, and he'd been very thin, approached him. His broad face was grave, and his eyes were rimmed with the darkness of fatigue.

"*Sinjoro* Burton! *Mi dezirus akompani vin.*"

"You'd like to go with me? Why?"

"For the same reason that drives you. I want desperately to know what has gone wrong. I've always wanted to know, but I told myself that it was much more important to raise the ethical level of the *kas*. Now . . . I don't know. Yes, I do! If we are to have faith, we must also have knowledge. I mean . . . faith is the only thing to cling to if you can't know the truth. But now . . . now . . . it may be possible to *know!*"

"What does La Viro think of this?"

"We've quarreled, something I thought I'd never do. He insists that I go with him down-River. He intends to travel to the mouth of The River, even if it takes him three hundred years, preaching all the way. He wants to restore the faith of the people . . ."

"How does he know that it needs restoring?" Burton said.

"He knows what's been happening downstream for as far as a hundred thousand miles. What's happening there must also be happening elsewhere. Besides, didn't you notice that there's been much doubt, much falling away from the Church, while you were traveling on the boat?"

"I noticed some but didn't think much about it," Burton said. "It's to be expected, you know."

"Yes. Even some of the Virolanders have been troubled, and they have the presence of La Viro himself to strengthen them. However, I believe that the best course is to get into the tower and determine exactly what has happened. That will insure that the Church is right, and when that happens, all of the people will have no doubt and all will come to the Church."

"On the other hand," Burton drawled, "what you find there may blow your religion to bits."

Göring shuddered and closed his eyes. When he opened them, he said, "Yes, I know. But my faith is so strong that I am willing to chance it."

"My middle name is Francis," Burton said, grinning. "So I'll be frank with you. I don't like you. I never have. You've changed character, true. But I can't forgive what you did to me and my friends. It's a case of forgiving but not forgetting. Though I suppose that fundamentally the two are the same."

Göring waved his hands imploringly.

"That is the burden I must carry. I deserve it, and I won't be able to put it down until every person who knows my evil deeds has truly forgiven me. But that is not the issue now. What is, is that I can be of great help. I am quick and strong and very determined and not unintelligent. Also . . ."

"Also, you're a Second Chancer, a pacifist," Burton said. "What use would you be if we have to fight?"

Göring said, fiercely, "I won't compromise my principles! I will not shed the blood of another human! But I doubt very much that you'll have to fight. The area upstream is thinly populated and becoming thinner every day. Haven't you seen the many boats coming through the strait? The news is out that the Virolanders are leaving. The people up-River are deserting their cold land to settle down here."

"There may well be a fight," Burton said. "If we catch up with those agents, we'll try to make them talk. And when we get into the tower . . . who knows what we'll find there? We may have to battle for our lives."

"Will you take me?"

"No. That's final! I don't care to discuss this anymore. Ever!"

He strode away while Göring roared, "If you won't take me, I'll go alone!"

Burton glanced back then. The man's face was red, and he was shaking his fist. Burton smiled. Even the ethically advanced bishops of the Church could get angry.

When Burton looked back once more, he saw Göring walking swiftly toward the temple, his face set. Evidently, he was on his way to tell La Viro that he was not obeying his orders to go down-River.

That night, the eleven, headed by Burton, overpowered the guards on the *Post No Bills*. They came up from The Riverside, having swum silently to the railing, and boarded the port side. Two of the guards were sitting on the starboard railing and talking. These were grabbed from behind, and their noses and mouths were gripped until they passed out from lack of air. At the same time, Joe Miller entered the launch from the bankside. After a few words with the remaining sentinel, he seized him and carried him struggling to the bow and cast him into the water.

"Jethuth!" he called out to the yelling guard. "I hate to do thith, Thmith, but I got a higher duty! Give my regretth to Kimon!"

After the guards had been thrown off, Burton's group carried aboard their grails and other possessions and some long ropes and tools which had been brought up by divers from the *Not For Hire*. Aphra Behn turned on the electricity. As soon as the last of the supplies had been thrown onto the deck and the tie lines loosed, she took the boat away. It was shortly going at its top speed while behind them torches flared and men and women yelled.

It was not until the launch had gotten through the strait that Burton felt they had really begun the next-to-last stage of the long, long journey.

Burton thought briefly about X. According to Cyrano's story of X's visit to him, X had told him to relay to the recruits that they should wait a year for X at Virolando. Burton didn't want to do this and neither did his colleagues. They were going on *now*.

Traveling against the shoreline current at thirty miles per hour and only stopping for two hours each day, the *Post No Bills* averaged 660 miles every twenty-four hours. When they had to abandon the boat, they still had some distance to go, the most difficult part of the journey. Before that, they'd have to stop and catch fish to smoke and make acorn bread and collect bamboo tips. These would not be all they'd have to eat, though. They carried twenty "free grails" some of which they'd owned and some of which they'd stolen. They planned to fill these before getting to the final grailstone in order to have extra provisions. The food which would decay swiftly would be kept in the launch's refrigerator or dragged behind in a cask in the cold water.

As they went north, The Valley became broader. Apparently the Ethicals had made it wider so that it might receive more of the weak sunlight. The temperature was tolerable during the day, which was longer than those in the regions behind them, reaching as high as sixty-two Fahrenheit. But it would get ever colder the farther north they went. The fogs lasted longer, too.

Göring had been right about the scarcity of people. There were only approximately a hundred per square mile. This number was being cut down daily, as the many boats going down-River showed.

Joe Miller, standing in the bow, looked longingly at the titanthrops they passed. When the launch landed for recharging, he went ashore to talk to any he could find. The conversations were in Esperanto, since none knew his native tongue.

"Jutht ath vell," Joe said. "I've forgotten motht of it anyvay. Jethuth H. Chritht! Ain't I ever going to find my parentth and my friends, my own tribethpeople?"

Fortunately, the titanthrops were amiable. They were by now far outnumbered by the "pygmies," and most of them had been converted to the Chancer faith. Burton and Joe tried to recruit some, but failed. The giants wanted nothing to do with the beings in the tower.

"They all dread the far north," Burton said. "You must have shared their fear. Why did you go with the Egyptians?"

Joe swelled his gorillalike chest. "I'm braver than thothe otherth. Thmarter, too. Though, to tell the truth, I came near thyitting down my leg vhen I thaw the tower. But any man vould. You jutht vait until you thee it."

The tenth day, they stopped for a shore leave of several days. The locals were a few titanthrops with a majority of Scandinavians, ancient, medieval, and modern. Among them were, however, people from many different times and places. The men who had no cabinmates immediately started looking for overnight stands. Burton walked around inquiring if anybody had seen the men and women who'd been forced to abandon the launch from the *Rex*. There were plenty, and all said that these had gone up-River in boats, all of them stolen.

"Have any others come along who've said they were on the *Not For Hire*?" Burton said. "That's the giant metal riverboat like the *Rex*, propelled by paddlewheels and driven by electric motors."

"No, I've not seen or heard of anybody like that."

Burton didn't expect that the deserters would advertise their identity.

Nor would the agents who'd left Clemens' vessel before the battle be any more open.

However, getting descriptions of those who had gone northward during the past few weeks, he recognized those who'd fled the *Rex*. De Marbot, who was also questioning, recognized from the descriptions all who'd deserted the *Not For Hire*.

"We'll catch up with them soon," Burton said.

"If we're lucky," the Frenchman said. "We may pass them at night. Or they might get word of our coming and hide while we go by."

"In any event, we'll get there first."

Twenty days passed. By then the agents from both boats had to have been behind them. Though Burton stopped the launch every twenty miles to question the locals, he could find none of those he sought.

In the interim, he watched his crew. Only two matched the short massive physique and facial features of the Ethicals Thanabur and Loga. The man who called himself Gilgamesh, and the man who called himself Ah Qaaq. But both were very dark and had dark brown eyes. Gilgamesh had curly, almost kinky, hair. Ah Qaaq had a slight epicanthic fold which made him look as if he had some recent Mongolian ancestors. Each spoke his supposed native language fluently. Unlike the agent Spruce, who had claimed to be a twentieth-century Englishman and whose very slight foreign accent had betrayed him to Burton, these two lacked any trace of such. Burton didn't know Sumerian or ancient Mayan well, but he knew enough to recognize a non-Sumerian or non-Mayan pronunciation and intonation.

That only meant that one of the two, possibly both, had completely mastered the tongues. Or it meant that both were innocent and what they claimed to be.

Twenty-two days after he'd passed through the strait in an area where there weren't more than fifty people to a grailstone, Burton was approached by a tall skinny woman with big eyes and a big mouth. Her white teeth shone in the black African face.

She spoke in Esperanto affected heavily by a backwoods Georgia accent. Her name was Blessed Croomes, and she wanted to go on the boat as far as it would go. Then she'd go on foot to the headwaters.

"That's where my mother Agatha Croomes went. I'm looking for her. I think she must have found the Lord and is now living at His right hand, waiting for me! Hallelujah!"

41

IT WAS DIFFICULT TO STOP HER FLOW OF TALK, BUT BURTON FINALLY said, loudly and sternly, that she had to answer his questions.

"Okay," she said, "I'll listen to the wise. Are you wise?"

"Wise enough," he said, "and mighty experienced, which is the same thing if you're not stupid. Let's start at the beginning. Where were you born and what were you on Earth?"

Blessed told him that she was born a slave in Georgia in 1734 in the house of her master. Come early, caught her mother in the kitchen while she was helping prepare the evening meal. She'd been raised as a house slave and baptized into the faith of her father and mother. After her father had died, her mother had become a preacher. She was a very devout and very strong woman who scared her flock, though they also loved her. Her mother had died in 1783 and she in 1821. But both had been resurrected near the same grailstone.

"Of course, she wasn't an old woman anymore. It was strange seeing my old momma a young woman. That didn't make no difference to her, though.

She was as holy and righteous and filled with the spirit as when she'd lived on Earth. Why, I tell you, when she preached in church there she had white folks come for miles around to listen to her. Most of them were white trash, but she converted them, and then they got in trouble . . ."

"You're wandering again," Burton said. "That's enough of your background. Why do you want to go with me?"

"Because you got that boat that can travel faster than a bird."

"But why do you want to go to the end of The River?"

"I would have told you if you hadn't interrupted me, man. You see, my mother being here didn't shake her faith at all. She said that we were here, all of us, because we were sinners on Earth. Some worse than the others. This was really Heaven, the outskirts of it anyway. What sweet Jesus wanted was that the real believers should go up The River, the sweet Jordan, and find Him at the end. He was up there, waiting to embrace those who truly believed, those who'd go to the trouble of seeking Him out. So she went.

"She wanted me to come with her, but I was scared. I wasn't sure anyway that she knew what she was talking about. I didn't tell her that. It would've been like hitting her in the face, and nobody has guts enough to do that. Anyway, it wasn't just that that kept me from going with her. I had a mighty sweet man, and he wouldn't go with her. He said he liked things fine as they were. So I let my pussy do the thinking for me, and I stayed with him.

"But things went bad with me and my old man. He started chasing other women, and I got to thinking that maybe this was a judgment on me for not obeying my momma. Maybe she was right, maybe Jesus was waiting for the truly faithful. Besides, I really missed my momma even if we do go around and around like wildcats sometimes. So I lived with another man for a while, but he wasn't any better than the first. Then, one night while I was praying, I saw a vision. It was Jesus Himself, sitting on His diamond and pearl throne with the angels singing back of Him, all in a blaze of glorious light. He told me to quit sinning and to follow my mother's footsteps and I'd get to Heaven.

"So I went. And here I am. It's been many years, brother, and I've suffered like one of God's own martyrs. I've gotten bone-weary and flesh-sick, but here I am! Last night I prayed again, and I saw my mother, only for a second, and she told me to come with you. She said you weren't a good man but you weren't bad either. You were in between. But I would be the one to bring you to the light, save you, and we'd go together to Kingdom Come and sweet Jesus would wrap His arms around us and welcome us to the glory throne. Hallelujah!"

"Hallelujah, sister!" Burton said. He was always willing to throw himself into the form of a religion while laughing at its spirit.

"It's a long long trip yet, brother. My back hurts from paddling my canoe against the current, and I hear that it's foggy and cold most of the way from now on and not a living soul to be seen. It'll be very lonely there. That's why I'd like to go with you and your friends."

Burton thought, Why not?

"There's room for just one more," he said. "However, we don't take pacifists since we may have to fight. We don't want any deadweight."

"Don't you worry about me, brother. I can fight like an avenging angel of the Lord for you, if you're on the side of good."

She put her few possessions on the boat a few minutes later. Tom Turpin, the black piano player, was happy to see her at first. Then he found out she'd taken a vow of chastity.

"She's crazy, Captain," he told Burton. "Why'd you take her on? She's got that good-looking body and she'll drive me crazy her not letting me touch her."

"Perhaps she'll talk you into taking the vow, too," Burton said, and he laughed.

Turpin didn't think that was funny.

When the boat pulled out after a four-day, not a two-day, leave as planned, Blessed sang a hymn, Then she shouted, "You needed me, brother Burton, to complete your number. You were only eleven and now you're twelve! Twelve's a good, a holy number. The apostles of Jesus were twelve!"

"Yaas," Burton said softly. "And one of them was Judas."

He looked at Ah Qaaq, the ancient Mayan warrior, a pocket-sized Hercules gone to pot. He seldom offered to start a conversation, though he would talk fluently if he was cornered. Nor did he draw back if someone touched him. According to Joe Miller, X, when visiting Clemens, had not wanted to be touched, had, in fact, acted as if Clemens were some sort of leper. Clemens had thought that X, though soliciting the help of the Valleydwellers, felt that he was morally superior and that if one touched him he was somehow fouled.

Neither Ah Qaaq nor Gilgamesh acted as if they must keep others at a proper distance. In fact, the Sumerian insisted on being very close when conversing, almost nose to nose. And he touched the other speaker frequently as if he had to have flesh contact also.

That insistence on closeness could be overcompensation, though. The Ethical might have found out that his recruits had noted his dislike for near proximity and was forcing himself to get close.

Long ago, the agent, Spruce, had said that he and his colleagues loathed violence, that doing it made them feel degraded. But if that were so, they had certainly learned to be violent without showing any repulsion. The agents on both boats had fought as well as the others. And X, as Odysseus and Barry Thorn, had killed enough to satisfy Jack the Ripper.

Possibly, X's avoidance of touch had nothing to do with a personal feeling. It might be that a touch by another human being could leave some sort of psychic print. Perhaps psychic wasn't the right word. The *wathans*, the auras that all sentient beings radiated, according to X, might take a sort of fingerprint. And this might last for some time. If so, then X would not be able to return to the tower until the "print" had vanished. His colleagues would see it and wonder how he'd gotten it.

Was that speculation too bizarre? All X had to tell his questioners was that he'd been on a mission and had been touched by a Valleydweller.

Ah! But what if X was not supposed to have been in The Valley? What if he had an alibi for his absences but it didn't include a visit to The Valley? Then he could not explain satisfactorily why his *wathan* bore a stranger's print.

This speculation, though, required that an agent's or Ethical's prints be different from those of resurrectees and instantly recognizable as such.

Burton shook his head. Sometimes, he got almost dizzy trying to think through these mysteries.

Deciding to abandon the wandering of the mental maze, he went to talk to Gilgamesh. Though the fellow disclaimed any of the adventures attributed to the mythical king of Uruk, he liked to boast of his unrecorded exploits. His black eyes would twinkle, and he would smile when he told his wild tales. He was like the American frontiersmen, like Mark Twain, he exaggerated to an incredible extent. He knew his listener knew he was lying, but he didn't care. It was all in fun.

The days passed, and the air became colder. The mists hung more heavily, refusing to dissipate until about eleven in the morning. They stopped more frequently to smoke the fish they caught by trolling and to make more acorn bread. Despite the thin sunshine, the grass and the trees were as green as their southern counterparts.

Then the day came when they arrived at the end of the line. There were no more grailstones.

From the north, borne by the cold wind, came a faint rumbling.

They stood on the forward deck, listening to the ominous growling. The now ever-present twilight and the mists seemed to press upon them. Above the soaring black mountain walls the sky was bright, though not nearly as bright as in the southern climes.

Joe broke their silence.

"That noithe ith the firtht cataract ve'll come to. It'th big ath hell, but it'th only a fart in a vindthtorm compared to the one that cometh from the cave. But ve got a long hard vay to go before ve get to that."

They were robed and hooded in heavy clothes and looked like ghosts in the thin fog. Cold moisture collected on their faces and hands.

Burton gave orders, and the *Post No Bills* was tied to the base of the grailstone. They began unloading, finishing in an hour. After they had set all their grails on the stone, they waited for it to discharge. An hour passed, the stone erupted; the echoes were a long time stopping.

"Eat hearty," Burton said. "This will be our last warm meal."

"Maybe our last supper, too," Aphra Behn said, but she laughed.

"Thith plathe lookth like purgatory," Joe Miller said. "It ain't tho bad. Vait until you get to hell."

"I've been there and back many times," Burton said.

They made a big fire of dried wood they'd been carrying in the boat and sat with their backs to the base of the stone while it warmed them. Joe Miller told some of his titanthrop jokes, mostly about the traveling trader and the bear hunter's wife and two daughters. Nur related some of his Sufi tales, designed to teach people to think differently, but light and amusing. Burton told some stories from the *Thousand and One Nights*. Alice told some paradoxical tales which Mr. Dodgson had made up for her when she was eight years old. Then Blessed Croomes got them to singing hymns, but she became angry when Burton inserted slightly off-color lines.

All in all, it was fun, and they went to bed feeling cheerier. The booze also helped to raise their spirits.

When they arose, they ate breakfast over another fire. Then they loaded up with their heavy burdens and started off. Before the stone and the boat disappeared in the mists, Burton turned for a last look. There were his final links with the world he'd known, though not always loved, so long. Would he ever see a boat, a grailstone again? Would he soon never see anything?

He heard Joe's lion-thunderish voice, and he turned away.

"Holy thmoke! Look at what I got to carry! I got three timeth ath much ath the retht of you. My name ain't Thamthon, you know."

Turpin laughed and said, "You're a white nigger with a big nose."

"I ain't no nigger," Joe said. "I'm a packhorthe, a beatht of burden."

"Vhat'th the differenthe?" Turpin said, and he ran laughing as Joe swung a gigantic fist at him. The towering backpack unbalanced him, and he fell flat on his face.

Laughter rose up and bounced off the canyon walls.

"I'll wager that's the first time the mountains have made merry," Burton said.

After a little while though, they became silent, and they trudged onward looking like lost souls in a circle of the Inferno.

They soon came to the first cataract, the little one, Joe Miller said. It was so broad that they couldn't see the other end, but it had to be ten times the width of Victoria Falls. At least, it seemed so. It fell from the mists above in a roar that made conversation impossible even if they shouted in each others' ears.

The titanthrop led the way. They climbed upward past the waterfall, spray now and then falling over them. Their progress was slow but not overly perilous. When they had gotten to perhaps two hundred feet up, they stopped on a broad ledge. Here they let down their burdens while Joe climbed on up. After an hour, the end of a long rope fell through the fog like a dead snake. They tied the packs, two at a time, to the rope, and Joe pulled them bumping and swinging into the mists. When all the packs were on top of the plateau, they worked their way carefully up the cliff. At the top they resumed their burdens and walked on, stopping frequently for rests.

Tai-Peng related stories of his adventures in his native land and got them to laughing. They came to another cataract and quit laughing. They scaled the cliff beside it, and then decided to call it a day. Joe poured some grain alcohol over wood—a frightful waste of good booze, he said—and they had a fire. Four days later, they were out of wood. But the last of the "small" cataracts was behind them.

After walking for an hour over a stone-strewn gently sloping-upward tableland, they came to the foot of another cliff.

"Thith ith it," Joe said excitedly. "Thithe ith the plathe vhere ve found a rope made out of cloththth. It vath left by Ekth."

Burton cast his lamp beam upward. The first ten feet was rough. From there on up, for as far as he could see, which wasn't far, there was a smooth-as-ice verticality.

"Where's the rope?"

"Damn it, it vath here!"

They went out in two parties, each going in opposite directions along the base of the cliff. Their electric lamps were beamed ahead of them, and they traced their fingers along the stone. But each returned without finding the rope.

"Thon of a bitch! Vhat happened?"

"I'd say that the other Ethicals found it and removed it," Burton said.

After some talk, they decided to spend the night at the base of the cliff. They ate vegetables which the grails had provided and dried fish and bread. They were already sick of their diet, but they didn't complain. At least, the liquor warmed them up. But that would be gone in a few days.

"I brought along a few bottleth of beer," Joe said. "Ve can have one last party vith them."

Burton grimaced. He disliked beer.

In the morning the two groups went out along the base again. Burton was with the one that went eastward or what he thought was that way. It was difficult to tell direction in this misty twilight. They came to the bottom of the huge cataract. There was no way for them to get across to the other side.

When they got back, Burton spoke to Joe.

"Was the rope on the left or right side of The River?"

Joe, illumined in the beam of a lamp, said, "Thith thide."

"It seems to me that X might have left another rope on the right side. After all, he wouldn't know if his henchmen would come up the right or left side."

"Vell, it theemth to me that ve came up the left thide. But it'th been tho many yearth. Hell, I can't be thyure!"

The little big-nosed dark Moor, Nur el-Musafir, said, "Unless we can get to the other side—and it doesn't seem possible—the question is irrelevant. I went westward, and I think that I may be able to get up to the plateau."

After breakfast, the entire group walked five miles or so to the corner of the mountain and the cliff walls. These met at an approximately 36-degree angle as if they were the walls of a very badly built room. Nur tied a very slender rope around his waist.

"Joe says that it's about a thousand feet up to the plateau. That's his estimate based on his memory of its height, and at that time Joe didn't know the English system of measurement. It might be less than he remembers. Let's hope so."

"If you get too tired, come back down," Joe said. "I don't vant you to fall."

"Then stand back so I won't strike you," Nur said, smiling. "It would hurt my conscience if I hit you and both of us died. Though I think that you wouldn't be injured any more than if an eagle defecated on you."

"It vould hurt me a lot," Joe said. "Eagleth and their crap vere taboo to my people."

"Think of me as a sparrow."

Nur went to the angle and braced himself, his back against one wall and his feet against the other. He slowly worked his way up the angle, holding his feet against one wall, the left foot extended a few inches more than the right. When his footing was secure, he slid his back upward as far as he could before losing his bracing. Then he would slide one foot up until his knee was almost to his chin. Keeping the one foot against the wall, he would slowly work the other up. Then he would slide his back up, and repeat the same maneuvers.

It wasn't long before he disappeared into the fog. Those below could tell his progress by the rate at which the slim rope was pulled up. It was very slow.

Alice said, "He'll have to have tremendous endurance to get to the top. And if he doesn't find a place to tie his rope to so he can haul up another, he might as well come back down."

"Let's hope the cliff isn't that high," Aphra Behn said.

"Or that the corner doesn't widen out," Ah Qaaq said.

When Burton's wristwatch indicated that Nur had been up for twenty-eight minutes, they heard him shout.

"Good luck! There's a ledge here! Large enough for two people to stand on, if you don't count Joe! And there's a projection I can tie the rope to!"

Burton looked at the titanthrop.

"Evidently the cliff isn't glass smooth."

"Yeah. Vell, I mutht have gone up on the right thide of The River, Dick. That'th thmooth all the way up. At leatht, the part I vent up on vath ath thlick ath a cat'th athth."

The Ethicals hadn't bothered to make the cliff unscalable all the way. They'd made the lower part smooth but had left the upper part, invisible in the fog, in its original state.

Had X been responsible for that decision?

Had he also arranged it so that the corner here, and perhaps the corner across The River, was angled so that a small light person could use his back and legs to get up the angles?

It was very probable.

If he had done so, then he'd planned on arranging this angle before it had been formed. This was no natural formation. The Ethicals had designed and built these mountains with whatever vast machines they had used.

Nur called down for them to fasten a heavier rope to the end of the light one. They did so, and presently he called down that the second rope was secured.

Burton hauled himself up on it, bracing his feet against the cliff, his body extended almost at right angles to it. He was panting and his arms hurt by the time he reached the ledge. Nur, surprisingly strong for such a skinny little man, helped him get up onto the ledge.

Then they hauled up the backpacks.

Nur looked up through the fog.

"The face is rough," he said. "It looks like I could climb up on the projections if I used the pitons."

He removed a hammer and some pitons from the pack. The latter were steel wedges which he would drive into the surface of the rock wall. Some of them contained holes through which a rope could be passed.

Nur disappeared into the mists. Burton heard his hammer now and then. After a while, the Moor called down for Burton to come on up. Nur was on another ledge.

"Actually, the surface is so irregular that we might be able to climb just using our hands. But we won't!"

By then Alice had climbed the rope up to the projection on which Burton stood. Burton kissed her and went on up after Nur.

Ten hours later, the entire group sat on top of the cliff. After they'd recovered, they walked on looking for a place to shelter them from the wind. They found none until they had traversed at least three miles. Here they came, as Joe said they would, to the base of another cliff. To their left The River, some miles away now, roared as it hurtled over the lip of the falls.

Joe played the beam of his lamp along the rock.

"Damme! If I did go up along the right side of The River, then ve're thcrewed. The tunnel ith on that thide, and ve can't get across The River!"

"If the Ethicals found X's rope and removed it, then they must have found the tunnel," Burton said.

They were too tired to search for the fissure which would be the gate to the tunnel. They walked along until they came to an overhang. Joe used some of his few remaining sticks to make a small fire, and they ate supper. The fire went out quickly. They piled heavy cloths on the rock floor and more over them and slept while The River thundered.

In the morning, while they were eating dried fish, pemmican, and bread, Nur said, "As Dick's pointed out, X wouldn't know which side his recruits would come up. So he must have left two ropes. Therefore, he must have made two tunnels. We should find one on this side."

Burton opened his mouth to say that that tunnel, if it existed, would also have been plugged. Nur held up his hand to forestall him.

"Yes, I know. But if the plug is thin, we can locate it, and we have the tools to dig through it."

One search party hadn't gone more than twenty feet from the camp when it found the plug. It was a few feet inside a fissure broad enough for even Joe to enter.

Great heat had been applied to melt the round plug into the surrounding quartz.

"Hot dog!" Joe said. "Thimmety tham! Maybe ve got a chanthe after all!"

"Perhaps," de Marbot said. "But what if the entire tunnel is plugged up?"

"Then we try the corner. If X was smart enough, he would've figured out that the tunnels might be found. So he would have arranged for a climbable angle here just as he did at the other place."

Burton scanned the face of the cliff while his lamp poked a bright hole through the fog. Ten feet from the base, the rock was wrinkled and fissured. But it abruptly became as smooth as a mirror from there to as far as he could see.

Joe swung his hammer against the plug. Burton, his ear close to the rock, said, "It's hollow!"

"Jutht great," Joe said. He removed several tungsten-steel alloy chisels from his backpack and began hammering. When he'd cut out enough of the quartz to make six holes, he and Burton inserted plastic explosive into them. Burton would have liked to daub clay over the plastic, but there wasn't any.

He stuck the ends of wires into the plastic and retreated along the face of the cliff, rolling out the wires. When the group was far enough away, he pressed one wire of his small battery against another. The explosions deafened them, and pieces of quartz flew out.

"Vell," Joe said, "at least my burden'll be lighter now. I von't have to carry thothe canth of plathtik and the battery anymore. That'th the end of them."

They went back into the fissure. Burton shot his light across it. The holes made by Joe had been enlarged. Several of them were big enough for him to see the tunnel beyond it.

He said, "We've got about twelve hours more work, Joe."

"Oh, thyit! Vell, here goeth nothing."

Shortly after breakfast, the titanthrop hacked out the last piece of rock, and the plug fell out.

"Now cometh the hard part," Joe said, wiping the sweat off his face and his grotesquely long nose.

The tunnel was just large enough for Joe to crawl up it, but his shoulders would rub against the sides and his head against the ceiling unless he lowered it. It went at an approximately 45-degree angle upward.

"Wrap clothth around your kneeth and handth," Joe said. "Othervithe, you're going to rub them bloody. You'll probably do tho anyvay."

Frigate, Alice, Behn, and Croomes returned just then with canteens refilled at The River. Joe half-emptied his.

"Now," he said, "ve thyould vait avhile until everybody'th taken a good healthy thyit. Vhen I vath vith thothe Egyptianths, ve neglected that precauthyon. Halfvay up, I couldn't thtand it no longer, tho I emptied my bowelth."

He laughed thunderously.

"You thyould have heard thothe notheleththth little fellowth cuthth! They carried on thomething terrible. They vath hopping mad vith no room to hop! Haw, haw!"

He wiped the tears from his eyes. "Jethuth! Did they thmell bad vhen they finally crawled out! Then they got even madder when they had to vath themthelveth off in The River. That vater'th ath cold ath a velldigger'th athth, ath Tham uthed to thay."

More tears flowed as he thought about Clemens. He snuffled, and he wiped off his proboscis on his sleeve.

Joe hadn't exaggerated the hardships. The tunnel was at least one mile long, every inch forward was an inch upward, and the air became increasingly thinner, though it howled through the shaft, and they had to drag their very heavy packs behind them. Moreover, for all they knew, the other end might have been plugged also. If it were, they would have to return to the base of the cliff.

Their joy at finding that the tunnel wasn't sealed renewed their strength for a while. However, the palms of their hands, their fingers, their knees, and their toes were skinned, bleeding, and hurting. They were unable to walk steadily for some time.

The wind was stronger and colder here despite its thinness. Joe sucked the oxygen-scarce air into his great lungs.

"Vone good thing about it. Ve only need one drink, and ve're loaded out of our thkullth."

They would have liked to make camp there, but the place was too exposed.

"Cheer up," Burton said. "Joe says that it's only a ten-mile walk to the next cataract."

"The latht vone, the biggetht. You think the otherth vere noithy. Vait until you hear thith vone."

Burton strapped on his pack and staggered on, his knees feeling as if they'd rusted. Joe came close behind him. Fortunately, the tableland was comparatively level and free of rock rubble. However, Burton had only the tremendous thunder of the falls to guide him through the fog. When the sound became stronger, he veered back to the left. When it was weaker, he went back to the right. Nevertheless, he was probably making a fifteen-mile hike out of a ten-miler.

All had to stop often because of the lack of oxygen and to make sure that no one straggled. Every fourth person in the line kept his lamp on until Burton stopped and swore.

"Vhat'th the matter?"

"We're not thinking straight in this air," Burton said, gasping. "We only need one light. We're wasting electicity. We can use a rope for all to hang onto."

With the line tied around his waist and the others grasping it, they went on into the cold grayness.

But after a while they were too weak to go a step more. Despite the wind, they lay down on and under cloths and tried to sleep. Burton awoke from a nightmare and turned his light on his watch. They'd been here ten hours.

He got them up, and they ate more than the rationing schedule allowed for. An hour later, the blackish face of a rock wall loomed out of the mists. They were at the foot of another obstacle.

42

JOE MILLER HADN'T COMPLAINED MUCH THOUGH HE HAD GROANED softly for the last half of the hike. He was ten feet tall and weighed eight hundred pounds and was as strong as any ten of Homo sapiens put together. But his giantism had disadvantages. One was that he suffered from fallen arches. Sam often called him the Great Flatfoot, and with very good reason. It hurt Joe to walk much, and when he was resting his feet still often hurt.

"Tham alvayth thaid that if it hadn't been for our feet, ve vould've conquered the world," Joe said. He was rubbing his right foot. "He claimed that it vath our broken-down dogth that made uth ekthinct. He may have been right."

It was obvious that the titanthrop needed at least two days of rest and therapy. While Burton and Nur, amateur but efficient podiatrists, worked on Joe, the others went out in two parties. They came back several hours later.

Tai-Peng, the leader of one, said, "I couldn't find the place Joe told us about."

Ah Qaaq, the other leader, said, "We found it. At least, it looks as if we could climb up there. It's very near the falls, though."

"In fact, it's so close," Alice said, "that it can't be seen until you're almost on it. It'll be dreadfully dangerous though. Very slippery with the spray.

Joe groaned, and said, "Now I remember! It *vath* the right thide that ve vent up on. The Egyptianth vent on it becauthe the left vath unlucky. Thith path mutht be one Ekth plathed here in cathe . . ."

"I wouldn't call it a path," the Mayan said.

"Vell, if it'th like the other plathe, it can be climbed."

It was, and it could be.

Seven days later, they were on top of the mountain. Snow and ice had made the dangers even greater than anticipated, and the air enfeebled them. Nevertheless, they had struggled up to another plateau. The River was far below, covered by fog.

After a few miles, they descended on a far easier slope. The air was thicker at the bottom and warmer, though still cold. They advanced through an ever-increasing and ever-louder wind until they came to another mountain.

"No uthe even thinking about climbing thith vone. Ve're lucky, though. The big cave of the vindth thyould be to our right a few mileth. Vell, maybe not tho lucky. You'll thee vhen ve get there. But that can vait avhile. I got to retht my thon-of-a-bitching feet again."

The River poured out in a vast and thick stream to descend swiftly down a gentle slope. The roar of water and wind was deafening, but at least it was warmer here. Joe, the veteran of the passage through the cave, led the way. A rope was tied to his waist and tied to the wrists of the others.

Warned by Joe to hang on tight, they went around the corner into the Brobdingnagian hole. Alice slipped and fell off the ledge and was pulled, shrieking, back up. Then Nur, even smaller than she, was blown off, but he too was hauled to safety.

The torches of the Egyptians had been extinguished by the wind when Joe had led them through the bellowing cave. Now, he could see, though not very far. Also, he shouted back to Burton, this ledge was broader than the one on the right.

"Boy, ve'd have been thyit out of luck if the Ethicalth had melted down the ledgeth! I guethth they thought that no vone vould ever get thith far after they took the ropeth avay and plugged the tunnel!"

Burton only heard part of what Joe said but filled in the rest.

They had to stop twice to eat and sleep. Meanwhile, The River gradually dropped away and finally disappeared. Burton, curious to know how deep it was, sacrificed a spare lamp. He counted seconds as its beam turned over and over and became a thread of light before it plunged into the blackness. It had fallen at least three thousand feet.

At last, the grayness that heralded the end of the cave appeared. They came out into the open air, misty but brighter. Above them was a sky which blazed with a multitude of giant stars and gas sheets. The thin cloud closed around them but didn't block their view of the mountain wall to their right. They were almost on the lip of the abyss at the bottom of which The River ran.

"Ve're on the wrong thide here," Joe said. "Ahead, on thith thide, a mountain blockth uth. If ve could only get acrothth to the right thide. But then maybe the Ethical left a vay for uth on thith thide."

"I doubt it," Burton said. "If he did, we'd have to circle completely around the inner wall of the mountains ringing the sea to get to the cave at the bottom. Unless . . ."

"Unlethth vhat?"

"Unless X made two caves and put boats there, too."

Nur said, "One rough ledge they might overlook. But two?"

"Yeah," Joe said. "Tell you vhat. The two thideth of The Valley here get very clothe at the top. The vallth mutht arch over, lean out. There'th only about tventy feet betveen the edgeth at the top. Here. Let me thyow you."

He walked slowly ahead and after about sixty feet stopped. His beam, added to theirs, clearly showed the other side of the gap.

"God Almighty!" Aphra said. "The Ethical surely didn't expect us to jump across it?"

"The other Ethicals wouldn't think anybody would dare it," Nur said. "But I think X expected us to, yes. I mean, he knew that at least one, maybe more, of any party that got this far would be able to leap across. After all, he picked some very athletic people. Then that person or persons would tie a rope to a rock, and the rest would go over on it."

Burton knew that he couldn't jump that far. He might get close, but close wasn't good enough.

Joe was stronger than two Hercules melded, but he was far too heavy. Ah Qaaq and Gilgamesh were also very strong but too squat and heavy. Good long jumpers weren't built like them. Turpin was tall but too muscular. Nur was very light and had a surprising wiry strength, but he was too short. The two white women and de Marbot were also too short and weren't good jumpers. That left Frigate, Croomes, and Tai-Peng.

The American knew what Burton was thinking. His face was pale. He was even better at long jumping than he'd been on Earth and had once leaped there to an unofficial distance of twenty-five feet during a practice jump but a wind had been behind his back. His normal distance was about twenty-two feet on Earth and twenty-three here. Nor had he ever jumped under such bad conditions.

"We should have brought along Jesse Owens," he said faintly.

"Hallelujah!" Croomes shrieked, startling the others. "Hallelujah! The Lord saw fit to make me a great jumper! I'm one of His chosen! He saw to it that I could leap like a goat and dance like King David for His glory! And now He gives me a chance to jump over the pit of Hell! Thank you, Lord!"

Burton moved close to Frigate and said, softly, "Are you going to allow a woman to jump first? Show you up?"

"It wouldn't be the first time," Frigate said. He shrugged. "Why shouldn't I let her go first? The problem here is not one of sex but of ability."

"You're scared!"

"You bet I am. Anybody but a psychotic would be."

He went to Blessed Croomes, though, and questioned her about her record. She said that she hadn't done much jumping on Earth, but, when she was living in a state called Wendisha, she had made twenty-two feet a number of times.

"How did you know it was that?" Frigate said. "We had an exact system of measurement on the *Rex,* but very few places would have such."

"What we did," Croomes said, "was guess what a foot was. It looked pretty close to me. Anyway, I know that I can do it! The Lord will buoy me up on the wings of my faith, and I will skip over it like one of His sweet gazelles!"

"Yeah, and you'll fall short, too, and smash your brains out against the edge of the gap," Frigate said.

"Why don't we mark out a distance?" Nur said. "Then you three can practice-jump, and we'll see who's the best."

"On this hard rock? We need a sand pit!"

Croomes said that they should throw a lantern over to the other side to provide a marker. Frigate cast one attached to a rope, so that it lit near the edge, rolled back, then stopped on its side several inches from the dropoff. Its beam pointed at them over the black abysm.

He pulled it back with the rope and threw it again. This time it rolled, but by whipping the rope he got it to an upright position and the light shone at right angles to them.

"Okay, so it can be done," Frigate said. "But I'll pull it back now. Nobody can jump until he's had a good night's sleep. Anyway, *I'm* too tired now to try it."

"Let's line up the run path with lanterns," Blessed said. "I'd like to get a good idea of how it'll look."

They did so, and Frigate and Croomes paced to where they would start their run, if they did. The marker for the leap was a lantern a few inches from the edge.

"It has to be a one-time thing," Frigate said. "We'll really have to warm up first. This cold air . . . On the other hand, the air is thinner and offers less resistance. That probably helped that black jumper—what's his name? such is fame—make that fabulous twenty-seven feet and four and a half inches in the Olympics at Mexico City. But, back to the first hand, we haven't really gotten acclimated yet to the high altitude. And we're sure as hell not in training."

Burton had said nothing to Tai-Peng since he wished to give him a chance to volunteer. The Chinese had been watching the procedure. Now he strode up to Burton and said, "I am a mighty jumper! I'm also sadly out of practice! But I will not allow a woman to be braver than I! I will make the first jump!"

His green eyes shone in the lantern beam.

Burton asked him what distance he'd cleared.

"More than that!" Tai-Peng said, pointing at the gap.

Frigate had been throwing pieces of paper up in the air to test the wind. He came up to Burton then, saying, "It blows on our left side and so it'll carry us a little to the right. But the mountain blocks most of it. I'd say it's a six- or seven-miles-an-hour wind."

"Thanks," Burton said. He kept his gaze on the Chinese. Tai-Peng was very good in athletics but not as good as he claimed to be. No one was that good. However, it was his life he was risking, and no one had asked him to do so.

Frigate spoke up loudly.

"Look! I'm really the most experienced jumper! So I should be the one to do it! And I will!"

"You've gotten over your fear?"

"Hell, no! What it is . . . I don't have the guts to let someone else do it. You'd all think I was a coward, and if you didn't, I would."

He turned to Nur.

"I failed to act rationally and logically. I failed you."

Nur smiled grimly at his disciple.

"You didn't fail me. You failed yourself. However, there are so many aspects to consider . . . anyway, you *should* be the one to jump."

The little Moor went up to the titanthrop and raised his head under Joe's vast nose.

"It may not be necessary for anyone to jump. Joe, do you think that I weigh as much as your pack?"

Joe frowned, and he picked up Nur with one hand under his buttocks. He held him out at arm's length and said, "Not by a long thyot."

When Nur was back on the ground, he said, "Do you think you could throw your pack across to the other side?"

Joe fingered his receding chin. "Vell, maybe. Thay, I thee vhat you're getting at! Vhy don't I try it? It von't make no differenth if the pack'th over there and ve're over here. Ve got to get acrothth anyvay."

He lifted the enormous pack above his head, walked to the edge, looked once, swung the pack twice, and heaved it. It fell a foot beyond the other edge.

Nur said, "I thought so. Joe, you throw me across now."

The titanthrop picked up the Moor with one hand against the little man's chest and one under his buttocks. Then he swung him back and forth, saying, "Vone, two, three!"

Nur arced across the abyss, landed on his feet a yard beyond the lip, and rolled. When he got up, he danced with joy.

Joe then cast Nur's lantern at the end of a rope. Nur caught it though he staggered back a little.

Nur came back out of the fog a few minutes later.

"I found a big boulder to tie the rope to, but I can't move it by myself! We'll need about five strong men!"

"Over you go!" Joe said, and he swung Burton back and forth. Though Burton wanted to shout that he was much heavier than Nur, he refrained. The gap looked twice as broad as it had up to that moment. Then he was shot up and outward while Joe yelled, "Vatch your athth, Dick!" and his laughter bellowed. The many-thousands-feet abyss was beneath him for a frightening second, and then Burton struck on his feet and was propelled forward. He rolled, but even so the rock thumped him hard.

A moment later, his pack followed. Joe then threw all the packs across, and he lifted Frigate and hurled him on over.

One by one, they followed until Ah Qaaq and Joe were the only ones left. Shouting, "Tho long, fatty!" the titanthrop hurled the Mayan. He hit closer to the edge than anyone but had a foot to spare.

"Now vhat?" Joe yelled.

Burton said, "There's a big boulder that must weigh almost as much as you, Joe. Go roll it up here, and then tie the end of the rope around it."

"That'th half a mile back," Joe said. "Vhy didn't you all thtay here and help me before you vent over?"

"Didn't want you to be too tired from moving the rock to throw us across."

"Jethuth H. Chritht! I do all the hard vork."

He disappeared with his lantern into the fog.

Some of them were bruised and with torn skin, but all were able to do their share. They followed Nur to the boulder and, after a long rest, they began rolling it over the flat stone surface of the plateau. It wasn't easy since the rock was irregularly shaped and probably weighed more than all of them together. Rests were frequent because of the thin air. They finally got it near the edge and then collapsed for a while.

A minute later, Joe rolled the boulder from the mists.

"I vath hoping I could beat you runtth to it," he shouted. "I vould've, too, if my boulder had been ath near ath yourth." He sat down to pant.

Blessed Croomes complained that she had been cheated out of the chance to jump and so demonstrate her faith in the Lord.

"Nobody stopped you," Frigate said. "Although, to tell the truth, I was disappointed, too. The only thing that kept me back was that, if I did miss, the group would be just that much weaker. Maybe I'll try it anyway just to show I can do it."

He looked at Tai-Peng, and they both burst out laughing.

"You ain't fooling me none," Croomes said in English. "You two men was skeered to do what a woman wasn't afraid to do."

"That's the difference between you and us," Frigate said. "We're not crazy."

When they all were restored, they tied the ends of the long heavy rope around the boulders and chocked them with smaller stones. Joe let himself down over the edge backward, grabbed the sagging rope, and hand-over-handed across it. His friends seized the rope to insure that the boulder wasn't moved by his enormous weight, though it wasn't necessary. When he got quickly to the edge, some left the rope and helped him get up over the edge.

"Boy, I hope I never have to do that again!" he gasped. "I never told you guyth thith before, but vhen I get on a real high plathe, I alvayth have an urge to jump off."

43

GETTING TO THE LEDGE THAT LED ALONG THE MOUNTAINSIDE TO THE SEA took them ten hours.

"Thith ith narrow enough now, but vhen ve get to the plathe vhere thothe two Egyptianth fell, man, that'th thomething!"

Several thousand feet below was a mass of clouds. They spent eight hours sleeping and continued after they'd had their monotonous breakfast. Though the Egyptians had crawled along this trail, the group faced the rock and edged along, their fingers gripping the holes and small outthrusts of the rock.

The air became somewhat warmer. Here the water still had heat to give up after its long wandering through the arctic regions and its passage through the polar sea.

The ledge was safely traversed. They went on another plateau and came to where, as Joe had said, they would be near the sea. He walked painfully to the edge of the mountain and pointed his lantern beam down on still another ledge.

It began about six feet below the edge of the cliff, was about two feet wide, and continued downward with the same breadth until it was lost in the thin clouds. It sloped at a 45-degree angle to the horizon or would have if there had been one.

"We'll have to abandon some stuff and make our packs smaller," Burton said. "There isn't enough room for them otherwise."

"Yeah, I know. Vhat vorrieth me ith that the Ethicalth might've cut the ledge in half, Jethuth, Dick! Vhat if they found the cave down there?"

"Then we'll have to trust to the inflatable kayak you're carrying to get two of us to the tower. I've mentioned that before."

"Yeah, I know. But that ain't going to keep me from talking about it. It helpth relieve my tenthyon."

The sun never came above the top of the circling mountains. Despite this, there was a twilight illumination.

"I fell off the ledge before I got too far," Joe said. "Tho I don't know how far the path—thome path!—goeth. It may take a whole day, maybe more, to get to the bottom."

"Tom Mix said that Paheri, the Egyptian, told him that they had to stop once and eat before they got to the bottom," Burton said. "That doesn't mean much, though. The journey was fatiguing, and so they'd get hungry sooner than they usually would."

They found a shallow cave. Joe, with the help of the others, rolled a big boulder to partially block the entrance and keep the wind out. They retreated to it to eat their meal. Two lamps kept the hollow bright, but they weren't enough to cheer them. What they needed was a fire, the ancient shifting brightness and crackling warmth which had cheered their Old Stone Age ancestors and every generation since.

Tai-Peng was the only one in high spirits. He told them stories of his antics and those of the Eight Immortals of the Wine Cups, the companions of his old age, and cracked many a Chinese joke. Though the latter couldn't adequately be translated through Esperanto, they were good enough to cause some, and especially Joe Miller, to shout with laughter and pound their thighs. Then Tai-Peng composed some on-the-spot poems and concluded by brandishing his sword at the tower somewhere ahead of them.

"Soon we will be in the fortress of the Big Grail! Let those who've meddled with our lives beware! We will conquer them though they be demons! Old Kung Fu Tze warned us that humans must not concern themselves with spirits, but I was never one to pay attention to that old man! I listen to no man! I follow my own spirit! I am Tai-Peng, and I know no superior!"

He howled, "Watch out, you things that hide and skulk and refuse to face us! Watch out! Tai-Peng comes! Burton comes! Joe Miller comes!"

And so on.

"Ve thyould fathe him our vay," Joe whispered to Burton. "Ve thyure could uthe all that hot air."

Burton was watching Gilgamesh and Ah Qaaq. They reacted just like the others, laughing and clapping Tai-Peng on. But that could be just good acting by one or both. He was worried. When they got to the cave—if they did—he would have to do something about them. Even if they were innocent, he would have to try to determine if one of them, or both, was X. Either of them could be Loga. Either of them could be Thanabur.

How could he do it?

And what—if anything—was one, or both, plotting?

He ran a scenario through his mind. When they started down the trail, he'd arrange it so that Joe Miller would be in the lead. He'd be second. Ah Qaaq and Gilgamesh would be in the rear. He didn't want them to be the first to get to the cave—if it was still there and not plugged up.

The Mayan and the Sumerian—if they were such—would come in last, and they'd be disarmed as they entered the cave. They carried long knives and .69-caliber plastic-bullet revolvers. Joe and de Marbot would see that they were relieved of them. He would warn Nur and Frigate about the deed, but he wouldn't have them in on it. He still wasn't sure about the American or the Moor. His experience with the agent, the pseudo-Peter Jairus Frigate, had made him very wary of the real Frigate, if he was indeed the original. Nur seemed to be what he claimed he was, but Burton trusted no one. Even the titanthrop might be an agent. Why not? He was intelligent and capable despite his grotesque size and facial features.

Burton had to trust someone, though. There were two, himself, and, after so many years of intimacy, Alice. The others—ah, the others! He'd have to watch them closely but his instincts, whatever that much-abused term meant, and it probably didn't mean much, told him that all but two were what they said they were.

With their much-reduced packs, Joe still carrying the largest, they let themselves down on the last ledge. Moving sidewise on the toes and front of their feet, their arms extended parallel to their shoulders most of the time, they held on to whatever grip they could find. It wasn't long before they came around the curve of the mountain, perhaps two hours, though it seemed like a very long time. Then Joe stopped, and he turned his head.

"Qviet, everyone. You might be able to hear the thound of the thea beating againtht the bathe of the mountainth."

They listened intently, but only Burton, Nur, and Tai-Peng heard the waves against the rock and that might have been their imagination.

When they came around the shoulder, however, they could see the relatively bright heavens and, looming faintly in the upper regions, the hulk of the mountains that ringed the sea on the far side.

Of the tower, there was no indication, not even a dim bulk. Yet it was in the center of the sea according to Joe's own story and the reports from the airship *Parseval*.

Joe called, "Here'th vhere I came acrothth a grail thomebody left. Here'th vhere I thaw a thudden blathe of light vhen the Ethical'th aircraft came down to the top of the tower. And here'th vhere I thtumbled over the grail and fell to my death."

He paused.

"It ain't here now."

"What?"

"The grail."

"The Ethicals must've removed it."

"I hope not," Joe said. "If they did, then they knew that people could get here, and they vould've trathed the ledge down to the bottom and found the cave. Let'th hope that thomebody elthe came along and removed it. Maybe the Egyptianth did after I fell."

They moved on the seemingly thread-thin wet-slippery footing. The mists became thicker then, and Burton couldn't see more than twenty feet ahead with the aid of his lantern, which he had to lift from his belt hook when he wanted more visibility.

Presently, Joe stopped.

"What's the matter?" Burton said.

"Thyit! The ledge runth out. Vait a minute. Lookth—and feelth—like it'th been melted down here. Yeah! It hath! The Ethicalth've cut the ledge out right here! Now vhat do ve do?"

"Can you see how far the melt goes?"

"Yeth. It lookth like it thtopth about forty feet from here. Might ath vell be a mile, though."

"How far up or down does the melt go?"

A minute passed.

"For ath far ath I can reach. Vait a minute. I'll thyine my light."

A few seconds passed.

"There'th thome fiththyureth about four feet above my fingertipth."

Burton removed his pack and got down on his hands and knees. Nur, who'd been just behind, crawled slowly over him. Joe and the Moor did a circus-acrobat balancing act while Nur climbed to the titanthrop's shoulders. Presently, Nur said, "It looks as if there are some fissures on a straight line. Enough for our pitons."

Nur continued standing on the titanthrop's shoulders. Burton handed the steel wedges and a hammer to Joe, who passed them on to the Moor. While Joe held Nur's legs firmly, Nur's hammer drove in two wedges. Burton sent up the end of a rope, thin but heavy enough, to Nur. He passed this through the eyes of the wedges and secured the end at the most remote piton.

The Moor got down onto the ledge by Joe's side where Burton held him from falling off while he put on a harness much like that which parachutists wear. These were made of fish leather and metal and had been part of the launch's stores. On the webbing on the chest were buckles to each of which strong plastic ribbons were attached. At the end of each was secured a small metal device containing a wheel.

Nur climbed back up on Joe. When he stood up on the titanthrop's broad shoulders, he passed one jaw of the wheeled device around the horizontal rope held through the eyes of the pitons. He snapped the device together and locked the jaws with a lever. Now he could slide along the rope attached to the cliff face. When he got to the first piton, he locked the left-hand wheeled block to the part of the rope beyond the first piton. Then he unhinged the first block and slid along to the second piton.

Bracing his feet against the cliff wall, he leaned outward, supported by the ribbons, and began hammering the third piton into a fissure. This was hard labor and required many rests. The others needed food, but they were too concerned about Nur to have any appetite.

It took five hours for Nur, working patiently, hammering at the pitons, to reach the area above the ledge where it resumed. By then he was too exhausted to drive in another piton. He dropped down along the face of the cliff to the projection.

Burton went next, climbing up on the giant's back to his shoulders, no undangerous feat. Without Joe's height and strength, the entire party would have been stopped at this point with no alternative except to go back. They would have starved then, since they did not have enough rations for the return trip.

Burton moved along the cliff face as Nur had and presently was at the other ledge. Nur caught and steadied Burton as he released the block and slid down with his hands extended to slow down his descent by their friction. Fortunately, the ledge here was broader than on the other side of the melt.

Those on that side had another problem. That was getting the heavy packs across. There seemed nothing else to do but to get rid of all except the most essential items. Unpacking was difficult, though, because of the very small space for footing. They helped each other, one clinging with a hand to a roughness in the wall while he or she reached over and opened the pack on the back of his neighbor. The items had to come out one by one and be dropped into the sea or placed on the ledge for repacking.

Everything went except the knives, firearms, the ammunition, some long heavy cloths, some rations, and the canteens. Part of those were placed in their grails. Alice and Aphra, the lightest, were to bring over what was left in Burton's and Nur's packs in their own.

Joe called across the abyss and asked if he should leave the inflatable kayak behind. Burton said that it shouldn't be discarded. But since Joe weighed so much, it'd be best to have de Marbot carry it in his pack. The contents of the Frenchman's pack should be parceled out between Croomes' and Tai-Peng's.

Burton didn't want the titanthrop to bring across anything but himself. So far, the pitons had given no indication of coming loose. But he didn't know what eight hundred pounds would do to them.

One by one, the others came until only Ah Qaaq and Joe Miller were left. When the Mayan made the passage, he used his hammer to drive each wedge in more securely.

Joe reached down gingerly and picked up his huge canteen. He emptied it and placed it back on the ledge. He shouted, "I vant to get acrothth fatht! Tho I ain't going to bother vith my harnethth! I'll thving over, hand over hand."

He leaped up and grabbed the rope by the first piton.

He moved swiftly, his long arms reaching out, grabbing the rope ahead of him and then sliding the other along. He used his knees to brace himself so he could lean outward.

Halfway across, a piton skreeked as it pulled out from its hole.

Joe was motionless for a moment. Then he extended a long arm to the rope on the side nearest him from the next piton.

The loosened piton came free with another screech. Joe dropped down, clinging to the rope, and swung like an almost-stopped pendulum.

"Hang on, Joe!" Burton said.

Then he screamed with the rest of the party as the second wedge tore loose and the others followed.

Bellowing, shrouded in white cloths, Joe Miller dropped for the second time into the dark sea.

SECTION 13

In the Dark Tower

44

BURTON WEPT WITH THE OTHERS. HE'D LIKED THE HUGE MAN, HAD perhaps loved him. With his death the group had lost much courage, much morale-boosting, much strength.

After a while they turned around, cautiously, and continued the slow still dangerous descent. When six hours passed, they stopped to eat and sleep. The latter was difficult, since they had to lie on one side and make sure they didn't roll over while sleeping. They put their pistols against their backs so these would, they hoped, be so uncomfortable that they'd wake them immediately. Excretion was not easy either. The men could face the outer side of the ledge to urinate, though the updraft sometimes caused the liquid to blow back on their cloths. The women had to hang their posteriors over the ledge and hope for the best, which often didn't happen.

Alice was the only modest one. She required that the others look away while she was relieving herself. Even then, their near presence made her inhibited. Sometimes, though, the mists thickened enough to give her privacy.

They were a gloomy party, still numbed by Joe Miller's death. Also, they could not help dwelling on the strong possibility that the Ethicals had found the cave and sealed it.

The sound of waves crashing against the base became louder. They descended into the thick clouds; the cliff face and the ledge became even wetter. Finally, Burton, in the lead, was wet by spray and the sea boomed around him.

He halted and sent his lantern beam ahead of him. The edge ran into the black waters. Ahead was an outcropping, and, if what Paheri had said was true, the mouth of the cave would be on its other side.

He called back to those behind Alice, telling them what his light had revealed. He walked into the water, which was only knee deep. Apparently, the shallow ledge went a long way out since the waves were weak here, though powerful on both sides not far away. The water was very cold, seeming to turn his legs into icy clumps.

He came back to the black projection and worked his way around it. Alice came closely behind him.

"Is there a cave?" Her voice trembled.

He shot the beam ahead to his right. His heart was hammering and not just from the shock of the cold water.

He breathed out, "Ah!"

There it was, the long-imagined hole at the base of the mountain. It was arched and low and would require that even Nur stoop to get through it. But it was wide enough for the boats which Paheri had described to pass through it.

Burton shouted back the good news. Croomes, fifth in line, screamed, "Hallelujah!"

However, Burton was not as exultant as he sounded. The cave could still be here, but the boats might not be.

He led Alice along on the rope still connected to her belt and bent down to enter the mouth. A few feet inside, a smooth stone floor sloped upward at a 30-degree angle, the hollow broadened, and the ceiling rose to twenty feet. When they were all gathered inside, he ordered that they disconnect the rope. They shouldn't need it now.

He shone his light on their faces, pale and tired-looking but eager. Gilgamesh was on his far right, and Ah Qaaq stood on the left behind the rest. If Burton had not abandoned his plan to seize the two, the time to do so would be near. But he had decided to improvise when he had to.

He turned and led them up the floor to a tunnel. It curved gently to the right for over three hundred feet, and the air became warmer as they advanced. Before they got to its end, they saw light.

Burton could not resist running toward the illumination. He burst into a very large dome-shaped chamber and almost stepped on a human skeleton. It lay face down, its right armbones stretched out as if reaching for something. He picked up the skull and looked within it and at the floor beneath it. There was no tiny black ball.

The light came from huge metal balls, each on one of nine black metal tripods about twelve feet high. The light looked cold.

There were ten black metal boats on V-shaped supports and one empty support. It had held the vessel that the Egyptians had used to get to the tower.

The boats were of various sizes, the largest able to hold thirty people.

At the left side were metal shelves holding gray tins—the Americans would call them cans—each about ten inches high and six inches wide.

It was as Paheri had said it was.

Except that three human skeletons clad in blue clothes lay by one of the large boats.

The others moved in, talking in low tones. The place was certainly awing, but Burton ignored its effect to examine the unexpected remains.

The clothes seemed to be one-piece suits, pocketless, seamless, and buttonless and with pants legs. The material felt glossy and filled out where his fingers had depressed it. He rolled the skulls to one side and shook the bones from the garments. One individual was tall and had heavy bones and a thick supraorbital ridge and heavy jaws. He had probably been an early paleolithic. The bones of the other two were of the modern type, and the pelvis of one was a woman's.

Inside each skull was a very tiny black sphere. If he hadn't been looking for them, he wouldn't have noticed them.

There was no evidence of violence. What had struck these agents down? And what vehicle had brought them here?

He would have expected one of the flying vessels he'd glimpsed many years ago. But there had been none outside the cave mouth. Could it have floated away?

What or who had interrupted the three? Why hadn't the people in the tower come after them after a certain amount of time?

They hadn't because they were having troubles of their own. Or they were dead, slain by the same thing that had felled these three.

X had to be responsible for this.

Burton reasoned that the same event that had downed these three had also resulted in stranding X and all the other Ethicals and agents in The Valley.

That meant that no craft could fly out from the tower to pick them up. Nor could the renegade fly one of his hidden vessels to the tower. He'd been forced, as Barry Thorn, to go on the airship built by Firebrass. And he'd failed to get in the tower.

From Burton's viewpoint, the event had made certain advantages for him and for X. The agents had obviously discovered the cloth-ropes hanging down from the cliffside and the tunnels, and they'd found out that the very narrow ledge had been used by people from The Valley. They had probably found the cave last, after trying to make sure that passage would be impossible for any more of the unauthorized.

If the three hadn't been killed, the cave entrance would be plugged up.

He strode to the shelves filled with tins. At the corner of each shelf was a plastic sheet about twelve inches by twelve inches. On it were figures of a man demonstrating how to open the tins. Burton didn't need the pictures since he knew from Paheri's story what to do. He passed a fingertip completely around the upper rim and waited for a few seconds. The top, seemingly of hard metal, quivered, shimmered, and turned into a gelatinous film. His finger penetrated it easily.

Burton said, loudly, "X forgot all about eating utensils and plates! But that's all right! We can use our fingers!"

Famished, the others quit looking at the objects in the cave and followed his example. They scooped out the beef stew—warm—with their fingers and, from the tins marked by a bas relief of bread, brought out loaves. They ate voraciously until their bellies were stuffed. There seemed no reason to ration themselves. The supply was more than plentiful.

Burton, sitting on the floor, his back against a wall, watched the others.

If one was X, why didn't he reveal his identity?

Was it because he had only recruited The Valley people to have a backup team? People who might pull his chestnuts out of the fire for him if he was in a situation where he was helpless without them?

If so, why hadn't he told them more of what he expected from them?

Or had he meant to do that but events had happened unexpectedly and too swiftly? And now he was in a position where he didn't need their help? Might, in fact, believe them to be a hindrance?

And why was he a renegade?

Burton didn't believe X's story about why the other Ethicals had resurrected the Terrans.

Indeed, he wasn't sure that he hadn't been allied with someone whose true goals he would loathe if he knew them.

Perhaps that was why the Mysterious Stranger had been so mysterious, why he'd not told them the truth, why he was still in disguise.

If he were.

Whatever the truth was, it was long past time for the Ethical to reveal himself. Unless . . . unless X knew that some of this party were agents or other Ethicals. He would then believe that he had to keep his disguise until they were in the tower. Why in the tower? Because there he had means to overpower or kill his enemies. Or anyone else who would try to keep him from carrying out his schemes, beneficent or malignant.

These might require that his recruits be among the removed. He'd needed them only to get to the tower.

Why would he ever have thought that he might have to have their help?

Well . . . when Spruce had been interrogated, he'd said something about the Operator of a giant computer. Burton didn't know who the Operator was, but a computer might have been used secretly by X when, or before when, the resurrection project began. He might have put into it all the probabilities he could think of regarding his unlawful project and asked for an estimate of their happening. Perhaps, the computer might even have been able to come up with some that X couldn't think of.

One of the items offered by the computer was a situation or situations in which X might need recruits.

Burton couldn't imagine what it was, unless it was the present one.

Good enough.

And so X had gotten his recruits, and he'd erased all his questions and the answers from the computer. Somehow, he'd done it without the Operator's knowing about it. That is, all this had happened if Spruce hadn't lied and there were indeed such things as an Operator and computer.

As of now, Burton's big problem was that X hadn't told him who he was. Which meant that very soon X would be acting, not for his recruits but against them.

Burton thought that they should get some sleep before they ventured out on the boats. All agreed, and so they laid out their heavy cloths on the floor and rolled up others for pillows. Since it was warm here, they didn't even have to cover themselves with their eskimo-suit-type garments. The hot air came from slits along the bases of the walls.

"Probably powered by nuclear energy," Frigate said. "The same goes for the lamps."

Burton wanted to set two-hour watches with two guards each.

"Why?" Tai-Peng said. "It's evident that we're the only ones around for twenty thousand miles."

"We don't know that," Burton said. "We shouldn't get careless now."

Some agreed with the Chinese, but it was finally decided that they should take no chances. Burton picked the sentinels and appointed Nur to be Gilgamesh's partner and himself as Ah Qaaq's.

The Moor wasn't likely to be taken by surprise; he had extraordinary perceptions of others' attitudes and feelings; he could often tell by subtle body language what others intended to do.

It was possible that Nur was an agent or that Gilgamesh and Ah Qaaq were in cahoots. One might pretend to sleep until his colleague who was on watch attacked his partner.

The possibilities were numerous, but Burton had to take chances. He couldn't do without sleep all the time.

What worried him most, though, was that X, if he was here, might take a small boat during the night and get to the tower ahead of the others. Once there, he would make sure that the entrance at the base couldn't be entered.

Burton gave de Marbot, Alice's partner for the first duty, his wristwatch. Then he lay down on his cloths, which were near the entrance to the tunnel. His loaded pistol was under his pillow. He had trouble getting to sleep, though he wasn't the only one if the sighs and mutterings he heard were any indication. It wasn't until the first two hours were almost over that he slid into an uneasy sleep. He kept starting awake; he had nightmares, some of them recurrences for the past thirty years. God, in the garments of a late Victorian gentleman, poked him in the ribs with a heavy cane.

"You owe for the flesh. Pay up."

His eyes opened, and he looked around. Tai-Peng and Blessed Croomes were on guard now. The Chinese was talking in a soft voice to the black woman not ten feet from Burton. Then Croomes slapped his face and walked away.

Burton said, "Better luck next time, Tai-Peng," and he went back to sleep.

When Nur and Gilgamesh were on watch, Burton roused again. He slitted his eyes so that they would think he was still sleeping. Both were in one of the big boats, sitting on the raised deck by the controls. The Sumerian seemed to be telling a funny story to the Moor, if Nur's smiles meant anything. Burton didn't like their closeness. All the very strong Gilgamesh had to do was to reach out and seize Nur's throat.

The Moor, however, seemed very much at ease. Burton watched them for a while, then nodded off. When he awoke again, with a start, Nur was shaking him.

"Your watch."

Burton rose and yawned. Ah Qaaq was standing by the shelves, eating bread and stew. He gestured at Burton to join him. Burton shook his head. He didn't intend to get any closer to him than he had to. Stooping, he withdrew the pistol from under the pillow and placed it in his holster. Ah Qaaq, he noted, was also armed. There was nothing significant in this. The guards were supposed to carry their weapons.

Burton got within six feet of Ah Qaaq and told him he was going outside to urinate. The Mayan, his mouth full, nodded. He'd lost weight during the hard journey and now seemed determined to make up for it.

If he's X pretending to be a compulsive eater, Burton thought, he's certainly an excellent actor.

Burton went through the tunnel with frequent looks behind him and stops now and then to listen for footsteps. He didn't turn on his lantern until he reached the cave. The lantern, set in the mouth on the sloping floor, beamed past him. The cold fog pressed wetly. Having finished his business quickly, he went back into the cave.

Now would be a good time for Ah Qaaq to sneak up on him. But he neither saw nor heard anything except the crash of waves against the rocks some distance away. When he cautiously returned, he found Ah Qaaq sitting with his back against the wall, his eyes half closed, his head drooping.

Burton moved over to the opposite wall and leaned against it. After a while, the Mayan stood up and stretched. He signaled that he was going out to the cave. Burton nodded. Ah Qaaq, his heavy dewlap bouncing, waddled out through the tunnel. Burton decided that he'd been overly suspicious. A minute later, he thought that he hadn't been suspicious enough. What if the Mayan was X, and he had another cave nearby in which was a boat? It might be behind a narrow fissure, an opening to which Ah Qaaq could wade through the shallow water on the shelf.

Ten minutes went by, not an unreasonable time for the absence. Should he go after Ah Qaaq?

While Burton was trying to make up his mind, he saw the Mayan enter. Burton relaxed. The watch was half over, and the others would be in the more shallow phase of sleep and thus more easily awakened by noise.

Also, it would be logical for X to wait until the tower was entered. Here, he would have to deal with many. There, he would be on familiar ground.

When the six hours had passed, Burton aroused everybody. They went out to the sea in two groups according to sex and returned complaining about the cold. By then Burton and Ah Qaaq had poured water from the canteens into the cups provided by the grails and were ready to add the instant coffee which also heated the water. They drank and talked softly for a while and then ate breakfast. Some left for the sea again. Croomes insisted that it was a shame to allow skeletons to lie unburied. She made such a fuss that Burton thought it would be better to mollify her. A delay wasn't going to make any difference anyway.

They trouped out with the bones and hurled them into the sea while Croomes said a long prayer over them. The skeleton nearest the tunnel had to be Blessed's mother, but no one mentioned this, and she would certainly have wept if she had suspected it. Burton and some of the others knew from Paheri's story that, when the Egyptians had come here, they'd found some pieces of scalp which hadn't rotted away entirely. These had held black kinky hair.

They returned and loaded up one of the thirty-person boats with their possessions and sixty cans of food. Four men picked up the big but very light craft and carried it down the tunnel to the cave. Two men and two women brought out a smaller one to be attached by a rope to the other.

When asked why the extra was needed, he replied, "Just in case."

He had no idea what the *case* might be. It couldn't hinder them, though, to take extra precautions.

The last to leave the chamber, he gave it a final look. It was very quiet and eerie here with the nine glowing lamps and the empty boats. Would anyone follow them? He didn't think so. This was the third expedition and the most successful, so far. Things went by threes. Then he thought of Joe Miller, who had twice fallen into the sea. Surely he wouldn't do it again?

Not unless *we* give him a chance, he thought.

All but Ah Qaaq and Gilgamesh got into the big boat. They pushed it into the water, climbed aboard, and began drying off their feet. Burton had studied the picture-chart in the craft until he knew what to do by heart. He stood on the raised deck behind the steering wheel and punched a button on the control panel. A light sprang out from the surface of the panel itself, a glow which enabled him to see the buttons. They had no markings, but the diagram showed the location and purpose of each.

At the same time, a bright orange outline of a cylindrical shape, the tower, sprang out on a screen just above the panel.

"We're ready," he called back. He paused, punched another button, and said, "We're off!"

"Off to see the Wizard of Oz, the Fisher King!" Frigate said. "Off to find the holy grail!"

"May it *be* holy," Burton said. He burst out laughing. "But if it is, what are *we* doing there?"

Whatever the propulsive power was—there was no trembling of the boat from propellers nor wake from a jet—the vessel moved swiftly. Its speed was controlled by a curious device, a plastic bulb attached to the rim of the wheel on the right side. By squeezing or releasing his grip, Burton could control the speed. He turned the wheel until the image of the tower moved from the right to the center of the screen. Then he slowly increased the pressure on the bulb. Presently, the boat was cutting through the waves at an angle. Spray drenched those behind him, but he would not slow down.

Now and then he looked behind him. In the dark fog he could not even see to the stern of the boat, but its passengers were huddled closely at the edge of the control deck. They looked in their shroudlike cloths like souls being ferried by Charon.

They were as silent as the dead, too.

Paheri had estimated that it had taken Akhenaten's boat about two hours to get to the tower. That was because he had been afraid to make the boat go at top speed. The sea, as reported by the *Parseval* radarman, was thirty miles in diameter. The tower was about ten miles in diameter. So there were only about twenty miles to go from the cave. The Pharaoh's vessel must have crawled at ten miles per hour.

The tower rapidly grew larger on the screen.

Suddenly, the image burst into flame.

They were very close to their goal.

The direction sheet indicated that now was the time to punch another button. Burton did so, and two extremely bright bowlamps shot their beams into the mists and lit upon a vast curving dull surface.

Burton released all pressure on the bulb. The boat quickly lost speed and started drifting away. Applying power again, he swung the boat around and headed it slowly for the dim bulk. He punched another button, and he could see a big port, thick as the door in a bank vault, open in the seamless side.

Light streamed out through the O.

Burton cut off the power and turned the wheel so that the side of the boat bumped against the lower side of the open port. Hands seized the threshold and steadied the boat.

"Hallelujah!" Blessed Croomes screamed. "Momma, I'll soon be with you, sitting on the right hand of sweet Jesus!"

The others jumped. The stillness, except for the slight thudding of the boat against the metal, had been so impressive and their wonder that the way was finally open for them had been so overpowering, they felt that her cry was near sacrilege.

"Quiet!" Frigate shouted. But he laughed when he realized that no one could hear them.

"Momma, I'm coming!" Blessed shouted.

"Shut up, Croomes!" Burton said. "Or by God I'll throw you into the water! This is no place for hysterics!"

"I'm not hysterical! I'm joyous! I'm filled with the glory of the Lord!"

"Then keep it to yourself," Burton said.

Croomes told him he was bound for Hell, but she subsided.

"You may be right," Burton said. "Let me tell you, though, that we're all going to the same place now. If it's Heaven, we'll be with you. If it's Hell . . ."

"Don't say that, man! That's irreverent!"

Burton sighed. She was, on the whole, sane. But she was a religious fanatic who managed to ignore the facts of life and also the contradictory elements in her faith. In this, she was much like his wife, Isabel, a devout Roman Catholic who had managed to believe in spiritualism at the same time. Croomes had been strong, enduring, uncomplaining, and always helpful during their struggles to reach this place except when she was trying to convert her crewmates to her religion.

Through the port he could see the gray-metaled corridor which Paheri had described. Of his companions who had collapsed near its end, there was no sight. Paheri had been too frightened to follow the others. He'd stayed in the boat. Then Akhenaten and his people fell to the floor, and the port had swung shut as silently as it had opened. Paheri had been unable to find the cave, and he had finally gone over the first of the cataracts in his boat and had awakened on some far bank of The River. But now there were no more resurrections.

Burton unbuttoned the strap on his holster.

He said, "I'll go first."

He stepped up over the threshold, Moving air warmed his face and hands. The light was shadowless, seeming to emanate from the walls, floor, and ceiling. A closed door was at the end of the corridor. The entrance port had been opened by thick gray-metal curving rods that disappeared inside a six-foot-high cube of gray metal by the outer wall. The base of the cube seemed to be part of the floor. No welding or bolts held it.

Burton waited until Alice, Aphra, Nur, and de Marbot had entered. He told them not to go more than ten feet from the port. Then he called out, "You fellows bring in the small boat!"

Tai-Peng said, "Why?"

"We'll wedge it in the door. It should keep the door from swinging shut."

Alice said, "But it'll be crushed."

"I doubt it. It's made of the same substance as the grails and the tower."

"It still looks awfully fragile."

"The grails have very thin walls, and the engineers in Parolando tried to blow them up, to crush them with powerful machinery, and to dent them with triphammers. They had no effect whatsoever."

The corridor light shone on the faces of the men in the boat below. Some looked surprised; some, delighted; some, emotionless. He wasn't able to determine by their reactions who X might be.

Only Tai-Peng had questioned him, but that didn't mean anything. The fellow was always wanting to know the why.

With the help of all, the vessel was lifted up and gotten halfway through the port. It was just wide enough to stick in the middle of the O, leaving room for those outside to crawl in underneath after they'd passed in the packs and tins.

Burton backed away as they came in one by one. He held his pistol in his hand, and he told Alice to bring hers out. The others, seeing the weapons trained on them, were astonished. They were even more so when he told them to put their hands on top of their heads.

Frigate said, "You're X!"

Burton laughed like a hyena.

"No, of course not! What I'm going to do now is to root X out!"

45

NUR EL-MUSAFIR SAID, "YOU MUST SUSPECT ALL BUT ALICE OF BEING X."

"No," Burton said, "some of you may be agents, and if you are, speak up. But I have seen the Ethicals in their Council, and there are only two in this group whose physiques resemble the person I think might be X!"

He waited. It became evident that if any were agents none was going to admit his or her identity.

"Very well. I'll explain. It seems obvious that X was Barry Thorn and perhaps Odysseus. Thorn and the self-proclaimed Greek were short and very muscular. Both had similar features, though Odysseus' ears stuck out and he was much darker. But these differences could be due to disguise-aids.

"The two Ethicals who resembled them were called Loga and Thanabur.

"Two of this group could be either. Or both. I believe, however, that the engineer Podebrad, who was killed on the *Rex*, was Thanabur. I admit that it could have been Loga. In any event, we're not going one step further until I question—most severely—two of this group."

He paused, then said, "These are Gilgamesh, the self-proclaimed king of Uruk of ancient Sumeria, and Ah Qaaq, the self-proclaimed ancient Mayan!"

Alice said in a low voice, "But Richard! If you press him too hard, he can just simply kill himself."

Burton roared, "Did you hear what she said? No? She said that all X has to do to escape is to kill himself! But I know that he isn't going to do that! If he does, he can't carry out his plans, whatever they are! No more raising from the dead for him!

"Now . . . I've finally taken action because we are at a place where we can go no further without him. Only X knows how to cancel the gas or supersonic frequency or whatever that felled the Egyptians. And I want answers to my questions!"

"You're desperate, man!" Tom Turpin said. "What if none of us is X? You're skating on mighty thin ice."

"I'm convinced that one of you is he," Burton said. "Now . . . here is what I plan to do. If no one confesses, then I'll knock you, Gilgamesh, and you, Ah Qaaq, out. You're my prime suspects. And while you're coming out of unconsciousness, I'll hypnotize you. I found out that Monat Grrautut, the Arcturan, and the men who claimed to be Peter Jairus Frigate and Lev Ruach had hypnotized my friend Kazz. They're not the only ones who can play at that game. I'm a master hypnotist, and if you're concealing something, I will get it out of you."

In the silence that followed, the others looked uneasily at one another.

Croomes said, "You're a wicked man, Burton! We're at the gates of Heaven, and you talk of killing us!"

"I said nothing about killing," Burton said, "though I'm prepared to do it if I must. What I want is to clear up this mystery. Some of you may be agents. I implore you to step forward and confess. You have nothing to lose and much to gain. It's too late now to attempt to hide things from us."

De Marbot said, sputtering, "But . . . but, my dear Burton! You hurt me! I am not one of these damnable agents or Ethicals! I am what I say I am, and I'll strike the man who calls me a liar!"

Nur said, "If one or both of them is guiltless, then you will have injured and insulted an innocent. It would be brutal to do so. Moreover, you'll have made an enemy of a friend. Can't you hypnotize them without violence?"

"I hate doing this as much as any of you," Burton said. "Believe me when I say that. But an Ethical would be an excellent hypnotist himself, and no doubt his powers of resistance will be very strong. I must knock these two out so that they won't have these powers, catch them when they're halfwitless."

Alice said softly, "It *is* terribly brutal, Richard."

"Now," Burton said, "I want you to take out your weapons and drop them on the floor. Do it one by one and do it slowly. You, Nur, you be the first."

The knives and pistols clattered onto the gray metal. When they were all disarmed, Burton told them to step back while Alice picked up the weapons. In a short while there was a pile of them against the wall behind him.

"Keep your hands on your heads."

Most of their faces showed anger, indignation, or hurt puzzlement. The faces of Ah Qaaq and Gilgamesh were iron masks.

"Come to me, Gilgamesh," Burton said. "When you're five feet from me, stop. Then turn around."

The Sumerian walked slowly toward him. Now he was glaring. He said, "If you strike me, Burton, you will have made an enemy forever. I was once the king of Uruk, and I am the descendant of gods! No one lays a hand on me without punishment! I will kill you!"

"I am indeed sorry to have to do this," Burton said. "But surely you can see that the fate of the world is the issue. If we were in each other's shoes, I would not blame you for what you were doing to me. I'd resent it, yes, but I'd understand it!"

"After you've found I'm innocent, you would do well to kill me! If you don't, I'll kill you! I speak the truth!"

"We'll see."

Burton planned, if the Sumerian was not X, to install a posthypnotic command that Gilgamesh forgive him when he came out of the trance. He would have ordered him to forget the injury, but the others would no doubt remind him of it.

"Place your hands on the back of your neck," Burton said. "Then turn around. Don't worry about being hurt too much. I know precisely just how much force I'll need. You won't be unconscious for more than a few seconds."

Burton reversed the pistol and lifted it by its butt. Gilgamesh, bellowing, "No!", whirled, his arms flying out from his neck, and his hand struck the pistol and tore it from Burton's grip.

Alice should have fired then. Instead, she tried to beat the Sumerian on the back with her pistol barrel. Burton was very strong, but he went down under the herculean power of Gilgamesh and then was lifted up. He struck Gilgamesh in the face, making his nose bleed and bruising the skin. The Sumerian lifted him above his head and threw him against the wall. Stunned, Burton dropped to the floor.

The others were shouting and screaming, and Alice was yelling. But she managed to bring the butt of her weapon, now reversed, down on the head of Gilgamesh. He swayed, then began to crumple.

Ah Qaaq, swift despite his fat, ran by Alice, snatching the pistol from her hand, and continued toward the end of the corridor.

Though dazed, Burton struggled to get up, shouting, "Get him! Get him! He's the Ethical! X! X!"

His legs felt as if they were balloons out of which the air was whistling. He slid back down against the wall.

The Mayan—no, no Mayan he—slammed his palm against the wall on his left. Immediately, the door at the end of the corridor slid into a recess in the wall.

Burton tried to note the exact location of the area that X had struck. The blow had undoubtedly activated machinery behind the wall. And since it opened the door, it also was inhibited from releasing whatever it was that had felled the Egyptians.

Nur, a small skinny dark flash, scooped up a pistol as he ran by the pile. Then he stopped, and he lifted the heavy weapon in both hands. The gun boomed. The projectile struck the side of the door as X went around it. Pieces of plastic flew through the exit and against the wall opposite. X fell, though only his black-clothed legs showed for a moment. Then they were gone.

Nur ran after him but stopped at the doorway. He leaned out cautiously, and at once jerked his head back. The bullet fired by X smashed itself against the wall just outside the door. Nur got down on his knees and looked around the exit again. Another boom. Nur seemed uninjured.

By then the others had picked up their weapons and were running toward the doorway.

Though regrets were useless, Burton regretted that he had not chosen Ah Qaaq first for hypnotism.

He called to Alice, who was bending over Gilgamesh, to help him up. Weeping, she came to him and pulled up on his wrists. His head was clearing, and his legs seemed steadier. He'd be all right in another minute.

He called, "Frigate! Tai-Peng! Turpin! Get Gilgamesh out of here! Everybody else! Out! Out before he closes the door!"

Nur yelled, "He's gone now!"

The three men came running, and they picked the Sumerian's heavy body and bore it toward the doorway. Burton leaned on Alice, his arm around her neck, and they followed the others. By the time he got to the exit, he felt recovered enough to tell Alice that he could go it by himself.

Turpin placed his grail in the doorway so the door couldn't be fully closed. Just as Alice and Burton stepped into the corridor, the door shot back out of its recess, slammed into the grail, and stopped.

Nur indicated the blood on the floor by the doorway and the red spots farther along.

"The bullet smashed against the wall, but some of the fragments got him."

The corridor ran both ways as far as they could see. It was illuminated by the shadowless light and was forty feet wide and fifty high by eye estimate. It gently curved to follow the roundness of the exterior. Burton wondered what was between the outer wall of the corridor and the outer wall of the tower. Probably, some of it was empty, but other spaces might contain machinery of some sort or storage facilities. At irregular intervals, at his eye level, the walls held bas-relief letters or symbols some of which superficially resembled runes and others Hindustani characters.

Burton left a bullet by the wall to mark the entrance if the door should somehow close.

Shortly after the bloodstains ceased, the trackers came across a bay in the center of which was a circular hole about a hundred feet across. Burton stood on the edge and looked down. Lights streamed out along the black shaft from many levels, other bays or rooms. He didn't know how deep the shaft went, but he guessed that it was miles. When he got down on his knees, his hands gripping the edge, and looked up, he saw the same thing. However, the shaft could go up no more than a mile, the height of the tower from sea level.

By then Gilgamesh was recovering. He sat on the floor holding his head and groaning. After a minute, he looked up.

"What happened?"

Burton told him. The Sumerian moaned, then said, "And you didn't strike me? It *was* the woman?"

"Yes, I apologize, if it will do any good. But I had to know."

"She was only fighting to save her man. And since you did not hit me, there is no insult. Though there is plenty of injury."

"I think you'll be all right," Burton said.

He forebore to say that he had hit Gilgamesh in the face. Truth could be sacrificed in this situation. He'd gone through his life making enemies because he didn't care if he did and even got a certain satisfaction from it. But during the past twenty years he'd seen that he was behaving irrationally in this respect. Nur, the Sufi, had taught him that, though not directly. Burton had learned while listening to Nur's conversations with his disciple Frigate.

"I think," Burton said, "that X took a lift of some sort. I don't see any, though. Nor do I see any controls to bring one up or down to here."

"Maybe that's because there *isn't* any cage," Frigate said.

Burton stared at him.

Frigate took a plastic bullet out of the bag that hung from his belt. He threw it twenty feet into the emptiness. It stopped as if it were in jelly at the level of the floor.

"Well, I'll be damned! I didn't think it was so, but it is!"

"What is?"

"There's some kind of field in the shaft. So . . . how do you go where you want to? Maybe the field moves you according to a codeword."

"That is good thinking," Nur said.

"Thank you, master. Only . . . if one person wants to go down at the same time another wants to go up . . . ? Maybe the field can do both simultaneously."

If the shafts—there must be others—were the only way to get from one floor to another, they were trapped. All the Ethical had to do was to let them starve.

Burton became angry. All his life he'd felt caged and he had broken out of some of the cages, though the big ones had restrained him. Now he was on the verge of solving this great mystery, and he was trapped again. This one, he might not escape from.

He stepped out into openness, putting one foot down slowly until he felt resistance. When he'd determined that his weight was going to be held, he moved entirely into the shaft. He was near panic; anybody unfamiliar with the setup would be. But here he was, standing on nothing, apparently, and an abyss below him.

He stooped, picked up the bullet, and threw it to Frigate.

"Now what?" Nur said.

Burton looked up and then down.

"I don't know. It's not just like being in air only. There's a slight resistance to my movements. I don't have any trouble breathing, however."

Since it made him more than just uneasy to stand there, he walked back to the solid floor.

"It's not like standing on something hard. There is a slight give to my weight."

They were silent for a while. Burton finally said, "We might as well go on."

46

They came to another bay marked by characters in bas-relief and containing a lift-shaft. Burton looked up and down this, hoping that he might see something to help them. It was as empty as the other.

When they had left this, Frigate said, "I wonder if Piscator is still alive? If only he'd come by . . ."

"If only!" Burton said. "We can't live by *if only*, even if you do most of the time."

Frigate looked hurt.

Nur said, "Piscator, as I understand it, was a Sufi. That may explain why he got through the gateway on top of the tower. From what I've heard, I'd venture that there's some sort of force, analogous to an electromagnetic field, perhaps, that prevents those who haven't attained a certain ethical level from entering."

"He must have been different from most Sufis I've seen, yourself excepted," Burton said. "Those I knew in Egypt were rogues."

"There are true Sufis and false Sufis," Nur said, paying no attention to the sneer in Burton's voice. "Anyway, I suspect that the *wathan* reflects the ethical or spiritual development of the individuals and what it shows would make the repulsion field admit or deny entrance to a person."

"Then how would X get in that way? He's obviously not as ethically developed as the others."

"You don't know that," Nur said. "If what he says about the other Ethicals is true . . ."

He stopped talking for a moment. Then he said, "If the gateway field admits only the highly ethical, then X made his secret room to avoid that field. But he must have done it when the tower was built, must have planned it before then. So that even then he knew he wouldn't be admitted into the gateway."

"No," Burton said. "The others would have been able to see his *wathan*. If they did, they'd know that he had degenerated, changed, anyway. And they'd have known that he was the renegade."

Frigate said, "Maybe the reason his *wathan* looked okay was that he had some device to distort it from its natural appearance. I mean . . . from the appearance it would have had if he hadn't used some kind of distorter. That way, he'd not only have passed as normal among his fellows, he'd have fooled the gateway field."

"That is possible," Nur said. "But wouldn't his colleagues know about distorters?"

"Not if they'd never seen or heard of one. It may have been X's invention."

Burton said, "And he had his hideaway so that he could leave the tower without anybody else knowing it."

"That implies that there are no radar devices on the tower," Frigate said.

"Well?" Burton said. "If there had been, they would've detected the first and second expeditions when they came down the ledge. The radar might also have spotted the cave, though I suppose its operators wouldn't have thought anything about it if it had been noted. No, there was no radar scanning the sea and the mountains. Why should there be? The Ethicals didn't believe that anybody would get that far."

Nur said, "We all have *wathans*, if what the Council of Twelve told you was true. You saw theirs. What I don't understand is why they couldn't have tracked you down long before they did. Surely, a photograph of your *wathan* was in the records of that giant computer Spruce mentioned. I would suppose that everybody's was."

"Perhaps X arranged it so that the record in the computer wasn't a true image of my *wathan*," Burton said. "Perhaps that was why the agent Agneau was carrying a photograph of my physical person."

"I think that the Ethicals must have scanner satellites up there," Frigate said. "Maybe these could locate your *wathan*. But they couldn't find it because your *wathan* was distorted."

"Hmm," Nur said. "I wonder if distorting the *wathan* also results in distorting its owner's psyche?"

Burton said, "You may remember de Marbot's report of Clemens' analysis of the connection between the *wathan* or *ka* or soul, call it what you will, and the body? The conclusion was that the *wathan is* the essence of the person. Otherwise, it is irrelevant. It does no good to reattach the *wathan* to a duplicated body because the duplicate isn't the same as the original. Similar to the nth degree, yes, but not the *same*. If the *wathan* or soul *is* the persona, the seat of self-consciousness, then the physical brain is not self-aware. Without the *wathan*, the human body would have intelligence but no self-awareness. No concept of *I*. The *wathan* uses the physical as a man uses a horse or an automobile.

"Perhaps that comparison isn't correct. The *wathan*-body combination is more like a centaur. A melding. Both the man-part and the horse-part need each other for perfect functioning. One without the other is useless. It may be that the *wathan* itself needs a body to become self-conscious. Certainly, the Ethicals said that the undeveloped *wathan* wanders in some sort of space when it's loosed by the body's death. And then the *wathan* is not just unaware of its own self but of anything. It's unconscious.

"Yet, according to our theory, the body generates the *wathan*. How, I don't know, don't even have a hypothesis. But without the body, a *wathan* can't come into existence. There are embryo *wathans* in the body embryos, and infant *wathans* in the infant body. Like the body, the *wathan* grows into adulthood.

"However, there are two stages of adulthood. Let's call the later stage super*wathan*hood. If a *wathan* doesn't attain a certain ethical or spiritual level, it's destined to wander forever after the body's death, unaware of itself.

"Unless, as happened here, a duplicate body is made and by some affinity the *wathan* reattaches itself to the duplicate body. This duplicate body would be intelligent but would have no concept of *I*. The *wathan* attached to it would have the self-awareness. But it couldn't have it until it interacted with the body.

"Without *wathans*, humans would have evolved from apes, would have had language, would have had technology and science, but no religion, yet would not have had any more knowledge of the self than an ant."

Frigate said, "What kind of language would that be? I mean, try to imagine a language in which no pronouns for *I* and *me* exist. And probably no *you* or *yours* either. To tell the truth, I don't think they'd develop language. Not as we know it, anyway. They'd just be highly intelligent animals. Living machines which would not depend upon instinct as much as animals do."

"We can talk about that some other time."

"Yeah, but what about the chimpanzees?"

"They must have had a rudimentary *wathan* which had a low-level consciousness of their *I*. However, it was never proved that apes did have language or self-awareness.

"The *wathan* itself can't develop self-awareness unless it has a body. If the body has a stunted brain, then the *wathan* is stunted. Hence, it can attain only to a certain low ethical level."

"No!" Frigate said. "You're confusing intelligence with morality. You and

I have known too many people with a high intelligence and low ethical development and vice versa to believe that a high I.Q. is a necessary accompaniment to a high moral quotient."

"Yaas, but you forget about the will."

They came to another bay. Burton looked along the shaft. "Nothing here."

They walked on while Burton resumed the role of Socrates.

"The will. We have to assume that it's not entirely free. It's affected by events outside the body, its exterior environment, and by internal events, the inside environment. Injuries physical or mental, diseases, chemical changes, and so forth, can change a person's will. A maniac may have been a *good* person before a disease or injury made him into a torturer and killer. Psychological or chemical factors may make multiple personalities or a psychic cripple or monster.

"I suggest that the *wathan* is so closely connected with the body that it reflects the body's mental changes. And a *wathan* attached to an idiot or imbecile is itself idiotic or imbecilic.

"That is why the Ethicals have resurrected idiots and imbeciles elsewhere—if our speculations are correct—so that these may get special treatment. Through the medical science of the Ethicals, the retarded are enabled to have fully developed brains. Hence, they also have highly developed *wathan*s with a full potentiality for a choice between good and evil."

"And," Nur said, "the opportunity to become super-*wathan*s and so reunited with God. I've been listening carefully to you, Burton. I don't agree with much of what you've said. One implication is that God doesn't care about His souls. He wouldn't allow them to float around as unconscious things. He has made provision for all of them."

"Perhaps God—if there is one—*doesn't* care," Burton said. "There is no evidence whatsoever that He does.

"Anyway, I argue that the human being without a *wathan* has no free will. That is, the ability to make choices between or among moral alternatives. To surpass the demands of body and environment and personal inclination. To lift one's self, as it were, by the self's bootstraps. Only the *wathan* has the free will and the self-awareness. But I admit that it has to express these through the vehicle of the body. And I admit that the *wathan* closely interacts with and is affected by the body.

"Indeed, the *wathan* must get its personality traits, most of them, anyway, from the body."

Frigate said, "Well then. Aren't we back where we started? We still can't make a clear distinction between the *wathan* and the body. If the *wathan* furnishes the concept of the *I* and the free will, it's still dependent upon the body for its character traits and everything else in the genetic and nervous systems. These are actually images which it absorbs. Or photocopies. So, in that sense, the *wathan* is only a copy, not the original.

"Thus, when the body dies, it stays dead. The *wathan* floats off, whatever that means. It has the duplicated emotions and thoughts and all that which make up a persona. It also has the free will and the self-awareness if it's reattached to a duplicate body. But it isn't the *same* person."

"What you've just proved," Aphra Behn said, "is that there is no soul, not in the way it's commonly conceived of. Or, if there is one, it's superfluous, it has nothing to do with the immortality of the individual."

Tai-Peng spoke for the first time since Burton had brought up the subject.

"I'd say that the *wathan* part is all that matters. It's the only immortal part, the only thing the Ethicals can preserve. It must be the same thing as the *ka* of the Chancers."

"Then the *wathan* is a half-assed thing!" Frigate cried. "A part only of me, the creature that died on Earth! I can't truly be resurrected unless my original body is resurrected!"

"It's the part that God wants and which he will absorb," Nur said.

"Who wants to be absorbed? I want to be I, the whole creature, the entire!"

"You will have the ecstasy of being part of God's body."

"So what? I won't be I anymore!"

"But on Earth you as an adult weren't the same person you were at fifty," Nur said. "Your whole being, at every second of your life, was and is in the process of change. The atoms composing your body at birth were not the same as when you were eight. They'd been replaced by other atoms. Nor were they the same when you were fifty as when you were forty.

"Your body changed, and with it your mind, your store of memories, your beliefs, your attitudes, your reactions. You were never the *same*.

"And when—or if—you, the creature, the creation, should return to the Creator, you will change then. It will be the last change. You will abide forever in the Unchanging. Unchanging because He has no need for changing. He is perfect."

"Bullshit!" Frigate said, his face red, his hands clenched. "There is the essence of me, the unchanging thing that wants to live forever, however imperfect! Though I strive for perfection! Which may not be attainable! But the striving is the thing, that which makes life endurable, though sometimes life itself becomes almost unendurable! I want to be I, forever lasting! No matter what the change, there is something in me, an unchanging identity, the soul, whatever, that resists death, loathes it, declares it to be unnatural! Death is both insult and injury and, in a sense, unthinkable!

"If the Creator has a plan for us, why doesn't He tell us what it is? Are we so stupid that we can't understand it? He should tell it to us directly! The books that the prophets, the revelators, and the revisionists wrote, claiming to have authority from God Himself, to have taken His dictations, these so-called revelations are false! They make no sense! Besides, they contradict each other! Does God make contradictory statements?"

"They only seem contradictory," Nur said. "When you've attained a higher stage of thinking, you'll see that the contradictions are not what they appear to be."

"Thesis, antithesis, and synthesis! That's all right for human logic! But I still maintain that we shouldn't have been left in ignorance. We should have been shown the Plan. Then we could make our choice, go along with the Plan or reject it!"

"You're still in a lower stage of development, and you seem to be stuck in it," Nur said. "Remember the chimpanzees. They got to a certain level, but they could not progress further. They made a wrong choice, and . . ."

"I'm not an ape! I'm a man, a human being!"

"You could be more than that," Nur said.

They came to another bay. This, however, led not to a shaft but to an entrance, huge, arched. Beyond it was a chamber the enormity of which staggered them. It was at least half a mile long and wide. Within it were thousands of tables on each of which were devices the purposes of which were not obvious.

Skeletons by the hundreds lay on the floor and the upper parts of more hundreds were on the desks or tables. Thigh bones and pelvic bones lay on the seats of chairs, and beneath the seats were more leg bones. Death had struck instantly and en masse.

There wasn't a single garment anywhere. The people working the experiments had been nude.

Burton said, "The Council of Twelve which interrogated me was clothed. Perhaps they donned their outfits so they wouldn't offend my sense of modesty. If so, they didn't know me well. Or perhaps they were required to wear garments when they were in session."

Some of the equipment on the tables was still running. The nearest to Burton was a transparent sphere the size of his head. It was seemingly without an opening, yet large bubbles of different colors rose from its top, floated up to the ceiling, and burst. By the sphere was a transparent cube in which characters flashed as the bubbles ascended.

They walked on murmuring about the strangeness of the devices. When they'd gone a quarter of a mile, Frigate said, "Look at that!"

He pointed at a wheeled chair which sat in a broad aisle between tables. A jumble of bones, including a skull, lay on the seat, and leg and foot bones were at its base.

47

THE CHAIR WAS OVERSTUFFED AND COVERED WITH A SOFT MATERIAL marked with thin alternating pale-red and pale-green zigzagging lines. Burton brushed the bones from the seat with a callousness which drew a protest from Croomes. He sat down, noting aloud that the chair fitted itself to his body. On the top of each massive arm, near the end, was a wide metal circle. He gingerly pressed down on the black center of the white disc on his right. Nothing happened.

But when he pressed on the fingertip-thick center on the left, a long thin metal rod slid out.

"Aha!"

He pulled back slowly on the rod.

Nur said, "There's a light coming from beneath the chair."

The chair lifted soundlessly from the floor for a few inches.

"Press on the forward edge of the disc on your right," Frigate said. "Maybe it controls the speed."

Burton frowned because he did not like anyone telling him what to do. But he did use a fingertip to push the metal as suggested. The chair moved toward the ceiling at a very slow rate.

Ignoring the exclamations and several more suggestions, he pushed the lever to dead center. The chair straightened out at a horizontal level, continuing to move forward. He increased its speed, then moved the left-hand rod toward the right. The chair turned with the rod, maintaining its angle—no banking as in an airplane—and headed for the faraway wall. After making the chair go up to the ceiling and then down to the floor, whirling it a few times, and speeding it up to an estimated ten miles per hour, Burton landed the chair.

He was smiling; his black eyes were shiny with eagerness.

"We may have a vehicle to lift us up the shaft!" he cried.

Frigate and some of the others weren't satisfied with the demonstration.

"It must be capable of even greater speed," the American said. "What happens if you have to stop suddenly? Do you hurtle on out of the chair?"

"There's one way of finding out," Burton said. He made the chair lift a few inches, then accelerated it toward the wall, half a mile distant. When he was within twenty yards of the wall, he removed pressure from the right-hand disc. The chair at once slowed down but not so quickly that its passenger was in danger of being ejected. And when it was within five feet of the wall, it stopped.

When he returned, Burton said, "It must have built-in sensors. I tried to ram it into the wall, but it wouldn't do it."

"Fine," Frigate said. "We can try to go through the shaft. But what if the

Ethical is observing us now? What if he can cut off the power by remote control? We'd fall to our deaths or at least be stuck halfway between floors."

"We'll go one at a time. Each one will stop off at a floor before the next one goes. He won't be able to catch more than one of us, and the others will be warned."

Though Burton thought that Frigate was too cautious, he had to admit to himself that his speculations were well founded.

"Also," Frigate said, "The two chairs must have been moving when their occupants died. What made the chairs stop?"

"Obviously, the sensors in the chairs," Burton drawled.

"Fine. Then we'll each get a chair and find out how to get used to handling it. After that, what? Up or down?"

"We'll go to the top floor first. I feel that the headquarters, the nerve center of these operations, must be there."

"Then we should go down instead," Frigate said, grinning. "Your predictions were always of the Moseilima type, you know. The opposite always happened."

The fellow had his way of getting back at him. He knew too much about Burton's Earthly life, knew all his faults and failings.

"No," Burton said, "not true. I warned the British government two years before the Sepoy Mutiny happened that it was coming. I was ignored. I was Cassandra then, not Moseilima."

"Touché!" Frigate said.

Gilgamesh pulled up his chair alongside Burton's a few minutes later. He seemed troubled and not well.

"My head still hurts bad. I see things double now and then."

"Can you make it? Or do you wish to stay here and rest?"

The Sumerian shook his massive taurine head.

"No. I wouldn't be able to find you. I just wanted you to know that I'm sick."

Alice must have struck him harder than she'd intended.

Tom Turpin called to Burton then. "Hey, I found out how they get their food here. Look!"

He'd been fiddling around with a big metal box which had many dials and buttons on it. It was set on a table and was connected by a black cable to a plug in the floor.

Turpin opened the glass-fronted door. Within were dishes and cups and cutlery, the dishes full of food and the cups full of liquid.

"This is their equivalent of the grail," Tom said, his pale yellow face smiling. "I don't know what any of the controls except this does, but I punched all the buttons and in a few seconds the whole meal formed before my eyes."

He opened the door and removed the contents.

"Wow! Smell that beef! And that bread!"

Burton thought it would be best to eat now. There would probably be other devices like this elsewhere, but he couldn't be sure. Besides, they were famished.

Turpin tried another combination of buttons and dials. This time, the meal was a mélange of French and Italian and Arabic cooking. All items were delicious, though some were undercooked, and the filet of camel's hump was too highly spiced for most of them. They tried other combinations with some surprising results, not all delightful. By experimentation, Turpin found the dial which regulated the degree of cooking, and they were able to get the meal well-done, medium, medium-rare, or rare. All except Gilgamesh ate voraciously, drank some of the liquor, and lit up the cigarettes and cigars also provided by the box. There was no lack of water; faucets were all over the place.

Afterward, they looked for toilets. These were in some nearby giant cabinets which they'd presumed had contained machinery. The toilets didn't flush; they were holes into which the urine and excrement disappeared before they hit the bottom.

Gilgamesh ate some of the bread, then vomited it up.

"I can't go with you," he said. He wiped his chin and squirted water from his mouth into a sink. "I'm just too sick."

Burton wondered if he were as ill as he said he was. He could be an agent and waiting until he could slip away.

"No, you go with us," he said. "We might not be able to find our way back to you. You'll be comfortable in your chair."

He led the others to the shaft. When he took the chair out over the emptiness, he extended a foot to touch below it. His toes met no slight springiness as in the other shaft. Perhaps the presence of the chairs automatically removed the field.

He pulled the rod back and tipped the disc. The chair moved slowly upward, then swiftly as Burton depressed the disc even more. At each bay he saw more corridors and some rooms. The latter were full of strange equipment, but there were no skeletons until he came to the tenth floor. The chamber he looked into was small compared to the one he'd left. It contained twelve large tables on each of which were twelve plates and twelve cups and some skulls and bones. Other bones lay on the chairs or at their feet.

A huge food-box was on a table in the corner.

Burton went on up, stopping now and then, until he arrived at the top of the shaft. The trip had taken fifteen minutes. On one side was another bay with a corridor outside. On his left was a small corridor which quickly opened into a giant one, at least one hundred feet square. After setting the chair down in the larger hallway, he leaned over the shaft and blinked his lantern three times. The answering flashes were tiny but sharp. Nur, the next one, would not make any stops and so would get to Burton in about twelve minutes.

Burton had never been patient except when it was absolutely necessary and often not then. He got back into the chair and moved down the hall. He'd take a six-minute tour and then return to the shaft.

He passed many open doors, all very large, giving him eye access to small and large rooms, some with equipment, some apparently for apartments. A number had many skeletons; some, a few; some, none. The corridor ran straight for at least two miles ahead of him. Just before it was time to return, he saw on his right an entrance with a closed door. He stopped the chair, got out, withdrew his pistol, and cautiously approached the door. Above it were thirteen symbols, twelve helices arranged in a circle with a sundisc in the center. There was no knob on the door. Instead, a metal facsimile of a human hand was attached to the door where a knob should have been. Its fingers were half closed as if about to seize another hand.

Burton turned it, and he pulled the door open.

The room was a very large, very pale-green semitransparent sphere surrounded by and intersected by other green bubbles. On the wall of the central sphere at one side was an oval of darker green, a moving picture of some sort. The odor of pine and dogwood rose from the trees in the background, and in the foreground a ghostly fox chased a ghostly rabbit. On the bottom of the largest sphere, or bubble, were twelve chairs in a circle. Ten contained parts of skeletons. Two were bare of anything, even dust.

Burton had to breathe deeply. This room brought back frightening memories. It was here that he had awakened after killing himself 777 times to escape the Ethicals. It was here that he had faced the Council.

Now those beings who had seemed so godlike to him were bones.

He put one foot beyond the threshold, poking it through the bubble with only a slight resistance. His body followed, feeling the same tiny push. Then his other foot came through, and he was standing on springy nothingness or what seemed to be nothingness.

He reholstered his pistol and passed through two bubbles, the surfaces closing behind him, but air moving past him, and then he was in the "Council room." When he got near the insubstantial chairs, he saw that he'd been mistaken. One of the seemingly empty seats held a very thin circular convex lens. He picked it up and recognized the many-faceted "eye" of the man who'd seemed to be the chief of the Council, Thanabur.

This was no jewel, no artificial device to replace an eye, as he'd thought then. It was a lens which could be slipped over the eye. It felt greasy. Perhaps it was lubricated so it wouldn't irritate the eyeball.

With some difficulty and revulsion, he inserted the lens under his eyelid.

The left eye saw the room through a distorting semiopaqueness. Then he closed his right eye.

"Oooohhhh!"

He quickly opened the right eye.

He'd been floating in space, in a darkness in which distant stars and great gas sheets shone and there was the feeling, but not the direct effect, of unbelievable coldness. He'd been aware that he was not alone, though. He knew, without having seen them, that he was followed by uncountable souls, trillions upon trillions, perhaps far more. And then he was shooting toward a sun, and it became larger, and suddenly he saw that the flaming body was not a star but a vast collection of other souls, all flaming, yet burning not as in Hell but with an ecstasy that he'd never experienced and which the mystics had tried to describe but was undescribable.

Though shaken and afraid, he was also pulled fiercely by the ecstasy. Moreover, he could not allow his fear to overcome him, he who had boasted that he had never feared anything.

He closed his right eye and was again in space in the same "location." Again, he was hurtling through space, far swifter than light, toward the sun. Again, he felt the innumerable presences behind him. The star swam up, grew larger, became vast, and he saw that the flames were composed of trillions upon trillions upon trillions of souls.

Then he heard a soundless cry, one of unutterable ecstasy and welcome, and he plunged headfirst into the sun, the swarm, and he was nothing and yet everything. Then, he wasn't he any more. He was something which had no parts and was not a part but was one with the ecstasy, with the others who were not others.

He gave a great cry and opened his eye. There were Alice and Nur and Frigate and his companions staring at him from the doorway. Trembling, he went to them through the bubbles. He was not so upset, however, that he did not notice that the Sumerian was missing nor that Alice was weeping.

He ignored their questions, saying, "Where's Gilgamesh?"

"He died on the way up," Alice said.

"We left him sitting in the chair in a room," Nur said. "He must have had a brain concussion."

"I killed him!" Alice said, and she sobbed.

"I'm sorry for that," Burton said, "but it couldn't be helped. If he was innocent, he shouldn't have resisted. Perhaps he really was an agent."

He put his arms around Alice and said, "You did what you had to do. If you hadn't, he might've killed me."

"Yes, I know. I've killed before, but those people were strangers attacking us. I liked Gilgamesh, and now . . ."

Burton thought it was best to allow her to weep out her guilt and grief. He released her and turned to the others. Nur asked him what he had been doing in the room. He told them of the lens.

"You must've been standing there for at least an hour," Frigate said.

"Yes, I know, but the state seemed to last only a minute."

"What about the aftereffects?" Nur said.

Burton hesitated, then said, "Apart from being shaken up, I feel . . . I feel . . . a tremendous closeness to all of you! Oh, I've been fond of some of you, but . . . now . . . I love all of you!"

"That must've been a shock," Frigate murmured. Burton ignored him.

The Moor held up the multifaceted device and looked through it with his right eye closed.

"I see nothing. It has to be fitted next to the eye."

Burton said, "I thought that the lens was something which only the chief of the twelve, Thanabur, would wear. I presumed that it was some sort of ritual token or emblem of leadership, something traditional. I may've been wrong. Perhaps everybody took a turn wearing it during the Council meetings. It may be that the lens gave all of them a feeling such as I had, a closeness and love for everybody in the room."

"In which case, X was able to overcome that feeling," Tai-Peng said.

"What I don't understand," Burton said, "is why the lens put me into a trance yet didn't seem to affect Thanabur."

"Perhaps," Nur said, "the Councilors were used to it. After wearing it many times, they got only a mild effect from it."

Nur fitted the lens under his eyelids and shut his right eye. Immediately, his face took on an expression of ecstasy, though his body remained motionless. When two minutes had passed, Burton shook the Moor by the shoulder. Nur came out of his trance and began weeping. But when he'd recovered and had taken the lens out, he said, "It does induce a state similar to that which the saints have attempted to describe."

He handed the lens to Burton.

"But it's a false state brought about by an artificial thing. It's not the true state. That can only be attained by spiritual development."

Some of the others wanted to try. Burton said, "Later. We may have used up time we sorely need. We have to find X before he finds us."

48

THEY CAME TO AN ENORMOUS CLOSED DOOR ABOVE WHICH WERE MORE OF the untranslatable characters. Burton halted the train of chairs and got out of his. A button on the wall seemed to be the only obvious means of opening the doors. He pressed, and the two sections slid away from each other into recesses. He looked into a wide hall ending in two more huge doors. Burton pressed the button by that.

They looked into a domed chamber which had to be half a mile across. The floor was earth on which grew a bright green short-bladed grass and, further on, trees. Brooks ran through it here and there, their sources cataracts forty or fifty feet high. Flowering bushes were many, and there were flat-topped rocks which had served as tables, if the plates and cups and cutlery on them meant anything.

The ceiling was a blue across which wisps of clouds moved, and a simulacrum of the sun was at its zenith.

They walked in and looked around. Human skeletons lay here and there, the nearest around a rock. There were also the bones of birds, deer, and some catlike and doglike and raccoonlike animals.

"They must've come here to get back to Nature," Frigate said. "A very reasonable facsimile thereof, anyway."

They had reasoned that X had transmitted a radio code which had activated the tiny black ball in the brains of the tower-dwellers and caused poison to be released in their bodies. But why had the animals died?

Starvation.

They left the chamber. Before they had traveled a mile, they came across another curiosity, the most puzzling and awe-inspiring of all. A transparent outward-leaning wall on their left revealed a Brobdingnagian shaft. A bright shifting light flared from below. They got off the chairs to look down into the well. And they cried out with wonder.

Five hundred feet below them was a raging furnace of many differently colored shapes, all closely packed but seeming to pass through each other or to merge at times.

Burton shaded his eyes with a hand and stared into it. After a while he could occasionally distinguish the shapes of the things that whirled around and around and shot up and down and sideways.

He turned away, his eyes hurting.

"They're *wathans*. Just like those I saw above the heads of the twelve Councilors. The wall must be of some material which enables us to see them."

Nur handed him a pair of dark glasses.

"Here. I found these in a box on a shelf near here."

Burton and the others put on the glasses and stared into the enormous well. Now he could see the things more clearly, the changing shifting colors in the always expanding-contracting shapes, the six-sided tentacles which shot out, flailed, waved, then shrank back into the body.

Burton, leaning out, his back pressed against the wall, looked up. The brightness showed him a ceiling of the gray metal about a hundred feet above him. He turned around and tried to see across to the other side of the well. He couldn't. He peered down into it. Far far below was a gray solid. Or was it his imagination, an illusion created by the metamorphosing horde, that made him now think that the solidity was pulsing?

He stepped back, removed the glasses, and rubbed his aching eyes.

"I don't know what this means, but we can't stay here any longer."

They'd passed a number of bays enclosing lift shafts with no upper passage. But after they'd gone a quarter of a mile, they came to one which extended up past their level.

"This may take us to the floor where the gateway is."

Again, they waited until each person had gotten safely up the shaft before the next flew up.

The bay opened onto another corridor. There were thirteen doors along this, each an entrance into a very large suite of luxuriously furnished rooms. In one was a table of some glossy reddish hardwood on which was a transparent sphere. Suspended in it were three doll-sized shapes.

"Looks like Monat and two other of his kind," Burton said.

"Something like three-dimensional photographs," Frigate said.

"I don't know," Alice said. "But there seems to be a family resemblance. Of course, I suppose they'd all look alike to anyone not familiar with the race. Still . . ."

Croomes had not said a word for a long time. Her grim face had indicated, though, that she was struggling terribly to accept the reality of this place. Nothing here had been what she expected; there had been no welcoming choir of angels, no glory-blazing God on a throne with her mother standing at His right hand to greet her.

Now she said, "Those two could be his parents."

There were many things to investigate in the rooms, but Burton hurried them on out.

They had gone about two hundred feet when they came to a bay, the first they'd seen on the right-hand wall. Burton got out from the chair and looked along the shaft. Its bottom was level with the floor; the top wasn't more than fifty feet up.

Wisps of fog rushed across it, apparently drawn from the outside and through vents in the wall opposite.

He withdrew his head.

"That might lead to the dome on the outside, the one which only Piscator could enter."

The Japanese had been intelligent and brave. He'd probably done as Burton had, tested the invisible field in the shaft, figured out that it would hold him, and then descended. But how could he have activated the field if he didn't know the codeword or whatever it was that operated it?

However, this shaft was different from the others. It was very short, and there was only one way to go if you were at its top. Sensors might determine that the field was activated if someone came in from the top. The sensors could detect that there was only one person and that he wouldn't be standing in the field unless he wanted to go down. To go up would require a codeword of some sort. Or maybe it didn't, the bottom part of the field would act like the top, only in the reverse direction.

Where was Piscator?

To test his theory, Burton stepped into the shaft. After three seconds, he was lifted slowly upward. At the top of the shaft, he stepped out into a short metal corridor. It curved near its end and undoubtedly opened into the corridor in the dome.

Fog billowed around the corner, but the lights were strong enough to pierce it.

He walked into the corridor and at once felt a very slight resistance. Its strength increased as he advanced struggling.

When he was panting and unable to go even an inch farther, he turned back. His way was unimpeded to the shaft. When he returned to the lower level, he gave a short report.

"The field works both ways," he concluded.

The Moor said, "According to the *Parseval* report, there was only one entrance. Yet . . . there must be an opening, a door of some kind, for the aircraft to come in. There were none on top of the tower. I think, however, that they just weren't visible. Also, there must be ethical fields in the entrances for the aircraft. Otherwise, anybody could go in that way. Including X. Surely he must have gone out on legitimate business from time to time in an aerial vessel."

"You forget about the hypothetical *wathan* distorter," Burton said. "That would've enabled X to get through the dome entrance, too."

"Yes. I know that. What I'm getting at is that if we could find the hangar for the aircraft, and then find out how to operate them, we could leave here at any time we pleased."

"They'd better be easier and simpler to fly than an airplane," Frigate said.

"No doubt they are."

"Say, I've got an idea," Frigate said, grinning. "Piscator was a Sufi, and he had no trouble entering. You're a Sufi and a highly developed ethicalist. Why don't you go out and try to get back in through the dome?"

The Moor grinned back at him.

"You'd like to see if I really am as advanced as I should be, wouldn't you? And what happens if I can't get out? Or, if I do, can't get back in? No, Peter. It would be a waste of time and an exhibition of pride on my part. You know that, yet you urge me to do it. You are teasing me. As a disciple, you sometimes lack the proper reverent attitude toward your master."

They returned to their chairs and flew slowly down the curving corridor. Burton was beginning to feel that their tour was very informative, even if often puzzling, but useless. This was no way to go about finding X.

What else could they do? There were no directories on the walls, and they couldn't read them if there were. It was frustrating and futile to proceed in this manner, yet they just couldn't sit around in one place and hope that X would find them. If he did, he'd be armed with some irresistible weapon. No doubt of that.

On the other hand, they had been fortunate in locating the residences of the twelve and of Monat Grrautut and the dome entrance. Perhaps, the place where X did his experiments or a control center he used might be near his apartment.

They came to a closed door and passed it. There would be many thousands of such in this vast place. They couldn't afford the time to open every one.

But when he was thirty feet beyond it, Burton raised his hand to signal a halt.

"What is it?" Alice said.

"I've a certain feeling, a strong hunch."

He lowered the chair to the floor.

"I'll just take a moment to check this out."

He pressed a button on the wall by the door, and the door slid soundlessly into a recess. Beyond was a cavernous room with much varied equipment on tables and, against the walls, many cabinets. There was only one skeleton. A violent explosion had evidently caught some one as he was passing by a cabinet or doing something with it. The top of the cabinet had been blown off, judging from the outwardly twisted metal, the pieces of some glassy substance on the floor, and metal pieces inside the skeleton. It lay twenty feet out from the wreck, and under the bones were dark bloodstains.

Just beyond the skeleton the blast had knocked a star-shaped metal construction from the top of a table. It lay on the floor emitting what looked like many-colored heat waves.

Straight ahead of Burton and near the center of the room was a flying chair. It was on the floor and tenantless, one side to him, and fresh bloodstains on the arm.

Just beyond the chair was a great revolving disc on a cylinder about two feet high. Cabinets and consoles were on its perimeter. In the center was a fixed platform. A man sat on a chair of some semitransparent stuff in the middle of the fixed platform. Before him was a console with a sloping instrument panel and several live screens. He was adjusting a dial, his eyes fixed on the largest oscilloscope. His profile was to Burton.

Burton put a finger to his lips and with the other hand gestured at his companions to get off their chairs. Then he unholstered his revolver and indicated that the others should do the same.

The operator had long fox-red hair, a pale white skin, and the eye presented to Burton lacked an epicanthic fold. If the man hadn't been so fat, Burton might not have identified him. Fat, however, couldn't be removed in such a short time.

Burton walked slowly through the door and toward the man. The others were fanning out, their guns ready.

When they were within sixty feet of him, the man saw them. He reared up out of the chair, grimaced, and sat back down. His hand shot out, dived into a recess under the panel, and came out holding a strange-looking device. It had a pistollike butt for gripping, a barrel about a foot long and three inches in diameter, and a sphere at its end the size of a large apple.

Burton cried out, "Loga!"

He ran forward.

49

THE ETHICAL ROSE AGAIN AND SHOUTED, "STOP! OR I'LL FIRE!"

They kept on running. He sighted along the barrel through the transparent sphere, and a thin scarlet line shot soundlessly from the sphere. Smoke curled up from the shallow arc drawn on the metal before the group.

They halted. Anything that could melt that metal was very impressive.

"I can cut you all into two with a single sweep of this," Loga said. "I don't want to. There's been far too much violence, and I'm sick of it. But I will kill you if I must. Now . . . all of you turn around in unison and throw your weapons as far as you can toward the door."

Burton said, "There are nine guns trained on you. You might get one or two of us, but you'll be blown to bits."

The Ethical smiled grimly.

"It looks like a Mexican standoff, doesn't it?"

He paused. "But it isn't, believe me!"

Croomes shouted, "No, it isn't! You Satan, you fiend from Hell!"

Her pistol boomed. The scarlet beam flashed out from Loga's weapon at the same time that eight other guns exploded.

Loga fell backwards. Burton ran, leaped upon the revolving disc, darted over it to the fixed platform, and pointed his revolver at the prostrate Ethical. The others crowded around him.

While Turpin and Tai-Peng picked up the bleeding and ashen-skinned man from the floor, Burton seized the sphere-ended weapon. Loga was seated roughly in his chair. He held his hand over a gushing wound on the biceps of his right arm. "He got Croomes!" Alice said, pointing. Burton looked once at the severed body and turned away.

Loga looked around as if he couldn't believe what had happened, then said, "There are three boxes in the upper-right-hand drawer in the console. Bring them to me, and I'll be all right in a few minutes."

"This isn't a trick?" Burton said.

"No! I swear! I've had enough of tricks and murder! I meant you no harm! I just wanted you to be disarmed so that I could explain without worrying about you. You're such a violent breed!"

"Look who's talking," Burton said.

"I didn't do it because I loved it!"

"Neither did we," Burton said, but he wasn't so sure that he was wholly truthful.

They brought out three silver boxes set with green emeralds. Burton opened each one slowly and inspected the contents. As the Ethical had said, each contained a bottle. Two held liquid; one, some pink stuff.

"How do I know they won't release some sort of gas?" Burton said. "Or that they aren't poison?"

"They won't be," Nur said. "He does not want to die now."

"That's right," Loga said. "Something terrible may happen soon, and only I know how to stop it. I may need your help."

"You could have had it all along," Burton said, "if only you'd told us the truth in the beginning."

"I had my reasons for not doing so," Loga said. "Very good reasons. And then things got out of hand."

He squeezed one of the bottles, and a clear liquid spurted out onto his hand. After rubbing it over the wound on his shoulder, wincing at the pain, he drank from the second bottle. From the third he poured out a pink gooey substance into his left hand and then pressed it over the wound.

"The first was to sterilize the wound," he said. "The second was to cancel the shock and give me strength. The third will heal the wound in a very short time. Three days."

Burton said, "Where did we wound you the first time?"

"The only bad wound was in my left thigh."

His grayness of skin had been replaced by a normal color within a minute. He asked for some water, which Frigate brought to him. Burton lit a cigarette. His questions were a logjam in his throat. Which one should he spit out first?

Before the inquisition, though, certain things had to be done. Burton held his revolver on Loga while the others brought their chairs in and Frigate made an extra trip to get Burton's. These were placed on the floor on the side of the disc where they'd be out of sight of Croomes' body. While this was being done, Loga was allowed to lift his bloodstained chair to a designated spot. The other chairs were then arranged closely in a semicircle facing the Ethical.

"I think we could all stand a little drink," Burton said.

Loga told them how to set the controls of a grail box to get their orders filled. His own was a yellow wine which the others had never found in their grails. Burton duplicated Loga's request and tasted the wine. It was comparable to nothing he'd ever had before, delicate yet pungent. For some reason it evoked a slowly receding tide of dark green waters above which flew giant white birds with crimson beaks.

Burton sat with Loga's weapon across his lap. His first question was how it was operated. Loga indicated the safety lock and the trigger, the use of which Burton had figured out for himself.

"Now," he said, "I think it best that we start out at the beginning. But what is the beginning?"

"Pardon me for interrupting," the Moor said. "We should establish one thing right now. Ah Qaaq . . . Loga . . . you must have a private resurrection chamber in the tower?"

"Yes."

The Ethical hesitated. "It wasn't just for me. Tringu also used it. He was my best friend; we were raised together on the Gardenworld. He was the only one I could trust."

"Was he the man called Stern who tried to kill Firebrass before the *Parseval* took off the tower?"

"Yes. He failed, as you know. So, when I saw that Firebrass was going to get into the tower ahead of me . . . and Siggen was too, I had to kill them both. Siggen had not told Firebrass who I was. She believed me when I told her that I'd abandon my plans and throw myself on the mercy of the Council. But only after we'd gotten to the tower and the Council was resurrected. She never would have agreed if I'd not lied, not told her that I'd put an inhibit on communication with the computer and that only I could break it. She said she wouldn't tell Firebrass about me until we were in the tower. But she then made arrangements to be in the tower ahead of me with Firebrass. She meant to check up on the truth of what I'd told her. Also, I was afraid that while she and Firebrass were in the helicopter on the way to the top of the tower, she'd change her mind and tell Firebrass. So . . . I set off the bomb I'd planted in the copter just in case . . ."

"Who's Siggen?" Alice said.

"My wife. The woman posing as Anya Obrenova, the Russian airship officer."

"Oh, yes," Alice said as tears ran down Loga's cheeks.

"It's obvious that your people found your private resurrector and deactivated it. Otherwise, you'd have killed yourself and been translated to the tower. Have you reactivated your resurrector?"

"Yes. Actually, I have two. But both were located and deactivated."

Burton said, "Then if we'd killed you just now, you'd have escaped us. Why didn't you let us do it? Or kill yourself?"

"Because, as I said, I may need you. Because I'm sick of this violence. Because I owe you something."

He paused. "I'd set up an inhibition in the general lazarus machinery long ago. It'd be activated at my signal, the same signal which would kill all within the tower, the underground chambers, and in the area of the sea. But Tringu and I had our private lines. One of them was in the room at the base of the tower. Sharmun, the woman in charge in Monat's and Thanabur's absence, told me that the two rooms had been found. She said that it would do no good to commit suicide in the hope that I could rise in the tower and continue my evil deeds. Me! Evil!"

"This is getting confusing," Burton said. "Start at the very beginning."

"Very well. But I'll have to be as brief as possible. By the way, where is Gilgamesh?"

Burton told him.

The Ethical said. "I'm sorry."

He paused, then said, "Like his mythical counterpart, he failed to find the secret of immortality."

Loga rose, saying, "I just want to see the screens. I won't go near them."

They kept their weapons trained on him while he limped to the edge of the revolving platform. It was useless to keep him in their sights, Burton thought. He could elude them at any time by making them kill him if he was telling the truth.

Loga limped back to his chair and eased himself into it.

"We may be able to do something. I don't really know. We do have some time, though. So . . ."

He began in the beginning.

When the universe was young, when the first inhabitable planets had formed after the explosion of the primal ball of energy-matter, evolution brought about a people on one planet who differed from those on other planets.

"I don't mean just in physical construction. All the sentient peoples have either bipedal or centaurine bodies, hands, stereoscopic vision, and so forth. They were intelligent but had no consciousness of self, no concept of the *I*."

"We speculated on that!" Frigate said. "But . . ."

"You must interrupt as little as possible. I'm telling the truth when I say that all sentient beings throughout the universe were without self-awareness. As far as we know, anyway. I know it's very difficult for you to believe. You can't conceive of such a state. But it was and is true—with exceptions now.

"The people who differed did not differ in their lack of self-awareness in the beginning of their history. They were like the others in this respect. However, they did have science, though they didn't go about dealing with it as self-aware sentients do.

"Nor did they have a concept of religion, of gods or of a God. That comes only with an advanced stage of self-awareness.

"Luckily for these people, called by those who followed them The Firsts, one of their scientists had accidentally formed a *wathan* during an experiment.

"It was the first indication The Firsts had that there was such a force as extraphysical energy. I use the term *extraphysical* to avoid any confusion with *paraphysical*, with such evidently existing but usually uncontrollable and elusive forces as telepathy, telekinesis, and other extrasensory perception phenomena."

Burton forebore saying that it was he who'd coined the term ESP on Earth, though he'd called it extra-sensuous perception.

"The *wathan* may be a form of this, but, if so, it's the only one that's controllable. This nameless scientist who accidentally generated a *wathan* from the extraphysical forces did not know what it was. He or she continued to experiment and generated more. I say generated because the equipment he was using formed the *wathan* from the extraphysical energy. Shaped it or perhaps plucked it from the field that exists in the same space as matter but usually doesn't interact with it.

"The first *wathans* probably attached themselves to the living beings in their proximity."

"All living creatures?" Nur murmured.

"All living individuals. Insects, trees, starfishes, all. After millions of years of experiments, we still don't know why the *wathans* are attracted to life energy. One of the hundreds of theories is that life itself may be a form of extraphysical energy. An interface, rather."

The effect of the attachments was not immediately noted. The *wathan* was the source and genesis of self-awareness. But it could not develop this except through living entities, and these had to have highly developed nervous systems if the potentiality for self-awareness was to be realized.

"But that also can't be realized if the *wathan* attaches itself to a human entity beyond the initial zygote stage. Beyond the fusion of spermatozoon and ovum. Don't ask me why. Just believe me when I say that it's true. Apparently, there is a *hardening* in the entity, a resistance to the interface."

The machine spat out billions of *wathans* during the experiments. Millions attached themselves to the zygotes of the sentients. And, for the first time in the universe, as far as anybody knew, self-awareness was born. Infants grew up with this, and neither the older nor the younger generation could understand that this was unique and new. Self-aware children and youths have always had difficulty understanding the adults, but never before had there been such an empathy gap, such lack of comprehension.

"Eventually, the unself-conscious people died out. It wasn't until twenty-five or so years after the first *wathan* was formed that the reason for self-awareness was discovered. Then it became a matter of necessity to keep producing *wathans*."

Centuries passed. Space flight via rockets came. After several centuries, a new form of propulsion was discovered. Interstellar flight became possible at speeds unheard of before when a method of sidepassing matter was invented. Even so, it took seven days of Earth-time to go a lightyear.

"The old science-fiction concept of going through other dimensions was realized?" Frigate said.

"No. But we don't have the time for the necessarily lengthy explanation of it."

By then The Firsts thought it was their ethical duty to bring immortality and self-awareness via the *wathan* to all other sentient people. Many expeditions set out to do this. When one found a planet with people whose brains were capable of developing self-awareness, *wathan*-generating machines were buried so deep in the earth that it was unlikely that they would be discovered by the aborigines.

"Why hidden?" Nur said. He was pale; he looked as if he'd been hard hit by Loga's revelations.

"Why hidden?" Loga said. "Why not just give the machines to the first self-aware generation? You should know why not. Consider your fellow human beings. The *wathan* generators would have been misused. There would be power struggles to monopolize them and through them the basest exploitation of others. No, the *wathan* generators can't be entrusted to people until they attain a certain ethical stage."

Burton didn't ask why The Firsts hadn't set up garrisons on each planet to insure that the generators were the property of all. With their scientific knowledge and ethical knowledge, they could have taught the aborigines to advance much more swiftly. But The Firsts would not consider that ethical. Besides, they wouldn't have enough of their own people to rule all the planets they found.

The faces of his companions reflected an agonizing struggle, though Frigate seemed the least affected. Nur, who had always been so flexible, so invulnerable to psychological shock, was suffering the worst. He could not accept the idea that *wathans*, call them souls, were synthetic. Well, not quite that. But they were formed by humanlike creatures through machines. They did not come parceled out by Allah. Nur had believed this far more deeply than some of the others who, though religious, had not had his firmness of faith.

Loga must have been aware of this.

He said, "There is no Creator unless we accept the creation, this universe, as evidence. The Firsts did, and we do. But there is no evidence whatsoever that It has any interest in Its creatures. It . . ."

"It?" Alice and de Marbot said.

"Yes. The Creator has no sex—as far as we know. The language of Monat's people has a unique neuter pronoun for the Creator."

"His people are The Firsts?" Tai-Peng said.

"No. The Firsts have Gone On long, long ago. Monat's people are the recipients of The Firsts' work through a line of five other peoples. These, you might say, have handed on the torch to others and then Gone On. Monat himself is just one of ten thousand of his own kind yet alive. The others have all Gone On.

"Some theologians say that the Creator has not done anything Itself to give Its sentient creatures *wathans*. Its divine plan leaves it to sentients to make their own salvation. But this isn't logical, since it was only an accident that the *wathans* were generated, and billions died with no chance of self-awareness or immortality before this. And billions, perhaps trillions, have died and will die, perished forever, before we Ethicals will have arrived to give them the *wathans*. So it looks as if the Creator is also indifferent to our self-awareness and immortality.

"It is up to sentients, however, wherever they live, to do what the primitive religionists believed was the Creator's prerogative."

50

Burton was much shaken, though he found the story perhaps easier to take than any of the rest, Frigate excepted. He'd always been intensely interested in religion. He'd investigated many faiths, especially the Oriental. He'd converted to Roman Catholicism, not only because it fascinated him but because doing so had gotten his wife Isabel off his back. He'd been initiated into the mysteries of Moslem Sufism, had earned the red thread of a Brahmin, had been a Sikh, and a Parsi, and had tried to convince the shrewd Brigham Young that he wanted to be a Mormon. Though he'd acted like a sincere convert and sometimes had surprisingly been overcome by patterned emotion, he'd always left the door of the faith as he'd gone in, a congenital infidel.

Even when he was very young, he had refused to accept the tenets of the Anglican Church. He'd infuriated his parents, and not even the enraged bellowings of and the thrashings given by his father had changed his mind. They *had* made him tend to keep his opinions and his questions to himself until he had gotten old enough that his father didn't dare attack him by word or fist.

Despite this, the orthodox concept of the soul and of its Donor had seeped through his being. Though he hadn't believed it, he hadn't thought of any other, and it hadn't been until recently that he had heard of one.

As that exasperating fellow Frigate had told him more than once when Burton was angry with him, he was a broad but not deep thinker. Nevertheless, the logical extrapolation of the concept of the soul he'd heard when with Frigate and the others had impressed him. Indeed, they had convinced him.

Loga's account was a shock. Not one, though, which stirred the depths of his mind. These had already been disturbed. So, next to Frigate, he was the one who could most accept this extraordinary history.

Loga continued, "It was Monat's people who came to Earth and set up the *wathan* generators. This would be, approximately, 100,000 B.C."

Frigate said, moaning, "And all those who'd lived before? Beyond saving? Gone? Forever?"

"Enough thought and grief have been expended on them," Loga said. "There is nothing you can do about them, so don't be self-sadistic. As you Americans say, tough shit. It sounds callous, but it's the attitude you must adopt if you don't wish to torment yourself needlessly. Better that some may be redeemed than none at all."

The *wathan* generators and the *wathan* catchers were buried far down, so deep that they were surrounded by a heat that would melt nickel-iron.

"Catchers?" Aphra Behn said softly.

"Yes. There is one in a big shaft in the tower. Did you see it on your way up here?"

Burton said, "We saw it."

"That is the very grave problem, the pressing problem which I shall get to after a while."

From that time on, the *wathans* fixed themselves to or integrated with the human zygotes. When a zygote or an embryo or any of any age died, their *wathans* were attracted to the buried machine and *caged*.

"So what the Church of the Second Chance preaches is not entirely true?" Burton said.

"No. It was I who came to Jacques Gillot, La Viro, and told him what we thought he should know. I didn't reveal more than half the truth, and I lied about some things. It was justifiable because you Valleydwellers were not ready for the full truth."

"That's debatable," Burton said.

"Yes. What isn't? But I did tell Gillot that the salvation of the *wathan* depended upon its attaining a certain ethical stage. That was no lie."

Monat's ancestors came from a planet of a star which was neither Tau Ceti nor Arcturus. They had found a planet which had no sentients as yet, and they had made it into the Gardenworld.

"After about ten thousand years, they began resurrecting the dead children of Earth."

"Including the miscarriages and abortions, etcetera?" Burton said.

"Yes. These were developed into full-term infants. I should say, were and are being. When I left the Garden, all those who'd died under the age of five before approximately A.D. 1925 had been resurrected."

The Gardenworld project had started during the tenth century B.C. The Riverworld project had begun in the late twenty-second century A.D.

Frigate said, "What century is it now in Terrestrial chronology?"

"When I left the Garden for here it was, let's see, umh, to be precise A.D. 2009. It took me one hundred and sixty Terran years to arrive here. It took fifty years to re-form this planet. The wholesale resurrection day took place twenty-seven years after that. That would be, A.D. 2246. It is now, I'm not sure about this, A.D. 2307."

"My God!" Alice said. "How old are you?"

"This is really irrelevant now," Loga said. "But I was born sometime during the twelfth century B.C. In that city which you call Troy. I was a grandson of the king Homer called Priamos. I wasn't quite five years old when the invading Akhaiwoi and Danawoi took the city, sacked and burned it, and slaughtered most of its people. I would've become a slave, I suppose, but I defended my mother. I stuck a spear into the leg of a warrior, annoying him so much that he killed me with his bronze sword."

Loga shuddered.

"At least, I didn't have to see her and my sisters raped and my father and brothers butchered."

Monat and his people raised several generations of Terrestrial children. After this, many of Monat's people left for other planets. Monat and some others stayed to supervise the human adults who'd grown up in the Garden and were now taking their turn in raising new generations. Monat had left the Garden, however, to accompany the human beings to the Riverworld.

"We sometimes referred to him as the Operator because he was head of the project and chief engineer of the biocomputer."

"The computer which Spruce mentioned?" Burton said. "The giant protein computer?"

"Yes."

"Spruce lied to us in other things, though," Burton said. "He said he was born in the fifty-second century A.D. and that a sort of chronoscope was used to record the bodies of those who'd died."

"We all had the same false stories if we should somehow get caught and were forced to talk. Of course, we could kill ourselves, but, if there was a chance of escaping, we'd stay alive. Anyway, when you questioned Spruce, Monat was present, and he led Spruce along, fed him the questions which had prepared answers."

"We've figured that out," Burton said.

"How do you record the dead?" Nur said.

"The *wathans* contain everything that the body contains. That is, the records of the body, including the brain, of course, and this recording is the basis for duplication of the body."

"But . . . but," Frigate said. "Then the duplicates, the resurrected, wouldn't be the *same* as the dead model! They'd just be duplicates!"

"No. The *wathan* is the source and the seat of self-awareness. That is not a copy. The *wathan* leaves the dead body, takes its self-awareness with it. But it is unconscious, most of the time, anyway. There are some indications that, under certain conditions and for a brief time, the *wathan* may be conscious after leaving the body. But we don't have enough evidence to state definitely that this can occur. This newly enfleshed *wathan* may be hallucinating.

"Anyway, the *wathan* furnishes all the data we need to make a new body, and then it attaches itself to the duplicate."

Burton wondered how many times this information would have to be repeated to some of the group before it was finally accepted.

"Why did you decide to carry out your own project?" Nur said.

Loga grimaced.

"I'll talk about that later."

The planet was re-formed into a Rivervalley many millions of miles long.

The tower and the underground chambers were constructed at the same time. The *wathans* were fed into the duplicate bodies made in the underground places. The physical defects of the bodies were rectified. Any metabolic disturbances were corrected. Dwarfs and midgets were given a normal height, but pygmies retained their original height. The *wathans* were attached to the bodies during this process, but the bodies had no self-awareness since the brains of the duplicates were kept unconscious. Nevertheless, the *wathans* were recording changes. Then, the duplicates were destroyed and, on general resurrection day, the bodies were duplicated again but along the banks of The River.

"My premature awakening in the chambers?" Burton said. "Was that an accident?"

"Not at all," Loga said. "I was responsible for that. You were one of those I'd picked to help me in my plan—if it ever became necessary that I'd need your help. I caused you to be awakened so that at least one of the group would have some inkling of what was being done to you people. It would also fire your determination. You have a vast curiosity; you would never be satisfied until you got to the bottom of this mystery."

"Yes, but when you visited us, you lied to us," Nur said. "You told us you'd picked only twelve. As it's turned out, you must have chosen many more than that."

"In the first place, I wasn't the only one who visited you. Sometimes, Tringu did. He was completely with me in my objections to some features of this project. He was the only one I could trust. I couldn't even tell Siggen what I was doing.

"In the second place, I couldn't limit the group to twelve. Chance alone was against that few ever getting to the tower, if I needed them for what I had in mind. So, I actually chose one hundred and twenty-four. I lied to you about the number because, if you were ever caught by my people, you'd not be revealing the full truth.

"That is also why I didn't reveal everything to you and why I lied about some things. If you'd been caught and your memories were read, you'd not be able to give them the complete plan. And you'd have contradictory stories.

"That is why, posing as Odysseus, I told Clemens that the renegade who'd visited me had claimed to be a woman."

Loga had awakened only one of his chosen group because that could be read by the Ethicals as an accident. More than one would arouse suspicion. But he'd made a mistake in arousing even one. Monat had investigated Burton's case, and, while he couldn't prove that someone had tampered with the resurrection machinery, he was on the lookout for more "accidents."

Loga had become very anxious when Monat said that he meant to be resurrected near Burton and to accompany him for a while. Monat also wished to study the lazari closely, and to do this he had to make up an acceptable story to account for his presence. Why not do both at the same time?

Loga hadn't warned Burton about this. He was afraid that Burton, knowing Monat's real story, might be self-conscious and act peculiarly. Or, even worse, try to take matters in his own hands.

"I would've," Burton said.

"I thought so."

"I don't like to interrupt," Nur said. "But do you know what happened to the Japanese, Piscator?"

Loga grimaced again, and he pointed to the wrecked equipment along the wall and the skeleton near it.

"That's what's left of Piscator."

He swallowed, and he said, "I didn't think that any Valleydweller would ever get to the top of this tower. The odds against it made it very improbable, though not absolutely impossible. I knew that the Parolanders might build an airship, but even so, how would they get into the tower? Only a highly advanced ethical person could enter. That wasn't likely, but it was possible. As it happened, one man from the *Parseval* did get in.

"So, just to make sure, or try to make sure that if someone like Piscator did enter, I put bombs in the cabinets along the wall and also in the cabinets in the revolving platform. Not just in this room. There are more in another control room past the apartments in the opposite direction. The bombs were explosives which were formed into instrument panels. Whichever direction the intruder took, he'd see a control room and go in. His curiosity would drive him to do so. He'd see screens still operating and the skeletons of those who'd been working in it.

"The sensors in the bombs would allow the bombs to go off only if the intruder's brain didn't contain the little black ball, the suicide mechanism."

"Piscator wasn't one of your recruits, was he?" Nur said.

"No."

"If I'd been on the airship and had gotten in, I'd have been killed."

Burton wondered briefly why Loga hadn't planted bombs in the secret room at the base. Then he realized that if Loga had done so and he'd been with the expedition, as he had, he, too, would've been killed.

"Did you deactivate the bombs when you came here?" Burton said. He was thinking of the control room with the open door they'd passed before arriving at the apartments.

"I did in this room."

Loga continued his narrative. He had made a *wathan* distorter to enter the tower and also to deceive the scanner satellites. And he had fixed the computer so that it couldn't notify the Council when Burton died and a duplicate body was being made for him.

"That's why you were able to kill yourself so many times and still elude the Council. But Monat sent word via an agent to inspect the place where your preresurrection duplicate would be made so that your fatal wounds could be repaired. The circuits were traced back to the inhibit I'd installed. That's why, the last time you committed suicide, you were caught."

In the frantic search to find out the identity of the renegade, the Council had agreed to submit themselves to the memory scanner. Loga had anticipated this, and he had fixed the computer so that it would show a false memory track.

"You understand that I couldn't do this for my entire track by any means. Only those memory sections for the times when we had to account for our absences were scanned. Even that took much time and hard work, but I did it."

The time came which Loga dreaded so much and hoped would not come. He had arranged for that, but he did not want to have to carry out his arrangements. It hurt him severely to do it.

"Monat decided that he would be picked up at night soon and return to the tower. At the same time, you, Burton, would be taken along for a complete scan of your time in The Valley. I think that Monat suspected that the renegade, I, had fixed it so that your memory of your questioning by the Council had not been removed. Also, the violence around him in The Valley was increasingly sickening him. He needed a vacation."

51

LOGA WAS FLYING TO THE TOWER, HAVING JUST COMPLETED A LEGITImate mission, when the two hidden resurrectors were found. At the same time, the engineers had discovered more evidence of Loga's tampering with the computer.

Monat, Thanabur, and Siggen were in The Valley then. The other Councilors sent out aircraft to pick them up and to give them the news. However, the Council had made an error in judgment. Instead of waiting until Loga arrived and then confronting him, they sent a message to him. He was told to expect arrest when he got home.

"It took me half an hour to work up my nerve to do what I'd long planned and had known that I must someday do. But I'd hoped I'd be in the tower when I had to do it."

He'd sent out a signal which had activated the codeword in the little black balls in the brains of those in the tower and the sea around it. They had made a mistake when they used one code instead of individual codes.

"But I also made a mistake when I didn't send the code down into The Valley. I'd thought of it, but I didn't want to kill any more than I had to. Also, I thought that those Ethicals in The Valley would be helpless. They couldn't get out to the tower, since I'd fixed it so that the signal also deactivated the aircraft. Those left in The Valley would have to try to get to the tower the hard way. By boat until they got to the headwaters and on foot over the mountains. Long before then, I'd have done what I had to do."

"But what if the aircraft had fallen into The Valley?" Nur said.

"They wouldn't. Before they hit the surface they'd have burned up. Those parked on top of the mountains along The Valley would have burned, too. I'd arranged that."

"How did their pilots get down the mountain and back up to the parked vehicles?" Nur said.

"The ships could be directed by remote control. They'd drop the pilots off in the foothills during a storm or hard rain and return to the mountain top. The pilot would bury the control if he was going to stay in the area or he'd carry it in his grail. It looked just like one of the cups found in all the grails."

There was nothing to stop Loga then from flying to the tower. But he'd underestimated the wiliness of Monat.

"At least, I believe it was he who took those countermeasures. He must have put into the computer all that had happened and had gotten a list of probabilities. The computer didn't betray me; it was inhibited. But it did all that Monat asked it to do. I think it did. Possibly Monat thought of it himself."

Loga was silent for so long that Burton had to jog him along.

"Thought of what?"

"Of their planting a device in my personal aircraft. When I sent out that signal, everybody in the tower and the sea area dropped dead, all other aircraft in flight were burned up, and the general resurrection machinery was shut down. It wouldn't start again until I signaled it to do so.

"But my own vessel had had a device installed in it. I found that out when I could no longer control it. It was flying automatically. It headed toward the top of the mountain range no matter what I did. At the same time, a recorded voice told me to wait there until I'd be picked up.

"Monat's voice!

"He'd had the stop-devices installed before he went into The Valley to accompany you, Burton. Of course, he must've had the devices put into every ship. If he'd suspected me only, he would've had me put under a completely exhaustive examination.

"What Monat hadn't reckoned on, though, was that there would be no aircraft or pilots to come to my rescue. That meant that I'd be stranded on the mountain top and would starve to death unless I could trace down the device and remove it.

"Though Monat had expected an aircraft from the tower to get to the guilty person's craft swiftly, he had also made sure that the culprit wouldn't be able to remove the device or cut it off. A few minutes before my machine would land, a recording told me that the device would burn up the moment contact with the ground was made and so would the motor."

Loga had cursed and raved. He briefly visualized what would happen. He'd die and so couldn't send false messages to the Gardenplanet. In one hundred and sixty years, the Gardeners would expect the automatically operated ship with the latest report. When it hadn't arrived after a reasonable time, the Gardeners would send people to investigate. They would arrive at the tower over three hundred and twenty years after the message-ship should have been launched.

"In one way," Loga said, "that was good. I had wanted the project to run far past the one hundred and twenty years allotted, though I hadn't dared say so. My colleagues said that that was more than long enough to weed out the people who would never get to the stage necessary to Go On. Now the project would run far longer than planned. And perhaps my father and mother and sisters and brothers and uncles and aunts and cousins would not be doomed."

Burton said, "What?"

Tears flowed down Loga's cheeks. He spoke in a strangled voice.

"It was strictly forbidden for anyone to locate any relatives resurrected in The Valley. The formulators of this policy were Monat's people. They said that experience had shown that Ethicals who found their loved ones among the lazari were too emotionally upset if these were evidently not going to make it. They'd interfere, they'd be tempted to reveal what was happening before the time was ripe for that. In a previous project, a woman had put her parents in a special place in the underground chambers and tried to force-feed, as it were, their ethical advancement.

"I was taught that when I was a young adult on the Gardenworld. I believed in the policy then. But later I couldn't endure not seeing my family. Nor could I endure the agonizing idea that they might not Go On. So, long before we left the Gardenworld, I had made my plans. Still, I wasn't sure that I could carry them out. But I did track down my relatives through the computer—that took a long long time, believe me—and I visited them in The Valley. I was in disguise, of course. They had no chance of recognizing me. I'd arranged it so that they'd all be resurrected in the same place. Also, if any moved away from there or was killed, I'd know where they were.

"I have almost photographic recall. Even though I'd died on Earth shortly before I was to be five years old, I vividly remembered my parents and all my other relatives.

"It was very hard on me to keep concealing my identity. But I had to. I did become good friends with them and even pretended to be learning their language. All this while engaged on an authorized project, you understand.

"I dearly loved my foster mother on the Gardenworld. But I loved my own mother even more, though she was not as spiritually developed as my foster mother, far from it.

"During several of my visits, in later years, I made sure that my relatives were introduced to the beliefs of the Church of the Second Chance. They all converted to it, but it wasn't enough. They were a long way from attaining that stage in which I could have hope that they'd advance even further.

"But I believed, and still believe, that if they're given enough time, they will do so."

Burton said gently, "You were just about to land on top of the mountain."

"Yes. But what I've told you about my relatives is highly important. You must also realize that I wasn't just distressed about my own family. I've agonized over all the others, the billions who are doomed. I couldn't even mention this once to my fellows, though. Except Tringu, of course, and I didn't bring up the subject until I was absolutely sure of him. If I'd said anything about it to the others, I'd have been suspected at once if it became known that there was a renegade."

Though he might be committing suicide, Loga did the one thing that would prevent his vessel from alighting on the designated place. He cut off the power.

"If Monat had thought that anyone'd do that, he'd have arranged it so that it couldn't be done. But he hadn't expected any such action. Why should he? The culprit would know that even if he killed himself, he'd be raised in the tower."

The craft had fallen at once and struck the side of the mountain just below the top. It was going slow, and Loga was in a buffer suit. Moreover, since the vessel was made of the almost indestructible gray metal, it was not even scratched by the impact.

"Even so, I would've been killed during the fall. But I turned on the power when it had hurtled for a hundred feet, and the craft started back up toward the top. I cut the power again, and I turned it on when I'd gone fifty feet. The craft started up again for its original destination. I cut the power once more."

By bone-jarring increments, Loga worked the vessel down to near ground level. Before this, he'd opened a port. When he thought that he was close enough, he leaped out the port, clutching the handle of his grail. He fell through the rain and the thunder and lightning, struck something, and was knocked unconscious.

When he awoke he was draped belly-down across a branch of an irontree. It was daylight, and he could see his grail a hundred feet below at the base of the tree. Though he was severely scratched and bruised and had some internal injuries and a broken leg, he managed to get to the ground.

"The rest I've told you or you've correctly inferred."

Burton said, "Not all. We don't have the slightest inkling what this terrible thing is which you mentioned. What you were saving for the last."

"Or what Going On really means," Nur said.

"Going On? When the body of a person who's highly advanced ethically dies, the *wathan* disappears. Our instruments can find no trace of it. If another duplicate body is made, its *wathan* doesn't return to it."

"What do you do with a *wathan*less body?"

"Only one experiment was made, and the *wathan*less was allowed to live out her natural span. That's never been done with human beings. The people who came before Monat's did that.

"The theory is that, though the Creator may appear to be indifferent to Its creatures, It does welcome and take care of the *wathan*s that disappear. What other explanation is there for that?"

"It could be," Frigate said, "that there's something about the extraphysical universe that attracts a *wathan* when it reaches a certain stage of development. I don't know why this would have anything to do with the extraphysical. But there could be some sort of magnetic pull caused by this, I suppose."

"That theory's been put forth. We prefer to believe that the Creator does it. Though It may do it through purely physical-extraphysical means and not by a supernatural act."

"In effect," Burton said, "you aren't relying on science but on faith to explain the disappearances."

"Yes, but when you get to the basics, infinity and finity, eternity and time, the First Cause, you must rely on faith."

"Which has led so many billions astray and caused such immense suffering," Frigate said.

"You can't say that about this situation."

Tai-Peng said, fiercely, "Let's get on with what's happening in this world."

"I recruited the lazari because there was a very slight probability that what has happened might happen. I put all the situations I could think of into the computer and told it to estimate their probability. Unfortunately, the computer cannot detect what sentient beings will think, what final choices they'll make, unless it has *all* the data and that's impossible. Well, not even if it had every item could it predict one hundred percent. Thus, Monat and the others did what I couldn't expect. Just as I did what he couldn't anticipate. Just as you did what I couldn't predict. The human, the sentient, mind is still a deep mystery."

"May it always be so," Burton said.

"It is, it is! That is why you can't predict the stage of development of any *wathan*. One may be rather advanced, yet go no further. Another may be in a low stage and, suddenly, almost overnight as it were, leap to a far higher state than the previously much further advanced. It's a quantum ethical leap. Also, people regress."

"Are you an example of regression?" Burton said.

"No! That's what Siggen accused me of being when we were living in that hut in Parolando. The truth is, I am more highly advanced than anyone else in the project. Isn't it much more ethical to give everyone all the time they might need to develop? Isn't it? Yes, it is! That can't be denied!"

Alice murmured, "He's crazy."

Burton wasn't so sure. What Loga had said seemed reasonable. But his ideas for insuring his plans didn't seem so. Yet, if he continued to send false messages, then the Gardenworlders wouldn't come to investigate. Loga might gain a thousand years. Surely, in that time, anybody would attain the stage desired.

His deep pessimism told him that it might not be so.

What was his own progress?

Or did he want to get to a stage where the essential part of him just disappeared?

Why not? It would be an adventure even greater than this one, the greatest in his life.

"Very well," he said. "I think we understand all that's happened. But you've hinted that you may not be able to carry out your plans even if you have no one to stop you.

"What terrible thing has happened?"

"It's my fault, mine only!" Loga cried. He rose from the chair and, despite his limp, paced back and forth, his face twisted and sweating.

"Because of what I did, billions may be doomed forever! In fact, almost everybody! Perhaps, everybody! Forever!"

52

THERE WAS SILENCE FOR A WHILE. LOGA CONTINUED HIS PAINFUL limping. Then Burton said, "You might as well tell us."

Loga sat down in his chair.

"My signal put an inhibit on the resurrection line. I didn't want any Ethical to commit suicide and get to the tower before I did. What I didn't know was that another Ethical had also commanded an inhibit on the resurrection line when I was found out."

The reason for this, Loga said, was that Monat didn't want the unknown traitor to gain access to the tower. There he or she might be able to carry out his plans—whatever they were—before his presence was known.

Monat's command overrode everybody else's.

"He was the Operator."

Moreover, Monat, through his proxy, had commanded the computer to obey no one else but him until normal operations were restored.

"I'm sure that if he'd known exactly what was to happen, he'd not have given such a command. But he had no more idea than I what course events would take."

"The universe is infinite, and the events in it are also infinite," Nur said.

"Perhaps. But you see, the computer uses the *wathans* as its . . . what shall I say? . . . *blueprints* to duplicate bodies. Once, records were kept of the bodies, but it was more economical to use the *wathans* themselves, as I've explained. There are no other records. So, if the *wathans* are lost, then we have no way to duplicate bodies anymore."

Burton rolled this around in his mind.

"Well, you *have* the *wathans*. We saw them in that enclosure in the middle of the tower."

"Yes, but when the computer dies, the *wathans* will be released! And there is no means then to resurrect the dead. They are lost forever!"

There was another silence. After a minute or two, Alice said, "The computer . . . is *dying?*"

Loga was almost choking. "Yes. It wouldn't be if it hadn't been left unattended so many years."

The machinery was built to last for centuries without any need for repair or replacement. Nevertheless, parts and units did malfunction now and then. That was why technicians inspected everything at regular intervals, and why there were so many self-repair capabilities. Machines, however, had a well-known but as yet unexplained obstinancy, a seeming tendency to break down of their own will or to refuse to operate. It had been jestingly observed that perhaps they, too, had *wathans* of a sort, and their free will was more ill will than anything else.

During the long absence of human supervision, a valve had quit operating.

"This is not a mechanical valve, you understand. It's basically a force field which shuts off or on to allow flow of sea water into the food-mixing chamber for the computer. The computer subsists on distilled water mixed with sugar and some traces of minerals. The shut-down valve is one of two. Its mate is for emergencies. It takes over should the main one go out. Then the technicians repair the field generator of the valve, and the backup one shuts down."

Unfortunately, the emergency valve did not admit enough water for a long term. And so the protein computer was dying.

"I could use the computer memory banks to furnish a model for a duplicate of it as the original before it was fed any data. Unfortunately, the computer contains the only memory banks of that. And it won't release the information so that I can feed it into the matter-energy converter."

"Why don't you repair the field generator?" Frigate said.

"For the good reason that the computer won't permit me to. Apparently, Monat ordered long ago that it be equipped with defenses. These weren't activated, though, until I was found out."

There was another long silence. Alice broke it, saying "Why don't you use one of those *wathan* catchers you told us about? The moment the computer died and released the *wathans*, the catcher could restrain them."

Loga smiled grimly.

"A very good idea. I've thought of that. Briefly. The only catcher is the computer. There are memory banks which I could tap to make a catcher. But these are also in the computer."

"Are the defenses absolutely invulnerable?" Burton said.

"It's easy to gain access to the field generator. I'd just have to pull out the malfunctioning module and replace it with another. But I'd be dead before I could do that. The computer would cut me down with beams. Just like those which my beamer shoots."

Nur said, "You used the computer at the same time that the others were. How did you keep them from finding that out?"

"In a sense, I made the computer schizophrenic. One part of it didn't know what the other was doing."

"That's it!" the Moor cried. Then his exultant expression was replaced by a frown. "No. You'd have thought of using it."

"Yes. I can't because the engineers apparently discovered the split mind. Now it's dominated by the main part."

"You said *dominated,* not *integrated,*" Nur said.

"Yes. The engineers didn't have time to remove the complex circuits which made the computer schizophrenic. But they did put in temporary bypass circuits to give the main part dominance. They would've integrated the parts later. But they were killed before they could do that."

"How do you know all this?" Burton said.

"The computer gave me that information. It doesn't refuse to communicate. It just won't obey any commands except those from Monat or whoever was authorized to act for him."

"There's no chance of finding out the codeword or whatever Monat used?"

"Not unless he recorded it somewhere. I doubt that he would. Also, the code would have to be accompanied by the voiceprints of Monat or his aide."

"Maybe there is no codeword," Frigate said. "Maybe the voice-recognition is enough."

"No. Monat would think of that. It'd be relatively easy to isolate phones from records of his speech and synthesize them to make new sentences. Also, Monat might've required that there be body recognition, too."

"Could you make a disguise of Monat to wear yourself?" Turpin said.

"I suppose so. But I'd use beam-simulators."

Loga seemed very weary now. Burton suspected that it was not the wound which had drained his energy. It was hopelessness and guilt.

"Well," Burton said. "We don't know but what voice and body recognition is all that's required. We must try to fool the computer even if it's wasted work."

Alice said, eagerly, "Have you told the computer that it's going to die?"

"Oh, yes. But it already knew it."

"Perhaps a man could get through the computer's defenses," Burton said, looking hard at Loga.

The Ethical straightened up a little.

"I know what you're thinking. Since I'm responsible for this horror, I should try to repair the valve generator. Even if there's an almost one-hundred-percent probability that I'd just be sacrificing myself. I would do that if I thought it'd do any good.

"But what if I succeeded and yet died? None of you would know how to operate the equipment here. You could do nothing to solve this problem.

"Moreover, if the computer lives, what then? The situation is unchanged only in that the computer lives and so the *wathans* won't be released."

Burton said that Loga must train them in the use of whatever instruments might be needed. He must because something might happen to him. Was there time for that before the computer died?

The Ethical replied that there might be. He'd have to teach them what the instrument markings meant. It would take too long to teach them the language used when talking to the computer, which was that of Monat's people and the primary one on the Gardenworld. But he could change the language converters and so allow them to use Esperanto.

"Excellent!" Burton said. "I think we should all go to bed now. We'll wake up refreshed and with clearer minds. Perhaps we can think of something to use against the computer then."

They moved into the Councilors' apartments. Loga went into his. Aphra Behn and de Marbot took one; Alice and Burton, another. Tai-Peng and Turpin shared a fourth apartment and Nur and Frigate the one next to it. Burton thought it best that none of their group be alone. He still didn't entirely trust the Ethical.

Before they went to sleep, Alice said, "Richard, there has to be a way to get around the computer. It was made by humans, so it should be mastered by humans."

"Why don't you appeal to its emotions?" Burton said. "You women are particularly good at that."

"No more than men, you braying arse! Anyway, I know there's no use appealing to the emotions of a thing that has none. Although I'm not so sure that it doesn't have some. Or analogies thereof. But since it operates purely by logic, why not use logic against it? Humans put human logic into it. We should be able to fight it or cozen it with logic."

"I'm sure that Loga has thought of that."

He kissed her on the cheek and turned away.

"Good night, Alice."

"Good night, Richard."

When he awoke some hours later, he found her staring up at the moving figures on the ceiling.

53

IN THE MORNING, THEY SHOWERED AND PUT ON CLEAN CLOTHS AND THEN went to a room which was used as a dining hall. Going past the control room, they saw that Croomes' body had been removed. There were no bloodstains on the floor, and all the skeletons were gone.

"Robots," Loga said. "I also sent one to take care of Gilgamesh's body."

"I didn't see any robots," Frigate said.

"You did, but they looked like large cabinets. Your beds are robots, too. They gently massage your muscles and manipulate your spinal cords."

"I didn't feel anything when I awoke during the night," Burton said.

"Nor I," Alice said.

"They're very subtle and only operate automatically when you're asleep. But if you want a massage while awake, you command them. I'll show you how."

Over the delicious breakfast, Alice told the others her thoughts about circumventing the computer with the very logic it used.

Loga shook his head. "It sounds fine, but it won't work."

"We can at least try," Alice said.

"We'll try everything, mental or physical," Loga said. "But, believe me, I've thought of everything."

"I don't doubt your intelligence," she said. "But nine heads are better than one."

"The nine-headed dragon!" Tai-Peng shouted. His face was flushed; he'd been drinking wine throughout the meal.

"I'll use one of the electronic computers in this room to set up a system," Loga said. "But it won't, I believe, be able to beat its own logic. A computer can calculate much faster than a human, if it has all the proper data. But it doesn't have an imagination. It's not creative. Still, its data might contain something I've overlooked. And it can be set to make combinations in a very short time which it would take me years to write out. Also, it does have some degree of extrapolation."

After going to his apartment, he went to the control room and seated himself in the chair in the center of the revolving platform. In a very short time, he called to the others.

"I couldn't resist asking the big computer how many *wathans* are now in the shaft."

"How many?" Nur said.

Loga looked at the screen again.

"Eighteen billion and twenty-eight. No. Add three more."

"Over half the people in The Valley," Frigate said.

"Yes. Add two more now."

Loga turned the display off.

"For every hour that passes, more people die, more *wathans* are caught. When the computer dies . . ."

His voice trailed off.

The Ethical had to have great courage, endurance, determination, and quick wits to do all that he'd done. But his guilt was too crushing for even him.

"Maybe," Turpin said, "you should throw in the towel. I mean . . . kill the computer now! That way, you won't lose any more, and you can continue the project."

"No!" Loga said, showing fire for the first time since they'd known him. "No! That would be monstrous! I have to save all of them! All!"

"Yes, and maybe you'll end up losing millions. Or maybe everybody on this planet."

"No! I can't!"

"Well," Turpin said, "I can't think of anything that'll help. This is all too deep for me."

He left for the nearby lounge to play on its piano.

"He's disgusted with me," Loga said. "But he doesn't know the loathing I feel for myself."

"Recriminations will do no good!" Tai-Peng said, waving a bottle in his hand. "But Tom may be right! I think I'll go to the lounge and enjoy myself, too! My head aches with thinking!"

"That isn't what's making it hurt," Alice said gently.

Tai-Peng just grinned and kissed her quickly on the cheek as he passed her.

Nur reminded the Ethical that he hadn't removed the bombs in the cabinets in the other control room.

"I'll just lock the door," Loga said. "Now for the logic-versus-logic program. Even if it will be a waste of time."

Those remaining went off to the language laboratory. The Ethical had given them instructions for the use of the equipment which would teach them to speak and read Gardenworldish or Ghuurrkh. There were also Esperanto-Ghuurrkhian grammars and dictionaries available.

Alice clutched Burton's arm.

"It is horrible, isn't it?" she said, her large dark eyes looking into his. "All those souls lost, and they had a chance for immortality! It's too horrible to think about!"

"Then don't think about it," Burton said. "Anyway, even the lost ones will be immortal. They just won't know it, that's all."

She shuddered and said, "Yes. But we could be among them. Do you think you're Going On? I'd like to believe that I am, but you practically have to be a saint to Go On!"

"Nobody has ever accused me of being a saint unless it was my wife," Burton said, grinning. "And she knew better."

Alice wasn't fooled. She knew that he was as desperate as she.

Two days passed. Loga ran out the results on the console screen while the others watched. When the display was ended, he shook his head.

"No use."

They conferred again and again and came up with many plans, but these were all dismissed because of flaws in logic or insurmountable facts.

The fourth day after they'd come to the tower, Frigate leaped smiling into the room.

"Hey, we're pretty dumb! The answer is right under our noses! Why don't you send robots in to insert the module?"

Loga sighed.

"I'd thought of that. It was one of the first things to occur to me. But even though the robots are made of *charruzz* (the gray metal), the computer's beamers will slice through them."

Frigate looked disappointed and a little foolish.

"Yes . . . but . . . if you send enough in, they'd knock out the beamers!"

"None of the robots have the functional structure to shoot beamers."

"Well, couldn't you convert them? And then program them?"

"It would take me ten days. If I'd started when I first got here, I couldn't have altered one in time."

He paused, then said dolefully, "I just checked on the time left before the computer dies. Five days!"

Even though they'd been expecting such an announcement, they were shocked.

Tom Turpin said, "At least we won't have that to worry about. The souls'll be gone, and there's nothing to do about it. But you can give those that're still alive a lot more time."

Loga turned some dials and punched a button. Ghuurrkhian numbers glowed on the screen. The others were advanced enough by now to be able to read them.

"Eighteen billion, one hundred and two," Aphra said.

"I should kill the computer right now," Loga said. "I've waited too long as it is. For all I know, my mother's soul was collected today."

"Wait!" Frigate said. "I've got an idea! You said you'd reopened your private resurrection chambers when you got here. Can they be fixed up so that we could be resurrected in them, too?"

"Why, yes. They could be. The resurrector catchers operate on a slightly different frequency from that of the computer. I had my *wathan* and Tringu's tuned to it. I could do the same for you. But why?"

Frigate started to explain, but Loga, Burton, and Nur comprehended at the same time what he meant to say.

They would go down in force, leaving several behind to do the necessary supervision. They would storm the room, and, though they might be killed over and over, they still could put out all the beamers of the computer.

"How'd you happen to think of that, Pete?" Tom Turpin said.

"I'm a science-fiction writer. I should've thought of it when I found out what the situation was."

"I should've thought of it, too," Loga said. "But we're all under great emotional pressure."

"You can duplicate these?" Burton said, holding up the pistollike sphere-ended weapon.

"As many as we'll need."

Within two minutes, the entire group was armed with the beamers. The Ethical then had his machine print out diagrams of the route to the valve room from the control room and from his private resurrectors. They studied the diagrams, identifying each corridor and chamber with the corresponding screen displays.

"There are video cameras on every wall in that area, including the valve room. Here's a picture of it from the files."

They studied the reproductions issued by the machine until they knew the room by heart. Then Loga commanded that a module be duplicated in the e-m cabinet, and he gave them the simple instructions for pulling out the old module and inserting the new.

Unfortunately, the Ethical was unable to get diagrams showing where the computer's defenses were located.

"That information must be in the computer's memory banks."

Nur said, "Why don't you ask the computer for it?"

Loga looked surprised, then laughed softly.

A moment later he had information, though it wasn't what he'd asked for. The computer refused to divulge where its weapons were.

"Well, it was worth a try."

They got into their chairs and followed the Ethical to a lift shaft. They descended in it far faster than they'd dared operate their chairs until then. When they'd gone a mile, he stopped and then went into a bay and from there into a corridor. After a few minutes Burton, who had an excellent sense of direction, realized that they were heading for the general area of the secret room at the base of the tower. At their speed, they quickly arrived at it.

The Ethical looked at the door, still kept from opening by the grail Burton had placed there. His face turned red.

"Why didn't you tell me that the doors were still open?"

"I thought about it, but it didn't seem important," Burton said.

"The agents could have come through!"

"No. They couldn't possibly have caught up with us in such a short time. They'll be using sailboats."

"I won't take any chances."

Loga turned the chair away from the door, then turned it back to face them.

"You get that boat out of the entrance while I'm gone."

"Where'll you be?" Burton said.

"I'm going to a control room so I can reactivate an automatically operated aircraft and direct it to the ledge. It'll melt it all down, and then it'll plug up the cave entrance."

"Go with him," Burton said to Tai-Peng and de Marbot.

Loga glared but said nothing, and his chair turned and flew down the corridor.

Burton led the others into the fog-shrouded room where, with much shoving, they got the boat out into the sea. Then they went back to the corridor, the larger ones squeezing themselves again through the narrow opening above the grail.

"We should've asked Loga to open it all the way," Frigate said.

"I don't think he wants us to know how he opens it," Burton said.

"Still doesn't trust us?"

"With the life he's led, he's conditioned to trust no one."

That, however, wasn't true. Loga, trailed by the Chinese and the Frenchman, returned after fifteen minutes. He got out of the chair and banged his fist on the wall a few inches from the door. At the same time, he said, clearly, "Ah Qaaq!"

The door slid back within the recess.

Burton made a mental note of the exact area struck.

"How did you know that someone wouldn't be coming along and catch you?" he said.

"This door is one big video screen. I also have other screens which look just like part of the walls. They're situated so that I can see up this corridor past its curves for some distance."

They followed Loga into the room. Halfway down it, he stopped, turned, facing the wall, and voiced the codeword again. An apparently seamless part of the wall moved back and they slid into a recess. The room beyond was well-lit and contained some equipment on tables, a large cabinet, and two skeletons. These were pointed toward the door as if they'd been about to leave the room. On the floor by bone fingers was a metal box. It had a number of dials, gauges, buttons, and a small video screen on one side and prongs on the other.

Loga said, "If only I could have sent that signal a few seconds earlier. I would've caught them before they removed the control box."

"But you wouldn't have known that," Burton said. "You would still not have been able to take the chance of killing yourself. By the way, why were the doors closed? Those two would've had to open them to get in."

Nur said, "Since they wouldn't have known the codes, how'd they get in?"

"After seventy-five seconds, the doors close automatically unless counter-manded. What happened is that the investigators located this room by tracing the circuits. That would've been a very time-consuming and arduous job because they couldn't use the computer to do the tracing. When they located this room, they must have been using magnetometers, too. They went back to find the tap-in source, and found the programmed open-shut code box. It wouldn't have taken them long to analyze the code."

"But what about the knock accompanying the code? How . . ."

"They figured that out, too, though it would've taken longer."

He pointed at the cabinet. "The resurrector."

He went in with Frigate at his heels. The American said, "You couldn't use your own power supply?"

Loga stopped and picked up the control box and then walked to the side of the cabinet. He inserted the prongs into receptacles on the side of the cabinet.

"No, I couldn't. I would've liked my own atomic converter so there'd be no wires to trace. But energy-matter conversion and *wathan*-attracting require enormous power. The physical-extraphysical interface alone uses enough power to blackout half of the cities of ancient Earth in the late twentieth century."

Frigate said, "How'd you prevent this power drain from showing up on meters?"

"I made arrangements for it not to. To get back to the original question. If the engineers had removed the code box, I wouldn't have been able to get out of the secret room into the corridor. The outer access door is activated by a signal going to another coder-decoder. It was very fortunate that the engineers didn't work on that before they were killed. I lost the signal-generator when I had to abandon my aircraft. But the boats in the cave contain generators. These are automatically started when the sensors detect that the tower is near."

"The door mechanisms wouldn't have used much power. Why didn't you use separate power generators for them?"

"I should have. But it was simpler and more economical to use the main power supply."

He smiled slightly. "I wonder what the engineers made of the codeword. Ah Qaaq is Mayan. The *Ah* is the article defining the name as masculine. *Qaaq* means *fire*. *Loga* is Ghuurrkh for *fire*. Perhaps that was what identified me. They might've put the Mayan name into the computer for a search. If they did, they got an answer within a second after insertion of the question.

"I outclevered myself."

He poised a finger over a button. "Gather around. I'll explain the simple operation twice so that there won't be any confusion. You're able to read the markings. When I press this button, that small silvery inset disc will turn on. That indicates that the power is on.

"That larger inset disc by the ON light is a readout frequency meter."

He pressed a button. The smaller disc glowed orange.

"Now . . ."

The light went out.

"*Khatuuch!* What is . . .?"

Loga put his hand on the box for a second, then ran around to the front of the cabinet. He opened the door and looked in. Even at their distance from it, the others could feel the heat.

"Run!" Loga said, and he limped as fast as he could toward the exit.

When Burton had reached the exit he looked at the cabinet. The control box was melting, and a large cube inside the cabinet was glowing red.

Loga swore in Ghuurrkh and then said, "Those . . . those . . . ! They fixed it so that when power came on it'd melt the converter!"

Except for Loga and Burton, who'd died so many times that they no longer feared the prospect of death, the others were relieved. Burton could see it in their faces. They knew they'd be resurrected with their *wathans* attached, but they still loathed the idea of dying.

Burton said, "We have the other resurrector."

"It'll be set up, too," Loga said. He was ashen.

"Can't you fix it so it won't melt?"

"I'll try."

But he failed.

Burton, looking at the molten mass, thought it was time to tell Loga something he'd put off revealing because the resurrectors were more urgent business.

He said, "Loga, when we left your secret room to go after you, I put a bullet by the door to mark its location. The bullet is gone."

There was a short silence. Frigate said, "A housekeeping robot probably picked it up."

"No," Loga said. "If the robots were programmed to do such work, they'd have disposed of the skeletons."

"Then someone else has gotten in!"

SECTION 14

Three-Cornered Play: Carroll to Alice to Computer

54

THEY WENT TO A LABORATORY. LOGA SAT DOWN BEFORE A COMPUTER AND worked furiously. Within a short time, all the cameras in the tower were operating. Two seconds later, the screen before him glowed with a display.

Burton whistled.

"*Frato Fenikso!* Hermann Göring!"

He was at a table eating a meal made by a grail-box. From his extreme thinness and the great black marks under his hollow eyes, he needed more than one meal.

"I can't see how he caught up with us so quickly," Loga said.

"The computer reports seeing no one else, but they may be out of camera range just now. And if they're agents, one might have the codeword. Monat could've passed it on to them in The Valley."

"Why don't we ask Göring?" Burton said.

"Of course. First, though, I'll ask the computer where he is."

Loga read the instructions, and they got into their chairs and flew out of the room. Ten minutes later, they were outside the laboratory down the corridor from Loga's hideaway. They set their chairs down softly and entered on foot. Though Göring was not armed, they couldn't be sure they wouldn't find others with him by now.

Burton bellowed, "*Achtung!*"

He laughed loudly when Göring jumped up, food spewing from his mouth, arms flying, the chair falling backward. Gray and trembling, he whirled around, his eyes wide. He seemed to be trying to say something, and then his face reddened, and he clutched his throat.

"My God! He's choking!" Alice said.

Göring was blue and on his knees by the time Burton hit him on the back and made him expel the food caught in his throat.

Alice said, "That wasn't at all funny, Richard. Quit laughing. You might've killed him."

Burton wiped the tears away and said, "I'm sorry, Göring. I guess I just wanted to pay you back for some of the things you'd done to me."

Göring gulped at the glass of water handed him by Aphra Behn.

"Yes, I suppose I can't blame you."

"You look near-starved," Nur said. "You shouldn't be eating so fast. Too much food too soon after a long starvation can kill you."

"I'm not that starved. But I seem to have lost my appetite."

He looked around. "Where are the others?"

"Dead."

"May God take pity on their souls."

"He hasn't and won't unless we do something fast."

"Göring!" Loga said sharply. "Did you come alone?"

Göring looked at him strangely. "Yes."

"How long have you been here?"

"About an hour."

"Were there any others close behind you when you were in the mountains?"

"No. At least, I saw no one."

"How did you get here so fast?"

Göring and other Virolanders had dived into the hold of the *Not For Hire* before it slipped over the shelf into the abyss. They had brought up some sections of the batacitor and rebolted them together in a wooden sailboat. They had also brought up two small electric motors, a spare propeller of the smaller launch, the *Gascon,* and other parts. They'd worked fast, and four left in the reconverted boat two weeks after the *Post No Bills* had departed.

Unlike Burton's group, they'd not taken days off for rest or recreation.

"Where are your companions?" Loga said, though he'd probably guessed their fate.

"Two quit early and went back. I went on with my wife, but she slipped and fell down the face of a mountain."

He made the circular sign, the blessing, used so much by the Chancers.

"You should sit down," Burton said kindly. "We have much to tell you."

When he'd heard Loga and Burton tell what had happened, Göring looked horrified.

"All those *wathans*? And my wife's among them?"

"Yes, and now we don't know what to do. Kill the computer so that no more *wathans* may be caught. Or hope that we can think of some way to countermand its prime command."

Hermann said, "No. There's a third choice."

"What?"

"Let me try to get the module in."

"Are you crazy?"

"No. I have a debt to pay."

Burton thought of his recurring dream of God.

"You owe for the flesh. Pay up."

"If you die, your *wathan* will be doomed."

"Perhaps not," Hermann said quietly. "I may be ready to Go On. I don't know that I am. God knows that I am far from a saint. But if I can save all those souls . . . *wathans* . . . then I will have made complete recompense."

No one argued with him.

"Very well," Loga said. "You are the most courageous person I've ever met. I think you clearly understand that you may have very little chance to succeed. But here's what we're going to do." ·

Burton was very sorry that he had played his little joke on the German. The man was risking his soul, would face the equivalent of damnation, if he failed. Loga was right. Göring was the bravest man he'd ever known. He may not have been once, but he was now.

Loga decided that they should return to the top level to be near their apartments. On the way, they stopped at a floor where Göring could see the caged *wathans*.

He gazed at the glowing, contracting-expanding swirling darting things for a few minutes, then turned away.

"The most beautiful, the most awe-inspiring, the most hideous."

He made the circular sign again, though Burton thought that this was more than a blessing. He caught intimations of a prayer for salvation and for stiffening of his determination.

When they got to the control room, the Ethical immediately set about working at the console on the revolving platform. After five minutes, he sent Göring into a cabinet. There his measurements were made by beams. Loga put more data into the computer, finishing in an hour.

He waited for a few seconds before punching another button.

He left the platform and limped to a large energy-matter converter. The others crowding behind him, he opened its door.

The parts of a suit of armor were on the floor. Loga picked them up and threw them to those ouside the cabinet. They put these on Göring and, when they were done, he looked more like a robot than an armored knight. The addition of the backpack, his air supply, made him resemble an astronaut.

Except for the narrow but long window in the front of the globular helmet, the suit was was made of the gray metal. Though thick, it weighed only nine pounds.

"The window isn't as resistant as the metal," Loga said. "And the beams will cut entirely through the metal if they're applied to one spot for more than ten seconds. So keep moving."

Göring tested the flexibility of the shoulder, wrist, finger, knee, and ankle joints. They gave him as much mobility as he'd need. He ran back and forth and leaped forward and sidewise and backward. Then he practiced with the beamer until he knew its full capabilities.

His armor removed, he ate again.

After Hermann had gone to an apartment to sleep, Loga took a chair off to a floor below sea level. He returned in an hour in a two-man research submarine which floated in the air.

"I didn't think of this until a couple of hours ago. This will help him get through the initial defenses. But he'll have to go on foot after that. The entrances won't be wide enough to admit the vessel."

During his absence, the others had been busy attaching beamers to the sides of the coffin-shaped clean-up robots and drilling the holes needed for passage of cables. Loga installed video equipment and trigger mechanisms. Then he programmed navigational boxes and installed them.

Burton went to wake up the German but found him on his knees praying by the bedside.

"You should've slept," Burton said.

"I used my time for something better."

They went back to the control room where Hermann ate a light meal before learning the route and the operation of the submarine. Loga showed him how to remove the old module and insert the new. The latter was a piece of the gray metal the size and shape of a playing card. Though it contained very complex circuits, its surface was smooth. One corner was nicked with a V, indicating that that end was to be inserted into the recess of the assembly. The code number was in bas-relief, and the card was to be put in with the code-side up.

"What could go wrong with a module like that?" Frigate said.

"Nothing," Loga said. "If it's inserted properly. I suspect human error. If the card was put in upside down, the circuits would operate properly. But every time there was a voltage surge, one of the circuits would be slightly damaged. There aren't many surges, but over a long period of time the damage would be cumulative. The error would have been noticed long ago—if the technicians hadn't been dead."

He put the card inside a metal cube and attached it to a leg-piece of armor just above the knee.

"All he has to do is press that inset button in the cube, and the magnetism will be canceled. The cube is thick enough to withstand many shots from the beamers."

All of Göring's armor was put on him except the globular helmet. Loga poured out the yellow wine into exquisite goblets brought from his apartment. He lifted his high and said, "To your success, Hermann Göring. May the Creator be with you."

"With all of us," Hermann said.

They drank, and the helmet was secured. Göring climbed up a short ladder into the top of the submarine and got himself with some difficulty into the hatch. Loga went up and, looking down into the hatchway, repeated the operation instructions. Then he closed the hatch.

Loga, as chief of operations, took the chair in the revolving platform. The others seated themselves before control consoles and began the adjustments taught them by the Ethical.

The first of the armed coffin-shapes lifted and headed toward the doorway. That was Burton's. Behind it came Alice's, then the others. They single-filed through the exit and turned right.

When all were out, the submarine rose from the floor and followed the robots.

The descent to the floor just below sea level took him fifteen minutes. He halted his robot before a closed door above which were letters in alto-relief. Burton activated the beamers, and presently the door was cut on one side from its top to the bottom. He moved his robot over and melted through another section. Then he rammed the machine into the middle, and the cut section fell backward.

Burton saw a gigantic room filled with equipment. He shot his machine toward a closed doorway in the opposite wall. Before it got there, sections of the wall slid back, and the sphere ends of beamers moved out. Scarlet lines spat from them.

Burton moved the controls on the panel so that his robot angled upward to the right. He held it then and pressed the trigger-activation button. Scarlet lines streamed out along the edges of the screen, and he had the satisfaction of seeing a globe explode. Fragments flew against the screen but did no damage.

A few seconds later, the screen went blank.

One of the computer's weapons had destroyed the camera on top of the robot.

Burton cursed, and he cut off the beamers. There was nothing he could do except watch. He pressed the button that would tie his computer in with one of Loga's cameras. Instantly, he could see from a camera on the wall above the doorway the robots had entered. His robot hovered ten feet above the floor, its front end pointed up at the beamers on the other wall.

The robots were in a semicircle so that they wouldn't get hit by their companions.

The last beamer in the room blew up, shifting the view from one camera to the next as one room after another was conquered. Alice's robot was melted down. De Marbot's camera was destroyed. Tai-Peng's was pierced by three beams at once, and it fell as some vital part was melted.

The others went dead one by one until only the submarine was left. The dirigible-shaped craft took over then, cutting through two doors, its thick hull drilled into by the computer's beamers.

The submarine came to a doorway wide enough to admit it but crossed by beams from ten weapons. Hermann shot his craft through it and came out into the next room with a small section of the stern cut off and many deep holes in the hull.

Ahead of him, at the opposite wall, was another entrance. Here was where he would have to abandon his craft. He drove it at great speed, slowed it a few feet from the doorway, and, while scarlet lines melted holes in the hull, climbed out. Immediately, the beamers transferred to him.

Göring fell out onto the floor, shielded from half of the weapons by the vessel but the target of the others. He got up slowly and staggered through the door entrance. Ranks of beamers turned toward him and tracked him as he ran toward the other doorway leading to the valve room. Just before he got to it, a door slid out from a recess and blocked the entrance. Ignoring the beamers, he began cutting through the door. He made a small hole, and he removed the cube holding the card and threw it ahead of him. Then he crawled through the hole, his beamer in his hand.

Burton and the others could hear his heavy breathing.

A cry of agony.

"My leg!"

"You're almost there!" Loga shouted.

Purplish vapors poured out through the hole.

"Poison gas," Loga said.

The screen shifted the view to the valve room. This was large and on the right-hand wall (from Hermann) a down-curving metal tube came out of the wall about ten feet above the floor. Near it was a small metal box on a table from which thin cables ran to another box. The front of the box had recesses from which the ends of modules stuck out.

Göring crawled to the cube as at least a hundred beamers poured their ravening energy into his suit.

His voice came to the watchers.

"I can't stand it. I'm going to faint."

"Hang on, Göring!" Loga said. "A minute more, and you'll have done it!"

They saw the bulky gray figure grab the cube, turn it over, and let the card module drop out. They saw Hermann pick it up and crawl toward the module box. They heard his scream and saw him fall forward. The module fell from his fingers at the foot of the table.

The scarlet lines continued their fire and did not stop until the armor was riddled with holes.

There was a long silence.

Burton heaved a deep sigh and turned his equipment off. The others did the same. Burton went up onto the platform and stood behind Loga. His screen was still alive, but now it showed a pulsing many-colored figure, a globe-shape with extending and withdrawing tentacles.

Loga was bent forward, his elbows on the edge of the panel, his hands against his face.

Burton said, "What's that?"

He knew it was the picture of a *wathan*, but he didn't know why it was on the screen.

Loga removed his hands and stared at the screen.

"I put a frequency tracker on Göring."

"That's he?"

"Yes."

"Then he didn't Go On?"

"No. He's with the others."

What do we do now?

That was the question of all.

Loga wanted to kill the computer before it captured more *wathans*, and then he would duplicate it at its predata stage. But he also hoped hopelessly that someone might think of something which would solve the problem before the *wathans* were released. He was mentally paralyzed and would evidently do nothing unless an impulse broke through and he pressed the fatal button.

The others were thinking hard. They put their speculations, their questions, into their computers. Always, there was some flaw in their schemes.

Burton went down several times to the floor below and stood or paced for hours while he gazed at the splendid spectacle of the swirling *wathans*. Were his parents among them? Ayesha? Isabel? Walter Scott, the nephew of Sir Walter Scott the author, and a great friend of his in India? Dr. Steinhaeuser? George Sala? Swinburne? His sister and brother? Speke? His grandfather Baker, who'd cheated him out of a fortune by dropping dead just before he could change his will? Bloody-minded and cruel King Gélélé of Dahomey, who didn't know that he was bloody-minded and cruel since he was only doing what his society required of him? Which was no acceptable excuse.

He went to bed exhausted and depressed. He had wished to talk to Alice, but she seemed withdrawn, foundering in her own thoughts. Now, though, she didn't seem to be in a reverie which would remove her from painful or distasteful reality. She was obviously thinking about their dilemma.

Finally, Burton slipped away. He awoke after six hours, if his watch was correct. Alice was standing over him in the dim light.

"What's the matter?" he said drowsily.

"Nothing. I hope. I just came back from the control room."

"What were you doing there?"

Alice lay down beside him.

"I just couldn't get to sleep. I kept thinking about this and that, my thoughts were as numerous as the *wathans*. I tried to keep my mind on the computer, but a thousand things pushed them aside, occupied me for a brief time, then slid away to be replaced by something else. I must've reviewed my whole life, here and on Earth.

"I remember thinking about Mr. Dodgson before I finally did sleep. I dreamed a lot, all sorts of dreams, a few good ones, some terrible. Didn't you hear me screaming once?"

"No."

"You must have been sleeping like the dead. I awoke shaking and perspiring, but I couldn't remember what it was that'd horrified me so."

"It isn't difficult to imagine what it was."

Alice had gotten up to get a drink of water. On returning to the bed, she again had trouble getting to sleep. Among other things, she thought of the Reverend Charles Lutwidge Dodgson and the pleasures from knowing him and from his two books inspired by her. Because she'd reread them many times, she had no trouble visualizing the text and Tenniel's illustrations.

"The first scene that came to me was the Mad Tea-Party."

Seated at the table were the Hatter, the March Hare, and the Dormouse. Uninvited, Alice sat down with them, and, after some insane conversation, the March Hare asked her to have some wine.

Alice looked all around the table, but there was nothing on it but tea.

"Actually," Alice said to Burton, "that wasn't true. There was also milk and bread and butter."

The book-Alice said, "I don't see any wine."

"There isn't any," said the March Hare.

Later there was a silence while Alice was trying to solve the riddle of why a raven was like a writing desk. The silence was broken when the Hatter turned to Alice and asked her what day of the month it was. He'd taken his watch out of his pocket and had been looking uneasily at it, shaking it and holding it to his ear.

Alice considered a little and then said, "The fourth."

The real Alice said to Burton, "Mr. Dodgson wrote that date because it was May in the book and the fourth of May was my birthday."

The Hatter sighed and said, "Two days wrong! I told you butter wouldn't suit the works!"

"It was the *best* butter," the March Hare meekly responded.

Burton got out of bed and began pacing back and forth.

"Must you go into such detail, Alice?"

"Yes. It's important."

The next scene she visualized, or empathized, since she became the seven-year-old Alice of the book, was from the Wool and Water chapter of *Through the Looking-Glass*. She was talking to the White Queen and the Red Queen.

"Can *you* keep from crying by considering things?" she (Alice) asked.

"That's the way it's done," the White Queen said with great decision. "Nobody can do two things at once, you know."

"Alice!" Burton said. "What's all this nonsense leading to?"

"It's not nonsense. Listen."

In her reverie, Alice leaped from the White Queen to Humpty Dumpty.

"Perhaps because Loga is so fat that he reminds me of Humpty Dumpty."

She, the book-Alice, was talking to the huge anthropomorphized egg sitting on a wall. They were discussing the meaning of words.

"When *I* use a word," Humpty Dumpty said in a rather scornful tone, "it means just what I choose it to mean—neither more nor less."

"The question is," said Alice, "whether you *can* make words mean so many different things."

"The question is," said Humpty Dumpty, "which is to be master—that's all."

Then the real Alice—But is she any more real than that other Alice? Burton wondered—flashed to the scene where the Red Queen asked her if she could do Subtraction.

"Take nine from eight," the Red Queen said.

"Nine from eight. I can't, you know," Alice replied very readily. "But—"

"She can't do Subtraction," said the White Queen to the Red Queen. She spoke to Alice. "Can you do Division? Divide a loaf by a knife—what's the answer to *that?*"

"Were there any more?" Burton said.

"No. I didn't think they meant much. They were just memories of some of my favorite sections."

She'd slept again. And then she awoke suddenly, her eyes wide. She'd thought she'd heard someone far off calling her. "Just over the horizon of my mind."

It sounded like Mr. Dodgson, but she wasn't sure.

She was wide awake, her heart pounding fast. She got out of bed and walked to the control room.

"Why?"

"It occurred to me that there were three key phrases in the scene. *The best butter. Which is to be master? Can you do Division?*"

Burton sighed. "Very well, Alice. Tell it as you must."

She had seated herself in Loga's chair and made the adjustments necessary to communicate directly with the computer.

"You realize that you're going to die in two days or less?" she said.

"Yes. That's redundant information. I didn't need to be informed."

"You were ordered by Monat not to resurrect anyone until he gave you the countercommand. What form does the countercommand take?"

Burton interrupted her. "Loga asked him that."

"Yes, I know. But I didn't think it'd hurt to try again."

"And the reply?"

As before, it had been silence.

Alice had then told it that there was an even higher command, and this had been given to it by Monat before the second order.

"What is that?" flashed on the screen. "I've been given many orders."

"The prime directive, the most essential, is to catch the *wathans* and reattach them to the duplicated bodies. That is what the project is all about. If Monat could have foreseen what his order would result in, he'd not have given it."

The computer said nothing.

Alice said, "Put me into communication with the section which Loga was using. That part of which Loga was the master."

Evidently, the computer had no orders to refuse communication with that part. Until Alice, no one had even thought about that possibility.

"My God!" Burton said. And then, "What happened?"

"I told it that it was going to die. It said that it knew it. In effect, so what? So I used my argument for the dominant part with it."

She followed that up with an order that it regain its former state, that it be independent.

"The dominant part did nothing during this time?"

"Nothing. Why should it? As Loga's said, it's a brilliant idiot."

"What happened then?"

"I told the dominant that it was its duty to resurrect Monat and confirm or invalidate the order not to resurrect anybody until it got the codeword or whatever it is."

"Then?"

"The screen went blank. I tried again and again to get it to respond."

The eagerness on Burton's face died away.

"Nothing?"

"Nothing."

"But why would it cut off communication? Its duty is to communicate."

"I hope," Alice said slowly, "that it's evidence of an internal struggle. That the dominated part is struggling with the dominant."

"That's nonsense!" Burton cried. "If what I've learned about computers is true, it couldn't happen."

"You forget that this is, in one sense, not a computer. Not the conventional kind, anyway. It's made of protein, and it's as complex as the human brain."

"We'll have to rouse Loga," Burton said. "I suppose it'll be for nothing, but he's the only one who can handle this."

The Ethical came from his sleep fully awake. He heard Alice out without any questions, then said, "There would be no struggle. Monat's order would have gone to the dominated part as well as the other."

"That depends upon *when* the order was given," she said. "If the circuits for domination were put in afterward, then the dominated part wouldn't have received them."

"But the dominant would have transmitted them to the schizophrenic part."

"Perhaps not!" Alice said.

"If it did happen, and I don't think there's the slightest chance it will, then Monat would be resurrected."

"But I *gave* that order to the *dominant*."

Loga quit frowning.

"Good! Still, if that's the only way to save the *wathans*, then it should happen. Even if . . ."

He didn't want to say what would happen to him.

They had breakfast in the dining hall except for Loga, who ate while in the control chair. Despite his efforts, he could get no direct response from the computer. One of his screens showed the enclosure of the *wathans*.

"When it becomes empty, we'll know that they're . . . lost."

He looked at another screen.

"Two more have just been caught. No. Three now."

While they were breakfasting in gloom, broken only now and then by halfhearted comments, Frigate said, "We do have something important to talk about."

They looked at him but said nothing.

"What's going to happen to us after the computer dies? Loga won't consider us ethically advanced enough to let us stay here. In his opinion, we won't be capable of running this operation. I think he's right, except possibly for Nur. If Nur could get through the entrance on top of the tower, he'd be allowed to stay."

The Moor said, "I've been through it."

They stared at him.

"When?" Frigate said.

"Last night. I decided that if I could get all the way out, I could get all the way back in. I succeeded, though it wasn't easy. I couldn't stroll through as a full-fledged Ethical would."

Burton growled, "That's fine for you. I apologize for what I said about all Sufis being charlatans. But what about the rest of us? Suppose we don't want to go back to The Valley? And if we do, then we'll tell people the truth. Not that everybody will believe us. There are still Christians and Moslems and so forth who've refused to abandon their religion. Also, I imagine there'll be many Chancers who'll cling to their tenets."

"That's their problem," Nur said. "However, I don't wish to stay here. I'll go back to The Valley willingly. I have work to do there. I must work until I Go On."

"That doesn't mean that you'll be gathered to the bosom of the Creator," Burton said. "Scientifically, all Going On means is that you will no longer be detectable by their scientists' instruments."

"As Allah wills it, so be it," Nur said.

Burton considered the prospect of staying here. He would have such power as nobody on Earth had ever had and few on the Riverworld.

To gain it, though, he would have to remove Loga. Kill him or imprison him. Would the others collaborate with him? If they didn't, he'd have to get them out of the way. He could resurrect them in The Valley, where they were going anyway. But he would be lonely. Alice wouldn't go along with him. No, he'd not be lonely. He could resurrect in the tower all sorts of agreeable companions, men and women.

He shuddered. The temptation had passed through him like a nightmare. He didn't want that sort of power, and he would forever feel he was a traitor if he did have it. Besides, it was evident that he couldn't be entrusted with it.

But what about Loga? Wasn't he a traitor?

Yes. In a sense. Burton, however, agreed with him that the candidates in The Valley should be given more, much more, time than the other Ethicals had planned. He himself, he felt, would need that extension.

He looked at the faces around the table. Were there thoughts such as his behind those dour expressions? Was one or more than one struggling with temptation?

He'd have to watch them. Make sure that they didn't try anything reprehensible.

He drank some of the yellow wine and said, "Is everybody agreeable to returning to The Valley? A show of hands, please."

Everybody raised their hands except Tom Turpin. They looked hard at him. Grinning, he raised his hand.

"I was thinking of all the good times I could have here. But I don't want to stay. Man, I couldn't handle it. Only . . . I wonder if Loga'd let me take a piano with me."

Alice burst into tears. "All those souls! I thought that I had an answer but . . ."

A screen on the wall glowed, and Loga's smiling face appeared.

"Come here!" he shouted. He laughed. "Come here!" He laughed again. "The dominant has just succumbed, and I've just gotten a message from the other! Alice, you were right! Oh, how you were right!"

They ran into the control room and gathered around the Ethical. There was the display on the screen, glowing with the most recent communication.

Then they cheered and whooped and flung their arms about each other and got off the platform and danced.

After a while, Loga shouted for attention.

"Remember, it's still dying! But it's given me permission to replace the module! I have to leave at once!"

It would be sadly ironic, thought Burton, if the computer died before Loga could get to it.

Ten minutes later, as they were waiting for his call in the dining hall, he appeared grinning on a screen.

"It's done! It's done! I've already given the order to start the resurrection again!"

They cheered and cried and embraced again. Turpin sat down at the piano and played the "St. Louis Rag."

"It's been a long, long River, but we made it to the end!" Alice shrieked. Her big dark eyes seemed to glow like a video screen, her whole being radiated joy. She had never looked more beautiful.

"Yes," Burton said. He kissed her several times. "We'll have to go back to The River, but that doesn't matter."

How strange and unforeseeable! The world had been saved, not by great rulers and statesmen, not by mystics and saints and prophets and messiahs, not by any of the holy scriptures, but by an introverted eccentric writer of mathematical texts and children's books and by the child who'd inspired him.

The little girl become a woman, dream-ridden Alice, had inspired the nonsense not really nonsense, and this in circuitous and spiraling fashion had inspired her to do what all others had failed to do, to save eighteen billion souls and the world.

While thinking this, Burton happened to look toward the door. Frigate had been whirling around and around and babbling nonsense all the way to the door. Now he was walking back from it and frowning.

Burton left Alice to go to him.

"Is something the matter?"

Frigate quit frowning and grinned.

"No. I thought I heard footsteps in the corridor. But I looked, and there was no one there. Imagination, I guess."